SPY IN
AMBER

Manohar Malgonkar (1913-2010) was an eminent post-Independence writer whose contribution to Indian writing in English is immense. A remarkable storyteller and a keen observer of social and political realities, Malgonkar is notable for his military thrillers, historical novels and adventure fiction. His major works include *The Men Who Killed Gandhi*, *A Bend in the Ganges*, *Spy in Amber*, *Combat of Shadows*, *The Garland Keepers*, *The Sea Hawk*, *Shalimar*, *The Princes*, *Cactus Country*, *Distant Drum*, *Bandicoot Run* and *The Devil's Wind*.

ALSO BY THE SAME AUTHOR

Combat of Shadows
The Garland Keepers

SPY IN AMBER

AMBER

MANOHAR
MALGONKAR

RUPA

Published by
Rupa Publications India Pvt. Ltd 2013
7/16, Ansari Road, Daryaganj
New Delhi 110002

Sales centres:
Allahabad Bengaluru Chennai
Hyderabad Jaipur Kathmandu
Kolkata Mumbai

First published by Hind Pocket Books (P.) Ltd in 1971.

ISBN: 978-81-291-2471-5

10 9 8 7 6 5 4 3 2 1

The moral right of the author has been asserted.

Typeset by Ninestars Information Technologies Ltd, Chennai

Printed at HT Media Ltd., Noida

AUTHOR'S NOTE

I was commissioned to write a movie story with a spy in it, and enjoyed myself writing *Spy in Amber*. My daughter, Sunita, who is weaned on spy fiction saw sufficient merit in the story to have taken it upon herself to transcribe the screenplay into the form of a novel.

Manohar Malgonkar

CHAPTER I

I

THE vastness of the Himalayas guards many secrets, Shangri-Las large and small, that are tucked away securely behind the impenetrable barriers of mountain and valley, great tracts of land still unsurveyed by man, and therefore merely blank spaces on maps.

On one of these blank spaces is the Ragyabas monastery, a stark and forbidding edifice of great antiquity, situated in a belt of territory which, though it is well within the Indian part of the range, is now virtually a no man's land, inaccessible to either China or India. On one side it stands on the sheer, cliff-like edge of the Indus valley at least two thousand feet deep. From the other side, it is cut off almost just as effectively by a series of rising chains of mountains. It is a land out of a nightmare, stark, rocky, barren, with not a tree to be seen. On the crest of a hill, accessible only by long winding trails through the mountains, is the monastery dominating the landscape.

It is said that Ragyabas was built two thousand years ago by a butcher who spent his life in lonely meditation. He acquired a following and established the order of the Amber Lamas, so called because of their cloaks of a translucent yellow colour. It is also said that the monastery was built on the site of an earlier structure. Since Ragyabas is the Tibetan word for butcher, it came to be called the Ragyabas monastery.

The small outcrop of mud and rocks, teetering over the edge of the cliff wears an air of time-defying solidity, indestructible as the mountains themselves. The sheer natural hill has been endlessly built upon so that the top is nearly flat and even, and the whole effect is that of some impregnable medieval fortress. A thin line of steps hewn out of living rock, hug the cliff precariously and run diagonally, winding up against the outer wall. At irregular intervals are minute black holes that are the air inlets for the cells of the monastery.

The massive Chorten or the Devil-gate at the foot of the edifice, is intended to keep evil spirits from slipping through, and behind the Devil-gate, the archway dug through rock is the entrance to the monastery itself. Right on top of the roof of the edifice is a platform surrounded by waist-high posts in the centre of which, resting against a wooden stand, is the ceremonial trumpet made of copper; a long slender horn, almost like the barrel of a gun.

Over the centuries, the monks of the Amber order have been working with mole-like industriousness to dig the mountain from within to make room for more cells and temples and passages and, from the material so excavated, to build yet more open halls and prayer rooms on top, so that now the entire hill is said to be quite hollow, with a maze of rooms and corridors running deep into the bowels of the mountain.

On the other side, there is nothing, for the valley plunges dizzily, as though through some fault in the structure of the earth itself, and far below is the faint glint of water, the thin line of the Indus river not far from its source.

II

AGAINST the receding panorama of the Himalayas, a small caravan of mules and sheep wound its way along torturous mountain paths. The two men who walked ahead of the caravan were obviously the leaders. Their faces were Tibetan, with wide cheekbones and narrow eyes. One of them, Pushkar Bhatta, was in his fifties, with a leathery face and grizzled hair. His companion Gomti Prasad, was a much younger man, under thirty, handsome, cocky, with merry, darting black eyes. They both wore rumpled nondescript suits of a Western cut.

Behind them stretched the caravan; the mules carrying bags of flour and salt and cans of oil; the bare necessities of a spartan way of life. The sheep were being taken for a year's supply of meat. The caravan was taking the annual supplies of rations for the monks of Ragyabas.

When they were within sight of the Devil-gate, both men, Bhatta and Gomti saw a yellow-robed monk going up the steps that ran along the outer walls. Bhatta pointed with his hand.

'There! He is taking the Head Lama's daily food.'

For a moment they both halted in their tracks, watching the man in the yellow robe going up the narrow, unrailed staircase that clung to the cliff. He walked with deliberate steps, as though he was used to the danger of the path. They saw him come up to one of the small square holes in the side of the hill and halt. He had brought with him a bowl of food and a brass vessel of water, and these he now placed on the ledge of the cavity. Then he bowed his head and chanted a prayer, 'Ooomm mani, padmi ahum.'

The sound of his voice lingered in the still mountain air, and before it had died out the two men watching from a distance saw a hand come out of the hole. It was muffled to the wrist in yellow cloth and looked like an insect that had crept out of a crevice, blinded by the light. Even as they were looking the brass pitcher and the bowl disappeared.

The monk waited for a second or two, his gown flapping in the mild breeze, almost as though he expected the hand to emerge again. Then he bowed his head reverently once again, and turning round began to descend the steps. His yellow robe ballooned in the breeze.

From where they were standing watching the scene, the younger man said, 'Amazing how anyone can do it. Stay sealed in like that for ten years, and just bread and water once a day, through that hole.'

'He is a very holy man,' Bhatta said. 'They don't need food and water and…and comforts as we do.'

'But fancy being locked in there, only to show himself once or twice every year, on the feast of the White Lion and the feast of the Green Serpent—then disappear—into that.' He pointed at the forbidding edifice before them and frowned. 'It's solitary confinement. I wonder if he looks forward to coming out?'

'I doubt it, he hardly stays out for an hour each time.'

'Or to the feast?'

'Haven't you noticed? He rarely touches the food,' Bhatta said. 'Just makes an appearance only because His Holiness had directed that it should be done.'

'I'd go crazy—wouldn't you? Thank God this is the last time. I've come to loathe this journey, it gets worse every time.'

'Come on,' Bhatta urged, resuming his walk. 'We've got to send the mule-men back before sunset.'

'I wonder if he is crazy,' Gomti mused, shaking his head and following the older man.

The caravan wound its way behind them like a sluggish snake.

III

AN hour or so later the caravan halted near the Devil-gate. Bhatta and Gomti supervised the unloading of the mules. The enormous spiked door guarding the entrance to the tunnel through the rock, creaked open behind them with a clang of many chains and four yellow robed monks came out. Without a word, or any manifestation of greeting, each picked up a sack and proceeded up the overhanging steps running along the outer wall.

It was nearly dark by the time the last pack-mule had been unloaded. Gomti paid the mule-men and waited at the Devil-gate until the caravan had gone a little distance. Then he turned and began to climb the steps. The gate closed behind him.

IV

THE next morning the eerie silence of the mountains was broken by the thin trembling wail of a copper trumpet blown by a lama in a yellow robe, silhouetted against the bright silver sky. The sound of the trumpet filled the air for about half a minute, after which the lama carefully placed the trumpet in its stand and walked briskly down the stone steps that disappeared under the platform on which he had been standing. He went through some open passages until he finally emerged into one of the main halls of the monastery; a large, rectangular room with delicately carved pillars. The other monks were waiting for him there.

In one corner of the room, near a window, a low table was laid; covered with a hundred different dishes, prepared overnight by the lamas for their annual feast, and all served in exquisite porcelain bowls. In the opposite corner was a plunger, its red handle attached by a wire to an array of dry batteries. On the wall near the handle was a red sign bearing a skull and crossbones and a written notice, under the heading: 'Danger'.

The nine men in the room were all grouped in the centre of the hall, under the stone ceiling delicately carved with an elaborate lotus design. The men squatted on the stone floor; the seven lamas in ceremonial robes and the two others, Bhatta and Gomti, still in their ill-fitting crumpled suits. The lama who had been blowing the trumpet joined the group, and for a while they all sat looking expectantly at a closed door in the wall. On the wall was painted a Tibetan wheel of life, a symbolic rendering of a rooster, and a snake and a pig chasing each other through cycles of life. The whole wheel was held by a terrifying demon-like figure.

All at once as though at some signal, the waiting men all prostrated themselves on the floor, touching their foreheads to the ground. They held this position rigidly for a few seconds, and then simultaneously, as though on cue, raised their heads.

The door before them stood open and the figure of a man stood framed in the black doorway. The Head Lama was wearing a gorgeous yellow silk robe. He looked very serene, almost spiritual, as though his prolonged stay within the mountain had made his skin luminous; his eyes shone unnaturally bright.

'I am ready, brothers,' he said in a dry crackling voice.

No one said anything. They all stared at the Head Lama as though hypnotized.

'Follow me, please,' he intoned. 'Keep close together. If you lose touch you may get lost. It may take days to find your way back, even weeks…but as you know the door will have closed.'

The Head Lama turned and the others made a chain behind him, clutching each others' hands. They followed him through the door and down a flight of steps that led into a long underground corridor lit only by the flickering flame of an oil lamp. Their leader picked up this lamp in his hand and made his way swiftly through a maze of rooms large and small. Finally they emerged into a large rectangular room where a little daylight filtered weakly through holes in the side of one wall.

The four walls were covered with Tibetan thangkas in rich silks, and flags with paintings on them of gods and goddesses; terrifying demon-like figures with faces of tigers and crocodiles. The floor along the walls was lined with chests and copper vessels filled with crude gold coins, trays of rare pearls, gleaming heaps of precious stones and ornaments of elaborate designs. There were at least thirty of these boxes and vessels, their lids open. The men looked incuriously into each one as they filed past in silent procession. In another room there was a collection of statues of the Buddha, each one kept in a cavity of its own, scooped out of the hillside. The statues gleamed dully, and their eyes made of jade or ambergris sparkled with the reflected light and seemed to stare angrily at the human chain shuffling past them. A group of figures in a special alcove were cut out of jade and studded with emeralds and rubies which gave them a fiery glow of their own.

Gomti took a quick look out of one of the holes in the wall. He drew his head back hurriedly for he could see only empty space below him, confirming his suspicion that the room in which they were was built on an overhanging cliff. Far below him Gomti had caught a gleam of water; a thin silver snake that was the river Indus.

'I take it that you are satisfied that it is all here, just as it was entrusted to us,' the Head Lama was saying.

'Yes, Eminence,' they all murmured in unison.

'Good. Then let us return to the waiting feast.' The chain of men filed quietly out of the room.

V

IN the room where the feast was laid out the door that led into the bowels of the hill was still open. The Head Lama hardly glanced at the elaborate spread before him. He picked up a cornmeal cake that was his daily fare and breaking it, put a bit into his mouth. He then took a sip of water before saying: 'This is an important occasion for us, brothers. The very last time we shall all be together. It has been ten years since His Holiness sent out his possessions to be cared for by us. And every year on the feast of the White Lion we all gather here to see that everything is in place.'

None of the others said anything.

'And now the time has come for us to deliver this into other hands as His Holiness had desired. It is a great relief—you will agree it has been a great responsibility. Ten years is a long time. Two of our brother monks who were with us are no more. We ourselves cannot live forever. His Holiness has not been able to come and claim what is his own. A pity! What is the news in Delhi?' he asked, turning to Bhatta and Gomti.

'They say,' Bhatta answered hesitatingly, 'that His Holiness himself is under pressure…virtually a prisoner.'

'A god cannot be made a prisoner by mere men,' the Head Lama pronounced. 'Have you heard the same thing, Gomti?'

'Yes. They say he has accepted Chinese overlordship…that he can never come out of our land.'

'In that case,' the Head Lama said, 'our orders are clear. We are to wait for another three months, till the feast of the Green Serpent. After that you, Bhatta, and you, Gomti, will together go to the Indian government. Tell them the facts. How His Holiness, the Panchen Lama sent out the most valuable of his possessions to India when the Chinese came, and hoped soon afterwards to come out himself. We were to guard this treasure until he came, but if His Holiness was not able to come out within ten years, we were to transfer it to the Indian Government for safekeeping. We will hand over the treasure to the Indian Government…unless…' He paused and took a sip of water.

The men all stared silently at his face.

'Unless, within those three months I receive some other orders.'

'You! Your Eminence!' Gomti could not help speaking out.

'Yes. This was arranged in my last interview with the Incarnation. His Holiness said that if for some reason he desired to countermand his earlier orders, he would send me a personal messenger…'

'But...but your Eminence is sealed in behind that...' Gomti pointed to the massive door. 'How can you receive a message?'

'There is a secret entrance to Ragyabas, an escape route that was hewn out of the rock during the Mongol invasion. A route no one knows. His Holiness is the only person in the world who has an exact plan. He can always entrust someone specially trustworthy to send me a secret message...even though I am sealed in there.' The Head Lama smiled benignly at Gomti.

None of the listeners said anything, and Gomti avoided the Head Lama's eyes.

'After three months then you are to proceed as arranged, without further notice. Make a report to the Indian Government, and bring their officials here, so we can pass on the burden to—to more capable shoulders than ours. Is that understood?'

'Yes, Eminence,' Bhatta said.

'But, Eminence...' Gomti began and then paused.

'Yes, Gomti?'

'But if Your Eminence has received some other orders by then?'

'Then there will be nothing here. Everything will have been shifted already. Only the Lamas of the Amber order will be here as ever.'

'I understand.'

'Meanwhile, I beseech you to take the greatest care, as in the past. Both of you must keep apart as far as possible, and meet only when it is absolutely essential. If anything should happen to one of you, the other will be there to carry out the allotted task.'

'Yes, Eminence.'

'Did you bring fresh batteries for that?' The Head Lama pointed a finger at the red plunger attached to a battery near one of the pillars.'

'Yes, Eminence,' Bhatta answered.

'The stairs running up the monastery are heavily mined as you know. In case any of the monks see strangers approaching they have orders to demolish the staircase so that no one can enter the monastery. We who are inside can carry on on the supplies stocked within, but we have to have fresh batteries every year.' The Head Lama rose. 'Go with luck,' he blessed Bhatta and Gomti. 'Till the feast of the Green Serpent, then,' he said to the eight lamas who had prostrated themselves once more. There was a gesture of blessing. A minute later when they raised their heads again the massive door with the Wheel of Life had closed silently behind him. The man who emerged from solitude only twice a year had been swallowed up by the hill.

CHAPTER 2

I

IT was six o'clock of an early March morning. A strong breeze blew a few white clouds across the sky. In the grey light of the dawn a green Ford Falcon driven at breakneck speed, swept along a winding dusty lane. The car skidded as it took a sharp turn, the tyres screeching in protest and raising a cloud of dust. It then righted itself and went bowling along at seventy miles an hour.

The Falcon screeched to a halt in front of an inconspicuous barnlike structure standing in its own compound, surrounded by a high hedge. On one side of the closed gates was a lopsided board which said:

FODDER DEPOT. MILITARY FARMS.

The door of the car opened and a man got out, wearing well-tailored blue-grey trousers, a thick polo-necked sweater, and a cloth golfing cap. At his approach the gate opened as though manipulated by some hidden device. He ran up the steps and knocked on the door which was instantly opened by a man in a black tracksuit and tennis shoes.

'Good morning, Colonel Jeet, that way please!' The man in the tracksuit pointed to a door on the left.

Jeet opened the door and hurried through a passage which opened out into a large room. Just as he reached the end of the passage, a figure rushed round the comer and charged at Jeet; the curved dagger in its hand made an arc of light.

Jeet checked his stride for a moment. He then stepped forward with his right foot, grabbed his assailant's wrist in his left hand and in the same fluid motion inserted his right hand through the crook of his assailant's elbow. With the left hand held firm, Jeet then began to press down the other man's arm with his right hand.

The man dropped the knife which fell on the wooden floor with a clatter, and as Jeet went on applying pressure, his knees bent forward, his face twitched and great beads of sweat appeared on his brow.

'Not so good!' said a dry voice. 'Clumsy! I saw you check yourself, as though you were startled by the attack…your assailant could have killed you if he had wanted to.'

'Yes, I know,' Jeet agreed, still holding on to his man. 'I…I was taken by surprise.'

'You must never allow yourself to be taken by surprise,' the voice continued. 'That's the whole point of this training; that you go into action absolutely without thinking, your response triggered by conditioned reflex.'

The voice which had at first come from the other end of the room came nearer and nearer. It belonged to a dark, square-faced man who seemed to come gliding through the semi-darkness. As he approached he could be seen more clearly. He was wearing a doctor's smock and was sitting in a wheelchair which he propelled with his hands.

Jeet released his assailant. The man immediately dropped to the ground and worked his arm up and down a few times to ease the pain. Then getting up he began to rub his shoulder.

Jeet put out his hand which the other man shook, and they both grinned at each other.

'Also you're late again,' the man in the wheelchair complained. 'Two minutes and twenty seconds. It…it upsets the schedule. I have a team of Navy Commandos scheduled to go through the Murder Alley this morning.'

'Sorry,' Jeet apologized, 'I drove very fast.'

'It's no use driving fast,' the man in the chair said, 'You must start earlier.'

Jeet laughed. 'I'll start at the same time and drive faster. I won't be late next time. This is new, isn't it? I didn't know we had to fend off attacks even before going into Murder Alley. I…I was hardly prepared.'

'That's the whole point, Colonel. We aim to train you to defend yourself when you are attacked…whenever you are attacked. Not just here, but anywhere at all; in the street, in a room, anywhere where your business takes you. You must go into these holds instinctively, without thinking. No one is going to warn you before you are attacked.'

'No, of course not.'

'We've combined Judo, the Japanese method, then Cheena di, the Chinese method, and our own Dangal to evolve this science. Any fool can defend himself with a pistol. We aim to train our men to kill without arms, without noise and without fuss. Clean and quick, like that!' He snapped his fingers.

'I know, I know. What special tortures have you laid on for me this morning in there?' Jeet pointed at a closed door.

'Oh, nothing really exciting, just routine stuff. Why have you removed your cap?' he asked abruptly.

'The cap? Oh!' Jeet pulled his cap out of his pocket where he had put it. 'Just habit I suppose, to take off one's hat indoors.'

'This is the Commando School, not the Gymkhana Club,' the instructor said dryly. 'Remember that here you are still outdoors, wandering in the streets, as it were.'

Jeet nodded and put on his cap. 'So caps on. That means you've got a man with a gun in there.'

'You'll find out.' The instructor pointed to the closed door at the other end of the room.

'Through there please. I have the next trainee coming up in ten minutes.'

Jeet waved a hand at the instructor and walked through the door. He was now in 'Murder Alley' designed as a sort of finishing school for all those who were trained to kill quickly and silently, and above all without weapons.

It was a brightly lit, twisting corridor with a few dark corners. Jeet strode along the corridor at a fairly brisk pace, whistling softly to himself. He paused to read a notice pasted on the wall, lit up by a bright naked bulb. The notice read: ATTENTION ALL TRAINEES. Below it was written in smaller letters:

'Remember that you are now beginning your stroll through Murder Alley. Remember that those who come to attack you are not your enemies but friends. Cause as little harm as possible.'

Even as Jeet stood reading the notice a man jumped out from the darkness behind him and locked him into a tight embrace. But Jeet had already ducked, thrusting his elbows to both sides to loosen the others grip, and then grabbing hold of his legs, succeeded in throwing the man high over his shoulder, so that there was a dull thump as he hit the ground. He gave a slight cry of pain and then lay still. Jeet frowned and bent over the prostrate figure.

'Are you all right? Sorry, I didn't mean to hurt you.'

Instead of answering, the man lashed out with his foot. Jeet doubled over with pain, clutching his stomach with both hands.

'Clumsy, no good!' came the mechanical voice of the Chief Instructor from just behind them. 'You asked for that. Go through that all over again, please,' he ordered.

They went through the routine again, the attack and the defence. While Jeet stood reading the notice the man crept up from behind and locked his arms to his side. Once again Jeet slipped out of the hold by pushing out with his elbows and ducking. He then grabbed the other man's legs and threw him over his shoulder and the man slumped to the floor and lay there limply. Jeet bent down.

'Are you all right?' he asked.

Again the man kicked, but this time Jeet bent right down, got his right hand below the other man's leg, and twisting his foot, put a hammer lock on it so that the man writhed on the floor.

'Better...much better!' pronounced the man in the wheelchair.

Jeet and the man who had attacked him let go of each other and stood up. They smiled and shook hands, and then without another word Jeet turned on his heel and went on along the corridor for the next hazard.

He had just turned a corner when he heard the quiet command: 'Put 'em up, buddy!' Hardly three yards away a man in a dark suit was holding a pistol steadily aimed at Jeet's stomach.

Jeet acted in a flash; while putting up his arms he whipped off his cap and flung it hard at the other man's face, momentarily blinding him. He then went at him with the speed of a panther, hitting hard at the hand that held the pistol with the edge of his right hand. The pistol clattered to the floor and Jeet then rammed his elbow into the other man's stomach.

Jeet's assailant bent double, clutching his stomach, his face white with pain. Jeet crouched over him, ready for anything.

'Bad, very bad!' pronounced the voice from the wheelchair.

'Why? What did I do wrong there?' Jeet swung round aggrieved.

'You didn't do anything wrong, but you certainly went all out—perhaps did things a shade too right...nearly broke the Havildar's wrist. Remember, however realistic we try to make it, this is still practice. Not the real thing. It is important here to use your skill with the utmost restraint.'

The instructor propelled his wheelchair towards the injured man who was now sitting up.

'Look!' he said reproachfully, pointing out an angry red swelling on the Havildar's wrist.

Jeet went over to the Havildar and patted his shoulder.

'Sorry,' he apologised. 'I didn't mean it, I can assure you.'

The Havildar grinned weakly and rose to his feet. 'That's all right, sir. My word, you hit hard...for a moment I really thought you'd broken my wrist.'

Both men smiled and shook hands.

'Carry on, please,' the instructor said. 'See me in my office when you've finished.'

II

AFTER he had finished his weekly workout at the Commando School, Jeet drove to the Delhi Gymkhana Club. As he passed through the entrance hall the hall porter said: 'Good morning, sir. There was a call for you. You were to ring back as soon as you came, I have the number here.'

Jeet frowned. 'Please get the number and put me through. I'll be in the dressing room.'

In the dressing room Jeet sat on a cane-backed chair near the telephone and peeled off his sweater, 'Run a nice hot bath for me, will you,' he told the attendant.

The telephone rang. 'I've been trying to get hold of you for a whole hour,' a familiar voice said. 'The chief wants to see you… He's been asking for you every few minutes.'

'Oh, no!' He moaned, frowning deeply.

'Oh, yes!' The girl from the duty room answered, imitating his tone. 'You're to see him right away.'

'In the office?'

'No. He's waiting for you in the bungalow…waiting impatiently.'

Jeet pulled on his sweater and dashed out. 'Bath ready, saar,' the attendant was saying behind him. 'Very hot bath ready.'

As Jeet's car came out of the club gate and on to the main road, it passed an autorickshaw that had been parked near the curb. Only after Jeet had gone as far as the circle at the end of the road did the engine of the rickshaw come to life. The rickshaw began to read its way through the traffic on Safdarjung road, following Jeet's car from a safe distance.

Five minutes later, Jeet's Falcon was turning into a bungalow on Akbar road. Here, in New Delhi's official colony, the roads were nearly deserted. It was nearly a full minute after Jeet had turned into the gate that the rickshaw drew up outside. The driver had a flat, mongoloid face and narrow slits for eyes, and his right cheek had a diagonal cut across it, nearly reaching his ear. He leaned out to look at the nameplate on the gate which read: Air Vice Marshal P. Kirpal.

The man in the passenger seat remained immobile, his felt hat pulled low over his eyes. What could be seen of his face was thin and deathly pale, as though he was recovering from some illness. The driver nodded to himself as he read out the name on the plate and then looked at his passenger and shook his head. Then he got out and trundled the rickshaw a few yards and began to tinker with the engine. The man at the back sat without moving as though he was asleep, or too ill to move.

III

THE head of MI 13, Air Vice Marshal Kirpal, better known as 'PK' was sitting in a canvas chair on the back lawn. The table by his side was piled high with newspapers, and on the other side of the table were two low cane chairs. PK was leaning back reading the *Sunday Times* which was held spread out in his hands. All that could be seen of him were his legs sticking out, clad in red and white striped pyjamas and his feet encased in highly polished Morocco leather slippers. As Jeet approached he sat up and lowered his paper. PK was a man about fifty years old, with greying hair and a strong face. He gave Jeet a quick grin and said, 'Ah! Jeet. They've been trying to get you for the past hour.'

'It was my day at Murder Alley,' Jeet explained. 'Your secretary caught me just as I was going in for a bath.'

'Bright girl,' PK said vaguely. 'Sorry to hound you like this, but I have one or two bits of awkward business this morning as soon as I get to office and I wanted to brief you before that. Would you care for a cup of coffee or something?'

'No, thanks,' Jeet declined, lowering himself into one of the chairs. 'Neither coffee nor something.'

PK picked up an envelope from the table and extracted a card from it about the size of a ladies' visiting card. He handed it to Jeet.

Jeet studied the card for a minute. On it was written in neat block capitals:

PREPARE FOR CHAUNG BRIDGE PARTY REUNION. WILL CONTACT AGAIN IF UNABLE TO ATTEND.

After this followed some dots and a dash. Jeet read the message aloud.

PK nodded. 'And the signature,' he pointed out.

'The signature? This?' Jeet pointed to the dots and dash.

PK nodded again. 'Three dots and a dash and another dot. Dot-dot-dot-dash-dot. The letters "V" and "E" in Morse code. V.E. stands for Victor Easy…an Anglo-Burmese sergeant.'

'I see,' Jeet said. 'Bridge party. I didn't know you played much bridge, PK.'

'Chaung Bridge,' PK explained. 'In the Shan hills in Burma. We blew it up during the war.'

'You and who else?'

'I and two others. This man Victor Easy, and another man…a Chinese officer called Chom Jung. We were para-dropped behind the Chinese lines. At the time as you know, the Chinese were our allies and the Japanese were the enemies. The three of us worked as a team destroying communications behind the Japanese lines.'

Jeet pointed to the card: 'Tell me more about this message.'

PK said nothing for a while. Then he said slowly. 'That it should have come at all is the important thing, it has come from Peking.'

'Oh! Is that where Victor Easy is…in China?'

PK nodded. 'He works for their Security Bureau.'

'For the Chinese Ministry of Interior?'

'Must be one of their star men. Smooth, daring and a real lady-killer too. He was given an American decoration during the war…a bronze star.'

Jeet was visibly impressed. 'Bronze star?' He whistled.

'Yes, no less. It must be some sort of an emergency for Victor Easy to have risked getting in touch with us. If he is caught they will shoot him for this. We have a sort of hot line with Peking, very tenuous. We can pass on just one message, in an emergency and hope for the best…knowing we can't send another message through the same channels.'

'What do you want me to do?' Jeet inquired.

'When he shows up I want you to handle him…on your own. As you know the Chinese have a network of agents here, and I don't want them to suspect that we have anything to do with this. For all we know it might be a double-cross. We have to go very carefully.'

'You mean he might really be still working for the Chinese?'

'Exactly! So I don't want this chap to have anything to do with us officially. I've sent back a message that you will be his contact and that he is to tell whatever he has to you.'

'You've sent a message to Peking?'

'Yes, it couldn't be helped.'

'And now that particular channel is compromised and you can't send another message on it, is that right?'

'Yes.'

'Supposing they've cottoned on to this already?'

'Then it means that they already know that you are to be his contact here.' PK replied calmly. 'But that risk we had to accept. In the past we've found that these channels are safe enough for two messages, one coming and the other going.'

'Why do you think he wants to see?' Jeet asked.

'It's difficult to say. It may be a trap of course, but on the other hand we might be able to pick up some valuable information. He's been working in Peking for some twenty years now and must know the whole set-up backwards. I want you to meet this man. I've given orders that the minute he shows up he is to be taken to you and from then on you handle him.'

'What about the other man?'

'What other man?'

'This Chomo, who helped you to blow up the bridges.'

'No one knows what happened to him. May have been killed by the Chinese Communists when they took over. So far as I remember he was far from a Communist sympathiser…very fond of the good things of life.'

'Have you any photograph or something,' Jeet asked.

'Yes, a wartime one. Here.' PK handed a folder to Jeet. Jeet opened the folder and looked carefully at the enlargement of a smaller photograph.

'This is Victor Easy,' PK explained, pointing a finger at the taller of the two men who were both wearing American camouflage overalls.

Jeet saw a tough, muscular man with frank eyes and a defiant, cocky look. Then his eyes turned to the other figure, shorter, heavy-shouldered, round-faced, with penetrating eyes and a sensuous mouth set in a perfectly round face. Jeet went on staring, fascinated at the dark, oddly soft, almost cat-like face.

'And this is Chomo,' Jeet said.

'Yes.'

'Quite a customer.'

'You're right. He was quite cold-blooded. Sometimes he gave me the shivers. I have seen him creep up to a Japanese sentry, put one hand over his mouth, and strangle him with the other hand. And do you know what he used to do while he strangled his victim? He whistled! I swear. He whistled to himself…and always the same tune too, some American marching song.'

'Victor Easy is good at his work, is he? I mean as an agent?'

'None better. He was trained at the OSS…the American Marine school that they set up in Thailand. It was the toughest training an agent could get.'

'The American Marines OSS. They were sort of Commandos, weren't they?'

PK nodded.

'Is there anything else?'

'The message says, "Will contact again if unable to attend." The words have a rather special meaning.'

'What's that?'

'In our service, during the war, if a person was unable to attend, it meant he was dead,' PK explained blandly.

'Dead,' Jeet repeated. 'How does a dead person send a message?'

'The message must have been sent already, with instructions that it should be delivered only if he did not show up by a certain date.'

'Oh, I see,' Jeet said. 'So from now on, if there is any further communication from your friend Victor Easy, it will mean that he is…'

'Dead!' PK finished the sentence abruptly.

IV

THE Chinaman tinkering with the engine of the autorickshaw didn't even glance at Jeet's car as it came out of the gates of the Air Vice Marshal's house, gathered speed and swept along Akbar Road. He gazed at the car receding in the distance and then squinted his eyes and nodded to himself. The man seated inside still had shown no signs of life.

CHAPTER 3

I

A murky light filtered through the narrow window set high into the wall. The room was small and drab and sparsely furnished. Apart from the steel sofa bed on which Pempem and Victor Esterhazy were sitting, there was a small table against the opposite wall, flanked by two bentwood chairs. On the table were a bowl and two plates containing the remains of an austere meal, and a bottle of sauce and two glasses. The walls were cluttered with small and large posters in bright colours, all showing Chinese troops and farmers vigorously engaged in nation-building tasks. On the wall above the sofa was a conspicuously large portrait of Mao Tse-tung. On one of the two chairs sat a large grey cat, delicately licking its paws.

Pempem sighed and snuggled into Victor's arms. 'You've given me the courage to break away from all this,' she purred, looking round the dreary room.

Victor said nothing, but went on stroking her hair with his powerful hands, as though his mind was far away.

She gave a faint smile and shook her head in disbelief. 'How I've longed for something like this to happen. I don't know how much longer I could have gone on enduring this. And yet…and yet, I can't help feeling worried… Oh, I'm so frightened, darling.'

He pulled her closer to him and gave her a peck on the cheek before answering. 'But what's there to worry about? It couldn't be more foolproof. Just leave everything to me. Everything is working out just as though we had planned it ourselves…'

The grey cat jumped down on to a wastebasket, upsetting it, and then perching itself on the arm of another chair, it settled down and stared at them unblinkingly.

II

IN a room at the other end of town, two men wearing Chinese uniforms, stood intently in front of a small loudspeaker on the table. At one end of the room a broad, plate-glass window overlooked the Suchow creek. Through the window could be seen an elbow of the river, crammed with the untidy traffic of sampans and barges. The room itself was luxuriously done up. An expensive Chinese carpet with an intricate design of dragons on it, covered the floor; two filing cabinets, an ornate desk and a few comfortable leather covered chairs, completed the furniture of the room. A very large map of the China-India border covered one entire wall. On the opposite wall hung an oil painting of Zhou Enlai.

The two men listened raptly to the loudspeaker.

'…worry about? It couldn't be more foolproof. Just leave everything to me. Everything is working out just as though we had planned it ourselves.' Then there was the sound of something falling.

'Ting-a-ling is always so restless when you're with me,' the girl's voice came clearly over the loudspeaker.

'I think the bastard's jealous! Looks most disapproving when I kiss you. There!'

There was a contented murmur from the girl, then she said: 'I don't see how it can fail. In any case we're both being sent on this mission to India. There we say goodbye to all this. Sometimes… sometimes I get a terrible feeling that it is all working out rather too smoothly…that there must be some catch in it somewhere.'

The two men listening in to the conversation looked briefly into each other's eyes and smiled grimly.

III

I N the dingy room Pempem trembled in Victor's arms.
'Once we're in Delhi we'll be OK,' he comforted her.
'It couldn't be too soon for me,' she sighed. 'And yet I feel so helpless…leaving my country for a strange land…friendless. No one whom I can turn to except you. And there's always the danger that they won't trust us. Do you think they'll be sympathetic in India? Have you any contacts?'

Victor laughed nervously. 'Oh it'll be all right. There's someone I knew…in fact he was a friend…during the war. We worked together quite a lot behind the Japanese lines.'

'Sabotage?'

'Uh huh, blowing railway-tracks and ammunition dumps and that kind of things. Seems incredible now, but we were working for the Americans then, during the war.'

'You still work for them, don't you?' she asked.

'Who?'

'The American OSS?'

'Don't be absurd! Whatever made you ask such a question?'

She patted his cheek affectionately and smiled. 'But even if you were, you wouldn't tell me, would you now? How silly of me to ask.'

'Darling, you know I have no secrets from you; neither of us can afford to be secretive. We're both too deep in this now…both wanting to break away.'

'And so hopelessly in love,' she smiled at him. 'And so fed up with…with all that,' she pointed a finger at Mao's picture.

He raised his head and started angrily at the picture and then his expression changed, almost as though he had seen a ghost. Almost fiercely Pempem pulled his head down to her and began kissing him.

For a moment there was silence as he nuzzled her neck. Then Pempem said. 'Tell me more about it.' Her voice had a tinge of urgency in it.

Victor did not answer her question but held her closer. 'What is there to say except that I love you,' he whispered.

'What happens in India?' she persisted. 'Have you already sent word to this friend of yours? Is he expecting you?'

'Look at your cat,' he said inconsequently. 'You know, he reminds me of someone. I can't think who…'

'Don't change the subject. What happens in India?'

'You leave it all to me,' Victor said comfortingly. 'Leave it to Victor Easy…that's what they called me during the war.'

'Victor Easy…' Pempem repeated with a smile. She wrinkled her nose and ran her fingers through his hair. 'And what was he called?'

'Who?'

'Your friend in India who used to blow up bridges with you.'

'Just a sec…,' he said raising his head.

'I feel so uncertain…so terrified,' she whispered softly. 'Supposing something does go wrong when we get there. Has he said anything to make you think…have you been in touch with him?'

'Wait!' Victor sat up abruptly and now a look of fear came over his face. He stared hard at Mao's picture and then at Pempem.

'What's the matter?' she whispered, pulling his head to her and smiling seductively.

'That picture,' he said hoarsely. 'I remember it always hung crooked…now it's straight. Who straightened it?'

'Don't be silly,' she laughed. 'Of course it was always straight.'

But Victor was not even listening. He pushed Pempem away and jumped off the sofa bed, all in one cat-like motion, and then, as though he was confronting some dangerous animal he inched closer to the picture of Mao hanging on the wall. Gingerly reaching out he took the picture off its hook and recoiled as he saw the tiny hole in the wall that it had concealed. Then he prodded with his finger and took out the small microphone, and tearing it away from its socket, he flung it on the floor.

His entire frame trembled and his shoulders drooped almost as though he had been hit physically. He turned to face Pempem, his features haggard with shock and disbelief. And then he saw the automatic pointed directly at his stomach. Pempem's face was hard and determined; her hand steady.

'You too?' He whispered in disbelief, pointing a finger at the portrait now lying on the bed.

She nodded.

'But…but how could you?' He gasped. 'With all your talk of making a break together. You led me into this, begging me to help you get out.'

Pempem laughed mirthlessly. 'Traitors to the People's Republic must expect no quarter,' she said harshly.

Victor pressed his fists into his eyes and slumped slowly down as if his legs were unable to bear their burden and fell in a pitiable heap before her, his hair brushing her bare legs. But the moment his head touched the floor, his arms shot out and he grabbed her legs; Pempem toppled backwards against the bed. Victor grabbed her wrist with his left hand and twisted it so that the shot she fired went wide, and the bullet lodged in the roof, chipping off some of the plaster. She struggled wildly as he kept her hand with the pistol pressed to the floor and pressed her body down with his.

'Do you know what I'm going to do to you now?' He grunted.

Pempem, her eyes terrified, struggled hard to escape from his powerful hold. Ting-a-ling sat unconcerned, looking away from the struggle, and delicately licking his hind paws.

'I'm going to choke the life out of that lovely neck of yours,' he told her. 'And I'm going to enjoy doing it too.'

Her face paled as his powerful hands closed around her naked white throat.

'That'll be enough!' said a voice behind them. 'You can get up now.'

Victor whirled, his hands still on Pempem's throat. In the open doorway stood a man with powerful shoulders and a round smooth face, holding a long-barreled automatic in a very steady hand. His face was urbane, quite unruffled and indeed there was a slight smile on it. Behind him were two men in uniform, carrying sten-guns.

'Oh, Chomo!' Pempem gasped in relief. 'I thought you were never coming.'

Victor glared at Chomo. 'Oh, my old friend Chomo Jung himself,' he said. 'I should have known. I didn't have much time… shouldn't have taken so long about throttling that bitch.'

Chomo slapped Victor across his face with the back of his hand and then delicately wiped his fingers on his sleeve, 'You couldn't have

done it,' he said matter of factly. 'We've been here for half an hour…
could have come in any time.'

'Well you were always thorough. Come on, let's get this over.'
Victor said, meekly putting out his hands to be hand cuffed.

Chomo stepped aside and motioned to his two soldiers to come
forward. Before they could reach him, Victor slammed the edge of
his hand into Chomo's, sending the revolver flying, and at the same
time kicked viciously at the first soldier, sending him reeling into
his comrade at the back. Victor dived for the open door, through
a scramble of bodies and legs, and might just have made good his
escape when Pempem brought her pistol cracking down on the back
of his head. He staggered and began to reel, backward and forward,
when she hit him once again. Even as he fell down, the others had
jumped on him and managed to pin him down. Once again Chomo
brought the back of his hand cracking across his mouth. Then they
pulled him up and made him stand against the wall.

His lips broken, blood streaming out of his nostrils, Victor stood
gasping for breath and cursed. Chomo gave curt orders and pointed
to the door, and the two guards propelled their prisoner towards the
landing. Just before he went out Victor turned to Pempem. 'Sorry
we were interrupted, sweet heart, but I shall be happy to wring your
neck some other day.'

'Some other day,' Chomo echoed. 'There is not going to be
another day for you…my men have orders to shoot you before
sundown.'

Pempem picked up her cat and began to stroke him.

IV

A squad of soldiers led Victor into the closed yard and made him
stand against the rear wall. The soldiers secured his wrists against
the steel rings that had been embedded into the wall, marched
back twenty paces and turned about and stood in a line. The guard
commander looked at his watch and glanced behind.

In the gallery that overlooked the courtyard stood Chomo Jung.
Chomo flashed his teeth in a grimace and then gave a curt order in
Chinese to the guard commander. The squad of soldiers raised their

rifles and aimed and the guard commander held up his hand high.

Chomo gave another order and the guard commander's hand dropped, as he yelled, 'Fire!' The rifles jumped in unison, making a short burp as the bullets were fired. Victor's body slumped against the wall and blood began to spurt out of it. Chomo grimaced again and wiped his hands delicately. Then he began to whistle to himself. It was the tune of the marching song of the U.S. Marines, 'From the Hills of Montezuma, to the shores of Tripoli.'

V

IN the elegant office overlooking the Suchow creek, the two men were once again bending over the now silent loud-speaker. The door behind them opened and Chomo Jung strode in. Both men snapped to attention and gave him stiff, formal bows. Chomo nodded curtly and went over to the chair behind the desk and sat down. 'Well?' he asked.

'She never got him to say whether he had already managed to contact them,' one of them said.

'That was unfortunate,' Chomo said. 'So we've nothing to go on beyond those two messages that were passed. Bring them here, please.'

'Here, Comrade Colonel,' the man placed a file on Chomo's desk.

Chomo opened the file and glanced at the messages. First the one in which Victor had asked for a contact in New Delhi. The second from New Delhi telling him to contact Colonel Jeet Mansingh. Chomo gave a tight-lipped smile. 'Fools! They didn't; know we had got on to their hot line. You got the dossier I asked for?'

'Yes, Comrade Colonel, it is on your table.'

Chomo opened the file before him. 'Good!' He nodded. 'Jeet Mansingh. So that's the man Victor was supposed to contact. Pity we don't know whether he managed to send any information to him or not.'

Chomo stared hard at the photograph of Jeet in the file, then after a while, snapped the file shut. 'Send word to Tien Aan to have this man eliminated…just as a precaution.'

His two subordinates nodded almost in unison.

'There must be no mistakes,' Chomo ordered, curling his lips.

'It shall be arranged, Comrade Colonel. Tien Aan is an expert. He has never slipped up so far.'

VI

JEET'S green Ford was parked under a tree on a lonely road outside a double-storeyed house in Friend's Colony. It was a dark night, and the dim street lamp shed little light on the Falcon.

A man crouched near the car, keeping a watch on the house. He had a thin face with a long scar on his left cheek and the cold, lustreless eyes of a killer. The driver's door was open and another man was doing something inside the car in the thin beam of a pencil torch. He worked with swift sure movements. This was Tien Aan.

He placed on the floorboard a small clamp made of steel strips and an empty cigarette tin. With a pair of pliers, he removed one of the small nuts from the back of the dashboard and fixed the clamp to the bolt. He secured it in place by putting back the nut and tightening it. Then from his pocket, he took out a dully gleaming, dark brown, segmented object as big as a man's fist. He examined the grenade in the beam of the torch and then carefully pulled out the pin, keeping the striker spring pressed down with one hand. He flung the pin out of the open door and carefully inserted the grenade into the cigarette tin. Then taking some steel wire out of a haversack, he ran one end of it through a hole in the bottom of the cigarette tin. Holding the clamp fixed behind the dashboard he measured out a length of wire to the brake pedal and snipped off the remaining wire from the end. He then tied the free end of the wire to the brake pedal and inserted the tin with the grenade inside, into the clamp behind the dashboard. Narrowing his eyes, Tien Aan examined his handiwork. The cigarette tin and the brake pedal were now joined by a thin steel wire, so that any pressure on the pedal would pull the tin away from the grenade and release the striker. Satisfied with what he had done Tien Aan slipped out of the car and closing the door softly behind him, he joined his companion in the shadows.

Now they both waited silently in the darkness, gazing intently at the house. About half an hour later the front door opened and a man and a girl stood in the lighted doorway. As they saw the man's face, the two men nodded to each other and faded away into the darkness.

Jeet walked briskly towards his parked car. At the gate he turned and waved at the girl who was still standing in the doorway.

'See you tomorrow,' she called.

'It's tomorrow already,' he pointed out, glancing at the luminous dial of his watch. 'Past two o'clock.'

The girl laughed gaily. 'Goodnight! Look after yourself.'

Jeet waved a hand and opened the gate. The girl shut the door and he waited till he saw the lights go off in the front room. Jeet smiled to himself as he got into the car. Starting the engine, he switched on his lights and drove off.

The car quickly gathered speed and Jeet whistled a tune as he drove. He slowed down to avoid a dog and then sniffed as he got a smell of burning. Suddenly he went rigid and jammed on the brakes. He pushed open the door and flung himself out of the car as it swerved wildly. It hit a roadside tree and went turning over and over. Even before it had settled down, flames burst through the engine.

VII

CHOMO sat at his elegant desk in the Security Bureau at Shanghai, talking busily into the telephone.

One of his two assistants walked briskly into the room, carrying a newspaper.

'It's the "*Delhi Chronicle*",' he said, putting it on the table before Chomo. Chomo glanced at the item heavily bordered in red ink. He barked some orders into the mouthpiece and put the receiver down before reading the item.

'CAR SMASH ON GURGAON ROAD

Colonel Jeet Mansingh of the artillery, died in a car accident on the Gurgaon road in the early hours of the morning, when the car he was driving crashed into a roadside tree and over turned.'

'Splendid!' Chomo pronounced. 'So the path is clear.' He pushed back his chair and walked briskly over to the enormous map of the India-China border. After studying the map for a while, he picked up a pointer staff and placed it on Shanghai saying: 'From here by jet to Lhasa. Then by car up to here,' he pointed to a spot on the Indian border, 'Then on foot,' he barked, stabbing the pointer on the Endee-la pass. 'Send the necessary instructions.'

His assistant nodded respectfully.

'I shall be there on the morning of the 5th of April,' Chomo continued. 'I shall cross no-man's-land between five thirty and six, the same evening. Is that clear?'

'Yes, Comrade Colonel,' the man replied, and slipped out of the room. Chomo stood gazing at the map for a little while; his eyes narrowed, his nostrils flared; as though savouring his thoughts and whistling softly to himself. It was a tune he had learnt long ago, as a young man: the marching song of the U.S. Marines. 'From the Halls of Montezuma, to the shores of Tripoli,' Chomo whistled.

VIII

I N her expensively furnished flat in New Delhi, overlooking the Jantar Mantar observatory, Pempem Kachin lay in bed. She was reading the headlines without much interest; then her face lit up as her eyes fell on a small item tucked away in one of the back pages. It stated that Colonel Jeet Mansingh had been killed in a motoring accident earlier that morning. Pempem smiled smugly and stretching out her limbs luxuriously, hummed to herself and gazed out of the window. Ting-a-ling, her Persian cat wriggled out from under the sheets and curled up against her shoulder.

CHAPTER 4

I

IN the special wing of a military hospital PK walked through polished corridors towards a ward reserved for VIPs. A nurse wearing a crisp white uniform came from the opposite direction and gave PK a warm smile.

She was small, with a trim figure and a light copper complexion. Her looks combined both beauty and an air of well bred distinction.

'How is he getting on?' PK asked.

'Doing very well,' she told him. 'Considering…'

'Will they have to…'

'No, they won't have to operate,' she broke in. Just a broken collar bone and flesh wounds. He must be made of hard rubber to have got off so lightly.'

'Oh good!' PK looked relieved. 'Sister, do you think I could have a word with him this morning…just a couple of minutes?'

'Only if it *is* a couple of minutes. The CO said to make sure that it wasn't more than five.'

'Thanks,' PK said. He showed her the newspaper he was carrying. 'I expect you've been told about this?'

She glanced at the newspaper and nodded. 'That's been taken care of. There are two of us in charge, the night sister and myself. No one else is allowed to see him.'

'That's good. Shall I go in now?'

'I'll just take a look.' She opened the door of the corner room very softly and then motioned to PK to go in.

Jeet lay on the high hospital bed, his chest and left shoulder swathed in bandages. He was propped up against a pile of snow-white pillows and looked quite cheerful. He grinned widely as PK walked in.

'Thank God they've let someone through. So far they haven't permitted a single visitor,' Jeet protested.

PK sat down gingerly on the edge of the bed. 'How do you feel?' he asked.

'I feel fine. But what's coming over Military Hospitals? The way they've been treating me here. No visitors, no phone calls; damn it, I'm not even permitted to write.'

PK lit a cigarette and handed it to Jeet who took a long drag on it before continuing.

'You've got to do something about it, PK. Speak to the CO or something. Pull your rank over them. The way they treat me, I might be a prisoner, damn it, held incommuni...incommuni...what's the blasted word?'

'Incommunicado,' PK suggested mildly.

'That's right. Damn it! Is this a Military Hospital or is this Belsen? For all anyone knows I might be dead.'

PK nodded slowly.

'Fine thing!' Jeet began again. 'Would you believe it? They don't even—' he stopped mid-sentence and stared hard at PK who had a slight grin on his face. 'My God! PK,' he said in a whisper. 'Don't tell me you've done this?'

PK said nothing, but gave another nod.

'Oh, no!' Jeet moaned. He lay back limply against the pillows and took a puff at his cigarette.

'They tried to murder you,' PK reminded him. 'Planted a grenade in your car. We had the ordnance people go over the wreck.'

'I thought I heard a clanging sound, and then I could smell something burning. I jammed on the brakes...then I don't remember what happened.'

'You, must have flung yourself out of the car...that's what must have saved you. The grenade remained stuck under the dashboard...

and exploded where it was. Even so, you're lucky to get away as lightly as you seem to have. They say you're making an excellent recovery…'

'They're not thinking of chopping anything, are they, PK?'

'No.'

'Truth?'

'Yes.'

'That's a mercy.'

'These miracle drugs…'

'Tell me more about this,' Jeet asked.

'There were two sets of footprints near where the car was parked. We also found a grenade pin and a bit of steel wire…that's what set us going. They must have used it to connect the striker pin to the brake pedal or something,'

'Clever bastards.'

'So, since they wanted to kill you, I thought it was just as well to play along and let them think they'd succeeded. Here!' He held out the newspaper to Jeet. Jeet read over the item ringed in blue and grinned.

'You think it might persuade them to go on with whatever they were doing?'

'It might.' PK agreed. 'It's worth a try anyway.'

'Which means…'

'That you'll have to go on staying here for a little while, even after you have recovered…until it's time to come out into the open.'

Jeet said nothing.

'I do hope they've made you comfortable here'

'Oh very,' Jeet said gruffly.

'The sister looks very pleasant.'

'She's terribly bossy.'

'You have everything you want?'

'I certainly don't have everything I want,' Jeet said ungraciously. 'Damn it, it may be weeks, even months before anything happens, while I have to lie here looking at the ceiling…' he spluttered.

'It's a rather nice ceiling,' PK commented. 'Anyway, I have a hunch it won't be long. I feel our friends out there are in a bit of a hurry.'

'What friends?'

'We put the dogs on to the scent of those footprints. Led us up to the Yang-tse restaurant. Then the dogs lost the trail.'

'Chinese?'

'Yes.'

'Could be anyone though; so many people go to Chinese restaurants.'

'Not this one. It's frequented mainly by the Chinese in the Chinese quarter.'

'Did Victor Easy show up at all?'

'No,' PK replied shortly.

'Do you think his little note might be tied up with this business?'

'Looks like it. It's quite unlike Victor not to show up after sending that message. Perhaps he was "unable to attend".' PK concluded.

Jeet nodded thoughtfully.

'Maybe they found him out…eliminated him. And maybe that's why they tried to eliminate you too…if they found out you were to be his contact here. It ties up…ah! That must be the sister coming to turn me out.'

The door opened and the nurse slipped in. 'You've been here exactly six minutes,' she told PK, and then as an afterthought added, 'Sir.'

'So I have,' PK said, getting up obediently. 'Get well soon,' he called to Jeet as he walked towards the door.

The nurse looked professionally at Jeet. 'You look tired,' she commented.

'Get well soon…get well soon,' Jeet repeated frowning and completely ignoring the nurse's remark. 'Tell me, sister, how can you get well after you've already been declared dead?'

The nurse said nothing but removed some of the pillows from the bed head so that he was forced to lie down. He looked contemplatively at the ceiling. 'Sister, do you think the ceiling is pretty?' he then asked.

'Oh yes, very pretty,' she replied, glancing up at the plain white washed ceiling.

'But you wouldn't want to go on looking at it for weeks, would you?'

'Well, not for weeks,' she conceded, smiling warmly at him.

'What's your name?' he asked.

'Nirupa Pandit.'

'Nirupa Pandit,' he repeated. 'Not Mrs. Eichmann?'

'No, why?'

'If this is Belsen, then it would have been right to have a Mrs. Eichmann.'

CHAPTER 5

I

IN the far distance, the Himalayan peaks sparkled with a hard, frosty glare, but the immense panorama of hills and valleys in the foreground was covered with an unending dark forest. And through this thick, matted forest ran the clean, wide belt that was no-man's-land. Here all the trees had been cut to the ground to provide a field for observation and fire. The forest on the other side of the line was Chinese, that on the nearer side, Indian. No wire demarcated either frontier, Chinese or Indian. On the farther side, in a clearing of the forest, was a huddle of tents surrounded by a few strands of barbed wire. A red flag with yellow stars flew in front of one of the tents.

On the nearer side, a young lieutenant and half a dozen jawans crouched behind an outcrop or rocks that overlooked no-man's-land and the Chinese outpost.

One of the jawans sat up with a jerk and nudged the officer. He pointed a finger in the direction of the forest, at a spot about a hundred yards to the West of the Chinese outpost. He said, 'I think we're going to have another refugee trying to make a bolt for it, sir.'

The officer trained his binoculars on the patch of forest. At first he could see only a smudge of yellow in the green of the forest. Then the figure of a man, wearing the saffron robes of a lama, came into view.

'The bloody fool!' he cursed. 'He's just asking for it. Those highly coloured clothes can be picked out a mile away. No chance at all.'

'Do you think they will fire at a lama, sir? A holy…'

'They don't worry about that,' the Jemadar interrupted. 'In fact I bet they'd rather shoot down a lama than an ordinary citizen. The lamas represent the old order.'

'Poor chap!' said the officer. 'I wonder if he realizes that he has nearly a hundred yards of open ground to cross.'

'And a whole platoon of trained soldiers firing at him.'

'We couldn't give him fire support, could we?' the jawan suggested tentatively.

'You know we can't fire beyond that line, as they can't fire this side of it,' the Jemadar said reprovingly.

'But they *do* fire beyond it at anyone crossing no-man's-land.'

'They do. They do,' agreed the officer. 'But we have a little more respect for human lives. No one goes from here to there luckily and those who come…we can always pass them on to our interrogation people…no need to murder them.'

On the opposite hill the yellow-robed figure walking serenely through the forest, seemed totally unaware of the danger.

'The Chinese guards still don't seem to have noticed anything,' the Lieutenant commented.

'Where he is now, is dead ground from the outpost, they can't see him from there.'

'They'll see him all right, the moment he steps into the fireline,' said one of the jawans pessimistically.

The lama came to the edge of the line and without a pause, entered the open ground.

'Oh, my God!' One of the jawans exclaimed. 'There's the alarm!'

There was a shrill whistle from across the hill and Chinese troops scrambled out of the shelters and took their positions. Without further orders they began to fire rapidly at the man who was now clearly visible in the open belt in the middle of the forest.

The lama began to run, fat and waddling. The bullets whistled and whined all around him, kicking up little spurts of earth. The lama kept on running, as though in utter panic, his fat arms flailing, his amber robe flying in the wind.

On the Indian side they cheered him silently. 'Don't run straight you bloody fool,' the Havildar cursed under his breath. 'Go zigzag.'

'He's still alive.'

'Won't be in a minute.'

'God, he must really be holy if he can come through that!' said the Jemadar through clenched teeth.

Bullets pinged all around the man in the yellow robe as he came clumsily on, and yet not a single bullet touched him. The lama had only another twenty yards to go when the rate of firing suddenly quickened.

'What poor shooting!'

'Hope they shoot like that when…'

'By God! He's made it.'

The guns abruptly stopped clattering as the lama reached the forest on Indian territory. He flung himself behind a tree and lay panting in an undignified heap; miraculously alive. The Indians watched him for a few seconds before the officer motioned with his hand to the Jemadar who ran to where the man was lying. Two Jawans followed him. The lama was still lying face down in a trembling heap when they reached him.

'It's over now,' the Jemadar said curtly. 'You've made it.'

The prostrate figure did not stir.

'You're in Indian territory now, don't you see?' The Jemadar continued. 'Sanctuary. Come on, you're safe now.'

'And lucky to be alive…God, you're lucky!' a Jawan put in.

The lama stirred. He touched the earth with his head, folded his hands in prayer and looked up.

Chomo Jung's recently shaved face was bathed in perspiration. Chomo Jung, Colonel in the Security Bureau of the Chinese Military of Interior had just managed to make a successful entry into India.

CHAPTER 6

I

JEET stood in the large hospital room, with a balcony that overlooked a luxuriant garden. In the distance the Qutub Minar was outlined starkly against the deep blue sky. Jeet, in a pair of peach and black pyjamas stood near a window, his hands held high above his head.

'Now bend both arms,' a feminine voice ordered.

Jeet tried to bend both arms at the elbows, and winced as pain shot through his left arm.

'No, no, no. Try again, like this.' Nirupa Pandit standing a little distance from Jeet raised both her arms in the air. 'Now try and do exactly what I do,' she ordered, bending both arms slowly.

Jeet once more found it impossible to bend his left arm.

'You *have* to try, otherwise you'll take ages to get back the use of your arm. Up! Now bring them down slowly. Don't think of your arm, think of something else.'

Jeet gritted his teeth and tried to follow his nurse's instructions. He gave up. 'I can't, Sister,' he grinned.

'You've been dying to get out of here, and you won't even do the prescribed exercises. The CO won't think of letting you go.'

'But I'm all right, Sister, I tell you. It's just the arm…and who wants to do anything with ones left arm, anyway?'

'You're not even trying. You don't obey orders.'

'Of course I do,' Jeet protested.

Shaking her head she came closer to him, a slight smile on her lips. Then she straightened her face and stood in a businesslike way in front of Jeet. 'Put your arm around me,' she ordered. 'No, the left one. That's right. Now bend it.' She told him as Jeet put his left arm behind her back.

Clenching his teeth Jeet began to bend his arm, pressing the girl closer to him. When she was a few inches away from him he stopped; beads of perspiration covered his forehead.

'Come on,' she prompted, her voice still very professional. 'Don't give up.'

The door at the side opened and PK stood blinking in the doorway.

'Just a little more,' Nirupa coaxed. 'Harder…more.'

Shutting his eyes against the pain. Jeet pulled her even closer until he was holding her firmly against his chest. He opened his eyes and grinned sheepishly.

'Ahem!' PK cleared his throat loudly.

Jeet whirled in confusion, but the nurse did not lose her professional poise even for a moment. 'See, you can do it,' she told Jeet with a smile of approval, not attempting to move away.

'Sorry,' PK apologised. 'I was told you were in here—doing exercises,' he added.

'I can't bend this arm,' Jeet explained sheepishly.

'You couldn't bend it any further without breaking the sister's ribs,' PK said.

Nirupa ignored PK's remark. 'Come on, try and straighten your arm now,' she said. 'Slowly now, don't jerk it.'

'I just can't,' Jeet said cheerfully, still holding her crushed to his chest.

'You've got to try,' she coaxed. 'Yes…oh, yes…you're doing fine.'

Painfully Jeet managed to straighten his arm until he was no longer holding her.

'That's better,' she complimented. 'Much better, you're doing very well today. Don't you think so Air Marshal?'

'Very well,' PK agreed dryly. He turned to Jeet. 'When you've finished this, er…exercising, I'd like a word with you.'

'Oh we're done for the day,' the sister said primly. She helped her patient into a towelling robe which was lying on a chair. PK nodded approvingly as she left the room.

'They certainly look after you well here, don't they?'

'Can't complain.'

'I should think not. Military hospitals have certainly changed a lot since my days; all for the better…yes, all for the better.' PK strolled over into the balcony, and stood leaning over the balustrade, looking at the Qutub Minar.

'I've got news for you,' he said softly, still looking into the distance. 'We may have a job for you.'

'Oh, good! I was beginning to get a little fed up with…with all this.'

'I'm afraid what we feared has happened.'

'Victor Easy?'

PK nodded.

'Killed?'

'I think so. There was a letter waiting for you at the club. I wheedled it out of the Hall Porter.' He handed an envelope to Jeet who read the message aloud.

'ESSENTIAL OBSERVE AND PROTECT HIGHEST CARE AND SECRECY. FIRST, PUSHKAR BHATTA, CLERK NIHALSINGH ESTATE, SECOND GOMTI PRASAD, KOSHABI HOTEL MAN-NAGAR. SORRY UNABLE TO ATTEND. BEST LUCK.'

'Poor Victor,' Jeet said quietly. 'So they got him. Any idea who left the letter?'

'It was on a dance night, busy day at the club. The Hall Porter thinks it was a foreigner…looked like an American, he says. Who knows, the Americans might be trying to help us out, but of course they can't do it openly. You know, I always had a feeling that Victor was still working for the OSS.'

'You mean he was one of their agents in China…right in the Chinese Security Bureau?'

'It's just a feeling.'

'That would certainly need a lot of guts.'

'Victor always did have a lot of guts.' PK said quietly. 'Now what do we do about this?' He pointed to the message. 'Keep a tail on these two men?'

'Without their knowing it. The message says 'highest care and secrecy'. Do these two individuals really exist?'

'Yes, we checked on that.'

'I could start tomorrow,' Jeet suggested eagerly.

PK shook his head. 'I was hoping for that, but the CO put his foot down. He won't let you get out for another ten days at least.'

'Nonsense! I'm perfectly recovered.'

'You know what these medics are, once they get you into their clutches…'

'But don't you see, PK, these men are not only to be kept under observation, but protected. Which means they are in some kind of danger.'

'I was thinking of that, but I'm afraid we'll just have to risk that, till they let you out of here. No use putting someone else on this at this stage. Besides, this is what we have been saving you up for—remember that for all they know, you're dead.'

'If you really think it can wait…' Jeet began doubtfully.

'Besides,' PK went on. 'I haven't got anyone senior enough free just now for this sort of work.'

'But ten days, PK.' Jeet protested.

'It may not be that long. I'll get working on the doctors again. Get the chief to speak to the DG if necessary. Perhaps they'll let you out if you always have a nurse or orderly with you for a few days. We might be able to work it out. In the meantime continue with your exercises,' he grinned before walking out of the room.

II

THE river rushed swiftly towards the waterfall where it fell a hundred feet with a deafening roar into the rocks far below. A narrow suspension bridge spanned the river, just above the waterfall. The bridge was extremely narrow, almost like a catwalk, supported by struts which reached up to the great twisted ropes of wire, stretched high above.

It was a dark evening with a lot of cloud in the sky and a strong wind blowing; the two electric lights at the entrance of the bridge were only foggy orbs in the semi-darkness. On the bridge there was barely enough twilight to show the swirling, dark grey water under the bridge. Nothing could be heard above the constant roar of the waterfall, and the sound of the rushing water.

Two figures approached the bridge, muffled up in raincoats and slouch-hats, carrying with them folded fishing rods and shoulder haversacks. One of the men, the burly and big-built man in the baggy suit, was Chomo Jung; the other thin and weedy was Pushkar Bhatta.

'I'm so glad I have been able to have this talk with you, even though your news is not what I had hoped for,' the thin one said.

'What sort of news had you hoped for?'

'That his Holiness had decided to come out, follow the Dalai Lama. Instead of going on living there.'

'Is that why you were so anxious to see me?'

'Yes. You are the most recent arrival from Tibet. I was anxious to find out things from you...to see if there was any hope.'

'So you sought me out, and asked me to go fishing with you?' Chomo asked.

There was a nervous laugh. 'I had to think of some place where we could talk undisturbed,' Bhatta told him.

'Clever,' Chomo murmured. 'Oh, very clever.'

'Actually I don't care for fishing at all. It was just an excuse to get you to myself...actually I don't think I shall go fishing again... far too strenuous, at my age.'

Chomo shrugged. 'I don't think so either.'

'What?'

'That you will *ever* go out fishing again.'

'You're quite right. It's been a long day, and I'm certainly looking forward to a bath and a drink. I'm not a young man, you know. Oh, I am tired!'

'Then why don't you rest awhile?'

'Here, in the middle of the bridge?'

'Why not?' The bigger man glanced up and down the bridge. 'Yes, do, let's stop for a bit, I'm tired too.' Chomo said.

Both men stopped and put down their bundles. The bridge swayed gently.

'So you want to go back to Tibet?'

'Yes,' Bhatta said. 'I want to be near His Holiness, be of some use to him.'

'Then why didn't you go all these years?'

'I couldn't. I have...there is something I have to do here. But it will be over within a few weeks. Then I can go. My wife and family are still there. Ten years now...my children won't even...'

'Have you got a cigarette?' Chomo asked.

'Yes, here.' The thin man rummaged through his pockets and brought out a packet of cigarettes and a box of matches. Handing the other a cigarette, he struck a match. The flare of the match lit up Chomo's face. What he saw made him gasp.

'Hey... What are you up to? Stop it!' The match died out. Bhatta screamed. 'Stop it damn you! Oh God help! Help! I'm being...' His last words ended in a terrifying shriek.

The murderer flexed his arms and wiped his hands, and briefly looked over the railings. All he could see was the swirlings black water below. He said in a dispassionate voice, 'No, Puskar Bhatta, you will never go back to Tibet...nor will you complete your unfinished business here.'

He then looked up and down the bridge which was slowly rocking as a result of their brief unequal struggle. No one was in sight. In a quick, smooth gesture, Chomo pushed Bhatta over the bridge. He then picked up Bhatta's bag and rod and threw them into the river too. Then after making sure nothing was left on the catwalk he strode briskly to the other end of the bridge, his head bent low, his hands thrust deep in his raincoat pockets. After a few paces he began whistling to himself.

CHAPTER 7

I

THE slanting rays of the early morning sun made Jeet blink. He turned in bed and then reached for the newspaper on his bedside table. He scanned the headlines and turning the page skimmed through the rest of the newspaper. He gasped as he sat up and the sudden movement sent a sharp twinge of pain through his left arm. The paper slipped from his hands and went fluttering under the bed. As he made a grab for it he knocked over a vase of flowers which went rolling across the tiled floor.

The door opened. 'And what may you be up to, Colonel?' Nirupa Pandit asked, stonily.

Jeet looked up sheepishly. 'The paper,' he pointed out.

'What about it?'

'I was reading it. It…it slipped.'

'Oh, is that all. I thought a squad of commandos was smashing things up…' she pointed to the deluge under the bed.

Jeet shrugged helplessly and gave her a bright smile.

'Look what you've done!' Picking up the paper she flounced out of the room.

'But, sister…' Jeet protested when she returned a moment later with a mop. 'I wanted to…'

'Then don't…I have half a mind to report you to the CO.' She shook a finger at him, and began to mop up the water.

'Oh don't do that. Things are bad enough already. If you won't let me read the paper at least will you read it out to me?'

She gave him a stony look.

'Oh, just a small item,' he continued. 'Only so big.' He held up two fingers about two inches apart to show her the size. 'Really teeny-weeny.'

She had finished mopping the floor now and returned his smile. 'Oh, all right, if it really is a small one.' She went and brought the paper. 'Which one is it?' she asked, settling herself in one of the bedside chairs.

'There at the bottom...no, in the middle there.'

'About the fishing tragedy?'

'That's the one.'

Nirupa began to read,

'Pushkar Bhatta, a clerk in the Ministry of Commerce died as the result of a drowning accident while he was fishing. His body was found floating yesterday evening. Medical examination showed that he had died of drowning about twenty-four hours earlier. So far as is known, Mr. Bhatta had no dependents.'

'That's all.' she concluded, looking up at Jeet's face. Her patient was glaring sullenly at the ceiling.

'I'm sorry,' she said softly. 'Was he a close friend?'

'Friend? No,' he said shortly shaking his head, his forehead creased in a frown. Then he gave a sharp exclamation. 'Look! Can you drive a car, sister?' He asked.

'Oh yes, but what...?'

'And you're cleared for all security risks, aren't you?'

'I should think so, to be able to attend to patients like yourself.'

'Look,' Jeet said excitedly. 'This is something really serious. Otherwise I wouldn't suggest it. Do you think you could take a week off to look after me?'

'But I *am* looking after you.'

'I mean outside, not here. You see, the CO won't let me out of here. If you're looking after me, maybe he'll agree to discharging me. Also I can't drive a car yet. It's important that I should get back to work, so...'

'It's quite out of the question,' the nurse said, with emphasis.

'But damn it! Do you know that this man might not have died

if I had been out of here two days ago?'

'But…he was drowned in a fishing accident…it says so.'

Jeet shook his head. 'No.'

'You mean he was…he was killed?'

'Yes.'

'Murdered?'

'Yes, yes,' he said with impatience. 'Now lets see…If PK were to tell your CO how urgent it all is, he just might agree to detail a security nurse to look after me. It's just worth trying.'

'It's never been done before.'

'I think we can leave that to PK to work out. The question is, do you want to come in on this?'

'Why…it might really be exciting,' she gasped.

'Dangerous too,' he warned her.

'Oh good!' She said, her eyes shining brightly.

'Then I'd love to. If you can really get me detailed…'

'I don't think that would be very difficult. We can get PK working on that.'

'Are you sure you should be going into this if, as you say, it might be dangerous… When you still haven't recovered from that dreadful car smash.'

'That was no accident either,' he said curtly. 'They tried to blow the car up…planted a bomb in the car.' He stared hard at her face.

'Oh!'

'I am telling you this because I want you to know how dangerous it might be. You still want to risk it?'

She nodded eagerly. 'Oh, but I do! Do you think that the CO will permit it?'

'OK. Hand me that telephone, will you?'

Even before Nirupa could reach the telephone it had begun to ring.

'That must be PK,' Jeet said.

Nirupa picked up the receiver. 'Hullo,' she said into the mouthpiece. 'Oh, yes, just a second. Air Vice Marshal,' she said handing the receiver to Jeet.

'Yes, I read about it,' Jeet said. 'I feel awful too. What? No, no. I'm getting out as soon as possible. It's all arranged. Listen PK, this is what you have to do. Ring up the CO and tell him…'

CHAPTER 8

I

Pᴇᴍᴘᴇᴍ Kachin lived in Olympic Chambers, an enormous, glass and concrete block, of new luxury flats. Her studio overlooked the entire complex of the Jantar Mantar.

Ting-a-ling, the cat, lay on the bed, curled into a tight ball, eyes closed and pink tongue protruding. Pempem herself, dressed in a pair of light blue pyjamas and a man's shirt knotted under her breasts, sat looking intently into large expensive looking radiogram. A shaded lamp threw a circle of light on a gleaming tape recorder and partly lit up her face, which betrayed anxiety, for her lips were pressed hard together and there was a furrow on her forehead.

A warm sing-song voice was on the air.

'This is a special feature bringing home news to our gallant soldiers in enemy hands...'

With the first word Pempem switched on the tape recorder and connected it to the radio. She then lit a cigarette and strolled into the balcony which overlooked the Jantar Mantar. Ting-a-ling noiselessly jumped off the bed and followed her, twining in and out between her legs and rubbing his head against her ankles.

Pempem threw away her cigarette and walked into the studio and switched on the lights. Paintings lined the walls: landscapes, portraits and posters were stacked all over. She walked up to the easel. It held a half-finished painting of a young man with centre-parted hair, close-set eyes and a weak mouth. The stiffly arched eye brows gave the face a permanently inquiring expression. It was a good likeness of Gomti Prasad, the Tibetan agent of the Panchen Lama in Delhi.

The voice on the air was saying,

'...ruled that the field which was taken over for the building of a people's kitchen, shall be given back to your eldest aunt, Wong Li so that she is compensated for the loss of both earning members of the family...'

Pempem lowered the volume of the radio and again stood in the balcony, gazing at the lights of New Delhi. After a while she realised with a start that the messages coming on the radio had stopped and that some Chinese music was now on the air. She switched off the radio, reversed the tape on the spool and played it back.

'...a special feature bringing home news to our gallant soldiers in enemy hands...'

Pempem nodded to herself in satisfaction as she switched off the machine.

II

GOMTI Prasad was riding a bicycle through Connaught Place. About two hundred yards behind him Jeet and Nirupa followed in a car which she was driving. Jeet, his left arm in a sling, sat beside her.

'Just keep him in sight,' Jeet said.

Gomti went along Parliament Street and then veered off along Jantar Mantar road. About half way down the road, they saw him turn into a gate. Parking his bicycle to one side he went into the building which was a large block of flats.

'Olympic Chambers,' Nirupa said as she drove the car a hundred yards beyond the gate and turned.

III

IN her studio Pempem was just slipping an artist's smock over her clothes when the doorbell rang. She shook her head impatiently, and as though making up her mind on the spur of the moment, replaced Gomti's portrait on the easel by a half-done poster and leaned the portrait against the wall. Then giving a quick glance round the room she went to the open door.

Gomti stood outside grinning widely. He said, 'Ten o'clock, on the dot.'

She kissed him on the cheek and stepped aside to let him into the room. Ting-a-ling came and began to rub himself against Gomti's legs, purring loudly.

'Shut the door, quick,' Pempem said urgently. 'Ting-a-ling will escape, he's always trying to run away.'

'Imagine, wanting to run away from you!' Gomti said looking at her fondly.

Pempem pointed at the poster on the easel. 'Look, Gomti… look at that,' she said complainingly.

'What?' he blinked innocently.

'That poster…I just have to get it finished this morning…you'll have to excuse me.'

'But, Pempem! You said ten o'clock and here I am. You said you were going to finish the portrait today, remember?'

'But don't you see? This poster…it has to be handed in this morning. They'll be sending for it soon.'

'But…but can't I sit here and watch you work?'

'But, darling! How can you expect me to work while you're around?' she said archly. 'I'll never be able to concentrate.' She put her head on his shoulder. 'Please, Gomti darling, just let me get this wretched thing finished…it'll be over by one.'

'One!' His face suddenly brightened, 'I'll tell you what! I'll go and buy something for lunch. We'll take lunch out, shall we? Let's go to the Qutub.'

'That would be just too wonderful, Gomti!' Pempem beamed. 'Oh how thrilling!'

Gomti stroked the cat at his feet. 'You know, this fellow reminds me of my friend Lama. They've both got the same sort of face.'

'Lama?' Pempem looked up, suddenly alert.

'Chomo Jung. He comes from my country, Tibet. He too has run away from Tibet because he could not tolerate the conditions there. Maybe the cat comes from there too.'

'From Tibet?'

'Yes,'

'Don't be absurd. Ting-a-ling is Persian.' She kissed him once more on the cheek, and leading him to the door, firmly shut it behind him.

IV

'JUST go and take a look, Rupa,' Jeet said to the girl. 'First see all the names of the residents... There may be some Chinese name, something that may ring a bell. Then go up to each floor and do the same... Study the name plates on each flat. I wish I could go myself...but not with this on.' He indicated his arm in its sling. 'I'd be far too conspicuous.'

Without a word, Rupa got out of the car and walked towards Olympic Chambers. She was just turning into the gate when she saw Gomti come out, trundling his bicycle. He hopped on to the seat expertly and went weaving in and out of the traffic, towards Connaught Place.

In the hallway next to the lifts, was a large board with the names of the residents, but none of the names looked odd to her. Then Rupa took the lift to the seventh floor and went along the corridor, studying the name-plates on the doors. After completing one side, she was returning to the lift when she heard the lift door open. A man got out and went past her. She only vaguely noticed that he was carrying a Baby Hermes typewriter and that he was whistling softly to himself a tune that was oddly familiar.

Chomo Jung edged close to the wall to allow Rupa to pass. As she waited for the lift which had gone down, she saw him ring the bell of a door right at the end of the corridor. The man was still whistling softly to himself.

V

As she heard the bell, Pempem, who had been lounging on the bed, rushed to the door and opened it. Chomo strode in carrying his typewriter. Without a word, he went and sat in a chair while Pempem shut and bolted the door. Then going up to the large open window, she began to draw the curtains.

'Don't draw all the curtains,' Chomo cautioned. 'It would look odd if all the curtains were pulled at this time of the morning. One has to be careful not to arouse suspicion.'

Pempem stopped, still holding the curtain.

'Tourists climbing the Jantar Mantar are always looking into the flat,' she complained. 'Some of them even look with binoculars.'

'That must only be when you are sun bathing, honey,' Chomo leered at her.

She looked at him coldly. 'Don't call me honey,' she snapped. 'So you don't want all the curtains, pulled?'

He shook his head. 'Just make sure that the place where we shall be working can't be seen from outside.'

Pempem drew the curtain behind the small dining table and going over to the radiogram, lifted out the turn table and put it on her bed. Then she reached down into the cavity and brought out a Baby Hermes typewriter, identical to Chomo's.

She put the typewriter on the bed and opened the case. Instead of a typewriter, the case contained a large square book covered in red calico. Very carefully she lifted out the book and taking it to the dining table, pulled up a chair and sat down next to Chomo who had also taken a similar book covered in yellow cloth out of his typewriter case.

Both books, when read together constituted a secret code; either book, if looked at separately was completely meaningless. Pempem was reading out a message which she had scribbled on a piece of paper.

'Aunt,' she read. 'There is also Only Aunt and Eldest Aunt. That's right, Eldest Aunt. Page thirty-one, entry number nine.'

Chomo opened his book. 'Got it,' he said. 'Helicopter.'

'Kitchen,' Pempem read. 'Then there is private kitchen and…
oh, here is Communal Kitchen.'

'What page?'

'Eighty-five, entry thirteen.'

'Here it is. Communal Kitchen means signal flare…red.'

It was a laborious business and they worked steadily, decoding
the message that had come over the radio the previous night.

VI

IT was nearly midday. Jeet sat in the car, frowning and impatiently
drumming his fingers. The car was parked in the yard of the Jantar
Mantar and he was watching Rupa who was trailing behind a group
of American tourists carrying PANAM overnight bags, being shown
round the Jantar Mantar. One or two of the more energetic tourists
had already reached the top and the others, including Rupa, were
still climbing up. She had an Air France bag slung over her shoulder
and as she climbed up, she took a pair of powerful binoculars out
of it. When she reached the top, she trained her binoculars on the
open windows of the building opposite. As the glasses swept over
the building, she saw a portrait of Gomti Prasad leaning against the
wall in one of the flats. Rupa quickly turned her gaze away and it
was not until she was ready to climb down, that she risked another
quick look at the flat. Besides the portrait she did not see anything
that struck her as unusual. Her glasses lingered a moment or two
on the empty typewriter case on the bed. As she looked once more
at Gomti's portrait, she saw a similar typewriter case on the floor
beside it. Thinking it a little odd that there should be two identical
empty cases, she trained her glasses alternately first on one and then
the other. While she was still looking, she caught a brief glimpse of a
woman walking towards the inner room, but before she could look
again the tourists had already begun climbing down the stairs, and
Rupa hurried after them.

CHAPTER 9

I

IN Pempem's flat they had finished their work and were now burning up the little bits of paper on which they had been scribbling. Chomo carried the ashes in a glass bowl into the bathroom and flushed them down the toilet. By the time he came out, Pempem had put her Hermes back into the radiogram. Chomo packed his part of the code into its case and snapped the lid shut.

'So things are beginning to warm up,' Chomo said. 'They're going to send the helicopter the moment we fire the signal flare.'

'And they want us to finish the whole thing before the thirteenth,' Pempem pointed out.

'Doesn't leave us much time, does it?'

'Why should it matter when they come? The sooner the better,' Pempem said. 'There's plenty of time.'

'It's just that...that I don't like to be rushed,' Chomo explained. 'The business here is still unfinished,' he said pointing to Gomti's picture.

'You can finish that today,' Pempem told him.

'Today?'

'This afternoon. We're taking lunch out to the Qutub. You might get an opportunity there.'

Chomo nodded slowly. 'That's an idea,' he agreed.

'Oddly enough he was talking about you,' Pempem said cattily.

'Said you reminded him of Ting-a-ling.'

'Oh, did he?'

'He still wants to pump you about Tibet?'

Chomo nodded.

'Anyway. I'm going to take my sketch book along. I'll ask him to leave me alone for some time while I sketch. After that it's up to you.'

'OK,' Chomo agreed. 'I'll manage.' He stood studying Gomti's portrait for a while.

'Anything worrying you?' Pempem asked.

'This message. The hurry…it's almost as though they don't trust us.'

Pempem grinned. 'Who would trust anyone when there are millions of pounds involved? The jewels alone, must be worth millions. One could easily carry away only a handful and live in the lap of luxury for ever…'

'But who would dream of such a thing?' He snapped, and there was a dark scowl on his face.

'Who indeed,' Pempem echoed. 'But we still have to be careful.'

Chomo checked his anger and studied her face for a few seconds, his nostrils flared.

'Have a good lunch, honey.'

'I thought I'd told you never to call me that…never!' She told him in an icy voice.

He grinned. 'You look very beautiful when you're angry, honey. Quite irresistible.'

She stared at him with contempt.

'And don't you forget your sketch book,' he reminded her.

'No, I won't Comrade Colonel.'

Chomo picked up his typewriter and Pempem turned to open the door. As she passed him, he put down the typewriter and grabbing her, pulled her to him and kissed her roughly on the mouth.

'How dare you!' She hissed, her eyes blazing, when he had released her. 'How dare you…you toad!' Then she slapped his face hard.

He stood looking at her with narrowed eyes. 'I'll make you wish you hadn't done that, honey,' he said very softly. 'I'll make you come crawling on your knees and begging forgiveness, begging to be kissed, begging to be made Mrs Toad.'

Picking up the typewriter, Chomo stalked out of the room, a look of hatred frozen on his face. Ting-a-ling tried to dart out of the open door, but Pempem managed to grab him by the tail as he flashed past. Quickly shutting the door she leant against it, her chest heaving. 'Mrs Toad!' she spat. 'I'll kill you before that. I'll kill you. I'd rather die than become Mrs Toad.'

II

Rupa grinned as she got into the car. She started the engine and began to drive before saying, 'I think we're beginning to get somewhere.'

'Come on, what is it?' Jeet asked impatiently.

'I've found the flat Gomti goes to,' she said triumphantly. 'There's a portrait of him there, so that must be it.'

'Oh, good. Now we have to find out whom the flat belongs to.'

'It belongs to a woman. I checked on that when I went up. It's a seventh floor apartment belonging to a woman called Pempem Kachin. Must be an artist…the room is littered with paintings.'

Jeet grinned and patted Rupa's shoulder approvingly. 'My word! You're certainly getting on. Anything else?'

'Well, nothing much. Just furniture and stuff, all very expensive; there were a couple of typewriters, that sort of thing.'

'You'll have to give it the once-over later.'

Rupa swallowed. 'What! You mean go in there and look around? Me!'

'Yes. It'll have to be you, since you people won't let me go.'

'Your people won't let you go either,' she pointed out. 'You're supposed to be dead and they can't have you walking around with your arm in a sling and a walking stick, attracting everyone's attention.'

'So, *you*.'

'Okay, *me*, I'll go, but you'll have to tell me what to do.'

'Good girl.'

'Where to, my master?' Rupa asked sarcastically.

'Drive back to the flat and keep going round and round till we can pick up Gomti again. I've an idea he'll show up soon.'

Rupa drove on, idly whistling the marching song of the U.S. marines to herself. 'You know,' she stopped whistling. 'I'm beginning to like this work…it's so unusual.'

'Dangerous too,' Jeet pointed out. 'Something pretty girls should not get mixed up with.'

'Do you think I'm pretty?'

'Ravishing.'

'But seriously, do you?'

'Seriously.'

'She is very pretty too, you know,' Rupa said pensively.

'Who?'

'This Pempem Kachin…oh, so smart in her tights.'

'You mean you saw her?' Jeet sat up.

'I just got a glimpse of her as she passed the window,' Rupa could have kicked herself for having forgotten to tell Jeet this.

'My God! Is there anything else you haven't told me?' Jeet asked in an irritated voice.

Rupa drove on in silence for a time. 'Do you know, if this was a job from which I could resign, I would do so now,' she said after a while.

'But I thought you were enjoying it.'

'I'm not used to being shouted at,' she said sullenly.

'I wasn't shouting.'

'You were, too.'

'All right, I'm sorry,' Jeet said, not sounding at all apologetic.

'And also,' she continued. 'I'm not as dumb as you think I am.'

'I never said you were dumb.'

'You didn't say it, but still you implied it.'

Jeet said nothing and Rupa drove on in silence. After a while she began whistling again.

Suddenly he sat up. 'Where did you learn that tune?'

'What tune?'

'The one you were whistling just now: "From the Hills of Montezuma".'

'Is that it? I didn't know.'

'But where did you hear it then?' He persisted.

A frown of concentration on her head, Rupa tried to remember. Then she shook her head. 'I can't remember…must have picked it up somewhere. Sorry. Are you angry again?'

Jeet did not answer her question. 'It's not a woman's tune,' he continued. 'It's a marching song, in fact. Can't you remember where you heard it? Try.'

Rupa shook her head once more. 'I'm sorry,' she laughed. 'I just can't remember. But why do you want to know? What's so special about it?'

Jeet frowned. 'That's just what I can't remember. There is something significant about it, but I can't…'

'There!' Rupa interrupted triumphantly. 'You can't remember either.'

III

JEET and Rupa followed Pempem's car at a discreet distance. Pempem in a pair of pink shorts and a light blue shirt, was driving and Gomti was sitting beside her. The road to the Qutub was almost empty of traffic and when they reached the Qutub, the place was almost deserted. Pempem parked the car while Gomti carried their picnic basket and Pempem's sketching materials to a grassy spot under a tree.

When they had reached the parking area near the Qutub Jeet told Rupa. 'Take the car to the back, behind the wall, will you.'

After Rupa had parked the car in a secluded place they got out and made their way into the garden from a side entrance. They strolled about until they saw Pempem and Gomti in the distance, eating their lunch and then sat down in the shade of a tree. Jeet lit a cigarette.

'Why didn't *we* think of bringing lunch,' Rupa said.

'We're not on a picnic,' Jeet pointed out, annoyed that he had not thought of giving Rupa some lunch. 'Beside, you have a job to do, remember?'

'Don't you wish we were just picnicking here, instead of… instead of doing whatever we are doing.'

IV

No sooner had Pempem and Gomti finished eating their lunch, than Pempem busied herself fixing the sketching paper on to the board.

'You and your sketching,' Gomti said in a complaining tone. 'I thought you'd done with work for the day. I was hoping you would climb to the top of the Qutub with me.'

'All the way up?' Pempem squinted and looked up at the top of the Minar. 'Oh, no Gomti.'

'But it's such fun,' he persisted. 'And I want you to see the view. It's magnificent.'

She gave him a dazzling smile and shook her head. 'I'll tell you what,' she said soothingly. 'You give me an hour for my sketching and after that we'll stroll in the garden. What time is it?'

'One thirty.'

'Give me till two-thirty. OK?' She sat down, resting her sketching board against her knees.

'OK,' Gomti agreed. 'I'll go up and take a look.'

'Don't fall off the top, or anything. Be here at half past two.'

'You bet.'

V

'Did you hear what time he said?' Jeet asked Rupa.

'Two thirty.'

'That gives us a full hour. So now you can drive back to her flat and give it a good look.'

'Me!' She gasped in horror. 'All by myself? But aren't you going to come too? At least sit in the car, while I...'

'One of us has to remain here,' Jeet explained.

'You mean I have to break into someone's flat on my own?'

'Only in the line of duty.' Jeet patted her shoulder reassuringly. 'You'll manage all right, don't worry. Here are the keys,' he said, handing her three keys on a ring. 'One of these should fit. If we'd been given more time we could have got the exact key, but for the moment you'll have to manage with these. Just keep your head and everything will be fine.'

Rupa got up reluctantly. 'Where will you be when I get back… if I get back.'

'Oh, right here!' Jeet answered. 'I'll just go along and take a closer look.' He indicated Pempem in the distance, busily sketching.

'I should have thought one could see quite enough from here.' Rupa said coldly.

'Hardly.'

'Those shorts! They couldn't be shorter.'

'She has the figure to get away with that sort of thing. Anyway, it's all in the line of duty,' Jeet grinned. 'But I've seen worse sights. See you at two thirty then. Be careful, and try not to touch anything… she mustn't know anyone's been inside her flat.'

VI

GOMTI was listlessly strolling towards the Qutub, idly kicking pebbles from his path, when he saw Chomo Jung on the lawn, bending over something on the ground. 'Hey lama…lama!' He called out as he crossed over to him. His face suddenly brightened; there was something he had been meaning to ask the lama, and this was a wonderful opportunity.

Chomo was still stooping, peering at a small snail on the grass, and did not look up till Gomti tapped him on the shoulder and said, 'What on earth are you doing?'

Chomo slowly straightened and turned ponderously to the intruder, a scowl on his face. Then recognizing Gomti, he grinned.

'Do you know I almost stepped on that,' Chomo said, pointing to the snail on the ground. 'I don't know what I would have done if I had crushed the poor thing.'

'But it's only a snail.'

'Only a snail?' Chomo looked at Gomti sternly. 'It's life… one of God's creatures. It should have been like killing a man.' He sounded close to tears.

'Never mind,' Gomti said soothingly. 'You didn't step on it, so why worry?'

'But still... I nearly did...'

'I'm going up,' Gomti interrupted, and pointed to the tower. 'Come on, you come too. It'll do you some good.'

'All the way up!' Chomo protested, shaking his head and patting his bulging stomach.

'It's not that bad,' Gomti laughed. 'Remember you came over the Himalayas.'

'They say there are five hundred steps...'

'Oh come on. You won't step on anything at least...there are no snails up there.' Gomti took hold of the lama's arm and guided him through the tunnel-like entrance door of the Qutub Minar.

The tower was completely deserted and the air inside was musty and cold. They had to pause a little before their eyes got accustomed to the darkness. Just as they began to climb the spiralling steps, Chomo asked, 'You were very close to His Holiness, weren't you?'

'Who?'

'The Panchen Lama. At least that's what I heard in Tibet.'

'Yes, I had His Holiness's confidence. Unfortunately they say he's decided to...er, collaborate.'

'Everyone says he sent out most of his money to India...in case he had to flee.'

'I really don't know,' Gomti replied guardedly. 'And in any case we shouldn't be speaking of such things here, should we now?'

'Why not? There's no one here,' Chomo pointed out.

'Walls have ears.'

'Not these walls, they're dead,' Chomo grinned. 'They're over six hundred years old, aren't they?'

By this time they had reached one of the galleries and stepped out into the dazzling sunlight, squinting their eyes against the glare. The trees and buildings below them were dwarfed by the height. Gomti could see the tree under which Pempem was sitting, but he could not see Pempem herself through the foliage. For a while he craned his neck and then turned to Chomo, who was standing stiffly against the inner wall.

'Dont you want to look at the view?' Gomti asked.

Chomo shook his head. 'Heights make me dizzy,' he said hoarsely.

'Oh come on. What's the point of climbing all these damned steps if you don't even look at the view. I'll hold on to your legs, come on!'

'You will?'

'Yes, yes. Come on.'

Hesitatingly Chomo shuffled forward and stood against the parapet, while Gomti held on to his legs tightly.

'Yes, it is a wonderful view,' Chomo conceded.

'You'll get an even better view from the top. Come on, let's go.'

VII

NIRUPA Pandit, was trembling with nervousness as she stood before Pempem's door, and her mouth had gone dry. For a whole minute, she stood where she was, hoping that something would happen to make her give up her quest. Then she braced herself and rang the bell.

Again she waited, her heart pounding hard, nervously clutching the keys Jeet had given her. Surely, if there had been anyone in the flat, the door would have opened by now. She inserted a key. It fitted the hole, but turned uselessly. The second key worked. The latch opened with a smooth click, giving her a start. She opened the door just a crack and stood as though rooted to the floor. Then she heard the whirr of the lift coming up, and quickly let herself in and shut the door behind her.

First she tiptoed quickly through the large room, making sure that she was alone, and remembering not to touch anything. Then she began to make a more careful search, going systematically from wall to wall, looking behind pictures and under chairs and tables. It would have been much simpler if she had some idea of what she was looking for.

'Anything unusual...anything that strikes you as odd,' she remembered Jeet telling her. Now, what was there that was odd?

The big green Venetian glass bowl on the table was too beautiful to have a sediment of ash sticking to its bottom. On a writing table there was a block of letter paper. Now that should yield fruitful results. And right enough, even though the top sheet was quite blank, it bore the impression of some writing that had been done on the preceding sheet. Only then did Rupa remember the pair of surgeon's rubber gloves that she had been given and which she had put into her handbag. She put on the gloves and taking the pad to the window tried to decipher the writing.

And then her blood froze and she was convinced she was going to faint. There was the creak of a door behind her, slight but quite unmistakable. She whirled, stifling a scream of terror and stared as though hypnotized at the inner door that was opening.

She could have fainted with relief as she saw a large Persian cat, stalking imperiously through the open door. Ting-a-ling came out, superior and disdainful, and perching himself on the fattest and softest chair, began to lick his paws delicately, completely ignoring the intruder.

Rupa tore off the top sheet from the block and put it away into her bag. As though outraged by the sound of rending paper, the cat was now looking accusingly at her. Rupa turned away and went into the room from which the cat had come out. It was the bedroom.

Even as she stood surveying the room, Ting-a-ling, who had followed her in, jumped on to a wicker basket which stood near the bed head. The basket which was stacked full of glossy magazines, slowly toppled, and the cat hastily jumped off it, on to the bed. Copies of *Life* and *Harper's Bazaar* littered the floor and from under the pile slid a gleaming black automatic.

Rupa stared at the black barrel as if it was a snake. Gingerly she picked up the pistol and put it back into the basket, rearranging the magazines on top of it.

Ignoring the cat's intent gaze, Rupa then went up to the tape recorder and switched it on. The machine took a little time to warm up and then a warm, lilting voice said,

'...a special feature, bringing home news to our gallant soldiers...'

Rupa switched off the recorder, and then hurriedly took a last-minute look around the flat. The travelling clock near the bed told her she had been in the flat for almost twenty minutes. The cat now lay sprawled on the pillows, his eyes closed, his pink tongue protruding slightly. She could not resist the temptation to put her own tongue out at him. Then she slipped out of the flat.

VIII

A few minutes after Rupa had left him, Jeet ambled across the lawn to where Pempem was sketching. He stood behind her for a while examining her sketch.

'Excellent!' He pronounced. 'Very good.'

Pempem turned in annoyance.

'Sorry if I gave you a fright,' Jeet apologised grinning disarmingly. 'But it really is a very good sketch…bold and clean.'

'You certainly did give me a start,' Pempem said, but she sounded placated.

'I didn't mean to. It's just that I was so taken by your sketch.'

'I'm glad you like it,' Pempem leaned back and studied her own work. 'Yes, it *is* coming out rather well.'

'Forgive my asking,' Jeet began hesitatingly. 'But do you…I mean do you…'

'Do I what?'

'Do you sell your paintings. It's just…'

'Of course I do,' she answered readily. 'That's how I make my living.'

'Good!' Jeet said, relieved. 'It's odd you know, but I've always wanted a sketch of the Qutub… It has such a stark beauty.'

'But this is merely an outline. I'll take it to my studio and transfer it on to canvas before…'

'Will you be making an oil painting of this?'

'I don't know…I might, if it still looks good tomorrow.'

'I'd like very much to see it again as a finished painting and… and if you haven't promised it to someone else, I'd like to buy it.'

'Then why don't you come to the studio sometime?' she offered, giving him a friendly smile. 'I have other paintings there. You might like one of them.'

'Oh, may I? I should love to,' Jeet said eagerly. 'I'd really like to see more of your work.'

'I live on Jantar Mantar road, Olympic Chambers. The name is Kachin, Pempem Kachin.'

'Why, thanks,' Jeet beamed. 'Most kind of you. Now I'm sure you want to get on with your picture. They say one should never distract creative artists…but you looked so attractive doing the sketch that I just had to come for a closer look.'

Pempem blushed prettily at the compliment and smiled her thanks.

Jeet turned and strolled away. He turned round once to find her looking at him and their eyes met briefly.

IX

CHOMO and Gomti stood on the highest platform of the Qutub and from where they were standing, everything looked minute. Chomo stood pressed against the wall, while Gomti leaned against the parapet and looked down. 'Come on, take a look,' Gomti invited.

Chomo rolled his eyes in terror. 'Not on your life!' He said emphatically. 'It was bad enough from below.'

Gomti turned and faced Chomo. 'I've been meaning to ask you something, Lama,' he said slowly. 'Was there much talk in Tibet about what the Panchen Lama intended to do?'

'What sort of talk?'

'Oh, anything at all.'

'There was some rumour about His Holiness having sent out his money to this country…why do you ask?'

'Because…er…because Bhatta too said something like that. He also said that the Chinese were going to make efforts to have the treasure brought back. But then poor Bhatta was the nervous type… always suspicious.'

'Was?'

'He died three days ago…drowned.'

'I *am* sorry to hear that. Was he a very close friend of yours?'

'Friend? Hardly. We saw each other only now and then. You don't know anyone else who came out recently, do you?'

Chomo shook his head.

'You know,' Gomti continued. 'I have a feeling that Bhatta was murdered…that the man he went to see, killed him.'

'How dreadful!' Chomo said very softly. 'But why should anyone have wanted to kill him?'

'Poor Bhatta, he was inclined to talk too much, you know…oh there!' He exclaimed suddenly, pointing a finger. 'I can see the tree now. Someone is talking to Pempem.'

'Who…where?' Chomo asked, suddenly animated. He shuffled forward to look out and bracing his knees against the parapet, he leaned over. Chomo blinked his eyes short-sightedly, and shook his head. 'I can't see a thing.'

'There, under that gulmohur. You can just see a part of him…a man with his arm in a sling.'

'No, I can't see a thing,' Chomo repeated as he straightened up.

'Oh, look!' Gomti said. 'There's a spider on the wall…such a pretty one too.'

Chomo frowned as he turned to look at the ancient, fragmented stonework. A small green and gold spider stared back at him from one of the slabs. Chomo quickly took out a folded newspaper from his pocket and, very casually swatted the spider.

Gomti once again turned and leaned over the parapet. 'Oh, there I think I can see the man now, he's walking away from the tree.'

'Here, Lama, grab my legs, will you, while I take a look.'

'Grab your legs?'

'Uh-hunh, so I don't fall over.'

'OK,' Chomo said without enthusiasm. He bent over and gingerly clutched Gomti's legs. 'Don't lean out too far,' he warned.

'No, I won't. But hold tight, don't let go.'

'OK, OK, I'm holding tight.'

'Oh, damn! He's walked out of my sight again…I can't see him at all now.'

For a while, neither said anything and when Gomti spoke again his voice held a note of uncertainty.

'You know Lama, at times you act so queer, that if I didn't know you were such a harmless man, even I would start getting suspicious.'

Chomo took a little time to answer. 'What do you mean queer?'

'Well, just inconsistent things, such as…'

'Finish looking please, my arms are getting tired.'

'Such as, well…you always said how terrified you were of heights, and yet when I said someone was talking to Pempem, you went and leaned right out.'

Gomti waited for Chomo to explain and when he remained silent, went on.

'And that snail…you were so worried you might have stepped on it. And then you went and swatted that poor little spider. Why? A lama never kills anything. To him all life is sacred, all living things… even ants and worms.'

Chomo said nothing, but strengthened his hold against Gomti's legs.

And then Gomti was saying in a hoarse, croaking whisper,

'You're hurting me now, dammit, Lama; there's something hard pressing against my legs…something in your pocket…' In the cramped position he was in, Gomti had to strain hard to look at the bending man and he saw that the thing pressing into his flesh was a pistol secured in a shoulder holster. 'My God! You carry a gun, Lama. Does that mean…oh, my God!' Gomti could feel the movement of the muscles like snakes coiling against his thighs and see the beads of sweat forming on the oily, hairless head of the man who was going to murder him.

'Who are you, Lama? A lama who carries a gun; and I thought you were a holy man. My God…was it you poor Bhatta went to see. Did you…oh God…did you kill Bhatta?'

'I did,' Chomo hissed through clenched teeth.

'Let me go. Please, let me go!' Gomti's voice was a terrified whine.

Chomo gave a quick upward heave, as though exulting in giving his powerful shoulder muscles their full play. Gomti's fingers clawed desperately at the stone parapet for a hold. His terrified shriek was drowned out almost instantly as he went hurtling down, as though the life had gone out of him long before he hit the ground.

Chomo stood breathing heavily, and then looked round to see if there was any evidence of their brief struggle. He took out a handkerchief and delicately wiped his fingers. Then he began to climb down the steps, whistling to himself the marching song of the U.S. marines.

X

RUPA parked the car behind the Qutub, exactly where she had parked it earlier. She was locking the car door, when she happened to glance at the top of the tower. The two figures silhouetted against the bright blue sky had suddenly fused, and then one of them came hurtling down. For a second, her frame went rigid, and then she began to run, trying to get to where she had left Jeet, stumbling over stone parapets and bristly bushes and cursing herself for having parked the car so far away. She had to negotiate the maze of high stone walls and corridors surrounding the Ashoka pillar before she could come out into the main gardens, and just as she was skirting a high stone wall, something brought her to an abrupt halt. On the other side of the wall someone was whistling; whistling a tune that was now familiar and oddly sinister.

Rupa scrambled over a stone heap in an effort to take a look, and then wasted a few more precious moments by attempting to scale the wall, before she decided to run all the way back and through the door to get to the other side. When she finally got to the other side of the wall, the place was quite deserted.

Rupa stood dejectedly for a moment, holding her forehead and panting. A slight sound behind her made her turn. In the harsh, afternoon sun, Jeet stood silhouetted against the pink wall. She ran up to him, and he folded her into his arms.

Gomti's body lay spreadeagled on the grass, the limbs twisted grotesquely. A kite circling lazily at the top of the tower, swooped down to investigate. Rupa buried her head in Jeet's chest as the kite dived.

Jeet stroked the girl's hair. 'Come on, we've got to get away,' he said urgently.

'Is it Gomti...the man we were watching?'

He nodded. 'Come on, we've got to keep out of this. Whoever murdered Gomti, it wasn't that woman. She has an accomplice; it's no use tipping our hand at this stage. Let them think we don't know anything yet.'

'But what happens to...to that?' Rupa whispered.

'The police will take over. An accident or suicide... It will be hushed up...like Bhatta's murder.'

Once they were back in the car and driving towards Delhi, Jeet said, 'I think I've managed to make friends with our Miss Pempem. I've even been invited to her flat.'

Rupa did not say anything, and for a long time they drove on in silence, aware of a new tension between them. It was not until they were within sight of Safdarjung, that Rupa gave a dry chuckle and said, 'Fine secret agent you are! You're told to look after two people. Given time to prepare; warned that they're going to be killed, and then what happens? One of them is pushed into a river and the other is murdered right under your nose, while you are trying to make friends with that...'

'Go on, rub it in!' Jeet snapped.

The ease with which she had managed to hurt him, made her contrite. 'I didn't really mean to be nasty,' she apologised. 'It's just the shock of seeing a body come hurtling down and falling with that terrible thud...'

'I know,' he said soothingly. 'Forget it.'

And then she remembered what she had to tell Jeet. 'That tune,' she said excitedly. 'The one I've been whistling...I heard it again, at the Qutub, after I'd seen the body falling down. Someone was whistling it on the other side of the courtyard where the Ashoka

Pillar is. I couldn't see who it was...I tried.'

'Oh, what a pity!' Jeet said reflectively. 'It's just a hunch I seem to have...that this tune is somehow closely linked up with–with whatever we are trying to tackle. And yet I can't imagine what it can be. If I could only remember where I'd heard it before, in what circumstances, it might help. Were you able to discover anything useful?'

'Discover?'

'In Pempem's apartment.'

'Oh, that! It had gone clean out of my mind. Well, I don't know if I found anything useful...'

'You'd better drive to Gallico's and tell me over some lunch. You must be famished.'

'I could certainly do with a cup of tea,' she said gratefully. 'I dont know whether I'd be able to eat anything though.'

XI

J EET and Rupa sat at a corner table with cups of tea before them. At that time of the afternoon the restaurant was almost empty and there was no danger of their conversation being overheard.

'She's been burning up some paper, definitely,' Rupa began. 'There were some traces of ash in a big glass bowl...and it certainly wasn't cigarette ash. And here,' she said handing him a piece of paper which she took from her bag. 'I tore the top sheet from a scribbling pad on the table. The page before this must have been written on with a ball-point pen, it's left deep marks.'

Jeet peered at the paper. 'I can make out an "E" and a "T". Then before that is an "I"...yes, I think it is an "I". What else?'

Putting her head close to his Rupa scrutinized the paper. "E" or "C"? I think it's a "C", don't you?'

'That's a "C" all right,' Jeet agreed. 'So now what have we got? Wait a minute, let me write it down.' Taking out a small diary and a pencil, Jeet wrote down: 'I C O T E.' 'Can you think of any word that contains 'ICOTE' not consecutively?'

Rupa frowned, shaking her head.

'Never mind. We can pass this on to the section. Let them work it out for us. Anything else?' He asked, folding the piece of paper and putting it in his pocket.

'The tape recorder.' Rupa continued. 'It played something peculiar when I switched it on. It just said: "…a special feature, bringing home news to our gallant soldiers in enemy hands…" Then I switched it off.'

'Some sort of broadcast. That too we can have checked up by the section. They can tape the same broadcast and see what they can find. What else?'

'Oh, yes. She keeps a pistol in a magazine basket near her bed. That's all,' she said shaking her head. 'I can't think of anything more. Poor you, it must be so disappointing for you. I'm sure you would have discovered all sorts of things if you'd gone yourself.'

'You've done very well,' Jeet told her patting her hand approvingly.

'Oh, wait,' Rupa suddenly remembered. 'There was nothing typed…nothing.'

'What do you mean, nothing typed?'

'That's just it. There wasn't a single piece of typewritten paper anywhere.'

'Should there have been?'

'But don't you remember! I told you. There were two typewriters in the flat, two. I saw them when I peeped into the flat from the Jantar Mantar.'

'Yes, of course,' Jeet said. 'So you did.'

'And not a single sheet of typed paper!'

'It *is* queer,' Jeet agreed. 'What sort of typewriters were they?'

'Hermes Portables.'

'Both of them?'

'Both. The other too was a Baby Hermes. Both exactly alike in olive green cases.'

'Odd,' Jeet mused. 'Very odd. You certainly are most observant. We'll soon have to give you a double-O card at this rate.'

CHAPTER 10

I

Later that same evening Jeet and Rupa sat in the office of Chief of Military Intelligence, Air Vice Marshal Prakash Kirpal. It was a large, air conditioned room, with two windows that overlooked the spacious lawns of Central Vista. Comfortable leather chairs were placed around PK's desk and book cases lined one entire wall. On the table before PK was a slim folder labelled:

TOP SECRET
DESTROY AFTER READING

The green telephone on the table shrilled loudly and PK picked it up irritably and said, 'Yes, certainly. In half an hour? I'll be there at seven thirty.' Putting down the receiver he glanced at the clock on the opposite wall which showed three minutes after seven. 'That was a summons from the Minister,' he told them. 'He's certainly not going to like it…I don't blame him either. We've certainly come off second best in this.'

'Second best!' Jeet echoed mournfully. 'We didn't even get started. They killed off both our leads right under our noses, as Miss Pandit has been telling me.'

'Well at least this last one, Gomti Prasad, was killed under our noses all right,' PK glanced at Rupa who was uncomfortably looking out of the small window on her right. 'He was pushed off the Qutub in broad daylight. God! The man must have nerve.'

'And that's all there is to go on,' Jeet said pointing at the folder on the table.

PK picked up the folder. 'I take it you have, er...digested what it has to say, so we can have it destroyed?'

Jeet nodded. 'I think so. Both Bhatta and Gomti were Tibetans who had come to this country ten years ago. Both names must have been assumed. They never seemed to get in touch with each other in Delhi, which is odd, because refugees rather tend to stick together. Anyway, no one ever saw them together. They both held fairly inconspicuous jobs, and yet managed to live very comfortably, as though they had some private money. Neither had families, at least not in India. And lastly, both took their leave in March every year, and went off to Chakrata for a whole month. That's about the only thing they had in common...that they both took their leave at the same time and went off to the same place...as though by arrangement.'

PK nodded. 'I have asked the SB to investigate and let me know what they did in Chakrata, whether they got together or not. In the meantime we're stuck.'

'Not entirely,' Jeet pointed out. 'We know the artist girl is implicated in this, she may know something. On the other hand she might only be a stooge, someone they engaged only to entice Gomti. She drove Gomti to the Qutub. We...Miss Pandit and I followed her.'

'She didn't know she was being tailed?'

No, I don't think so. Otherwise they'd hardly have gone through with the murder.'

'That seems logical enough,' PK agreed.

'Then Miss Pandit has been round the flat and has made some important observations which I want to follow up,' Jeet continued. 'I propose to take Miss Kachin up on her invitation to go to her flat. She may be trying it on, of course, but there's always a chance that she doesn't know who I am.'

'Do you want a watch kept on her?'

Jeet shook his head. 'Not at the moment; anyway. If I discover that she is deliberately trying to make my acquaintance, then we can put someone on to her. In the meantime I don't want to risk her being scared off.'

'OK, we'll leave Pempem entirely to you then,' PK said. 'And I must say I don't envy you.'

'Then again there's the Yang-tse restaurant. We'll have to see if that leads somewhere. Those men who planted a grenade in my car, you say the dogs scented out their trail as far as the Yang-tse?'

'I doubt if we'll be able to make much headway there,' PK said doubtfully. 'I've had the place watched for the last few days. Seems an ordinary enough eating place.'

'Meanwhile, we should get some dope from the Special Branch about whether there was anything significant in Bhatta and Gomti going to Chakrata at the same time. Of course, it might have been a coincidence.'

'A coincidence that was repeated year after year for ten years,' Rupa put in diffidently.

Jeet looked at her approvingly. 'That's our main hope really. Why did Bhatta and Gomti go on leave at the same time every year…and to the same place…to Chakrata, what did they do there?'

'Let's see what the SB is able to discover,' PK put in. 'I hope they are going to find that out in time for us to be able to do something. And what about the other complications?' he asked Jeet. 'First about your being reported dead…we can't keep that going for long, someone is bound to catch on. Any one of your friends who…'

'I'm keeping away from my friends, chief, and from my usual haunts. Just give me a few more days,' Jeet pleaded. 'A week at the most so that we can follow up the leads we already have.'

'I don't know what the Minister is going to say after this,' said PK. 'And in any case, are you really well enough to take this on? How are you feeling?'

'Oh, fine,' Jeet said with excessive heartiness. 'Very fit.'

'What do you think, sister?' PK turned to Rupa.

'Not so fine,' Rupa answered.

'The arm is as good as new,' Jeet protested, wincing slightly as he tried to prove his point by swinging his arm.

'They'll have to take another X-ray to see how it has set before deciding. Till then he mustn't drive a car, and mustn't get into any fights.'

'I'm only going to try and discover something from Pempem,'

Jeet said irritably. 'Not get into fights.'

'She keeps a gun,' Rupa pointed out.

'I could give you someone from Security, in place of Miss Pandit, who must be anxious to get back to her own work,' PK offered.

Rupa's face fell. She said, 'Can't I...I mean can't I go on being chauffeur and doing odd jobs? Sometimes it is...I mean, a girl can do some things that a man can't. Besides, Colonel Mansingh still needs medical attention,'

PK frowned, and looked at Jeet. 'It's up to Jeet,' he said.

'I don't know that we should expose you to any further risks. You've done quite a lot already,' Jeet said slowly.

'It's irregular too,' PK said reflectively. 'I mean, I agreed to it as a sort of emergency, but I can't really expect you to...' He smiled and added. 'Thank you for helping us out, Miss Pandit, but I really don't think it's a job for a girl.'

'But I'd like to very much,' Rupa persisted. 'I know much of the background already. Besides, they too have a girl working for them,' she added desperately.

'We don't have women working as agents,' PK said gently. 'They do.'

'But we should,' Rupa insisted. 'Think how useful this Miss Kachin has been to them. I doubt if anyone else, I mean any man would have been able to lure Gomti to his death as easily.'

'What do you say, Jeet?' PK asked.

Jeet shook his head, avoiding Rupa's eyes.

'I'm sorry,' PK said apologetically to Rupa. Then he turned to Jeet. 'I'll get Ramaswamy to tag along with you. OK?'

'Yes, Ramaswamy should be fine.'

Now that the decision had been made, both men turned to Rupa, who sat stiffly in her chair, avoiding their eyes, and looking out of the window. Jeet wished she would relax and smile and accept her dismissal with good grace. It was just as well that they didn't have women agents, he was thinking to himself.

Outside, the lights of New Delhi were coming on and the red sandstone buildings stood silhouetted against the silvery grey sky. Abruptly, Rupa got up and walking to one of the windows, stood staring at the sky. In the distance a lone helicopter droned through the twilight. 'Helicopter,' Rupa said excitedly, pointing to it.

Both PK and Jeet, stared at her blankly.

'It came over me when I saw the thing flying. Helicopter,' she repeated.

'What about it?' Jeet asked.

'The message on the scratch pad,' she told them breathlessly. 'ICOTE. It can only mean helicopter. Someone is sending a helicopter somewhere.'

The three people in the room looked alternately at each other for a few seconds. Then Jeet turned to PK saying, 'I would like to make a special request, PK, that we accept Miss Pandit's offer of help!'

II

IN a large department store, Jeet and Rupa stood before a display of typewriters. Jeet picked up a portable Hermes.

'It wasn't this one?' he asked.

Rupa shook her head. 'No. The case was olive green, I'm quite sure of that.'

'Are you quite certain that you *did* see two typewriters?' Jeet persisted. 'I've been in the flat three times now, and I haven't seen even one.'

Rupa nodded emphatically and then turned to the shop assistant who came up, wringing his hands and smiling.

'Have you the same model in a different colour?' she asked.

'Indeed, we do, madam. Two other shades: rust and olive green. Unfortunately the rust-coloured ones have been sold out, but I think we have one more left in olive green. Ah! Here it is.' He pulled out a cardboard case from the rack, put it on the table and took out the typewriter.

Jeet looked at Rupa. 'Yes, I'd like to buy it, please,' she told the assistant.

A little while later, Jeet and Rupa walked out of the shop, the cardboard case, tucked under Jeet's arm. They got into the car parked nearby and drove off.

'It's funny that I've never seen a typewriter in the flat,' Jeet mused.

'Obviously you've had other things on your mind,' Rupa told him.

'What do you mean?'

But Rupa said nothing and stared fixedly at the road ahead.

'Look, she's painting my portrait, that's all…I mean, I want to gain her confidence, so I can go snooping around her flat.'

'Of course,' Rupa murmered coldly.

As they turned a corner, a Chinaman trundling his bicycle across the road turned to glance at Rupa and then went pale as he saw the man on the seat beside her. Quickly getting on to his bicycle he pedalled away as though in a great hurry.

III

BY the time the cyclist had reached the Yang-tse restaurant, he was bathed in sweat and panting hard. Jumping off from the seat, the man did not even pause to put his cycle on its stand, but let it go, so that it fell over with a clatter. He rushed up the stairs three at a time, through the restaurant which was now empty and burst into the kitchen at the back. He spoke rapidly in Chinese to the three men busily working there, till the man who was chopping vegetables, looked up with a startled expression and told him in English to shut up. He dropped his heavy chopping knife, wiped his hands on his apron and led the cyclist into the backyard before he let him speak again. At the foot of the stairs, they talked in urgent whispers, all the while gesticulating wildly with their hands. Then having reached a decision, they both went up the staircase and gently knocked at the door on the landing.

The door opened immediately and both men slipped through and shut it behind them. They were now in an unpretentious office. Tien Aan sat behind a table, scowling at them with displeasure. 'I told you never to come here…never!' he said. His face was livid with anger.

Both men bowed very low, as slaves before their master. Then the man who had been cutting vegetables spoke. 'We had to come, Comrade Captain. It was an emergency.'

IV

CHOMO Jung bustled about in a tiny two-roomed flat in Jor Bagh. The open windows overlooked Safdarjung's tomb. A kettle of coffee bubbled merrily in the kitchenette and the aroma of freshly ground coffee filled the apartment. Chomo cut two slices of bread and popped them into the toaster. Just as he switched on the toaster he heard a noise outside his door. His first reaction was to throw open a drawer in the kitchen table and grab the small Smith and Wesson revolver it held. Over the barrel of the revolver, Chomo eyed the front door of his flat, ready to fire if necessary.

Three knocks sounded on the door, with long pauses between each knock. This was followed by two short raps. Chomo put away the revolver and went to open the door. He scowled angrily at Tien Aan but did not say anything till the door was shut again.

'Are you crazy?' he hissed. 'I told you never to come here.'

'But this was an emergency, Comrade Colonel.'

Chomo shook his head. 'Nothing can justify this, nothing. I am here to give you orders. It is not your place to give me advice.'

'I am quite aware of that, Comrade Colonel.'

'Then why you fool, why?' Chomo hissed.

'He is alive!' Tien Aan blurted out unhappily. 'We seem to have bungled. I didn't know…'

'Who's alive? What are you mumbling…speak up!'

'The man you ordered eliminated, Colonel Mansingh…'

'But you said it was done! You said so,' Chomo screamed. 'I even read it in the papers. How…' Chomo stopped mid-sentence and stared at Tien Aan. 'Oh, my God!' he gasped. 'Then they…' Then Chomo slapped the other man with the back of his hand, hard. 'Fool! You reported to the Security Bureau that it was done. They'll hold me responsible for this bungling…for your bungling,' he added savagely. 'Traitor!' Chomo spat, clenching and unclenching his fist

'Comrade Colonel,' Tien Aan whispered. 'There is something else I have to report. Something…' his face contorted pathetically and his eyebrows twitched.

'What else can there be after this?' Chomo snapped. 'All the plans so carefully made, falling down. Come on, what else?'

The other man hung his head low. 'I don't know how to say it, Comrade Colonel. But it looks as if they're on to something. I trailed him last evening to the house of…to…' Tien Aan's voice trailed off.

'Where you idiot, where?'

'To Madam Pempem's flat,' Tien Aan said softly.

Chomo pushed the other man so hard that he staggered back a step or two. 'Are you crazy?' Chomo breathed hard into Tien Aan's face. 'You saw him going to Madam's flat?'

'I followed him there, Comrade Colonel,' Tien Aan held his head down. 'They're very friendly, he was there for at least an hour last evening.'

Chomo flung himself into a chair. 'Sit down,' he ordered his visitor, who gingerly lowered himself on to the edge of a chair opposite him. Chomo said very slowly and enunciating his words carefully. 'Are you trying to suggest that Madam is a traitor? That she has gone over to their side?'

'It is not in my place to say, Comrade Colonel,' Tien Aan said avoiding Chomo's eyes. 'But it very much looks like it. It is true that he visits her place.'

V

FROWNING impatiently, Jeet sat in a quiet cafe, before an empty cup of coffee and a half-eaten plate of sandwiches. He looked up in relief as Rupa walked through the door, and got up.

'I thought you were never coming,' he complained, even before she could sit down. 'Coffee?'

'She's just left,' Rupa told Jeet, sitting down opposite him.

'When?'

'About ten minutes ago. Now's your chance.'

'Good girl,' Jeet said approvingly. He dropped a five-rupee note on the table and got up, picking up the briefcase lying beside him. Almost as an afterthought he gave her an affectionate pat on the shoulder and a fond smile. Then he walked out of the restaurant without another backward glance.

Once outside, Jeet hailed a passing taxi and got in. Telling the driver where to go, Jeet settled himself into the back seat and removing the sling that still supported his arm, put it into his pocket. He flexed his arm experimentally a few times.

At Olympic Chambers Jeet paid off the taxi and walked towards the lift, carrying his briefcase in his hand.

The cyclist who was following Jeet's taxi, went straight past the gate after the taxi had stopped, pedalling furiously. It was not until he saw Jeet safely inside the building, that he turned, and leaning his bicycle against the wall, sat down amidst the parked cars and lit a cigarette.

Jeet fitted the key into the latch of Pempem's door and turned the knob cautiously and pushed the door open. He then turned behind to make sure no one had followed him. It was then, when the door was open only a few inches, that Ting-a-ling flashed past him. He must have been waiting right behind the door and had streaked out the moment the door opened. Jeet never saw the cat go out.

Once inside, Jeet slipped on a pair of gloves. He had brought a flashlight with him, so that he should not have to put on any lights, and he ran the beam of the torch everywhere he thought a typewriter could be concealed. The beam played on the radiogram and went past, and then came right back.

Jeet threw open the lid of the radiogram and switched on the record player. Nothing happened. He frowned and switched it off. The machine looked too new for anything to have gone wrong with it already. Or was it a dummy? He bent over it, and gripping it firmly tried to lift it out. It came out smoothly and with startling ease. Jeet deposited the player on the bed and flashed the torch into the cavity of the radiogram. The thin beam of the torch fell on a green, Baby Hermes typewriter.

He took out the typewriter and placed it on the bed. Then from his briefcase, he took out the Hermes that he and Rupa had bought and deposited it within the cabinet. He replaced the record player on top of it and then put away Pempem's typewriter into his briefcase. Jeet gave a quick look round to see that he had not disturbed anything. Satisfied that everything was just as it had been, he let himself out and walked down the stairs instead of taking the lift.

The Chinaman sitting amidst the parked cars barely gave him a glance. It was only after he had seen Jeet get into a taxi that he ambled towards his bicycle.

VI

IT was not till long past ten that Pempem returned that night. Even as she walked down the corridor towards her flat, she realized that something was amiss. The sharp tap-tap of her heels on the tiled flooring suddenly came to a stop, and in the sudden silence she could distinctly hear a plaintive cry.

It was Ting-a-ling mewing, and as Pempem stood listening, from out of the darknes the cat came and began to rub his head against her legs with pleasure, purring loudly all the while. She picked up her pet and held him close to her.

For a moment she stood still, staring at the door, aware that her heart was pounding wildly and that her hands were suddenly trembling. She dropped the cat on the floor and removed her shoes. Then she inserted her latch key and flung open the door and switched on the light, all in one movement. She stood in the doorway and looked round the room, and then very quietly said:

'Hello!'

There was no one in the flat. In the mirror in the hallway, her own face looked haggard and drawn. Pempem took several deep breaths to try and compose herself. The cat had followed her in and she shut and bolted the door. Then, making up her mind, she went into the bedroom and put on the lights. Here too, everything seemed to be as it always had been. She went up to the radiogram and opened it. Now as she pulled up the player, her hands trembled uncontrollably. She almost dropped the machine in relief, when she saw the olive-green typewriter snug in its accustomed place.

So she had panicked for nothing. Ting-a-ling had gone out sometime when she herself had left the door open by mistake. It was the only explanation. In a burst of sheer relief, she picked up the cat and waltzed him round the room.

VII

'DID you see him? Did you actually see him?' Chomo asked excitedly.

'Yes, Comrade Colonel. I saw him go in and I waited at the street door. It was a long time before he came out, at least thirty minutes. He was carrying a briefcase.'

Chomo got up and walked thoughtfully over to the window. There was nothing of any value in the flat to Jeet Mansingh except for the code in the typewriter case; a Baby Hermes would fit snugly into a briefcase. After a long time Chomo turned tiredly towards Tien Aan.

'Thank you, Comrade, you have done well. Meet me tomorrow evening at eight o'clock at the India Gate. I shall have some instructions for you.'

'Yes, Comrade Colonel.'

'It looks as though we have even less time than I thought. You may go now. And remember, never come here again. Is that clear?'

CHAPTER 11

I

A few evenings later, Jeet, wearing a light blue knitted shirt and dark trousers, his left arm once more in a sling, sat comfortably in a high backed chair. Pempem stood a little distance away from him, facing an easel on which there was a half-done portrait of Jeet. She was dressed in a pair of oyster coloured silk slacks and a light pink shirt, knotted loosely at her waist. Turning towards Jeet, her brush held poised in one hand, she studied him professionally for a moment. Going up to him she raised his head slightly with her forefinger.

'Now try and hold that position,' she told him. Bending down, she loosened one of his shirt buttons. 'There! That's much better,' she exclaimed in satisfaction. 'Yes, that's it. You look like Byron, the great lover.'

'That's because I'm in love with you,' Jeet told her.

'But you haven't even known me for a week,' she protested.

'Must be love at first sight,' he told her seriously as she walked back towards the easel.

A few minutes later, Pempem stopped painting abruptly and looked dispairingly at Jeet's face. 'Try and relax,' she pleaded. 'You're too tense, too stiff.'

He gave her an apologetic smile and tried to change his expression. 'Better?' he asked hopefully.

'Worse.' Pempem shook her head.

'Why don't we call it a day?' Jeet suggested. 'You must be quite tired too. Why don't you relax?'

'All right,' Pempem agreed reluctantly. 'I think we'd better call it a day.' Putting away her brushes and palette, she came up to his chair. 'Would you like a drink?'

'Later,' he answered, taking out his cigarette case. He offered it to her and lit one himself.

Pempem bent over his chair. 'What's the matter with you today?' she asked. 'You're suddenly very preoccupied. Is there anything on your mind?'

'Yes, you,' Jeet told her lightly.

'You don't really expect me to believe that, do you?' she smiled.

Instead of answering, Jeet pulled her down to him and kissed her roughly on the mouth.

'Is this your idea of relaxing?' she whispered after a while.

He nodded. 'Now I'm ready for that drink, Scotch on the rocks, but topped with soda. Then I'm going to take you out to dinner.'

'Oh, lovely,' Pempem gave him a dazzling smile. 'Then I'll go and get dressed. Give me fifteen minutes to put on something decent. Then…'

'You look good enough to eat as you are.'

Pempem switched on the ceiling lights and went to mix his drink.

'Oh, wait! Just come here for a minute first,' he called to her.

Pempem came up to his chair with mincing steps. He stubbed out his cigarette and pulled her down to him and she tumbled lightly into his lap.

'I must be smelling of oil paint,' she whispered, toying with the buttons of his shirt.

Jeet said nothing, but went on brushing her hair with his lips.

Suddenly Pempem reached up and grabbing Jeet's face almost roughly, brought it down to hers.

Ting-a-ling stalked out of the bedroom and perched himself on a book case. Stretching his legs, he began to tidy his fur.

II

RUPA stood among the crowd of foreign tourists milling up the steps of the Jantar Mantar, her binoculars trained on Pempem's brightly lit window. She could clearly see Jeet and Pempem, kissing passionately. She shrugged her shoulders and tried to smile, realizing that she was on the verge of tears. She put her binoculars into the airbag slung over her shoulder and disconsolately began to climb down.

The semi-circular flights of pink stone steps joined the landing, forming a platform. She took the left staircase, and as she went down, hardly noticed the man in the dark grey suit going up the right staircase, whistling softly to himself.

By the time Chomo Jung reached the highest platform, he was breathing heavily and there were beads of perspiration on his forehead. For a time he stood still trying to regain his breath, then, taking out a pair of binoculars from his worn travel beg, he trained them on Pempem's flat. Chomo cursed under his breath at what he saw. Now he knew that Tien Aan had told him the truth. This was proof… proof but not evidence. Chomo hurriedly put away his binoculars and took out a gleaming Japanese camera fitted with a telephoto lens. For the next few minutes he clicked away, grimacing all the while. As he put away the camera, Chomo began to whistle to himself.

Rupa, sitting tired and dejected at the foot of the Jantar Mantar, glanced up in alarm. Someone was whistling that tune; the tune associated with Gomti's murder. Her skin prickled with fear, and yet she knew she had to find out who the man was – was he the mysterious murderer?

She had to force herself to go where the man was; get close enough to identify him in the darkness. And then once again her luck failed her. About halfway up the flight of stairs, she realized that the whistler was going down the other flight of stairs. She stood still and watched the man as he went down, merely an impression of bulk and strength, enclosed in nondescript clothes. Rupa had a moment of utter panic as the man stopped whistling and turned his head in her direction. She avoided his eyes and started to descend the stairs too. Rupa hurried down and waited for him at the foot of the stairs, but he had been even faster. She saw his dark form disappearing round the corner, towards the gate. She gulped hard, and sprinted after him, her heart pounding with fear. But as she reached the gate, she heard a motorcycle start, and saw the man in the suit getting on and riding off, blowing his horn at intervals.

III

In Pempem's flat, Jeet, his hair tousled and his shirt buttons open, sat on the long wide sofa, nursing a drink. Pempem who had slipped into a long quilted housecoat, bent to pick up her clothes lying strewn on the floor.

'Give me fifteen minutes to dress,' she smiled at him. 'Then you can take me out to eat…I'm famished.'

The telephone in the bedroom rang and Pempem blanched. 'Must be a wrong number,' she mumbled as she hurried into the bedroom, carefully shutting and bolting the door behind her.

It was Chomo Jung. His voice came mockingly over the telephone. 'Honey? Is that you, honey? And have you bolted the door?'

'Are you crazy to ring me up here?' She hissed.

'Honey,' Chomo continued. 'Who have you been to bed with?'

'That's none of your business,' she spluttered. 'Are you drunk? Don't forget your place. What does it matter what I do in my spare time. And don't call me honey.' Her whole body shook with anger.

'Wait a sec, honey,' Chomo cautioned. 'Just go and take a look at the man on your sofa. Do you know who he is?'

'Of course I do. Avinash Kapur. A friend…someone who's buying…'

'Honey, that's Jeet Mansingh. He works for MI 13 here.'

'Are you mad! He was killed… You told me so yourself.'

'It didn't come off, honey. And you didn't just meet him. He picked you up.'

Pempem's face went ashen. 'Oh, my God,' she whimpered.

'Listen, you little bitch,' Chomo said harshly. 'Get hold of yourself, we might still make it. This is what you have to do now. Ask him to take you out to dinner. You know where to take him.'

The Yang-tse?'

'Yes. They will be waiting for him there.'

'All right.'

'All right, what?' Chomo demanded arrogantly.

'All right, honey,' Pempem answered, almost choking over the last word.

'That's better, oh, much better. And listen. If anything goes wrong, you'd better come and see me. Go to the usual place first. If I'm not there, I shall be at...at the emergency meeting place. And be on time. You know when. We must both get there at the same time. OK?'

'OK, honey,' Pempem answered meekly.

'See that you're not followed, and remember don't do anything rash. I bet they're keeping your place under watch.'

'What about the phone? Do you think that's safe?'

'It's safe... They haven't tapped the line, but that doesn't mean anything. And in any case, you've already gone too far to worry about the telephone,' he added maliciously.

'What do you mean too far?'

Chomo sniggered. 'Committed too many indescretions, sweetheart. I'd hate to be in your place.'

'What?' Pempem almost squealed. 'What did you say? Listen, honey. Please!' But Chomo had gone off the line.

Pempem cradled the dead receiver and sat numbly for some time, looking very shaken. Then pulling herself together, she spoke loudly into the mouthpiece, 'I'll have it ready on Monday. Yes, certainly, you can call for the poster any time after twelve.'

When she went back into the sitting room, she found Jeet sitting exactly where she had left him.

'Tiresome people!' she shrugged, smiling brightly. 'Want a poster done in a hurry. I'll go and get changed, shall I? Then we can go out to dinner.'

'Don't be long,' he called after her. 'Is there anywhere special you want to eat?'

Pempem stood in the doorway. 'N-oo,' she answered uncertainly. 'We'll see what we feel like, shall we? Do *you* want to go anywhere in particular?'

'Well, I feel like having some Chinese food today.'

'Chinese food?' Pempem repeated after him.

'I thought we could go and have some, if you have no objection. There is a very good place, the Yang-tse.'

'The what?' Pempem gulped hard.

'Yang-tse,' he repeated. 'Why, is there anything wrong?'

'No, nothing. Is there any...er...special reason why you want to go to the Yang-tse?'

'No, no special reason. I just thought it would be nice to have some Chinese food and they say the Yang-tse is good. That's all. If there's anywhere else you'd like to go...'

'No, no, that would be fine,' she smiled nervously. 'Just let me get on some clothes.'

As she closed the door behind her, Pempem's face was livid with anger. First, she rushed to the bathroom and turned on all the taps. Then coming back into the bedroom she delved under the magazines in the wickerwork basket and fished out her pistol. Switching off the lights, she opened the door leading into the sitting room, just a crack, through which she trained the pistol on Jeet. For a whole minute she stood there, her face tense, her lips pressed close together, her chest heaving. Jeet was sitting where she had left him, sipping his drink and smoking a cigarette.

Pempem's fingers curled round the butt of the pistol. She saw Jeet stub out the cigarette in the ash tray and get up and walk towards the table, his glass in his hand. After filling his glass with soda from the bottle on the table, he walked back to his chair and drawing up his knees, shut his eyes.

Closing the door very softly, Pempem put away her pistol and peeling off her housecoat went into the bathroom.

IV

FIFTEEN minutes later, Pempem entered the sitting room dressed in a green chiffon sari and holding a strand of pearls in her hands.

'Did I take very long? Oh sorry, you dropped off to sleep.'

Jeet stirred and opened his eyes, blinking sleepily. 'Must have dozed off, sorry,' he apologized. 'May I use your telephone? I want to book a table.'

'At the Yang-tse?'

'Yes. Let's make sure we don't have to wait for a table.'

Walking up to him, she handed him her necklace. 'Could you do up the clasp of my necklace, please? It's rather difficult.'

While he was doing up the clasp, she said, 'Darling, do you particularly want to go to the Yang-tse? Would you mind if we go somewhere else, instead?'

'Certainly not. We'll go anywhere you like.'

'Let's go to the Dutch Oven...shall we?'

'Certainly. There, that's fixed, I think,' he gave the pearls a light tug.

'Thanks. Did you get yourself a drink?'

'I certainly did. And now let's go to the Dutch Oven. You look absolutely gorgeous, honey.'

'Perhaps we could go to the Yang-tse some other time?'

'Any time you like,' he assured her.

V

CHOMO Jung and Tien Aan sat on a stone bench near the India Gate, talking in low voices, even though at that hour of the evening, the lawn round them was quite deserted.

'I am most grateful to you Comrade, for giving me this other chance,' Tien Aan said humbly.

'Loyalty,' Chomo pronounced in a pompous voice. 'That is what I value above everything else. I feel I can trust you.'

'I am grateful, Comrade,' Tien Aan repeated.

'Here it is,' Chomo said, handing the other man a small packet. 'It is a roll of film, already exposed. Send it to Peking through the usual channels. But not another week, that is important.'

'It shall be done, Comrade Colonel.'

'And search his rooms for a baby Hermes typewriter. He might still have got it there... Get it back if you can.'

Tien Aan nodded.

'You had better go now and make preparations. I have arranged for him to come there tonight. I don't want any bungling this time. I want him taken captive and questioned. Don't have any qualms about the methods you use. He has threatened one of our most carefully laid plans, so give him the works. Do what you like, but find out how much he knows. Find out particularly what Madam Pempem has told him and what steps they have taken to upset our plans. Send a full report to Peking.'

'Don't you want a report yourself, Comrade?' Tien Aan asked in a puzzled voice.

Chomo shook his head. 'No, I shan't be here…my time here is over, I am leaving within the hour. But make the fullest report so that they…they realize the full enormity of the offence. The roll of film here will corroborate your report.'

'Yes, Comrade Colonel.'

'And after you have done the questioning, finish him off. That is important too. The man must not be alive tomorrow.'

'It shall be done,' Tien Aan's teeth flashed in a sinister smile.

'Is everything clear?' Chomo asked. 'Can I trust you not to bungle it again?'

'You can trust me, Comrade Colonel. This time there shall not be any mistake.'

'I shall recommend that the last lapse on your part be condoned,' Chomo said magnanimously. 'But that depends entirely on how this job is done.'

'You are very kind, Comrade.'

'You may go now,' Chomo dismissed him.

Obediently Tien Aan got up. 'Good bye, Comrade Colonel,' he murmered, 'and thank you for everything.'

For a long time Chomo went on sitting on the stone bench, glancing at his watch now and then. Then he got up and walked into the darkness, whistling his favourite tune.

CHAPTER 12

I

IT was nearly midnight when Jeet saw Pempem back to her apartment. She opened the door with her latchkey and said, 'It really was a wonderful evening. See you tomorrow.'

If Jeet had expected to be asked in, he did not show it. 'Ten o' clock?' he asked.

'Yes, ten would be fine. We'll finish the portrait tomorrow.'

He said goodnight to her and walked towards the lift which was still on the seventh floor. Only after he had got in and the lift had gone down, did Pempem go into her flat. She bolted the door and then rushed to the radiogram and lifted the lid. Her fingers shook as she took out the record player and her breath came in quick gasps. She could have cried with sheer relief when she found the Hermes in its accustomed place. She put back the turn table and picked up Ting-a-ling who had come rubbing himself against her legs, and carried him into the next room.

At the door she nearly dropped the cat. She wheeled round and darted back to the radiogram and again removed the player. She pulled out the typewriter and put it on the bed and threw open the lid. Her face went ashen as she stared at the gleaming new machine inside. The code had gone. Pempem viciously flung the typewriter across the room and throwing herself on the bed, burst into uncontrollable sobs. Ting-a-ling, sensing that something was wrong, began to purr loudly to attract her attention and then snuggled against her.

In the distance, a clock struck twelve. Pempem sat up with a jerk. She got up and emptied the wickerwork basket and placed it before Ting-a-ling, who recognizing his travelling carriage, eagerly jumped into it, still purring happily. After fastening the lid, Pempem went to a cupboard and taking out a warm coat she put it on. Delving under the pile of magazines on the floor, she picked up her pistol and slipped it into her handbag. Then with the basket under her arm and carrying her handbag, she let herself out of the flat.

Once on the road, she gave a quick glance all round to see that no one was following. She let three cruising cabs pass and hailed the fourth.

Pempem dismissed the taxi in the yard of the New Delhi railway station and mingled with the crowd round the ticket windows. After a few minutes she came out again and took an autorickshaw as far as Connaught Place. She paid off the autorickshaw and walked briskly as far as the next block before she slid behind a dark archway. She flattened herself against the wall and, groping inside her handbag, took out the pistol.

She did not have long to wait. A man reeled drunkenly out of the shadows and went past. She could not see his face, but the man was not Chomo. All the same she kept him covered with her pistol right from the time he emerged from the darkness, till he passed out of the circle of light. He never came close to her.

From nearly fifty yards away, glued to the wall under another archway, Chomo watched his pretty accomplice and cursed under his breath. So she had intended to kill him…the bitch! He would teach her yet. He grimaced to himself and scowled, then he wheeled round and disappeared into the darkness.

Pempem still held her pistol aimed rigidly at the drunk who had paused under the next street lamp to light a cigarette. The man took three matches to light his cigarette and in the flare of the matches she could see Tien Aan's lean, hawklike face. Instead of replacing the packet in his pocket, he threw it on the curb. She could have sworn he glanced in her direction. Then he was gone.

Pempem shrugged and put away her pistol. She waited till the sound of Tien Aan's footsteps had died away and then went and picked up the cigarette packet. She groped in the darkness for the twist of paper she knew would be inside, and taking it out, peered at the message.

'ONE AM PHASE TWO MEETING PLACE.'

Pempem took out her cigarette lighter and burned the message. Then she picked up Ting-a-ling's basket and began to walk in the direction she had come from. What had gone wrong? Why had Chomo himself not come to their accustomed place of meeting? Did he suspect something? Pempem had a feeling that things were somehow coming to a head; and yet she had enough confidence in her own abilities to cope with whatever might come up. A wave of anger passed over her when she remembered how Chomo had spoken to her over the telephone...Chomo, her subordinate, whose proper role was to take orders from her...not to presume to give them.

II

As she came up to the main gate of the Purana Quila, Pempem glanced at the luminous dial of her watch. It was exactly forty minutes past midnight. She quickened her pace and took the path that went up to one of the ramparts. The only light came from a six-day old moon and she had to pick her way cautiously. A stone tower loomed before her, and she began to climb the ancient uneven steps, still clutching the basket with the cat in it, now and then groping cautiously with her free hand to feel the way.

By the time she had reached the observation tower, her strength almost gave way and she sat down on a low stone slab. The railway line passed a hundred feet below her and way beyond the line, gleaming in the moonlight, was the curve of the Jumna.

Pempem glanced at her watch again and stood up. There was no time to lose. She deposited Ting-a-ling's basket among the cobblestones and went and stood in the shadows against the inner wall. Then she took out her pistol and held it aimed at the entrance.

In the distance a train whistled mournfully. The strong beam of the engine's light came slicing through the darkness, before she heard the lazy clanging of the carriages. Then the train swung into view; only from the corner of her eye could she see the first blaze of light and the gleaming black engine and the lighted carriages looking like toys, for her eyes were glued to the arc of faint light through which Chomo would appear. She found herself gulping hard as the seconds passed, thankful for the protecting darkness.

Over the rumbling of the train, Pempem heard a swish and something hit hard against her wrist, sending the pistol flying, and making her cry out with pain. But her sharp scream of anguish was drowned by the thunder of the train and then a powerful hand closed over her mouth.

She struggled wildly, trying to reach the pistol that lay gleaming dully in the moonlight on the beaten-earth floor. Like a cat playing with a mouse, Chomo let her reach the pistol and then brought his foot down hard on her outspread fingers. Again she screamed. Chomo Jung's enormous round head was silhouetted against the sky, the powerful shoulders loomed over her.

'So you were all ready to kill me,' Chomo said evenly. 'That's why you got here early...so you could shoot me as I came up the steps.'

Pempem curled and uncurled her bruised fingers.

'Speak, honey, say something,' Chomo taunted. 'Why didn't you show up at the Yang-tse? The reception was all arranged for your friend. You went to the Dutch Oven instead. I had you followed there and your conversation was recorded. It was clear that he had left the choice to you. You could have taken him to the Yang-tse where the arrangements for finishing him off were ready. Everyone was ready and waiting. Why...'

'You fool!' Pempem snapped. 'I had to do my best to head him off the Yang-tse. It was he who suggested going there, which meant that they had some plans of their own. There was danger in going there, danger for us. Are you too dumb to see that? They'd have nabbed the whole lot of us...all in one go.'

'I may be too dumb, but those who judge you when the time comes won't be so dumb, don't you see, sweet...'

'What do you mean, judge me?' Pempem gasped, suddenly afraid.

'You gave him a copy of the code, too, didn't you?' Chomo

continued as if she hadn't spoken. 'That too has been reported to Peking.'

'I didn't give it to him. You know that. They must have stolen it from my flat. You know that I'd never betray…'

'I do, honey, I really do,' Chomo said menacingly. 'But will they believe that in Peking? Will they believe that you didn't give away the code to be copied and then put back? Particularly after they have seen photographs of you two making love…' Chomo stopped mid sentence.

'Photographs!' Pempem's voice came out as a croak. 'What photographs?'

'The ones I took, honey. That's proof enough. You know what they do to traitors, don't you? The lovely Miss Pempem Kachin, number two in security and mistress of Lee Hung, won't look so lovely after being subjected to our traditional methods of torture. The scorpion and the snake chamber,' he droned on. 'The little bits of skin removed from your face by hungry ants while you are doped and lying unconscious; the red hot irons…'

'Stop it! Oh, stop it,' Pempem pleaded.

'Now, honey,' Chomo said. 'Listen to this, and you'd better listen carefully. From now on you're going to play the game by my rules. I'm the boss, see? Not your subordinate. Forget that you were number two in security and I was way down the list; that you were Miss Peking University 1960. All that is over. You burnt your boats the moment you began behaving like a cheap little whore.'

'Stop drivelling,' Pempem snapped with a little of her old assurance. 'It would never have happened if you hadn't bungled. You told me back in Peking that he had been killed off. I had never seen him before, not even a photograph. I'll show you when we get back. Let's see who is believed and who isn't. Who is given the torture. Who…'

'Sorry to disappoint you, honey,' Chomo interrupted. 'But let me make it clear that you are never going back, never. The evidence against you is too glaring to be ignored, even by your friends in the bureau. You know it too. In any case, you're not going back.'

'What do you mean?' Pempem asked anxiously. 'Are you going to kill me?'

Chomo did not answer for a while, savouring his power over the woman who had always treated him with contempt. 'It depends, darling. I never kill anyone unless I have to. There is an alternative for you,' he said after a time.

'What alternative?'

'I can make you Mrs Chomo Jung, mistress of my house.'

'What house?' Pempem asked scornfully. 'Your two roomed flat in the Security Barracks?'

'No, honey,' he smirked. 'Not my mean little apartment in Peking, but my villa in the South of France, my chalet in Switzerland, my castle in Spain, my rancho in Argentina. Take your choice. Money, servants, cars, jewellery, anything your heart desires; and somewhere safe...safe, and away from all this.' He had almost forgotten her presence and was talking more to himself, than to her.

'But how? I know you have no money and the Americans won't pay you that kind of money. Or, are you...oh, my God! You don't mean to tell me...' she looked at him in horror.

Chomo, obviously pleased at the effect he was causing, nodded slowly. 'That is exactly what I *do* mean, honey.'

'But they'll never let you get away with this...never.'

'I've already got away,' he told her smugly. 'I'm never going back and I'm not letting you go back either. So take your choice, honey. Make up your mind quickly. Will you or will you not share my life?'

'And what's the alternative?' Pempem asked in a trembling voice.

'This,' Chomo replied. Opening the lid of the wicker-work basket, he lovingly picked up Ting-a-ling and began to stroke him gently. In the distance the whistle of another train cut through the silence and the bright, probing light of the engine, knifed through the darkness. As though hypnotized, Pempem watched Chomo hold the cat over the parapet, then she screamed.

'Oh, no, Chomo, please, no! I'll do anything; anything you say, not Ting-a-ling, please.'

Without saying anything Chomo dangled the clawing animal over the hundred foot drop.

'That's what will happen to you. *That's* your alternative.'

'You swine!' Pempem hissed. 'You horrible beast!'

'You're looking beautiful,' Chomo said narrowing his eyes. 'You always look beautiful when you're angry.'

For a moment or two she stared at him in helpless anger and then covering her face with her hands, began to sob.

'And another thing,' Chomo continued. 'I shouldn't try any of your little tricks any more. There just isn't any way out for you other than sharing my life, and becoming Mrs Toad, ha-ha. Madam Toad, Lady Toad, Princess Toad! What they will do to you if you ever get back to Peking, will be far worse than just being pushed down that parapet.'

Pempem went on sobbing softly.

'They'll go by evidence. You made friends with Colonel Jeet, allowed him to make love to you. The films are there. You were the one who kept him away from the Yang-tse when he was going to be killed. You let him take the code...'

'I didn't. You know I didn't.'

'I know, honey. But will they? Certainly not the Green Dragon or Lee Hung. Now will you come with me, share my life? Yes?'

Pempem said nothing for a time, her face was blank and her lips trembled as she wiped her eyes. Then she stared hard at Chomo. 'All right,' she agreed. 'So you win.'

Chomo inflated his chest. 'All right what?' He demanded, drawing himself up to his full height.

'All right, honey.'

Chomo crooked his little finger. 'Come,' he ordered. 'Come and kiss me. A nice juicy one! Like the one you gave that Indian. Come on.'

Obediently Pempem went up to him and raised her face up to his to be kissed. Instead of kissing her, Chomo slapped the upturned face, hard. 'That's going to be your treatment from now on,' he told her dispassionately. 'Just get that clear. I call the tune and you play it, understand? I slap you when I want to, I make love to you when I want to.'

Pempem nodded, trying hard to give him a cheerful smile.

'That's better. Now let's go and see if that cat of yours really has nine lives.'

CHAPTER 13

I

THE men at the office had done a quick job of microfilming the entire code, and now, within hours, it was back in Jeet's safe as though it had never left his flat. Jeet took it out of the safe and put it on the side table in his sitting room. Then he threw open the curtains. The morning sunlight came streaming in. Jeet hung about in the balcony, watching the road below and now and then glancing at his watch. He saw Rupa's car in the distance and as she drove into the entrance and honked, he leaned out and beckoned to her to come up.

Rupa was whistling as she came up the stairs, and the first thing Jeet said to her as he threw open the door was, 'Please don't stop whistling. Just go on; it…it's coming back!'

For a moment she paused, taken aback, and then the urgency in his voice made her stop on the landing and go on whistling for a few seconds. Then feeling slightly ludicrous, she stopped and said, 'What on earth is all this? It's nine thirty-five and you'll have to hurry if you're going to keep your ten o'clock appointment.'

He was still gesturing impatiently as though entreating her to go on whistling, but Rupa had no intention of obliging him. Instead she scowled and said, 'You told me you were expected at Pempem's flat at ten…something about a portrait.'

He snapped his fingers and beamed. 'Come right in,' he invited. 'Gosh! I think I've got it now.'

'Got what?'

'That tune, don't you know? Come in and I'll tell you all about it.' He shut the door behind her and made her sit on the sofa. 'That tune...the one you've been whistling, it's associated with...with killing. I think I know who used to whistle it. It's a long chain, but it might just fit in. I remember PK telling me about it. There was this Chinese agent...an officer really...who was with PK in Burma during the war. An absolute wizard at his job; a killer who used to whistle as he did his job. PK had forgotten what the tune was, but he said it was some American marching song...'

'But...but it all looks so far-fetched,' Rupa pointed out.

'Does it? Well to me it seems to fit in perfectly. A man whistling a tune...a man somehow connected with a killing. Even among Chinese agents they can't have many of those. I'll check up with PK right away.'

'Sorry to interrupt you,' Rupa said. 'But aren't you going to be late for your appointment this morning?'

'Appointment?' he frowned. 'Oh, that! It's all off.'

'Off?'

'Oh, yes. Madam Pempem's gone.'

'What do you mean gone?'

'Just that. Bolted. Run away. She and her boyfriend, both. They've given us the slip.'

'Then what is there to laugh about?' Rupa demanded in exasperation. 'If they've given you the slip.'

'They certainly have.'

'You mean you let them give you the slip...oh, how could you! When you had all the proof you needed. You went into her room and brought out the code in the typewriter...is that it on the table?' She asked, pointing a finger at the Baby Hermes on the table.

'Unh-hunh,' he said casually.

'But how careless,' she exploded. 'To leave it lying about like that....anyone can see it from the windows of the next flat.' She shrugged her shoulders as though appalled at his carelessness. 'It... it makes one wild with rage!' For a minute Rupa stared at Jeet in helpless anger and then said, 'How did they get away? And when?'

'At midnight last night. I thought she might try something like that, so I tailed her. She took her cat in a basket and went in a taxi as far as New Delhi station. From there she took an autorickshaw and went to Connaught Place. There she must have been given some message to go to the Purana Quila, but that's only guesswork since I couldn't get close enough to discover if anyone met her. I had to keep my distance. At about a quarter to one she entered the Purana Quila by the main gate. After that they gave me the slip. I hung around until dawn, but I didn't really expect them to come out the same way. They must have climbed down the wall where it's broken or they may have taken one of the underground passages. The fort is riddled with them.'

'Who's the "they"?' Rupa asked.

'Pempem and her contact; who ever it was who had asked her to meet him there.'

'But surely...surely you could have caught them there. You could have called the police and had them arrested.'

'I suppose I could have,' Jeet agreed.

'And you didn't. And they escaped!'

He nodded.

'You don't seem terribly distressed about it,' Rupa said derisively.

'Should I be?'

'Oh, it makes me want to cry,' she burst out. 'You had them in your hands and you let them get away.'

He shrugged his shoulders nonchalantly. 'Yes, we do seem to have bungled...don't we,' he agreed. 'It's just one of those things.'

'But how absurdly careless!' she protested. 'Pardon my saying so, but I really don't think you people are a match for the other side. Such bungling! Look at that Hermes for instance, right there in the open. Anyone might run away with it.'

Jeet smiled sheepishly. 'Yes, they might,' he agreed.

Rupa went on staring at Jeet's face searchingly for a few seconds. Then she said, 'You don't mean to say...you can't mean that you deliberately let them get away.'

Jeet smiled wearily. 'You're getting a bit too close to the truth, you'd better not ask any more questions.'

'Just tell me one thing,' she pleaded. 'You could have caught them both, couldn't you...if you had wanted to.'

'Oh, yes, quite easily.'

'That means you didn't want to.'

'That's question number two,' he pointed out. 'You were only allowed one, but I'll give you the answer. You see, it was no use catching these two, not at this stage anyway. We are still not sure what they are up to, so it seems sensible to give them more rope and let them play their hand, and then catch them.'

'But they might not do anything more…you might never be able to pick up their trail again.'

'We have to chance that.'

'But they are murderers, don't you see,' Rupa protested. 'And you had them in your hands. Two murders, and then the attempt to kill you. And yet you say they may escape.'

'Murders,' Jeet said softly. 'One mustn't get heated up about murders. What is more important is to find out what the murderers are up to.'

'In the meantime they can go on killing innocent people!' Rupa retorted.

'Not innocent people,' Jeet pointed out gently. 'Only those who are involved in this game, the insiders. A spy never kills wantonly, or in passion, but always in cold blood; only out of necessity.'

Rupa sat silently for some time, digesting what Jeet had told her. 'Do you really think you'll be able to lay your hands on them again? Before they have accomplished whatever it is they're up to?'

'We should be able to. There's an even chance.'

'Do you at least know where they are headed for?'

He shook his head. 'No, not at the moment. But we should in a day or two.'

'And what do we do in the meantime?'

'Nothing, we just sit and wait. Personally, I propose to sleep through the day and in the evening I want to take a look at the Yang-tse, see if I can find out anything there. Excuse me,' he apologised, stifling a yawn.

Rupa stared professionally at his tired face. 'What time did you go to sleep last night?'

'I got back from the Purana Quila at about six this morning, and after that I had one or two things to do.'

'You mean you haven't slept at all?'

He shook his head. 'I have the whole day to catch up.'

'Most irregular!' she pronounced in her nurse's voice. 'Especially as you haven't been well. And have you had breakfast?'

'I had a cup of tea with PK at about seven.'

'You poor thing, let me make you some coffee and toast. Would you like that? Then you can go off to sleep.'

'Oh, no,' Jeet protested. 'I'd never dream of…'

'Don't forget you're still in my charge,' she reminded him. 'Is that the kitchen there? And have you got any eggs in the flat?'

'I think there are some eggs, but…' Jeet protested feebly.

'Then I'll make you an omelette, ' she announced, getting up from her chair. 'I make excellent omelettes. Just show me where everything is and I'll make your breakfast. And in the evening you can take me out to dinner, OK?'

He gave her a startled look. 'Wait a minute. You know that I can't take you out in the evening, I'm going to the Yang-tse.'

'I know,' she answered, smiling at him. 'I'd like some Chinese food too.'

Jeet looked at her speculatively. 'Remember, what I told you about their not harming outsiders? The more you become involved in this, the more you become an insider.'

'I want to become an insider, Jeet,' she said softly. 'Unless you think I'd be a nuisance.'

'No,' he told her after thinking for a moment. 'No, I think you would be quite a help. It's more natural to take a pretty girl out to dinner than to go one's own. It's just that I was thinking of the risks.'

'Then stop worrying about the risks,' she told him gaily. 'Come and show me where everything is.'

'Just a second, I must ring up PK and tell him about Chomo Jung.'

'Chomo Jung?' she asked. 'Who is he now?'

'The man who whistles that tune…you heard him behind the wall at the Qutub Minar, remember?' he said, going over to the telephone and dialling a number. 'Not in yet? Please tell him to ring me back the moment he arrives. Tell him it's important.'

II

RUPA opened the kitchen door and came out carrying a tray loaded with cups and saucers and a pot of coffee. Jeet, who had already fallen asleep in his armchair, twitched his nostrils appreciatively. Rupa cleared a place on the low table in front of him and began to lay the things for breakfast.

The telephone rang. Jeet jumped out of the chair and picked up the receiver. 'Please speak to Air Vice Marshal Kirpal, sir,' the girl from the office was saying.

'Oh, PK, I've been trying to get hold of you... What? You too? Oh, good! Good news? Oh, I see, not so good! Yes, certainly, right away. I'll be there in five minutes.' He put down the receiver and even as he began to put on a coat and tie, called out to Rupa, 'That was PK. He wants me in his office.'

'What about breakfast?'

'I'm afraid it'll have to wait. Pity…'

'But why not have breakfast and go? It won't take ten minutes.'

'I'll be back in twenty minutes…I promise. Half an hour at the most. Then we can have coffee in peace, instead of rushing.'

At the door he stopped and came and gave her an impulsive peck on the cheek. 'Thanks for whistling,' he said, and darted out.

III

IN his office, PK stood in front of a wall map of the Himalayas. Behind him the intercom box on his table gave a soft burr and a girl's voice said. 'Colonel Mansingh is here sir, I've sent him in to you.'

The door opened and Jeet walked in.

'Ah! There you are. I'm afraid you're not going to like this,' PK said, beckoning Jeet to the map on the wall.

'What's wrong? Have the SB drawn a blank?'

'Not quite, but things don't look all that good. Take a look.' PK pointed to Chakrata on the map. A red ring had been drawn around the name. 'Chakrata,' PK said. 'That's where Bhatta and Gomti used to go for their leave every year at the same time. Seven thousand feet high, and deep in the Himalayas. It seems that they not only met there, but always booked rooms at the same hotel—The Snow View—weeks in advance. The money was paid in advance too.'

'So it was a sort of rendezvous.'

'Yes. It was also a starting point. In Chakrata they hired a mule-caravan and went off into the mountains, ostensibly for a trek. They used to carry a whole lot of supplies with them, far more than they could possibly use up themselves. You know, things like bags of flour, tins of kerosene and cooking oil, salt, sugar, a few boxes, things like that. Their caravan used to be out from between sixteen to eighteen days. Giving eight days travelling time each way, their destination must be around a hundred and fifty miles from Chakrata, somewhere in this circle.' PK pointed to a portion of the map that was ringed around with red pencil.

'That's not much to go on, is it? Anywhere within a hundred and fifty miles just isn't good enough, even Simla falls in that radius.'

PK smiled ruefully. 'There's a bit more. It seems that the caravan always returned on its own. Bhatta and Gomti stayed back for a few days and then followed on their own. They checked in at their hotel on their way back and then dispersed.'

'Only to meet the next year.'

'That's right.'

'And we have no indication at all as to where they used to go?'

'No. All we know is that it was some place in all this vastness; some of the most difficult terrain on the face of the earth. It's a maze of mountains and valleys and a few spidery tracks.'

'What about the mule-men?' Jeet asked. 'Were they the same lot every year?'

'Oh yes, the same lot every year. Evidently they too were engaged well in advance and held in readiness for the expedition.'

'So it should be fairly simple to find out the mule-men and ask them where they went.'

PK stared at him oddly for a moment. 'It would be fairly simple,' he agreed. 'If only we could find the mule-men first. That's just it, they aren't there.'

'Oh!'

'They were hired only three days ago and have already left.'

'Who hired them?'

'No one knows. It could have been any one at all.'

'But one can guess,' Jeet argued.

'What's your guess?'

'That the mule-men have been deliberately sent out in a different direction. Just to mislead us, in case we've caught on.'

'You mean they haven't been taken to the usual place, where Bhatta and Gomti used to go?'

Jeet shook his head. 'No. A caravan slows one's pace, besides it can be spotted from the air.'

'The SB have already asked for an aerial reconnaissance,' PK interrupted.

'Pempem and her boyfriend are not the sort of people to put their whole scheme in danger by setting out with a caravan. They're too clever for that. Especially as they know we might be...' he broke off suddenly. 'Remember telling me that this man who was with you in Burma used to whistle as he strangled people?'

'Yes, Chomo Jung,' PK said, slightly puzzled. 'But where does he come in?'

'What was the tune he whistled?'

'Some marching song...but what has it got to do with this?'

'You said he was trained at the American Marine Commando school. Now did the tune he whistled go something like this?' Jeet hummed the first two bars of the marching song of the marines.

'By Jove, you're right!' PK exclaimed, his face lighting up. 'That's Chomo's tune, of course. How did you...'

'Then I think Pempem's companion is Chomo Jung,' Jeet stated.

PK waited for him to go on.

Jeet continued, and proceeded to tell PK how he had reached this conclusion.

'So you think the man we were looking for here is Chomo?' PK said after Jeet had finished talking. 'It certainly fits in with his methods. The ruthlessness, the skill, the way every detail had been thought of, and always managing to keep one jump ahead; like this business with the mule-men.'

'I thought you might recognize the pattern,' Jeet said.

'And the tune! I can still hear it even though it was more

than twenty years ago. I remember Victor and I were covering the approach while Chomo went forward to finish the sentry. One hand on his mouth, the other pressing the windpipe, and while the victim was strangling, choking to death, Chomo whistled. It brought on the shivers!'

For a second or two the two men studied the map in silence, both concentrating, thinking of the next move.

'Don't the SB hold out any hope at all? They've been pretty good in the past,' Jeet said.

'Oh they're trying hard. They've sent out their best men in all directions, and there's an aerial recce going on to locate the caravan. Once they've spotted the mule-men, it will be simple enough for someone to go and grill them and find out where Bhatta and Gomti used to go.'

'Do you think they'll be able to catch up with the mule-men in time?'

'I hope so,' PK replied not very confidently. 'We could do with a lucky break.'

'Lucky break!' Jeet made a wry face. 'We haven't had one for a long time. Just a long run of rotten luck.'

'Don't forget your escape from being blown to bits,' PK reminded him.

'That was my stupidity, really, to have fallen for such a stunt. Then again,' Jeet continued, 'I should have cottoned on long ago that it was Chomo Jung operating here. Rupa has been whistling that tune for days.'

'I must say, I think, we're very lucky to have Miss Pandit coming in on this,' PK said. 'I have half a mind to make her an offer.'

'Offer?'

'Ask her if she would give up nursing for good and join our set-up. We need a few girls like her.'

IV

IN the second storey flat across the road from Jeet's apartment, three men waited anxiously in an empty room, facing a dark green curtain which had been pulled across a large glass window. Two of them were keeping a watch on Jeet's flat through tiny holes cut into the material; the third man restlessly paced the room.

'Nothing doing?' he asked, coming up to the window.

The two men shook their heads.

'This Colonel Mansingh sometimes gives the most idiotic orders,' the other continued disrespectfully. 'I doubt if anyone is going to be so foolish as to risk it in broad daylight.'

'You never know. He's got a hell of a reputation.'

'With what? Women? We saw that woman go in half an hour ago. She's still inside even though he's rushed off somewhere.'

'I wouldn't rush off anywhere in a hurry if I had a dame like that tucked away in the flat.' All three men laughed.

V

RUPA was tidying up the kitchen and humming softly to herself. Removing the apron she had put on, she folded it and put it away neatly in a drawer when she heard the key being turned in the door.

'You're back?' she called out happily. 'Good. I'll just bring your breakfast.'

There was no answer.

'Jeet,' Rupa called softly. 'Jeet?' Turning away from the gas range she opened the door into the sitting room. 'Oh!' she gasped, stopping in her tracks.

'One word from you, and I'll slash your face to ribbons,' Tien Aan hissed. He was holding a long bladed knife, steadily between her eyes.

Rupa stared at him in horror, her shoulders trembling slightly. She remembered what Jeet had said about their killing only insiders; well she was an insider now.

'Now take it easy, lady,' Tien Aan said softly. 'Dont complicate things by fainting or screaming, because then I'll have to fall you, see?'

Rupa went on staring numbly at the thin, expressionless face behind the knife.

'Put your hands out, come on, quickly,' he ordered. There's not much time.'

Almost involuntarily Rupa put out her hands and Tien Aan bound them securely with a length of cord which he took from his pockets. 'Now turn,' he ordered.

Mechanically Rupa obeyed and before she could realize what was happening he had drawn a large silk scarf across her mouth and knotted the ends behind her head. Catching her by the shoulders, he roughly spun her round so that she was facing him. 'Stand there now and don't move,' he told her harshly.

Tien Aan left her standing helplessly by the kitchen door and looked round the flat. He pounced on the Hermes that was lying on the table and grinned to himself in satisfaction when he saw the code was still inside. As he glanced round the room once more his eyes rested on Jeet's raincoat hanging on a hook near the entrance door. Taking it off the hook Tien Aan closely examined the dark grey, knee-length Burberry. Then he brought it over to Rupa and draped it around her, carefully arranging the hood round her head. 'Come on,' he ordered gruffly. 'Walk by my side, and keep your head down.' Then with the typewriter in one hand, he carefully guided Rupa out of the flat with the other.

In the room across the road the three men watching the flat nodded to each other in satisfaction as they saw Tien Aan help Rupa into the waiting car. Without a word two of the men instantly left the flat, leaving only one behind to observe the now empty apartment.

After driving about for a little while to make sure that he was not being followed, Tien Aan drew the car to one side of the road and stopped. He opened the glove compartment from which he took a green bottle filled with a liquid some of which he sprinkled on the silk scarf tied over Rupa's mouth. Then recorking the bottle he held a handkerchief over his own nose while he watched Rupa fall under the effect of the anaesthesia. When he was quite sure she had passed out, he started driving once again.

VI

J EET walked jauntily into the flat, a smile on his face. He paused at the door and sniffed appreciatively at the scent of coffee which still lingered in the air.

'Rupa,' he called out softly, 'Rupa.' Then suddenly anxious he ran into the kitchen. It was empty. A glance at the table showed him that the Baby Hermes was also missing. So the Chinese had snapped at his bait. But then he had not meant Rupa to be in the flat when they came to take away the typewriter.

The telephone in the entrance hall rang, and Jeet ran and picked it up on the second ring. 'Yes,' he said.

'I saw you come in, sir,' a man's voice said. 'It was just as you expected. A man came, driving an Austin A-Forty, and let himself into the flat. He took away a typewriter case.'

'When?'

'Five to ten. He was inside for hardly five minutes.'

'What did he look like?'

'A thin man in a dark-brown suit, a felt hat, a slightly stooping gait. Might have been a Chinaman.'

'Good!' Jeet pronounced.

'And, sir, the lady went with him.'

'I see. Any idea where they went?'

'Two men are tailing them, sir. They'll make a report as soon as they have anything to say. In the mean time I'm keeping a watch here.'

'I don't think that's necessary any more, you can go now. Wait a minute. The lady; did she go on her own?'

'She just walked away with him, sir. She was wearing a raincoat and had the hood pulled well over her face.'

'You're sure she wasn't carried or anything?' Jeet persisted.

'Oh no, sir, I saw her walking myself.'

'That'll be all, thank you.'

Jeet rang off and after deliberating for a moment or two, dialled a number. 'Dolly! Put me through to the Chief, will you.' He waited for the line to be connected, then, 'Oh PK, do you remember that Hermes?'

'Yes.'

'I used it as a bait after the Photostat boys had finished with the code. I carried it back to my flat rather openly and left it on a table. It seems to have worked, a man broke in and took it away. Two men from the SB are tailing the man, and will report later.'

'Oh good,' PK said exultantly, 'Oh, very good!'

'Not so good.'

'Why not?'

'They've gone and kidnapped Rupa.'

'When? How?' PK's voice came anxiously over the phone.

'She was in my flat when the man came,' Jeet answered glumly.

'What on earth was she doing in your flat?'

'Making breakfast.'

'What?'

'What I said, PK, she was making breakfast. She'd come to drive me over to Pempem's place and since I didn't have to go she stayed on to cook me some breakfast…'

'My god, this certainly complicates matters, doesn't it.'

'You can say that again,' Jeet said feelingly.

'If she talks she might blow up the whole thing—she knows too much.'

'That's only if she talks,' Jeet said.

'They'll make her talk,' PK prophesied glumly. 'You know how they work. What do you propose to do now?'

'I'm going to stick right here until the SB people give me a ring. Then I'll decide what I'm going to do. I'll let you know my plans,' he said ringing off. As he put down the receiver, Jeet flopped into a chair and shut his eyes tightly, running his fingers distractedly through his hair.

CHAPTER 14

I

JEET drove past the bright red sign reading: 'Yang-tse and took a right turn. After driving round the block twice, he came back to the Yang-tse again and parked his Fiat a little distance from the entrance. He checked his Mauser to make sure that the chamber had a round in it, and the magazine was in place.

The main room of the restaurant was not crowded, since most of the Yang-tse's customers preferred to sit in the privacy of the cubicles that lined the walls on either side. The two men sitting at the first table near the door casually looked up at Jeet as he entered, before turning back to their bowls of soup. The head waiter detached himself from a knot of waiters at the back of the room and hurried over to Jeet.

'Just yourself sir?'

'Yes.'

'This way if you please.' The waiter guided Jeet to one of the cubicles at the far corner and opened the door with a flourish. He waited for Jeet to sit down before taking out his order pad.

'A bowl of sweet corn and chicken soup, and some noodles with shrimps and some sweet and sour pork,' Jeet said without consulting the menu. 'And could you bring everything at the same time, please?'

'Certainly, sir,' the head-waiter bowed himself out of the room, shutting the door behind him.

Jeet lit a cigarette and examined the tiny room. The partitions were solid and a grill in the wall filtered in cold air. On the walls were a few conventional Chinese prints and in the middle of the table was a plant growing in a gaudily coloured Chinese bowl. Soft music came out of the loudspeaker cleverly concealed in the screen of heavily carved woodwork behind Jeet's chair.

In the kitchen, the head waiter made a sign to one of the cooks and drew him to one side.

'I've put him in the special room,' he whispered.

'Good.' The other man nodded in approval. They spoke in excited whispers for a few seconds and then hesitatingly went out of the back door and up the stair-case to Tien Aan's office. The cook knocked discreetly on the door.

'Who is it?' a voice asked.

The waiter spoke softly in Chinese and the door opened automatically from within. The two men went in and emerged after a minute or so.

The cook held up a small yellow bottle with a glass stopper.

'Remember, two drops in the soup and three in the noodles.'

II

THE head waiter pushed open the door of Jeet's cubicle with his shoulder and set down a tray of steaming bowls round Jeet's plate. He brought up a glass of water and a bottle of sauce.

'Anything else, sir?' he asked.

'I don't think so, this looks fine,' Jeet told him as he ladled a generous portion of soup into his bowl. He tasted a spoonful and said. 'Excellent!'

The waiter bowed and went out and shut the door, but for a while lounged close to the door, listening to the rhythmic tinkle of spoon against plate. Then he hurried to the kitchen at the back and, catching the eye of the head cook, gave him a slight nod and raised his thumb.

The men who were sitting near the door were wolfing down large platefuls of fried prawns. They did not even look up as the head waiter came back and raised the volume of the music that was being piped through all the rooms. By the time their prawns were finished, their waiter had brought them an enormous bowl of Chinese fried rice. The head waiter went up and down past the closed door of Jeet's room very silently, and then, as though satisfied with whatever he had heard or observed, went out by the back door. In the veranda, he was joined by the head cook. Side by side, they both went into the closed courtyard at the back and stood there smoking in silence, glancing at their watches every now and then. Then the cook said, 'This should be it…fifteen minutes. It's guaranteed to take effect in ten minutes, even if he's eaten no more than a portion of either the soup or the chow.'

'He was eating with appetite. Let me go and see.'

Inside the cubicle the bowls of food were half empty. A little food remained on the plate, uneaten. The fork Jeet had been using had fallen to the floor and Jeet himself lay slumped in the chair in an unnatural position, breathing stertorously, his eyes half open. A single blue bottle trapped in the room, darted away from his hand where it had been sitting and perched on the remains of the noodles and shrimp. It buzzed about for a few seconds, making short darts, and then suddenly dropped down on the marble surface of the table. Circling groggily for a moment or two, it flopped over on its back and died with a faint stirring of wings.

The head waiter, watching through the slightly open door, seemed satisfied with what he saw. He hurried back to the courtyard, where the cook was waiting for him.

A short while later, the Chinese screen at the back of Jeet's chair, silently swung open and the waiter and the cook entered the cubicle.

'Must have taken quite a load of the stuff,' the waiter remarked.

'Hope he doesn't die yet,' the other said. 'He doesn't want him dead.'

'Probably just passed out,' the waiter shrugged. 'Come on, let's take him away.'

One picking up his legs and the other his shoulders, they carried Jeet out of the room, up the stairs at the back and through the door that had opened for them as they reached the landing. They went through a dimly lit passage into a room at the end where there was an old sofa with sagging springs, and some discarded furniture heaped in a corner. The only window was heavily curtained and the two bracket lamps on the wall threw a harsh glare over the shabby room. They dumped Jeet unceremoniously on the dilapidated sofa and left the room.

A faint muffled scream came from the other end of the building as the two men left the room, but Jeet lay without stirring, his breath coming in choking gasps.

III

RUPA sat on a straight backed cane chair; her hands tied securely behind her. A man with a shaved head and square, deadpan face stood behind her chair, and Tien Aan sat on low stool facing her, a cigarette dangling loosely from his lips.

The man behind Rupa opened her fingers and inserted the barrel of a revolver between the second and third fingers of her left hand. With his other hand he began to squeeze her fingers.

The pain made Rupa wince and brought tears to her eyes. 'I tell you I don't know anything,' she said again. 'They didn't tell me anything, I just drove the car.'

'Oh, I see,' Tien Aan said very softly and nodded to the man behind the chair. The grip on her fingers suddenly tightened. Rupa's body writhed in pain and her lips trembled.

'Who sent the information from China?' Tien Aan asked. 'What was the man's name? Who brought the message?'

All she could do was to shake her head wearily.

Tien Aan very casually lifted her bare foot and thrust the burning cigarette into the sole and slowly ground it out. It was a gesture almost of disgust...of contempt. He had no time to waste on small fry. Rupa's scream of agony was immediately stifled by the bald man.

'No use wasting time on her,' Tien Aan said delicately wiping his fingers. 'Let's finish her off...get her out of the way.'

'Okay, boss.' His assistant went over to a cupboard built into the wall and took out a hypodermic syringe and a box of amber ampoules which he took over to Tien Aan.

'I wonder if the gallant Colonel has recovered from his knock out drops,' Tien Aan said almost to himself as he took the syringe and box of ampoules from his subordinate.

IV

THE head waiter walked into the main room of the Yang-tse, beaming happily to himself. Going into the cubicle in which Jeet had been eating, he began to clear the table. He stacked the bowls and plates on to a tray. Half-way through his work, he suddenly stiffened as his glance fell on the bowl with the potted plant. A thin trickle of pink sauce oozed out of a crack in the side of the porcelain bowl. He looked at it in horror and then parted the leaves of the plant. Inside the bowl was a mess of noodles and sweet and sour pork and corn soup. The waiter stared at the contents of the pot as though hypnotized and then, with a start dumped the tray on the table and darted out of the cubicle. As he flung open the door, he was brought to an abrupt halt. Two men barred his way, and both were holding ugly automatics in their hands. He recognized them as the two customers who had been sitting near the door and guzzling implausible quantities of food. He goggled as they bore down upon him and pushed him back into the cubicle. Everything had been done so quietly, so quickly that not a single customer of the Yang-tse realized that anything was amiss. The music in the room changed over from 'Limelight' to 'Come September'.

V

WITH professional competence, Tien Aan filled the syringe from one of the ampoules while the other Chinaman held Rupa's arm in a vicelike grip. Rupa watched the two men helplessly, her face white, her eyes staring in terror. A strip of sticking plaster had been taped across her mouth to prevent her from crying out.

Tien Aan pressed down the plunger to clear the air from the end of the needle, when the door behind him opened with a slight click.

'Has the man come out of his coma?' he asked without turning round. 'I would like him to see this, it might prompt him to speak.'

Receiving no answer, Tien Aan swung round in irritation only to see Jeet crouching in the doorway. The needle dropped from his fingers, the glass breaking with a tinkle, while his right hand whipped down to his side for his revolver, when Jeet sprang.

Jeet jabbed at the Chinaman's face with the edge of his hand and in the same action, brought his elbow crashing into his stomach just as Tien Aan had swung his revolver into an arc and squeezed off. The shot went wild, chipping some of the plaster from the roof. Before Tien Aan could press the trigger again, Jeet was on to him like a panther, lashing wildly with his knee into his groin. The force of the kick lifted Tien Aan clean off his feet and sent him crashing against the medicine cupboard.

Jeet swung back at a noise behind him and realized it was too late. The other Chinaman had flung a chair wildly at him and it caught him just below the knees, making him reel and lose his balance. And then the two Chinamen jumped on him and held him pinned to the floor. They were like wild animals tearing up a victim. Rupa watched in horrified fascination as Tien Aan picked up his fallen revolver and brought the butt sharply against the side of Jeet's head; Jeet slumped slowly forward, his legs sliding from under him. The two men dragged him to a comer and dumping him onto a chair, bound his arms behind him.

'Why not finish him off, boss,' the Chinaman suggested to Tien Aan. Both men were breathing in great lungfuls of air.

'In a moment,' Tien Aan answered. 'I want to do a little questioning first. He couldn't have eaten any of the food…go and find out what went wrong, will you. Get both Wong and Lee too report to me. Bring me that pitcher of water before you go.'

Handing Tien Aan the pitcher of water, the other Chinaman hurried out of the room. Tien Aan poured a stream of water on to Jeet's face. Jeet's eyes fluttered.

'Come on. Wake up,' Tien Aan said in an urgent voice. 'See this hypodermic needle? It's loaded with a special pesticide…something like rat poison. It's guaranteed to bring on the most painful death, quite quickly. The eye balls shrink and blood spurts out of them, and there is a roaring fire in the body, and the limbs begin to twist and twist, and the pain is so intense that the victim howls like an animal. Not for long though, death comes within ten minutes.'

Jeet went on looking blankly at Tien Aan, his eyes glazed and dull. Tien Aan slapped his face hard and cursed.

'Wake up, damn you!' He splashed the remaining water in the pitcher on Jeet's face. 'Now, listen. You're both going to get this, but ladies first,' he sniggered and bowed courteously in Rupa's direction. 'Unless you're ready to talk.'

'And what will you do if I talk.'

'If you tell me the things I want to know, I might let her go.'

Jeet shook his head.

'No? How ungallant!' Tien Aan mocked. 'I thought you would want to save the girl's life. You don't care if she dies first?'

'Of course I do,' Jeet said.

'Then, Colonel, come on, be reasonable now. Why not?' Tien Aan said wheedlingly.

'Because her life is no longer in danger, you slob; it's your life that's in danger now. That door behind you is opening; and two of our best men from the SB are covering you…incidentally they're both crack shots. Come on, take a look,' Jeet invited.

'Stop playing for time, Colonel,' Tien Aan jeered. All the same he turned and glanced behind him.

The two men who had been in the restaurant below, were standing in the open door-way, their long-barrelled pistols held steadily pointing at Tien Aan's stomach.

'You bastard,' Tien Aan spluttered, and like a flash his hand went to the needle lying next to him. But the men had seen his movement and were taking no risks. The man on the right fired, and the steel nosed .38 bullet went clean through Tien Aan's outstretched hand, smashing the heel of the hand.

'I told you they were both crack shots,' Jeet said quietly.

VI

JEET anxiously paced up and down the length of his verandah, glancing at his watch every few minutes, while Rupa sat at a low table, concentrating on a large jigsaw puzzle. They both looked at each other for a second, when the telephone rang, and then Jeet jumped to answer it.

'Yes? I'll be there in ten minutes,' he said into the receiver. 'Anything new? Oh, I see. Tell PK I'll be right there. And listen, please say I'd like to ask a few questions of the man myself.'

Putting down the receiver, he walked over to Rupa. 'PK's secretary,' he explained. 'They might have discovered something about where Bhatta and Gomti used to go.'

'You think so?' Rupa asked eagerly.

'Well she says there's an officer from the SB specially flown over from Chakrata. He's with PK just now. It seems hopeful. Come on, let's go.'

'You really want me to come with you?' she asked looking up at him.

'Just for luck,' he grinned. 'Things always seem to happen when you're around.'

CHAPTER 15

I

AROUND the tower of the Ragyabas monastery, the Himalayas ranged in all their icy splendour. The thin trembling wail of the ceremonial trumpet sounded forlorn in the vast emptiness breaking the silence of the dawn. Within the walls of the monastery the lamas prepared quietly for the feast of the Green Serpent.

As the first slanting rays of sunlight touched the white peaks, the sound of the trumpet ceased and the yellow-robed lama who was announcing the birth of a new day reverently deposited the trumpet in its stand. He gave a last look down into the valley where the steps went plunging crazily down in a spiral, precariously clutching the sheer wall of the mountain, then walked down the steps going into the bowels of the mountain.

In the main marble hall below, the seven other yellow-robed lamas were already at prayer, all grouped under the marble lotus in the ceiling. The Lama whose duty it had been to sound the trumpet quietly took his place in the group and knelt down, praying softly.

Behind the kneeling lamas, along one wall, the low tables were loaded with an array of exquisite porcelain bowls, filled with dishes lovingly prepared by the monks in honour of the feast. This was the second time in the year that the Head Lama of the Amber Order made an appearance in the central hall. Across the hall from the tables of food incongruous in these peaceful surroundings, was the plunger handle attached to dry batteries. Over its red handle was the sign of the skull and cross bones and the one word of warning: DANGER.

Now, as by some common impulse, all the lamas stared at the closed door in the wall. Then with one accord the eight yellow-robed figures prostrated on the floor, touching the cold marble with their foreheads. The door before them opened and the monks simultaneously raised their heads.

Chomo Jung stood in the doorway, arrayed in the ceremonial robes of the Head Lama. In his hands he held a gleaming stengun, its barrel pointed at the centre of the group. The nose of the barrel jumped and there followed a long single burp as Chomo shot at point-blank range into the huddled group, killing all eight lamas almost instantly.

He stopped shooting only when the magazine had run out, and then calmly strode into the hall, barely glancing at the bodies of the fallen lamas, some of them twitching feebly. Behind him in the open doorway, stood a woman, dressed in the gorgeous silk robes of a Tibetan queen, a glittering crown on her head. Pempem Kachin, looking aloof and slightly contemptuous, surveying the scene of carnage without visible dismay.

Chomo strutted around the marble hall self-importantly, and paused briefly to read the notice hung below the red plunger. He leaned his still smoking stengun against the plunger and walked over to the tables laden with food.

'Wonderful!' he sniffed, bending down and picking up a morsel of fried mountain trout. 'Delicious! Real Tibetan food…food fit for kings. I haven't tasted anything like this for months. Come on, honey, let's begin the feast.' He began circling the table, sampling dish after dish and smacking his lips appreciatively, while Pempem stood stock-still in the doorway, looking implausibly beautiful in the outlandish attire. For a moment her eyes flashed and she scowled in disgust as she watched Chomo bending over a tray of eggs; but her expression immediately changed to a submissive smile for Chomo had turned and was looking at her and his face was wreathed in a smile.

'Ah, the eggs…they're said to be two hundred years old…the most exotic delicacy in the world, Chinese preserved eggs! To think that these eggs were fresh when the Manchus ruled in Peking.' He popped an egg into his mouth and swallowed it like an oyster and took a deep breath. 'Come on. I don't think you have ever tasted food like this. They've always been famous for their cooking, these Amber Lamas. It is said they cooked for the Mings and preserved the art,' he waved a podgy hand at the bodies lying on the floor. None of them now showed a spark of life.

Pempem obediently shuffled forward but at the edge of a trickle of fresh blood that was beginning to spread into a pool, stopped uncertainly.

'Sit at the other end,' Chomo ordered, and his voice was edgy. 'At the other end, as befits a loving wife. This is quite an occasion; the beginning of a new life…a life of immense riches, the wealth of Croseus, of Monte Cristo; a life without care. Let us celebrate its coming with proper seriousness.'

Pempem came up to the low table and primly sat at the end as ordered.

'Come here,' Chomo commanded in a throaty whisper as soon as she had sat down. Pempem got up immediately and went to him. Taking her cheek between his thumb and forefinger, he squeezed it until she winced and a moan escaped her lips. 'Dont look so mournful, honey. Learn to smile. Come on, smile!' He released her cheek and the marks of his fingers showed up red against her pale skin. All the same she smiled.

'That's better, much better! That's the proper mood for a victory celebration. Something I have been planning for years. Success! Success! I don't want you spoiling it by being glum.' Picking up the golden goblet that was placed beside the Head Lama's plate he examined it appreciatively. 'Ah! A loving cup! he exclaimed, smacking his lips noisily. 'A loving cup for a loving couple. Come on, let's drink as lovers should.' He poured himself a drink from one of the tall porcelain pitchers on the table. 'This wine is said to be a hundred years old,' he said, taking a sip from the goblet. 'Heavenly!' he pronounced as he passed the goblet to Pempem. 'Now you drink out of it and then pass it back to me,' he ordered.

Pempem meekly took a sip of the wine before passing the cup back to Chomo. As he took the cup from her hand, he roughly gathered her into his arms and kissed her on the mouth. Then abruptly pushing her away, he drank noisily from the cup. 'Now go and sit there,' he said without looking at her. 'And keep smiling, you slut!'

Pempem shuffled over to the other end of the table and sat down, the smile on her face more strained than ever.

Chomo looked at her speculatively. 'You're quite happy, aren't you?' he asked her,

Pempem nodded.

'You should be too,' he jeered. 'Sharing the life of Chomo Jung instead of going back and slogging for a pittance, spouting patriotism.' He picked up a crisp roll and nibbled at it. 'Delicious! Don't you agree?'

Pempem dutifully picked up a roll and bit into it. 'Yes, excellent.'

'You look very lovely, my dear, in that costume. The headdress alone must be worth thousands...more than you could have earned in a lifetime. I don't know what I have longed for more. You, or the Panchen Lama's treasure. Now I have both...yes, both. Money! All in diamonds and rubies and emeralds, all we can carry away on our mules. The gold we must leave behind, it is too heavy to carry...pity!'

'Lee Hung is going to be very angry when he finds out,' Pempem said.

'How I wish I could be there to see his face,' Chomo chuckled with his mouth full. 'His chief agent gets away with the Panchen Lama's treasure and his most trusted female spy too. I've always longed to get away from China, but what was the use of getting out when one had no money? Where could one go? Then they put me in charge of this operation...to bring back the Panchen Lama's treasure to China. That was the answer. Why take it to China when I could take it to some other country...wherever I wanted to go: Brazil, France, Argentina, somewhere really far away, out of their clutches. To live the life I've always wanted to lead. Champagne and caviar and a string of race horses, a chauffeur driven Rolls...and a beautiful wife.' Chomo winked broadly at her. 'And they even gave me the plan of the secret entrance into this place. Otherwise it would have been impossible. And now no one can come in,' he smirked, pointing to the plunger. 'I just have to press that and bang, anyone who is on the stairs is blown to eternity,' Chomo chuckled evilly to himself.

'And I've even got you where I wanted, by sending them the fullest proof of your treason and making it impossible for you to go back to China. Nor can you go anywhere else without money. And who can afford to give you as much as I can? Did you see those boxes down there, honey? Crammed with diamonds and rubies. Now all you've got to do is to keep close to Chomo,' he tapped his chest importantly.

'We leave within the hour, loading as much as possible on to our two mules. Once we're out of the country, we can stop worrying for ever.'

Hearing a slight sound, Pempem cocked her head to listen properly, a frown of concentration on her forehead.

'Stop frowning,' he snapped. 'This is a time to...why, what's the matter?'

Pempem put a finger to her lips. 'Can't you hear?' she whispered, a frightened look on her face.

Chomo listened carefully, a half-eaten chicken bone still held in his hand. Suddenly his expression changed. 'Oh God!' he whispered as he heard a faint throbbing sound which soon became a deafening roar. 'Damn!' he exclaimed. Jumping up he picked up his gun before walking briskly to the open side of the hall to look out.

The helicopter hovered uncertainly over the top of the monastery, searching for a place to land. Chomo watched it intently, his face contorted with anger. Then he turned and glowered at Pempem.

'But the signal said that they were going to send the helicopter only after we had fired the flare. Does that mean that Lee Hung has anticipated my move? Have you anything to do with this, you cheap little...'

'Don't be so absurd!' Pempem hissed. 'I don't think it is one of ours...it's got different markings.'

'You mean it's an Indian one?' Chomo asked in disbelief.

Pempem slowly nodded.

II

THE helicopter descended jerkily, like a huge ungainly insect that had lost its wings. It landed in a cloud of dust on the hard, beaten earth of the top of the mountain. The big blades of the main rotor stopped whirling and the cockpit cover was pushed open and a short rope ladder was thrown over the side. A man in a parka and goggles started to descend. Halfway down the swaying ladder, he turned to give a hand to a woman dressed in a hooded parka and a pair of sky blue slacks. Once on the ground they stood for a while beside the machine, looking at the gorge of the Indus far below.

'My word!' Jeet said in an awed voice. 'Just look at that view!'

Rupa went on staring, fascinated. 'It all looks so quiet,' she said after a while. 'Why is everything so quiet?'

'Maybe we've come too late,' Jeet looked round and then briskly gave his orders. 'You know what you are to do. Stand right here guarding the helicopter. If anyone comes near, you shoot. OK? Don't wait to ask questions, I'm going to take a look.' Patting her on the shoulder, he grinned at her brightly and was gone.

III

In the hall Chomo flared his nostrils and grimaced, accepting this new challenge. 'You were quite right,' he said turning to Pempem. 'It's the boy friend you picked up so conveniently...only he's brought his own girl with him.' He chuckled. 'There are only two of them. You stay right here and shoot anyone who comes. Though no one will,' he added. 'I'll see to that.'

He inserted a fresh magazine, then without looking back, went out through one of the numerous exits of the main hall.

Chomo stalked along the dark corridors, his expression grim; like that of a hunter who has sighted his quarry.

IV

The staircase out into the rockface hung over emptiness. On one side was the sheer wall of the hill with a few overhanging boulders jutting out and poised precariously for a plunge into the valley, but held in place by twisted roots of gnarled and leafless trees that still survived in the most unlikely crannies.

Jeet tried each step for firmness before putting his full weight on it. He was carrying his long-barrelled .22 in one hand and trying to balance himself with the other. He came up to a place where the steps cut into the rock had almost completely crumbled away.

Hovering in the helicopter, he had seen little black slits in the wall of the hill which must have been windows to let in light and air into the monastery. Now, even though he had descended at least fifty feet, there was no sign of an inlet. He craned his neck around a jutting stone and quickly looked away. There was a sheer drop into nothingness, and in the valley, far below, hawks were going round in lazy circles, looking like tiny specks.

And yet he had seen what he was looking for, a black rectangle a few feet to his right and some twelve feet below his present position. He gritted his teeth, tucked his pistol carefully into its holster and reached out with both hands for a gnarled root that had broken through a crevice in the rock. If he could hang on to the root, he might just be able to slide down onto the parapet of the opening. He had managed to grip the root and was groping with both feet for a foothold.

Jeet's foot never reached the jutting boulder he had seen. For when he looked again, he saw the perforated barrel of an automatic weapon pointed at him, glinting evilly in the blinding sunlight.

'Ha ha ha ha ha,' there was a short peal of grotesque laughter from below. 'Don't move, stay just where you are,' Chomo said. 'It couldn't be better! Ha ha ha ha ha!'

'I don't see anything funny,' Jeet snapped, his fingers clawing desperately for a firmer grip on the roots he was clinging on to.

'Don't you?' Chomo smirked. 'But then you can't see yourself. Such a pity. Like a lizard against a wall…fully exposed, not knowing how many seconds you have to live.'

'How many?'

Chomo pretended to deliberate. 'Maybe ten, certainly not more,' he said slowly. 'I want to shoot you from about ten yards away. Near enough to make sure, but not too near for you to try any of your tricks. I want to watch you drop off the hill, go hurtling down into the gorge. Pity I won't be able to see you splash into the river.'

V

WITHIN the many-pillared banquet hall in the bowels of the monastery, Pempem fumed, stalking up and down the marble floor like a caged tigress. She stamped her feet in anger and kicked hysterically at the brocade cushion on which Chomo had sat down to his feast. The golden goblet was still lying where he had left it, half-full with wine. 'Loving cup!' she hissed venomously and picked up the cup and hurled it against the stone wall. Then, as though finding release in the gesture of defiance, she took off her jewelled crown and smashed it against the massive stone pillar that supported the centre of the domed roof. The precious stones cracked and splintered and rolled on the floor, a great red ruby came spinning back at her feet like a child's top. For a moment she stood rigidly staring at the ruby as though at some instrument of destruction. She picked it up and flung it out through the window into the valley below. Then she suddenly sat down as though her legs had folded under her, and began to sob convulsively.

She sat up, listening. Somewhere far below, at the outer edge of consciousness, there was the sound of rude laughter, like the chirping of some insect. Chomo's laughter. She jumped to her feet and ran to the window that overlooked the valley.

She stared aghast at the figure of the man struggling desperately to keep his hold of the root in the hillside, his feet kicking wildly to find a toehold, Jeet, a spider waiting to be swatted. And not more than twenty feet below him, Chomo, moving up step by step, the stengun held like some toy in the immensely powerful hands. And the sound of the whistled tune came up to her, the tune that went with the words, 'From the Hills of Montezuma, to the shores of Tripoli.' Chomo, the man who had humiliated her, had ruined her life, who was holding her captive.

And suddenly Pempem began to laugh. She ran back through the hall, stepping lightly over the contorted bodies of the holy men, slipping in the pools of blood, kicking aside the tables with their priceless porcelain, but still laughing weirdly. The red handle of the plunger beckoned; the skull over the crossbones grinned. The demonic grin on her own face hardened and her teeth bit into her lips as she reached for the red handle and pressed it down with all her strength.

VI

CHOMO waddled up the stair case, taking each step carefully. When he was about ten yards away from Jeet and slightly below him, he stopped. He braced his legs and steadied the gun in his hands. He pushed forward the safety with unhurried deliberation, as though savouring every moment of his triumph, almost as though he was reluctant to bring down the final curtain too soon. And Jeet heard him whistling his tune of death.

Then the earth beneath his feet shook, dust crept out of crevices like smoke spurting. And with a rumble and a roar that became a deafening explosion the entire length of the staircase winding round the tower went tumbling down the valley. The cloud of dust thickened and the thunder of crashing rocks and falling debris continued in a chain reaction long after the first explosion.

Slowly the dust began to settle. Where the staircase had been there was nothing, just a yawning emptiness. A jagged line running diagonally up in a spiral showed where the hill-face had been cut.

Jeet still dangled by the protruding roots he had been clutching, his feet beating against the crumbling hillside for a foothold. He kicked again and again with his toes and heels, each time dislodging a few pebbles and earth till he had managed to scoop out a niche in which to plant his feet firmly. Now, with some of the weight supported by his feet, he backed himself against the hill and looked desperately for a way of escape. His face was covered with sweat and grime and his eyes were blurring. But a little below him and to the left was a jutting out slab of rock. He had no time to debate with himself whether he could slide down on to the ledge and still manage to keep his footing, for his trembling arms could not have held his weight much longer. He gritted his teeth and took a deep breath. Then he released his hold and slid down. He landed with both feet onto the narrow ledge of rock, teetered precariously for a few seconds, falling his arms in the air, and then managed to regain his balance.

Immediately under the ledge was another protruding root, and from there to the inlet through which the Head Lama was given his food was a fairly easy drop. He bent over and caught at the root and slid down till his feet rested on the edge of the window.

CHAPTER 16

Rupa had stayed obediently at her post near the helicopter, keeping both the staircases under observation; the one going directly into the hill, the other running along the outer wall. Over the eerie silence, she heard what she could have sworn were human voices. She went to the edge of the precipice to look.

About fifty feet below, Jeet was straddled against the hillside, his hands held high above him, gripping a root. Below him was a yellow-robed lama, clutching a short-barrelled sten. He was moving up the stair case with chilling deliberation. Her cry of warning froze in her mouth as she saw the holy man stop and take aim, and heard him begin to whistle his tune.

Then she heard the deafening explosion and under her very eyes everything seemed to break up into fragments. A thick cloud of dust shot up from the side of the hill.

Rupa leaned forward to see what was happening. The staircase had vanished, and small and large stones were still dislodging themselves and hurtling down the gorge. And then the dust came up and enveloped everything. For a moment she stood where she was, as though paralysed, then she turned and rushed, to the other staircase, the last remaining outlet.

Two flights of stairs and she emerged into the main hall where the bodies of the lamas lay stiffly, their yellow silk robes stained with widening patches of blood. A cry of dismay escaped her lips as she took in the scene and then she ran on, through the open door that led into the main part of the Ragyabas monastery. She ran without knowing where she was going, taking the corridors as they came, groping her way through the pitch-dark narrow passages towards faint glimmers of light in the distance.

Now she was in a large room again, perhaps an underground vault. A room with statues ranged on shelves, with open boxes glinting mysteriously in the dim light of an oil flame lamp placed on a shining pedestal. Feeling her way as she went she stumbled past the treasure of the Panchen Lama towards a faint glimmer of light, hoping against hope that there must be a way out. The corridors must lead out of the bowels of the hill and into the fresh air.

And abruptly, as though pulled by a chain, she halted in her tracks, realizing, only after she had drawn back against the clammy wall, what it was that had made her stop.

She had heard a click, an unmistakable metallic sound...a sound magnified by the cavernous stillness. It was the sound of a safety catch being slid forward. She froze against the wall and listened, trying to locate the source of the sound.

In the dimness, her own face as rigid as the two devil masks on either side, stood Pempem, her automatic at the ready, waiting for Rupa to come out of the darkness to where there was a little light.

Rupa stood glued to the black wall, convinced that the girl with the pistol could hear the hammering of her heart. The room was full of strange whispering sounds; sounds made by birds of darkness disturbed in their slumbers. Shadows went flitting past through the dimness, almost brushing her body. And then Rupa saw that a low door at the far end of the room was opening ever so slowly, as though pushed by an unseen hand. An object like a black, furry hand came crawling along the floor through the chink in the door...

Rupa screamed. Then screamed again and stifled her scream as she realized that the object that had terrified her was a cat...a cat that had shot up into the air when she first screamed and had turned before touching the ground and bolted back through the open door. And then a figure had emerged out of the shadows and flashed past.

Ting-a-ling. Ting-a-ling, already terrified by the explosion and the mysterious echoing whispers made by the bats, must have been shaken out of his wits by Rupa's screams, for he squeezed out of the chink in the door and was gone like a flash. And cursing under her

THE BEST AMERICAN

NONREQUIRED
READING
2002

THE BEST AMERICAN

NONREQUIRED READING

2002

■

EDITED AND WITH
AN INTRODUCTION
BY

DAVE EGGERS

MICHAEL CART,
SERIES EDITOR

HOUGHTON MIFFLIN COMPANY
BOSTON • NEW YORK
2002

Visit our Web site: www.houghtonmifflinbooks.com.

ISSN 1539-316x
ISBN 0-618-24693-2
ISBN 0-618-24694-0 (pbk.)

Printed in the United States of America

Book design by Robert Overholtzer

DOC 10 9 8 7 6 5 4 3 2 1

CONTENTS

Contents / ix

FOREWORD

The word *reading:* by itself, it describes one of the most pleasur-
able, stimulating, rewarding, exciting, even joyful acts we human
beings are capable of. Yet put one single adjective — *required* — in
front of it and you suck all the joy out of the process, turning it into
drudgery.

That's the reason that reading has always been too closely linked
with schoolwork and the other stuff that life requires. In fact, in a
recent national survey of people under twenty-five, conducted by
SmartGirl.com and the American Library Association, more than
80 percent of respondents said the books they read are "assigned
for class."

That's the bad news. The good news is that 65 percent also said
that "outside of class" they read books "for pleasure." Even more
read magazines, newspapers, comics, graphic novels, and Web
zines and a host of other on-line publications. Not only are they
reading more than ever, the under-twenty-five population is now,
according to the *Wall Street Journal,* actually buying books for leisure reading "at three times the rate of the overall market."

Oh, sure, this book-buying is partly because of the fact that
young people have more disposable income than ever before —
teenagers spent an average of $104 a week in 2001, according
to Teenage Research Unlimited — but it's also because of the
fact that more good stuff is available now than ever before. I

mean, there is more reading material, regardless of format, that addresses — with authentic wit, lively style, unsparing realism, and urgent relevance — the real interests and real lives of real readers.

Sometimes this material is pulled from the headlines, but more often it is ripped from the heart of matters that have to do with the emotional, developmental, intellectual, and yes, even survival, skills of fifteen- to twenty-five-year-olds.

This was not always the case.

Not long ago, publishers were publishing "young adult literature," an unfortunate phrase that always made the work sound like adult literature in training wheels. Even worse, in the 1930s and early 1940s there was a category patronizingly called "the junior novel." For too many years this "literature" for young adults bore about as much resemblance to reality as the Cleaver family. Part of this may have been the result of a collective exercise in wishful thinking, and of an adult desire to "protect" young readers from the grittier realities of life.

No wonder that Chris Lynch, one of the most important younger writers for these readers (*Gold Dust, Dog Eat Dog, Slot Machine*), observed as recently as 1994 that "when writers hear the term Young Adult, they get the feeling the 'the gloves are on.'"

The gloves finally came off sometime in the middle of the 1990s, and writers were at last permitted to match the sophistication of their readers with the sophistication of their material and their creative ambition. Or, to put it another way, writers were at last allowed to respect their readers, their readers' abilities and inherent savvy. Gone was the traditional insistence on a simplistically happy ending. Instead, writers for young people began to bring ambiguity and uncertainty to their work, to acknowledge the presence of darkness in human affairs as well as the persistence of light. Previously taboo subjects such as abuse and incest could now be addressed. Of equal importance, writers were permitted to flex their literary muscles, bringing to their work newly complex characterization, themes, and settings along with stylistic and structural innovation.

Other reasons for this newfound freedom include the sheer growth in the numbers of younger Americans — there are now 34 million people under twenty in the United States — their media-driven sophistication and curiosity; their increasing access to books, thanks to the rise of superbookstores and virtual booksellers; the willingness of a generation of young editors to take creative risks; and more. Much more. Just as the demands of the increasingly vocal 1960s generation for more realistic fiction gave birth to the first authentic young adult novels, so similar demands today are giving rise to a "gloves-off" literature that challenges readers to reexamine their lives and the world in which they live.

As for "young adults" — if they were once defined as twelve- to eighteen-year-olds, that too is no longer the case. Such labeling, though convenient for publishers and librarians, can't do justice to the complexity of a new literature that has intrinsic appeal to a cross-generational readership as young as fifteen and as (relatively) old as twenty-five.

The gloves are off, so read on.

But first a few words about how this inaugural edition of *The Best American Nonrequired Reading* was put together. As the series editor, I examined, surveyed, combed, and read nearly 140 magazines, newspapers, and zines that publish material either for or of interest to readers ages fifteen to twenty-five. I found approximately 125 stories and articles that, in my opinion, could be described as "the best." These I sent to the guest editor, Dave Eggers, who added even more pieces to the "best" pile, based on a process he describes in his introduction, and who chose the twenty-three selections that are published in this book. Our collaboration was, I think, a creative one that has resulted in an outstanding inaugural collection, which will set a very high standard for the volumes to follow in succeeding years.

We are now asking editors to submit what they consider to be the best "nonrequired reading" for *The Best American Nonrequired Reading 2003*. These submissions may be fiction or nonfiction but must be published in the United States during the year 2002. Reprints and excerpts from published books are not accepted. Each submission must include the author's name, the date of publication, and the publication's name and must be submitted as tear-sheets, a copy of the whole publication, or a clean, clear photocopy of the piece as it originally appeared.

All submissions must be received by February 3, 2003. Publications wishing to be sure that their contributions will be considered should include this anthology on their subscription list. Submissions or subscriptions should be sent to Dave Eggers, c/o Editor, *The Best American Nonrequired Reading 2003,* Houghton Mifflin Company, 222 Berkeley Street, Boston, MA 02116.

I want to thank Deanne Urmy and Melissa Grella of Houghton Mifflin for their insights, enthusiasm, and support, which made this anthology possible. They were a joy to work with. And thanks too to the writers whose work is represented here, who have so artfully demonstrated the joy of nonrequired reading.

MICHAEL CART

INTRODUCTION

Instead of an introduction I give you this:

The pool lights were never on but always there was other light,
from streetlamps or from the moon, round and toilet-tank white
and licking itself felinely, and the light, whatever its source, would
allow us to see the pool's edges and each other. This was high
school and it was humid. In the pools someone would always float
as if he were dead. Someone would lurk like a squid in the deep
end and yank your legs from below. Then you would yelp or someone would scream or giggle or trip over a sprinkler and someone
else would whisper-yell *Quiet!* and we'd have to get out and get any
clothes we'd taken off and then jump the fence or the hedge or the
wall and get back to the car before the pool owners awoke or the
cops came. The convertible we'd borrowed was wet and cool, and
we sank down into the seats, six of us squirming together for
warmth, Drew starting the car and going, keeping the headlights
off for a block, the wind cooler now. Lying on top of each other
while horizontal in the back seat, watching the tops of trees as we
passed underneath, the car so quiet, so quiet — I don't know why
it should have been so quiet, such a big car and so full of people,
but I remember no noise in that car, from pool to pool to pool.
By the end of the night we would be swimming naked. Jumping
the fence and then pushing our clothes down our bodies and onto

the ground, and then a brief look around to catch what we could of our friends' naked bodies, and then into the pool. Water so cool down there. No matter the temperature of the water, always that river down there was cooler, was maybe not a river but a cool hand grabbing around there, forward and back as I swam, the grip of the hand shifting slightly, as anemones shift in the winds under water. Some water was warm, the pools heated during the day, but those were rare and strange anyway, the water hotter than the warm humid July air — it hardly felt like swimming at all, felt like the move from sauna to hot tub, which was lung-squeezing and seemed like too much work or like dying. Some pools were too cold, so cold, not heated but cooled, seemingly — we could never figure out why some pools were so cold but we would jump in; we were not allowed, did not allow ourselves, to feel the water first — and as I would run toward the edge ready to jump someone ahead would already be in with his head popped out and gasping and exhaling *Jesus* in disbelief and it would be too late to stop; I'd be in the air, doing my nice dive, seeing their big wide eyes as I would break through the water and freeze up everywhere immediately, the cold not on my skin but in my heart, always a seizing first of my heart.

But most of the water was the same, was pool water in July, a coolness to it that was . . . when you were in this water you knew you were in water but were not suffering or tired. It made your arms move and you would push your hair from your face and smooth it in back, then let your chin drop into it so the water would come into your mouth and you could spit it out slowly down your neck and you might picture the microbes in that stream of water, sliding down your chin, that they were either having fun doing this, as one would on a waterslide, or that this was for them a tidal wave, terror, the end of the world.

My friend Hand had this convertible only that summer — it was our first summer driving, and at the end of August he would try to cross a swollen creek with it, down near school, and it would flood and soon enough be abandoned. The car could fit eight of us, all small people at that point, and we would go three in the front and four in the back, Hand driving, insisting we call him Captain.

Then the car would go again, smooth and wide. It was so hot that summer, the humidity like breathing through mittens. We would meet at Annie's house, in her older brother's room, Hand and me and Dean dunking on and almost always breaking the cheap Nerf hoop attached to his door, the ball moist from the mouth of Tiger, their dog, now exiled, scratching from the door's other side.

Ritual dictated the stopping first at Hand's aunt's pool, for good luck, even though there was no risk factor — she knew we would come and didn't mind — and so we would jump the fence and run quickly through her yard, jump the hose, dive in, swim across and sling ourselves out in one motion, and continue, around the side of the house, the grass cool and itchy, over the wood log fence into the neighbor's and then through their side garden and to the street and into the boatcar again. If it all went off hitchless, no cuts or loud sounds, we would know the night's luck would be good.

We were all horny little people and looking to make mistakes. Hand and Jennifer were together so the variables were Dean and the rest, really, because I wasn't someone they were interested in. Sometimes Frankie came out too, and that's why the girls even bothered, to get a shot at either of them, Dean or Frankie, or to get a look at Hand's dick, which was supposed to be huge but wasn't really, or maybe it was — I'm the wrong one to ask, I guess. I still have no idea how it all worked, who decided on whom and how. I was always ready for anything, for any of the girls, who were all out of my league, and I was supposed to know this but kept forgetting.

Diving boards were as much curse as blessing — they made us loud and lazy and loose, and that's how we got caught. We stopped at a nice pool that night, by the unincorporated land, the water clean and arctic blue, only our second one that night. The house looked empty; no cars in the driveway, no lights on except one in front but no one in that room so we figured we had time. Hand was doing his serious diving, and Dean was doing his Dean Martin thing where he pretended to fall off with a drink in his hand, and everyone was shrieking, which is a stupid thing to do.

Soon the yard lights came on; a silhouette in the porch door. We were quick. Dean was over the fence and Hand right behind him but Ellen and I were smack in the middle of the man's pool still and he was right there, now by the edge, in a polo shirt and khakis and holding a tumbler full of something tinkly. He crouched down slowly and looked in his water.

"Are one of you Shannon?"

I know now that he was tipsy and nearsighted and thought that his niece, who went to our school, had come to use the pool, but I didn't know these things at the time and Ellen didn't say anything, so I said, "We all are."

I didn't know yet that there were only two of us left. But I figured we were caught anyway and so we might as well have fun. I went on: "Who are you? That's the real question."

There was a long pause. The trees everywhere were black.

"Who am I? I am the owner of this pool!"

Honking was coming from the street. Everyone was in the car and waiting. We should have just run for it.

"Property is theft," offered Ellen.

The man said nothing. He stood up again and now was looking into the woods. It was strange.

No one was talking. I thought maybe he would shoot us. I dropped under the surface and sank, cross-legged, until I was sitting on the bottom, hoping by the time I came up everything would be settled — either we'd be free to go or he was calling the cops. I sank to the bottom. My leg was rubbed by a white tube attached to a kind of sentient floor-cleaner, moving slowly along the pool's sandpapery bottom, of its own accord. I tried to ride it but it stopped when I stood on it. I ran out of air. I came up under a raft. Ellen, now in a towel, was sitting with the man at the patio table. I couldn't hear what they were saying.

They saw me under the raft.

"Get out — it's okay," Ellen said. I did, and put on my shorts. Ellen watched me. The man pointed to a towel on a chair.

He wasn't mad. Ellen had told him we were classmates of Shannon's. I sat down, warm in the thick soft towel, and told him I had Shannon in Trig and she was cool. The man liked that.

"You kids want some pop or something?"

"Sure," Ellen said.

"No thanks," I said, staring at her. I wanted to be gone.

"I want some," she said, louder.

We followed the man through his kitchen and into his living room. He didn't say anything about us being wet so we forged ahead, dripping on his tile, on his clean rugs. He went to a bar area, fancy with crystal decanters and everything like *Dynasty*, and poured us something from a carafe. I smelled it. Pepsi. The TV was on. We sipped our Pepsi and watched a dog bite a baby's face, an audience laughing.

The man sat on his coffee table and sighed.

"So where did the others go? It sounded like there were about ten of you."

"They had to go study," I said.

"Hmm." He sipped his drink. Then he looked at us — Ellen, then me. "You kids do drugs?"

I froze. Uh-oh, he was going to offer us drugs. Just like the lady the football players went to, the one they called Big Joan, who gave them beer and pot and ran card games. Did every town have one of these people, so lonely that he let teenagers do things like that in his home?

"No thanks," I said. "Not tonight."

The man looked confused.

We watched the TV a little more. The man was wearing athletic socks under his sandals. I was about to announce our departure when the man said, "Well, I'm going to go to bed. Leave the TV on when you go."

He went upstairs.

"Should we go?" I asked.

"Let's stay," Ellen said.

We waited until the car stopped honking and they figured we were caught and we settled in, in our bathing suits, on the couch of Shannon Wharton's uncle, and after watching the news we kissed.

It didn't go far and never happened again. Ellen with her coal eyes and perfectly tanning arms.

What this has to do with this collection I will never know.

About this collection:

1. It's not scientific.

These collections, the Best Americans, usually comprise work that first appeared in American periodicals in a given year. In this case, two of the pieces — by Adrian Tomine and Zoe Trope — didn't technically appear in any magazine but were instead published on their own, by small presses.

Also, we didn't look at every last thing published in every last periodical in 2001. The idea for this collection came about late in the year, and we scrambled to get it done in time and get the mix right, even if it meant bending some rules.

Rodney Rothman's "My Fake Job" has two qualification problems. First, it was actually first published at the tail end of 2000. Second, when it was published, labeled as nonfiction in *The New Yorker*, it subsequently turned out that there were fictional elements to the story. The author describes getting a massage from a masseuse — I won't give anything else away — and this massage never, in fact, happened. This is the primary offending portion, and while we don't for a second condone adding fictional elements to something called journalism — and *The New Yorker*, which has the most exacting factual standards, justifiably disowned the piece — we feel the story is a valuable and extremely funny one, with a lot to say about the dot-com boom, and maybe even why it went bust. Read Rothman's story as a piece of fiction, though one based extremely closely on real life.

2. The order is alphabetical.

The Best American collections are almost always printed in alphabetical order, by the author's last name. This is the easiest way to do it, of course, and the most elegant, but it means that stories shouldn't necessarily be read in order. In the first half of this collection, you get a good deal of hard journalism, primarily about war and refugees, from Afghanistan to the Sudan, followed immediately by a number of less serious pieces, about malls and Marilyn Manson. We didn't group anything by theme, and won't be offended if you skip around.

3. We had a lot of help with this.

Out here in San Francisco, we recently opened 826 Valencia, a writing and tutoring lab for young students in the Mission district. We offer drop-in tutoring, in-class workshops, free classes and vocational training, and scholarships. We work a lot with another group, Youth Speaks, which helps students interested in spoken-word poetry, among other things. When I was asked to edit this collection, I immediately asked the students of Youth Speaks and 826 Valencia — all of them high school age — to help find and judge the work we were sifting through.

They did an amazing job. We had stacks all over the office, three and four feet high, and the job of the student readers was to read the pieces, talk about them, vote on them, and let us know what they thought would be good in the collection. They spent countless hours at our Valencia Street space and at home reading the work we'd found, and when we felt we were still short of things we felt strongly about, they did research of their own. They took their task very seriously, and we took their opinions very seriously.

I'd like to thank Nico Cary, Rafael Casal, Katri Foster, Irene Garcia, Chinaka Hodge, Adam Tapia-Grassi, Janet Yukhtman, and my brother Chris for their honesty — their brutal honesty — and for their consistently hard work in making *The Best American Nonrequired Reading 2002* what it is. Also, a few dozen of the tutors of 826 Valencia spent long hours sifting and reading, and their work was essential. Extra thanks go to Kiara Brinkman, Janelle Brown, James Daly, Arne Johnson, Matthew Ness, Jenny Traig, and especially Jason Roberts and Kate Kudirka.

This collection: it's a strange and potent mix of stuff, always frank, never shrinking, all over the world and back — a collection we're really proud of. I hope you find something here that removes your head and flies away, or gets inside you and lights you up.

DAVE EGGERS

THE BEST AMERICAN

NONREQUIRED READING

2002

JENNY BITNER

■

The Pamphleteer

FROM *To-Do List*

"It is error only, and not truth, that shrinks from inquiry."
— Thomas Paine, author of *Common Sense*

I AM TRYING to devise the perfect pamphlet, a pamphlet that if given to enough people could change the world. I wonder if such a pamphlet is possible, and what it could say. I am intrigued by the belief that a pamphlet can change a life. I remember those given to me with images of a man burning amid fiery flames, and inside: "Change your life. Do you know you will burn in hell if you don't change your ways?"

I have read a lot of pamphlets: on menstruation, yoga, saving the redwoods, saying no to drugs, and breast implants. Pamphlets on sexually transmitted diseases that I read very carefully. I've been given pamphlets (often handed to me) about the first day of college, investing for retirement, and monkeys on Mars. I've also read a lot of pamphlets on getting rich: selling health supplies, makeup, healing magnets, bottled water, or Kambucha mushrooms. There are pamphlets for every religion. Well, except maybe the nonconverting sects, like the Amish. If something is important, there will be a pamphlet about it.

I wonder: If written in the correct order, could the correct words make a difference in someone's life? Could words stop her from doing something or make her a different person? Like the mo-

ment of epiphany in a great novel where the young man, seeing a
stranger stuff his pipe, suddenly has an insight about the nature of
death.

I play with words. I try arranging them in a way that might
spark a change in someone's brain — causing neurons to fire differently or altering those furry spots that make decisions about
who is sexy and what is good. Imagine a pamphlet that makes you
feel kind or makes you sexy. Read this.— and your life will trans-
form. But I can't figure out what it is I want to say. Late at night I
go down to the coffee shop where a girl gives me a cup of hot coffee. I make this pamphlet for her:

On the outside is a drawing of a girl one step up from a stick figure. She is wearing an odd cap, and the line that is her mouth
seems to be half grinning and half straight, as if she were on the
way into or out of a smile. She is giving a cup of coffee in a round
mug to another girl. The text inside reads:

> Maybe we always like people who give us coffee
> Maybe her eyes are the color of glacier melt
> Maybe we always like people who give us coffee

It's a personal communication. It is not art- or world-changing,
but perhaps it will make some difference to us.

I wake up in the middle of the night in a sweat. I am gripped by
the knowledge that I have nothing to say — that even if I could
write a pamphlet everyone in the world would see, I would fail.
That I can't say Love each other. Or Stop and look at things. Or
Don't concentrate wealth. Everything I have to say has been said a
million times and better. Plus it's a cliché. Plus — and here's the
kicker — it doesn't change anything. The inevitability of history
hits me like a mallet over the head. There is no room for a Thomas
Paine in the world today — even though I want to be the female
Thomas Paine, filled with Revolutionary zeal, making pamphlets
on a Xerox machine.

Oh, I guess I could inform people about something they were
clueless about, like U.S. involvement in _____, you fill in the atroc-

ity. But my pamphlet is not being written. I cannot write it, and the reason is this: pamphleteers are fundamentalists. They believe in something without a doubt. They know they are right. They know. They have the knowledge. They know what is what. They are not flounderers. They are not confused. Their message is not ambiguous. They know they know, and they share their fucking unequivocal knowledge. Can you imagine this state of mind? I can't. It must be close to religious conversion (in some cases it is). Ah, the sweet rested mind. The mind that knows and wants to share.

On the subway, a little boy is handing around a pamphlet that says he is a deaf mute. It says that this is how he makes his money and would you please give him some. I don't. I don't because I don't believe he is a deaf mute. Maybe I am wrong. There is room for doubt.

But I have to start my pamphlet from this state of confusion and ambiguity. It doesn't make a very strong pamphlet.

> Honor All Religions
> Don't Change Your Life
> Boredom Kills

These are more like bumper sticker slogans, and nothing is as boring as a bumper sticker. See it once, and it's interesting. After that, it becomes boring, annoying, pitiful.

I am not a genuine pamphleteer. I have nothing to write. Instead, I start drawing pictures and giving them to people. This gives people the impression that I am deaf or just extremely introverted. Neither is true. If I had something to say, I would be the first to say it, loudly, outrageously, and articulately, but I only have these pictures:

A little girl buying a hot dog from a guy with long greasy hair.
A pregnant woman getting her belly kicked (sorry).
Two people having sex while one is worrying about the other having sex with someone else.
A girl sleeping on three mushrooms.

These are the pamphlets I'm creating.

I am not at all sure that any one of them alters the world in any way.

There will probably be a gradual sea change. The way we all used to just drink tap water without thinking and now nobody does, but we hardly ever think about it.

Still, I start a regimen of giving these pamphlets to strangers. I have discarded the idea (did I ever have it?) that I have to give my pamphlets to everyone. Now I have a sincere and real belief that it is far better to give the pamphlet to just one person. That person, when handed her custom-made pamphlet, will wonder, "Was it written just for me? Was it written for anyone and I just happened along? Is this really ballpoint pen, or did she Xerox this in blue ink?"

These words, the singularity of the moment, the intimacy, I believe, will create the power I need — the power to change.

One day I'm hanging outside of Goodwill. (I still work, don't worry, it's Saturday.)

I see a woman I want to give one to. She looks like this: she looks like she's nice and she's working in a job she doesn't really like (what's new) and she has a boyfriend who is okay and she wanted to be a third-grade teacher in a small town but now she's living in San Francisco and is a little unsure how she ended up here. She's perfect. Her life is in need of a pamphlet.

I give her: a snail looking for something while a can of salt is falling out of the sky.

She reacts by looking at me like I'm homeless (I'm not) or crazy (who knows). Thanks, she says. The way we say thanks for something we don't really want.

I head down the street unruffled. The long-term effects of these pamphlets are unknown. I don't know, and frankly she doesn't either. We are clueless and naive about effects. We will unself-consciously watch a movie about something and then go do the same thing the next day, unaware. We will repeat things we've heard before without realizing it. I will on occasion reread my diary and realize that I had made the profound realization I thought I'd just made for the first time. We don't know what is ruling us. At least people who believe in the stars admit to the mystery of it all.

I have my own theory of where ideas come from. Messages come though me like garbled signals through a shaky television antenna. They come from the environment and are picked up on my clothing like minuscule hair fibers that later will tie me to the scene of a crime. For example, the way my window faces the street and not the back of the house affects my actions. I am in touch with the world: the late cries, the sounds of people wandering drunkenly to cars they should not drive, men harassing women, weird howls I don't know the origin of. The sounds sneak into my dreams with angry vulnerability.

I read about an artist in love with the purity of randomness, Zen-like. He liked chance occurrences more than intentional acts because he thought the ego is not involved in chance operations. But what if the ego isn't involved in either? Maybe my drawing comes from the noise across the street or the thoughts of someone walking by on the street. Maybe it's from a thunderstorm in Nebraska or a story I read when I was ten and forgot.

I fear that people would think — if they were to think about me — that I have unresolved communications issues. They would picture some dark secret in my past that hasn't been cleared up: a dead tyrannical father, a mother caught in an affair, a pedophile uncle, something of the deep and unearthed sort. But I prefer to think of myself as a remnant of a time when communications happened in person.

I decide, for obvious reasons, that people on the bus are the most in need of drawings. I try to give a drawing to a man on the bus who looks lost. I hand it to him.

"I don't have any change," he says.

"I didn't ask you for change," I say.

"Sorry, I don't have any," he says.

"I want to give this to you," I say.

He looks at the picture that is lying in front of him.

It is a monkey clinging to a telephone pole.

He looks up at me for a second and then looks down. "Sorry," he says, "I really don't have any change."

My career as a pamphleteer is in the pits. I realize that with communication at this level things are impossible for a pamphleteer. Everyone thinks I am insane. I decide that the only thing that will make anyone listen is a dramatic, sweeping motion.

I decide to give up my pamphleteer career and find a new one. The truth is I have always wanted to be a Pony Express messenger, but I'm afraid of horses. I am not only afraid of them, I loathe them as if they all represented a girlish sublimated sexuality that makes me uncomfortable. Why do only girls say they *love* horses? As in "Daddy, I love horses." But the horse is not what I really want. What I want is to deliver mail in person cross-country. I want to take my message every step of the way from this coast to the other.

I am disgusted by the quick and sloppy way communication is happening. We send those e-things effortlessly with a click and without thinking. We can even send groups of them that way. Like a swarm of flies descending on the victim. Like a mailbox full of messages that all say Urgent. Communication is urgent. Letters are slow. Postcards are whipped off, but messages in bottles I suspect are labored over a bit. A message that you know someone will have to deliver in person must be thought over. It must be important. It must be short and deep and true.

If we have to suffer to deliver mail, then it means something. If there are sores on the sides of my legs and horse smells in my clothes and the thought of another mile is a torture, then I will think about the words. Books are heavy from the ink. Ink weighs. It's like imagining we had to carry everything we owned with us. We would think about our purchases.

An 1860 California newspaper ad for Pony Express riders read: "Wanted: Young, skinny, wiry fellows. Not over 18. Must be expert riders. Willing to risk death daily. Orphans preferred."

I meet none of those qualifications; that's why I'm ripe for the new Pony Express. There is a message I want to deliver. I need to deliver. Tell you the truth, it would be preferable if I went back in time and delivered it several years ago, but that is not possible.

And so I decide to reinstate a one-woman Pony Express just to deliver this message from California to Virginia. It will be a long ride. I'm not looking forward to the Rocky Mountains. Is there something I will learn in the distance? I set out, it's spring, and I don't arrive until the deep winter. I pass highways and homeless people and McDonald's — so fucking many plastic slides and strip malls — and so many homes with people, and none of them belongs to me, and I belong to none of them. I used to be a pamphleteer, and now I'm a messenger. I wrote the letter too, and now after all these months I forget what it says.

People look at me oddly as I ride by on my horse with the leather carrier satchel, and when they see the words PONY EXPRESS on the satchel there is a look of slight wonder in their eyes. I think that they are hoping for a letter from someone, maybe even from someone dead or lost to them. I wish I had one. I wish I was the one to magically bring all of the letters people have hoped for.

As I enter Virginia it's snowing. I see the old house by the soapstone quarry where we used to let the dogs run in the fields and watch the seasons instead of TV. When I get closer, I see that the porch is falling in, and the paint is peeling from the house in long white curves, exposing gray, weathered wood. The porch swing hangs by three hooks and is covered in snowdrift. A thin flow of smoke is coming out of the chimney. She is not waiting for me; but how could she be? If we don't know where someone is, we always picture her in the last place we left her.

I tie up my horse and knock on the door. She answers in her nightgown, her long hair tied up in a knot. Her eyes are not as scary as I remember. She doesn't seem surprised to see me and even seems to be expecting me. The letter in my hand has not managed the trip so well. One corner is soggy, and one has a coffee smear on it. She sees the letter. Her hand reaches for it in a no-nonsense kind of way.

It's the moment I've been waiting for, and yet I feel like I am watching the scene from the top of the old maple tree: a girl on a horse and another in a nightgown. Their faces are hard to read but seem tired. The one in the nightgown takes the letter. She says thank you. I wonder for a second if she is sleepwalking. She turns and goes inside to read the letter.

I'm alone now. It seems I hardly remember how I got here. My eyes are not accustomed to the light, as if they had been focused on one small thing for so long and now that thing is gone. A squirrel in the yard near the oak tree watches me with a look of territorial fear. I notice that a forsythia bush has managed to hold on to some of its yellow flowers. I get on my horse and ride away.

SARA CORBETT

■

The Lost Boys

FROM *The New York Times Upfront*

ONE EVENING in late January, Peter Dut, twenty-one, leads his
two teenage brothers through the brightly lit corridors of the Minneapolis airport, trying to mask his confusion. Two days earlier,
the brothers, refugees from Africa, encountered their first light
switch and their first set of stairs. An aid worker in Nairobi demonstrated the flush toilet to them — also the seat belt, the shoe-
lace, the fork. And now they find themselves alone in Minneapolis, three bone-thin African boys confronted by a swirling river of
white faces and rolling suitcases.

Finally, a traveling businessman recognizes their uncertainty.
"Where are you flying to?" he asks kindly, and the eldest brother
tells him in halting, bookish English. A few days earlier, they left a
small mud hut in a blistering hot Kenyan refugee camp, where
they had lived as orphans for nine years after walking for hundreds of miles across Sudan. They are now headed to a new home
in the U.S.A. "Where?" the man asks in disbelief when Peter Dut
says the city's name. "Fargo? North Dakota? You gotta be kidding
me. It's too cold there. You'll never survive it!"

And then he laughs. Peter Dut has no idea why.

In the meantime, the temperature in Fargo has dropped to 15
below. The boys tell me that until now, all they have ever known
about cold is what they felt grasping a bottle of frozen water. An
aid worker handed it to them one day during a "cultural orienta-

tion" session at the Kakuma Refugee Camp, a place where the temperature hovers around 100 degrees.

Peter Dut and his two brothers belong to an unusual group of refugees referred to by aid organizations as the Lost Boys of Sudan, a group of roughly 10,000 boys who arrived in Kenya in 1992 seeking refuge from their country's fractious civil war. The fighting pits a northern Islamic government against rebels in the south who practice Christianity and tribal religions.

The Lost Boys were named after Peter Pan's posse of orphans. According to U.S. State Department estimates, some 17,000 boys were separated from their families and fled southern Sudan in an exodus of biblical proportions after fighting intensified in 1987. They arrived in throngs, homeless and parentless, having trekked about 1000 miles, from Sudan to Ethiopia, back to Sudan, and finally to Kenya. The majority of the boys belonged to the Dinka and Nuer tribes, and most were then between the ages of eight and eighteen. (Most of the boys don't know for sure how old they are; aid workers assigned them approximate ages after they arrived in 1992.)

Along the way, the boys endured attacks from the northern army and marauding bandits as well as lions, who preyed on the slowest and weakest among them. Many died from starvation or thirst. Others drowned or were eaten by crocodiles as they tried to cross a swollen Ethiopian river. By the time the Lost Boys reached the Kakuma Refugee Camp, their numbers had been cut nearly in half.

Now, after nine years of subsisting on rationed corn mush and lentils and living largely ungoverned by adults, the Lost Boys of Sudan are coming to America. In 1999, the United Nations High Commissioner for Refugees, which handles refugee cases around the world, and the U.S. government agreed to send 3600 of the boys to the United States — since going back to Sudan was out of the question. About 500 of the Lost Boys still under the age of eighteen will be living in apartments or foster homes across the United States by the end of this year. The boys will start school at a grade level normal for their age, thanks to a tough English-language program at their refugee camp. The remaining 3100 Lost Boys will be resettled as adults. After five years, each boy will be eligible for citizenship, provided he has turned twenty-one.

Nighttime in America?

On the night that I stand waiting for Peter Dut and his brothers to land in Fargo, tendrils of snow are snaking across the tarmac. The three boys file through the gate without money or coats or luggage beyond their small backpacks. The younger brothers, Maduk, seventeen, and Riak, fifteen, appear petrified. As a social worker passes out coats, Peter Dut studies the black night through the airport window. "Excuse me," he says worriedly. "Can you tell me, please, is it now night or day?"

This is a stove burner. This is a can opener. This is a brush for your teeth. The new things come in a tumble. The brothers' home is a sparsely furnished two-bedroom apartment in a complex on Fargo's south side. Rent is $445 a month. It has been stocked with donations from area churches and businesses: toothpaste, bread, beans, bananas.

A caseworker empties a garbage bag full of donated clothing, which looks to have come straight from the closet of an elderly man. I know how lucky the boys are: the State Department estimates that war, famine, and disease in southern Sudan have killed more than 2 million people and displaced another 4 million. Still I cringe to think of the boys showing up for school in these clothes.

The next day, when I return to the apartment at noon, the boys have been up since five and are terribly hungry. "What about your food?" I ask, gesturing to the bread and bananas and the box of cereal sitting on the counter.

Peter grins sheepishly. I suddenly realize that the boys, in a lifetime of cooking maize and beans over a fire pit, have never opened a box. I am placed in the role of teacher. And so begins an opening spree. We open potato chips. We open a can of beans. We untwist the tie on the bagged loaf of bread. Soon the boys are seated and eating a hot meal.

Living on Leaves and Berries

The three brothers have come a long way since they fled their village in Sudan with their parents and three sisters, all of whom were later killed by Sudanese army soldiers. The Lost Boys first survived a six- to ten-week walk to Ethiopia, often subsisting on leaves and berries and the occasional boon of a warthog carcass. Some boys staved off dehydration by drinking their own urine. Many fell behind; some were devoured by lions or trampled by buffalo.

The Lost Boys lived for three years in Ethiopia, in UN-supported camps, before they were forced back into Sudan by a new Ethiopian government no longer sympathetic to their plight. Somehow, more than 10,000 of the boys miraculously trailed into Kenya's UN camps in the summer of 1992 — as Sudanese government planes bombed the rear of their procession.

For the Lost Boys, then, a new life in America might easily seem to be the answer to every dream. But the real world has been more complicated than that. Within weeks of arriving, Riak is placed in a local junior high; Maduk starts high school classes; and Peter begins adult education classes.

Refugee Blues

Five weeks later, Riak listens quietly through a lesson on Elizabethan history at school, all but ignored by white students around him.

Nearby, at Fargo South High School, Maduk is frequently alone as well, copying passages from his geography textbook, trying not to look at the short skirts worn by many of the girls.

Peter Dut worries about money. The three brothers say they receive just $107 in food stamps each month and spend most of their $510 monthly cash assistance on rent and utilities.

Resettlement workers say the brothers are just undergoing the normal transition. Scott Burtsfield, who coordinates resettlement efforts in Fargo through Lutheran Social Services, says, "The first three months are always the toughest. It really does get better."

The Lost Boys can only hope so; they have few other options. A return to southern Sudan could be fatal. "There is nothing left for the Lost Boys to go home to — it's a war zone," says Mary Anne Fitzgerald, a Nairobi-based relief consultant.

Some Sudanese elders have criticized sending boys to the United States. They worry that their children will lose their African identity. One afternoon an eighteen-year-old Lost Boy translated a part of a tape an elder had sent along with many boys: "He is saying, 'Don't drink. Don't smoke. Don't kill. Go to school every day, and remember, America is not your home.'"

But if adjustment is hard, the boys also experience consoling moments. One of these came on a quiet Friday night last winter. As the boys make a dinner of rice and lentils, Peter changes into an African outfit, a finely woven green tunic with a skullcap to match, bought with precious food rations at Kakuma.

Just then the doorbell rings unexpectedly. And out of the cold tumble four Sudanese boys — all of whom have resettled as refugees over the past several years. I watch one, an eighteen-year-old named Sunday, wrap his arms encouragingly around Peter Dut. "It's a hard life here," Sunday whispers to the older boy, "but it's a free life, too."

MICHAEL FINKEL

■

Naji's Taliban Phase

FROM *The New York Times Magazine*

NAJI RECEIVED his first letter from Ali in early July. It was delivered by a man on a donkey. The man rode from the Northern Alliance positions in the brown hills outside the city of Taloqan, in northeastern Afghanistan, then across the dusty battle plains, and then farther, to the Taliban roadblock patrolled by Naji. Naji opened the letter, read it through, and tore it up. Then he struck a match and burned the pieces.

The letter was written by a midlevel Northern Alliance commander named Ali Ahmed. This was six months ago, when the Northern Alliance controlled only a tenuous pocket of the Afghan highlands and the United States military had scant interest in a far-off civil war. For Naji, the letter was completely unexpected; its mere delivery shot him with fear. "It was just a small letter," Ali says, speaking in Dari, the Afghan dialect of Persian. "I introduced myself. I sent greetings from my family, and I sent greetings to his family. I said I would be happy to hear back from him. Then I signed my name."

Naji's father and Ali's father are old friends. Both are in the textile business and occasionally share expenses on shipments from Pakistan. Naji and Ali had actually met, though only once, when they were young. The two boys were raised in the same region of northern Afghanistan, and both came from families of Tajik descent. Otherwise their lives had followed different trajectories.

Naji fought for the Taliban, and Ali was with the Northern Alliance. They were trying to kill each other.

Ali's letter was not written only out of kindness, and both soldiers knew it. Ali's "family greetings" were a veiled way of pointing out that the two men shared the same ethnicity. It did not need to be mentioned that most soldiers of Tajik descent had joined the Northern Alliance; the Taliban was dominated by Pashtuns from Afghanistan's southern provinces. Ali's invitation to write back was a way of expressing that the Northern Alliance would welcome Naji into its army. These meanings were clear to Naji, and potentially damning, which is why the note was promptly destroyed.

When Ali's letter arrived, Naji had been with the Taliban for nearly five years. He was twenty-four. His beard spilled from his face in a mass of black curls; he wore a dark blue turban. He was a low-ranking soldier, often positioned on the front lines. He'd been trained to shoot a Kalashnikov and a shoulder-mounted rocket launcher and a Russian-made machine gun called an RPK.

Naji had fought his way across Afghanistan. He had fought in Charikar, and in Bagram, and in Shir Khan and Kunduz and Mazar-i-Sharif. Death seemed to be around him all the time; it had become like a fog. By his count, he'd watched more than a hundred of his fellow soldiers die, and had inflicted no small vengeance of his own. He was never paid a salary — he was given only food and clothing and boots and weapons.

If you ask Naji about his experiences, he doesn't have much to share. "I spent a lot of time fighting," he'll say, then he'll look at you with the sort of tired expression that suggests either that he has pushed these memories into a far corner of his mind or, perhaps, that he has seen so little else in his life that he can't understand how war stories could be interesting. Naji has big, somber eyes, with lids that seem to furl no higher than half-mast. His countenance appears gloomy no matter his mood. When he is sitting in a room, away from the battlefield, it is difficult to picture him as a warrior. He has a habit of nibbling on the ends of his thumbs, and he speaks so softly that you have to lean in to hear him. He's a bit chubby. He has never been married; he says he has never had a girlfriend.

Last winter Naji's unit helped capture the city of Taloqan, forcing the Northern Alliance troops into the hills and casting thousands of families out of their homes. Though Naji didn't know it, one of these families was Ali's — Taloqan is his hometown. Ali has three wives and three children, a son by each wife. He is young — twenty-eight — and well educated, with a degree in pharmacology. He wears his hair in the sort of mop cut that was once popularized by the Beatles, and keeps his chin clean-shaven. One of his front teeth is capped in silver, lending an element of thuggishness to an otherwise boyish face.

In the Northern Alliance army, Ali ascended from foot soldier to officer in a matter of months; his brothers call him, with only a bit of facetiousness, the Commander. His favorite game is chess, and he plays in a style both meticulous and, even from the black pieces, almost invariably aggressive. When he takes a piece, he does it with fanfare, plucking up his opponent's piece and slamming down his, an action at once brash and daunting.

It was from his retreated position, in the hills, that Ali learned from his father of Naji's location and sent his first letter. Naji says that after he read it he felt suddenly anxious. He thought about things he had seen that he wished he had not seen. He had watched, more than once, as civilians were forced to leave their homes. He'd watched as bales of hay were lighted and then tossed into these homes. He'd watched as some of these fleeing civilians were murdered. "I saw children get killed," he says, "and I became sad and ashamed and I thought, This is not how Islam works."

Such thoughts, Naji says, are the main reason that the man on the donkey rode back to the Northern Alliance side a week later, this time bearing a note from Naji.

A donkey plodding past tanks and rocket launchers and front-line positions may seem a wildly incongruous sight. In Afghanistan, at least, it is not. Riding a donkey is the second most common way for Afghans to travel. Most common is by foot. Virtually all of Afghanistan is without a telephone system, or mail service, or electricity, or highways, or railroads. Villages are constructed entirely of baked mud and straw. The only resource the country seems to have in any surplus is dust. It's an amazing sort of dust — it hangs in the air like smoke, muting the sun, accumulating so thickly and rapidly that automobiles often drive with their windshield wipers on.

The country has been in a state of war for so long that war has been absorbed into daily life. Bomb craters fill with water and become drinking holes for cattle. Wooden ammunition boxes are used to construct window shutters. Food supply bags from relief agencies are sewn together to make tents. A burst of gunfire from a few yards away does not disturb a conversation.

During lulls in the fighting, there is often a steady stream of traffic passing through the front lines. Merchants drag burros laden with corn and rice and cooking oil and tea. Displaced families head to refugee camps, infants held to chests, possessions strapped to backs. Herdsmen guide sheep and goats and cows and camels. Women seem to float within their burkas, shapeless save for an exposed ankle or the dent of a nose against the scrim. Everyone tries to walk in tank tracks or footprints so as not to trigger land mines.

Amid such a flow rode the letter carrier. He delivered letters through the summer, as the Taliban surged forward, and then, after the September attacks in the United States, he delivered letters as the Taliban was pushed back. The notes grew longer, and more eloquent, and increasingly personal. Because there was distance between the two men, and because they did not know each other, the strictures of social conventions were loosened, and Naji and Ali could be freer with their thoughts, more opinionated — riskier — than they could with friends or family. "Sometimes," Naji once wrote, "I think about living in another part of the world." Ali wrote back: "I think about it always."

The letter carrier crossed the front lines almost once a week for nearly five months. There were letters about religion, and bigotry, and honor. The tone was sometimes frank and sometimes droll. And in this way, cumbersome but effective, a strange sort of friendship was forged.

When Naji was thirteen, he left home to get an education and ended up in a war. His given name is Najibullah; he prefers Naji, and like many Afghans, he doesn't use a surname. There were ten children in his family, and Naji was clearly one of the brightest, the only one his parents encouraged to seek schooling. This was the time of the Soviet invasion, and most schools in Naji's province were closed. He had an uncle who lived in Pakistan, where he could attend a madrasa free. So Naji walked east for seven days, over the Hindu Kush mountains and across the border.

Naji's family was Muslim, but at the madrasa he learned a new form of Islam. Here he was schooled in a puritan interpretation of Islamic law — a version that preached that music and dancing were anti-Islamic; that women should not work or attend school; that card playing and kite flying and most athletic pursuits were impure. Naji memorized large portions of the Koran. He studied the sayings of the Prophet Muhammad. He was told that the culture of the United States was "like a type of cancer." He was schooled by mullahs who saw no need to teach math or science or literature or history. He sensed that there was more to learn. He felt that there was a world just beyond his fingertips — but there was nothing he could do. It was the only education available to him.

Even the limited offerings of the madrasa were better than anything he could find at home, so Naji studied for six years. Then he was informed by the mullahs that he needed to fight. "I was told," he says, "that foreigners had overtaken my country; that non-Muslims were controlling Afghanistan. I was told that because I am educated I had to join the Taliban and purify my country."

And so he did. He returned to Afghanistan, to the Taliban capital of Kandahar. There he studied for a month with the movement's leader, Mullah Mohammed Omar. He learned about the value of the Taliban's ideals and the baseness of the enemy. "I concentrated with my whole mind on Mullah Omar," Naji says. The mullah, he says, had a quiet but addictively powerful charisma, a type he'd never before experienced. "You were pulled to him like a magnet," he says. When he speaks about Mullah Omar, the volume of Naji's voice drops by half, as if the mullah himself might somehow be listening. "I was ready to give my life for him." Then, armed with ideology and a Kalashnikov, Naji was sent off to war.

Until Ali's letters began arriving, Naji says, he believed that the Northern Alliance forces were composed primarily of non-Islamic, non-Afghan fighters. This idea, Naji says, was often repeated by the Taliban leadership. Ali's letters refuted it, and Naji became curious. He began to question a lot of what he'd been taught. In Taloqan, which was once the Northern Alliance capital, he spoke with civilians passing through his roadblock. "Everyone told me the same thing," Naji says. "They told me that all of the Northern Alliance fighters were Afghans."

Naji also had a troubling sense that as a Tajik in a Pashtun-controlled army, he was never afforded more than second-class status. "This is why I spent so many days on the front lines," he says. "This is why I was never made an officer." He felt somehow expendable; he worried that a Taliban victory might eventually exclude him. He discussed these ideas in his letters to Ali. They also corresponded about "the culture of Islam," as Naji puts it. "Ali wrote that a Muslim can have a long beard or a short one, can go to mosque or not, can wear a burka or not, and still be a good Muslim. I was very nervous to write this, but I said I agreed with him."

Then came September 11. Naji first learned of the attacks on America when U.S. planes dropped leaflets — "books that fell from the sky," he calls them. The books explained, in pictographs and simple language, a little of what had happened. "I had already seen my army burn our own people's houses, so I was not surprised that they would burn other people's houses," he says. "After the books came the bombs, and after the bombs I thought I was going to Allah."

In a matter of weeks, the momentum of the war shifted. The

Northern Alliance advanced on Taloqan, and Naji developed a plan: "I told my commander that I had an earache and that I had to go into the city to see a doctor." He left his post and did not return. Three days later, on November 15, as the city fell and Northern Alliance troops stormed in, the letter carrier was sent out with a final note — the twentieth, by Naji's tally. It was as short as the first. "I told Ali where I was staying," Naji recalls, "and then I said, 'I'm waiting here to greet you.'"

When Ali And Naji finally met, they kissed each other on the left cheek, in local fashion, and then Ali asked Naji if he'd like to stay at his house. Naji accepted. "In a minute, all my nervousness went away," Naji says. He moved into the two-story home, made of cinder block and cement, that Ali himself had just returned to. The house sits on a street lined with maple trees, where horse-drawn carriages, which serve as taxis in Taloqan, continually clop past.

On the first full day of his post-Taliban life, Naji visited a barber and had his beard cut to a reasonable length — an experience he found amusing, for one of his duties in the Taliban army was to punish soldiers whose beards were "shorter than a man's fist." He also shed his turban. He now covers his head with a *pakool*, the brown beret that was worn by Ahmed Shah Massoud, the slain Northern Alliance general.

In Ali's home, as with most Afghan homes, there is no furniture — just thin cushions, large pillows, Persian carpets, posters of Koranic verses, and a prayer rug aligned with Mecca. In the evenings the men sit on pillows beside a kerosene lantern and eat rice and mutton, balling the rice in their fingers, then scooping up a bit of meat. Ali's wives never enter the room, but his three sons continually run about, and Naji appears to have developed a bond with the youngest, Bahman, who is three and whom Naji likes to chase down and tickle. Naji says that he hasn't felt so content since he left home to go to school.

Two days after his defection, Naji returned to the front lines — this time with the Northern Alliance, as they fought to capture the city of Kunduz, where most of the Taliban retreated after their defeat in Taloqan. Naji was armed not with a weapon but with a radio. He remained well back of the fighting, where a group of commanders sat cross-legged on a duff of straw, in a circle, talking rapidly and fingering prayer beads. As machine-gun fire was exchanged from positions on opposite hills, Naji spoke by radio with Taliban officers he had just served under. The negotiations took five days, during which a village that had the unfortunate luck to be situated between the front lines was more or less returned to the soil. Then two hundred soldiers defected, driving across the front lines in a convoy of Toyota pickup trucks that had been camouflaged in the Taliban style — smeared with a thick layer of mud. The soldiers carried their bedrolls and canteens and Kalashnikovs and rocket launchers. They were greeted by the Northern Alliance troops with smiles and waves.

The defectors were of many ethnicities, though all were Afghans. They were lodged in Northern Alliance barracks, permitted to travel home to visit their families, and allowed to keep their weapons. The defectors cut their beards, exchanged turbans for *pakools,* hung posters of Massoud on their pickup trucks, and swore death to Mullah Omar. Many vowed that they'd had a sudden and powerful change of heart. They said they were ready to return to the front and fire upon soldiers they'd shared foxholes with the day before.

"When someone switches sides," Naji says, "we forget all past hatred and accept each other like brothers." Ali repeats a Dari expression: *"Derose derose buth wah imrose imrose hast"* — "Yesterday was yesterday but today is today."

Such is life in Afghanistan. A generation of Afghan boys do not know how to farm; have not learned a trade; have no specialized skills. There is no chance for them to obtain a real education. They do not have employment opportunities. There is no way for them to earn money. All they know how to do is fight. There is nothing else for them. They have made a career of waging war. To them, switching armies most likely feels no different from a businessman moving to a rival company. They simply hope to be on the winning side.

From the more thoughtful soldiers, there is talk of wanting peace. Naji says that he may one day join his father in the textile business. Ali says that he'd like to continue his schooling and perhaps become a doctor. But both men acknowledge that they will most likely continue doing what they know best. "I will fight with Ali until the Taliban is gone," Naji says. "And if this does not bring peace, then I will fight some more."

MEENAKSHI GANGULY

■

Generation Exile

FROM *Transition*

LOBSANG STILL REMEMBERS his last winter in Lhasa. He was seven years old, his brother nine. They had been racing each other in the street outside when their father called Lobsang over. Lobsang didn't want to go; his older brother had teased him mercilessly and he was looking for revenge. But their father had an ugly temper, and just now he was looking particularly grim. His brother's taunts rang in his ears as Lobsang jogged off.

He never saw his brother again. Lobsang's father introduced him to a strange man. The man was an agent, and he had been paid to take Lobsang away to Dharamsala in India, where the Dalai Lama lived. "I was terribly excited," Lobsang remembers. "We weren't allowed to say the Dalai Lama's name in public. And here was my father, sending me to him." Today, Lobsang is a stocky seventeen-year-old, and he laughs off the agonizing journey across the Himalayas — the frostbite, the hunger, the blisters that refused to heal. "I don't think of those things," he says. The most painful part of his journey was not saying good-bye to his mother.

For years Lobsang lived on memories. He often thought of his mother and her dog-eared photograph of the Dalai Lama. Every night when they prayed, she would bring it out from a hiding place in an old chest. She had sworn her sons to secrecy, lest their Chinese neighbors find them out.

After a decade in exile, Lobsang decided to go back. Last year, during summer vacation, he trekked to Nepal disguised as a trader; after bribing the Chinese border guards, he crossed into Tibet. With little money and no identification papers, he hid out at a relative's house near Lhasa. But it's hard to keep a secret in Chinese-occupied Tibet, and shortly after his arrival, the police surrounded the house. His uncle argued with them at the front door while Lobsang escaped by sliding down a scalding stovepipe.

Eventually the teenager was reunited with his mother. She told him that she had been weeping inside since the day he'd left — and not only for him. Lobsang's father had been thrown in jail for supporting the cause of independence. He'd been released, but no one was willing to employ him now.

Lobsang's brother met a darker fate. The older boy had been sent to a faraway monastery. One day the young monk decided to display a picture of the Dalai Lama in his chambers. When the police heard about his act of defiance, they descended on the monastery. He was dragged outside and murdered in the street. "It's strange." Lobsang whispers. "He was so fast when we were kids." Lobsang falls silent for a moment. He brings out his brother's identification card, rubbing his fingers over the grainy photograph. "They stabbed him to death in front of a crowd," he tells me. "What has happened to Tibet, that a monk should be murdered in broad daylight and no one raises a hand?"

In 1950, when Mao's Red Army overwhelmed independent Tibet's poorly equipped troops, the Communists claimed they had taken the territory — a former possession of imperial China — in order to modernize its feudal society. They also claimed to value Tibetan Buddhism as part of China's own national culture. The Dalai Lama agreed that Tibet was backward, but he — and many ordinary Tibetans — bridled at Chinese moves to erode Tibetan autonomy. By the mid-1950s, Tibet found itself fighting a savage guerrilla war against the occupation. Finally, in 1959, mass demonstrations and violence engulfed the region. As the Chinese brutally suppressed the uprising, the Dalai Lama and his ministers fled across the Himalayas, to India.

In theory, Beijing officially tolerates Tibetan Buddhism even to-day, just as it tolerates the Islam practiced by the Uighurs in China's restive northwest province. In practice, tales like Lob-sang's abound. Although many Tibetans are resigned to life with China and live by the laws of the Chinese state, the maroon robe still commands respect. Monks and nuns are the intellectuals and the activists in this deeply religious society. They are the living link to the Dalai Lama. They are the dissenters of modern-day Tibet — and the Chinese brook no dissent.

The conspicuous symbol of Chinese oppression, here as else-where, is the reeducation camp. Chinese authorities escort Ti-betan officials to the sacred monasteries and convents and inun-date them with propaganda that portrays the Dalai Lama as an evil man and a traitor. It doesn't always take. With unnerving regular-ity, maroon-robed lamas demonstrate in the streets, chanting na-tionalist slogans until the police drag them away. According to hu-man rights activists, two thirds of Tibet's political prisoners are monks and nuns. The ones who make it out tell gruesome tales: nuns raped with cattle prods; monks hung up by their legs and whipped. Activists display photographs of spiked shackles that tighten as the captive struggles, harnesses that suspend prisoners over a blazing flame while hot peppers are rubbed in their eyes. In India, a hidden forest convent harbors more than a hundred nuns who have survived Chinese prisons. Screams echo through the halls at night.

"I knew that things were bad in Tibet," Lobsang says, "but noth-ing prepared me for the fear. On the surface everyone seems happy. But they are absolutely terrified of the authorities." The city looked different than he remembered, too. "The streets had all changed. The Tibetans still live in dirty houses, but there are grand Chinese buildings in front of them." These days, visitors to Lhasa behold Potala Palace, the former seat of the Dalai Lama, from a sterile public square. The ramshackle Tibetan neighbor-hood that once surrounded the palace is gone. Shiny stores have sprung up around the edges of the square, selling beer, pop music, and televisions.

The Dalai Lama has long struggled to understand this brutality. He often recounts a story from his childhood: As a boy, the greatest god of Tibet was accustomed to deference. Everyone did his bidding except his pet parrot: this bird often showed its clear preference for the monk who fed it. "I was jealous," the Dalai Lama says. "I tried to feed it once or twice, but I never got the same response. So I beat it." He giggles. "Then, of course, I got nothing." Suddenly his expression turns sad. "The Chinese want Tibetans to be loyal to them, but it is impossible to buy loyalty by using the stick."

And yet the stick has subdued Tibet. The old Lhasa — its ugliness and its beauty — is long gone. Chinese settlers play a greater role in Tibetan life than Tibetans. Nowadays, if you want to find the real Tibet, you have to go to India.

Young Lobsang was awestruck when he first arrived in Dharamsala. The Tibetans in India were wealthy. They ran stores and hotels and wore nice clothes. Pictures of the Dalai Lama were everywhere. "The first time I saw a school parade," he says, "I knew I wanted to be the boy who carried the flag."

Lobsang learned a lot about his homeland. "In Lhasa, no one talked about the invasion," he says. "Not until I came to Dharamsala did I understand that the Chinese were ruling us by force, that Tibet was not free." Like his classmates, Lobsang participated in Free Tibet rallies. He painted posters and smiled smartly when American movie stars visited his school. He listened carefully to the Dalai Lama: "His Holiness said that we children must use our education to preserve our culture and help make our country free again." Lobsang decided to study law so that he could argue Tibet's case before the United Nations.

The UN may not be the best forum for the cause of Tibetan independence. China's permanent position on the Security Council makes it difficult to air Tibetan grievances. The Dalai Lama wasn't even invited to the UN's millennium summit of religious leaders last year. But he remains one of the world's paramount spiritual leaders. Heads of state welcome him, diplomats happily endure the fourteen-hour drive from New Delhi to Dharamsala, and hardened journalists find themselves charmed by his self-deprecating jokes. Celebrities like the actor Richard Gere and the rapper Adam Yauch (of the Beastie Boys) consider the Dalai Lama their spiritual guide, and they use their celebrity to highlight his predicament. China's bid to suppress dissent has made the Tibetans poster children for religious freedom. The Dalai Lama has become a global saint, a computer salesman, a political icon: a celebrity himself.

The Dalai Lama, however, reminds Tibetans that it is up to them to win their country back. "I am nothing special," he says. "I am just another human being, just a Buddhist follower. Nothing else." His government in exile is a democracy; he has admitted that the feudal system he left behind in Tibet was unjust and exploitative. In Dharamsala, representatives are elected to parliament, though the office of His Holiness still nominates the cabinet ministers. Tibetans say that they like the idea of popular rule. "We have never had this system," says a man named Phurbo Thondup, who sells sweaters in Dharamsala. "Democracy is considered the best system in the world. So we must learn it." But what of the Dalai Lama? "We cannot do without the Dalai Lama," he says promptly. "Even after they are elected, these representatives have to consult the Dalai Lama about everything."

Whenever the Dalai Lama drives in or out of his monastery, the townspeople line the streets, incense sticks in hand, and murmur their prayers. The Dalai Lama's family wields inordinate influence, and the Tibetan government in exile is a farrago of bureaucratic inefficiency. "The Dalai Lama will lead us to freedom," says one watery-eyed vegetable seller in Dharamsala. "If not the fourteenth Dalai Lama, then the fifteenth, or the sixteenth, or the one after that."

When Lobsang made his perilous journey to Dharamsala a decade ago, he was welcomed into the exile community. Today most escapees are given a brief audience with the Dalai Lama and told to go home. With the town's resources taxed to the limit, Dharamsala is becoming a kind of exclusive political resort. The refugee reception center still allows children to settle in Dharamsala, since they are the best hope for a Tibetan future. But the only adult refugees who are allowed to remain are religious officials. Others can visit, but they can't stay.

Tourism has brought prosperity — and, perhaps, complacency — to Dharamsala. After all, the city is the Tibetan Babylon, filled with bars, Internet cafés, and curio stalls. "If they are building houses here, how can they be planning to go back?" wonders one frostbitten nun as she stares at the colorful shops. "Back in Tibet, we thought people here were fighting for our cause. But they're just making money."

Perhaps you have to go still farther south to find the real Tibet. Many of the earliest Tibetan refugees settled in the south of India, where they live in scattered villages seldom visited by Western spiritual pilgrims. The settlers here still speak Tibetan and wear traditional garb. They have recreated monasteries that were destroyed by the Chinese. The illustrious Sera Monastic University, once the main school for Tibetan monks in Lhasa, has opened again in Bylakuppe, a village in the Indian state of Karnataka. Nearly five thousand monks are enrolled today, many of them young boys fresh out of Tibet.

Life here has not been easy. Forty years have passed since the original exodus, and the restoration of the monasteries has done nothing to raise the hope of return. Most Tibetans in the south are poor: nobody — neither the Tibetans nor their Indian neighbors — expected the situation to last this long. One wizened old woman named Bhuti, who runs a grocery store in Bylakuppe, has been ready to go home since she fled Tibet in 1960. She left everything there, thinking she would be back in a year or two; now she knows that she will never return. "I would like to die in my own country, but there is no path for me to take and no place for me back in Tibet," she says. Bhuti doesn't even have any souvenirs from her childhood: she sold all her jewelry during her first years in exile. She keeps a tattered postcard picture of a Tibetan bride wearing a heavy necklace like the one she once owned. Prayer beads roll ceaselessly in her hand. What is she praying for? She smiles gently. "For the long life of the Dalai Lama."

In another village, called Kollegal, there's a farmer named Neadup who also fled Tibet after the Chinese crackdown. At the time, India was barely able to feed its own people. All the government could offer the Tibetan refugees was backbreaking work building roads in the Himalayas. Neadup was on a crew near Manali, an Indian hill town, when the young Dalai Lama came to visit. Distraught by the hardships his people faced, the Dalai Lama approached Neadup. Neadup weeps as he recalls the encounter: "His Holiness asked me, 'Why are you here in India?' I said, 'We came to see you, and live with you in exile.' The Dalai Lama was crying. He told me, 'Don't worry. I will ask the Indian government to help you.'"

Neadup was eventually given four acres of land. "It's been difficult," the old man sighs. "At first we knew nothing about the local crops. We were always sick, because it was so hot, and we weren't used to the low altitude." Sometimes elephants would come out from the jungle and trample the harvest. Neadup and his wife gradually grew accustomed to their new life — they even learned to make trenches around the fields to stop the elephants. But they had six children, and the land was never quite enough to support the family. Now, after years of farming, the soil has been depleted. Neadup's children have found other jobs. "These young people," he laughs. "Once they're educated, they don't want to be farmers." Like the old woman in Bylakuppe, Neadup knows he will probably die in India. His reverence for the Dalai Lama will see him through.

For some Tibetans, born in exile, it will not.

In the struggle for a free Tibet, the Dalai Lama has steadfastly adhered to the doctrine of nonviolence. A paragon of peace and virtue, he asks for patience. He admits that forty or fifty years is a long time for an individual, but he points out that in the history of a nation, it is nothing. "I think it is a mistake to say that only if something materializes within my lifetime, then I will struggle," he says. He counsels against violence, which he considers an emotional reaction. "We must combine our intelligence and our emotion," he says.

It's not widely known, but many Tibetans disagree with the Dalai Lama. There are those who fondly recall the guerrilla struggle against the Chinese in the 1950s. Some of the Tibetans in India are veterans of that war. At the refugee center in Dharamsala, a man sits quietly, smoking a pipe. He is an anti-Chinese agitator, and he has spent twenty-two of his sixty years in Chinese prisons. His wife and six sons are still back in Tibet, so he won't give his name. He participated in the armed resistance. "The Red Army was too big," he recalls. "Half of my friends were killed in the fighting. The rest of us were caught. But I think jail and torture is worth it. I have the satisfaction of knowing that I killed many Chinese."

The Dalai Lama has lent an appealing halo of nonviolence to his religion. But Buddhists have not always been pacifists. During the Tang Dynasty of the eighth and ninth centuries, Buddhist ministers were feared wizards, employed by the Chinese emperor to help vanquish enemy troops. In medieval Japan, Buddhist sects organized armies of monks who battled on behalf of one fiefdom or another. To be sure, the Tibetan guerrilla fighters of the 1950s were partly inspired — and bankrolled — by the CIA. But for many Tibetan Buddhists, there is nothing sacrilegious about armed struggle.

Today, young Tibetans are growing tired of pacifism. In the pubs of Dharamsala, young men talk wistfully of violent resistance. "I want to go and blow up a few bridges," says one of them. "Even if it doesn't bring us freedom, at least we will have hurt the Chinese. Right now they're not being challenged, no one is putting up a fight." These sentiments accompany a growing dissatisfaction with the clerical establishment in Dharamsala. "Our government has no sense of urgency," complained another pub-goer. "They're just busy adding to their bank accounts. They're not thinking about going back."

A lobby of college-educated exiles called the Tibetan Youth Congress is steadily gaining supporters. The group's president, Tseten Norbu, says that keeping the struggle alive for young Tibetans requires a more confrontational approach. "Two generations have been brought up in exile. They don't have a sense of belonging to

Tibet," he says. "We are paying the price of a peaceful movement. Our nonviolence seems like nonaction."

The Dalai Lama is revered by Tibetans and Westerners alike as the living incarnation of Buddhist virtue, but his virtues are not necessarily Buddhist. He is one of the twentieth century's great champions of universal human rights. As an icon of nonviolent resistance to oppression, he is more like Mahatma Gandhi or Martin Luther King, Jr., than any of his lama forebears. Whether that makes his philosophy the right one for Tibetan politics in the twenty-first century, or for the myriad Buddhist followers who still consider him a living god, is another question.

The Dalai Lama has tried to be a political modernizer as well as a human rights advocate. In practice, though, the government in Dharamsala has reproduced the political structure of old Tibet: a clerical elite holds sway, employing a class of bureaucrats to execute its orders. And it's difficult to reconcile the Dalai Lama's democratic leanings with the tortuous — and decidedly undemocratic — search for his successor.

The Tibetan system of succession is inexact and mysterious, relying on dreams, secret messages, and oracular pronouncements. But the basic principle is simple: after the death of a senior monk, the lamas head off in search of his reincarnation. China's Communists publicly scorn such superstition, but they have found the concept of reincarnation useful. Monks backed by Beijing have identified their own reincarnation of the Panchen Lama, the Tibetan monk second only to the Dalai Lama. In Dharamsala, the Dalai Lama has identified a different boy. Beijing installed its choice in the Panchen Lama's monastery, while the boy the Dalai Lama chose has vanished — probably into Chinese captivity.

The Dalai Lama is sixty-five years old now, and Tibetans are beginning to wonder how they're going to find his reincarnation. Traditionally, the Panchen Lama is responsible for authenticating the new Dalai Lama; Beijing is grooming its Panchen Lama to select a weak leader. In retaliation, the Dalai Lama has announced that he will be reborn in exile. It's not clear whether this signifies a decisive break with the Tibetan homeland.

There is one custody battle that the Dalai Lama appears to have won. But his victory may undermine his authority, and test his commitment to democracy, in ways he never expected. Both the Dalai Lama and the Chinese government identified Ugyen Trinley Dorje as the seventeenth reincarnation of the Karmapa Lama, head of the Kagyu sect of Tibetan Buddhism. The Chinese authorities installed the new lama in his monastery at Tsurphu; they even showed him off on government television. It was Beijing's way of displaying religious tolerance. By all accounts, the Chinese treated the young Karmapa well.

In January 2000, the Tibetan government in exile announced that the seventeen-year-old lama had escaped to Dharamsala. The Karmapa's first public statement made it clear that the Chinese had been wasting their time. "Over the last twenty to thirty years," he said, "Tibet has suffered terrible losses. Tibetan religious and cultural traditions are now facing the risk of total extinction." In Tibet, he felt stifled, unable to fulfill his religious vocation. Embarrassed by the Karmapa Lama's treachery, Beijing has insisted that the boy is only visiting India long enough to retrieve religious artifacts that belong to his earlier incarnation. Fearful of China's wrath, Indian authorities have kept the boy under virtual house arrest.

The Karmapa Lama is quickly becoming an icon for Tibet's generation exile. In Dharamsala, where years of contact with Westerners has produced scooter-riding, MTV-watching teenagers who seldom bother to visit a temple, the Karmapa Lama's public appearances are extremely well attended. Restless in his confinement, he has taken to writing poetry. The Tibetan Institute of Performing Arts has set his poems to music and released them on compact disc. He is an impressive boy: tall, good-looking, with a deep and purposeful voice. Accustomed to reverence, he already has the air of one who understands his own importance — he was, after all, born with seventeen lifetimes under his belt. Many young people see him as the future of Tibet.

Back in Kollegal, Neadup, the old Tibetan farmer, has a granddaughter who has just turned sixteen. Dolma knows what's going on in Dharamsala. "The Dalai Lama is growing old," she says sadly. "But now the Karmapa has come. He will help the Dalai Lama." Instead of speaking Tibetan, Dolma uses a smattering of Hindi, English, and the local Kanadda language. She prefers Indian movies, Western clothes, and rap music to Buddhist poetry. She wants to be a doctor and live in the city.

Young Tibetans like Dolma are leaving old settlements like Bylakuppe and Kollegal. Many are finding alternative ways to make a living, some with an eye toward moving to Tibet someday. Kunchok Gyurma, a nineteen-year-old dropout, trained himself as a hairdresser. Most of his clients are young Tibetans from the refugee camps. "I decided this was a good profession," he explains, "because eventually I can run a shop in Lhasa as well." Namgyal Phuntsok, a teenager, keeps cows. Of course in Tibet there are no cows, only yaks. What will he do? "I don't know," he shrugs. "I've only ever seen pictures of yaks. I hear they smell terrible." Tsering Dorje, twenty-nine, is a soldier. Does he believe he will ever see a free Tibet? "We have hope," he says. "That is all we have." When I ask him what Tibet must be like, he seems confused: "Like an Indian hill town?"

Other Tibetan youth are leaving for Europe and America. They're eager for sponsors who can get them into the United States; there, many will find work in — where else? — Chinese restaurants. They hope to marry a citizen and get resident status.

In the West, most Tibetans assimilate rapidly. They might turn up for Free Tibet rallies, but their children probably won't. Phurbu Sithar Dekhang, a Tibetan official in Bylakuppe, doubts that many of these exiles would return to Tibet even if China pulled out tomorrow. "As long as you don't write my name," says a young Tibetan woman who now lives in Europe, "I will tell you frankly that my brothers and I will never go back."

Is this really so bad? Shouldn't a free Tibet mean free Tibetans? Many of them are finding their freedom in exile; others are looking beyond the received wisdom of their elders. Do Tibetan youth need to wait for their own country before they can rebel against their parents?

Lobsang, the boy who wants to argue Tibet's case before the

United Nations, is looking forward to meeting the Karmapa Lama. They are both seventeen. Both are eager to complete their education and work for a free Tibet. But it remains to be seen how many of their peers will join the battle. Meanwhile, the land of Tibet is fast becoming a fantasy of Hollywood cinema — mysterious, distant, and Chinese.

KARL TARO GREENFELD

■

Speed Demons

FROM *Time*

JACKY TALKS ABOUT killing him, slitting his throat from three till nine and hanging him upside down so the blood drains out of him the way it ran from the baby pigs they used to slaughter in her village before a funeral feast. He deserves it, really, she says, for his freeloading, for his hanging around, for how he just stands there, spindly-legged and narrow-chested and pimple-faced with his big yearning eyes, begging for another hit.

She has run out of methamphetamine, what the Thais call *yaba* (mad medicine), and she has become irritable and potentially violent. Jacky's cheeks are sunken, her skin pockmarked, and her hair an unruly explosion of varying strands of red and brown. She is tall and skinny, and her arms and legs extend out from her narrow torso with its slightly protuberant belly like the appendages of a spider shortchanged on legs.

Sitting on the blue vinyl flooring of her Bangkok hut, Jacky leans her bare back against the plank wall, her dragon tattoos glistening with sweat as she trims her fingernails with a straight razor. It has been two days — no, three — without sleep, sitting in this hut and smoking the little pink speed tablets from sheets of tinfoil stripped from Krong Tip cigarette packets. Now, as the flushes of artificial energy recede and the realization surfaces that there's no more money anywhere in her hut, Jacky is crashing hard, and she hates everyone and everything. Especially Bing. She hates that sponging little punk for all the tablets he smoked a few hours ago — tablets she could be smoking right now. Back then, she had a dozen tablets packed into a plastic soda straw stuffed down her black wire-frame bra. The hut was alive with the chatter of half a dozen speed addicts, all pulling apart their Krong Tip packs and sucking in meth smoke through metal pipes. Now that the pills are gone, the fun is gone. And Bing, of course, he's long gone.

This slum doesn't have a name. The five thousand residents call it Ban Chua Gan, which translates roughly as Do It Yourself Happy Homes. The expanse of jerry-built wood-frame huts with corrugated steel roofs sprawls in a murky bog in Bangkok's Sukhumvit district, in the shadow of forty-story office buildings and glass-plated corporate towers. The inhabitants migrated here about a decade ago from villages all around Thailand. Jacky came from Nakon Nayok, a province near Bangkok's Don Muang airport, seeking financial redemption in the Asian economic miracle. And for a while in the mid-'90s, conditions in this slum actually improved. Some of the huts had plumbing installed. Even the shabbiest shanties were wired for electricity. The main alleyways were paved. That was when Thailand's development and construction boom required the labor of every able-bodied person. There were shopping malls to be built, housing estates to be constructed, highways to be paved.

Around the same time, mad medicine began making its way into Do It Yourself Happy Homes. It had originally been the drug of choice for long-haul truck and bus drivers, but during the go-go '90s, it evolved into the working man's and woman's preferred intoxicant, gradually becoming more popular among Thailand's underclass than heroin and eventually replacing that opiate as the leading drug produced in the notorious Golden Triangle — the world's most prolific opium-producing region — where Myanmar (Burma), Thailand, and Laos come together. While methamphetamines had previously been sold either in powdered or crystalline form, new labs in Burma, northern Thailand, and China commoditized the methamphetamine business by pressing little tablets of the substance that now retail for about 50 baht ($1.20) each. At first only bar girls like Jacky smoked it. Then some of the younger guys who hung out with the girls tried it. Soon a few of the housewives began smoking, and finally some of the dads would take a hit or two when they were out of corn whiskey. Now it has reached the point that on weekend nights, it's hard to find anyone in the slum who isn't smoking the mad medicine.

When the *yaba* runs out after much of the slum's population has been up for two days bingeing, many of the inhabitants feel a bit like Jacky, cooped up in her squalid little hut, her mouth turned down into a scowl and her eyes squinted and empty and mean. She looks as if she wants something. And if she thinks you have what she wants, look out. She slices at her cuticles with the straight razor. And curses Bing.

But then Bing comes around the corner between two shanties and down the narrow dirt path to Jacky's hut. He stands looking lost and confused, as usual. Jacky pretends he's not there. She sighs, looking at her nails, and stage whispers to me that she hates him.

Bing, his long black hair half tied into a ponytail, stands next to a cinder-block wall rubbing his eyes. Above his head, a thick trail of red army ants runs between a crack in the wall and a smashed piece of pineapple. He reaches into his pocket and pulls out a tissue in which he has wrapped four *doa* (bodies, slang for speed tablets). Jacky stops doing her nails, smiles, and invites Bing back into her hut, asking sweetly, "Oh, Bing, where have you been?"

This mad medicine is the same drug that's called *shabu* in Japan and Indonesia, *batu* in the Philippines, and *bingdu* in China. While it has taken scientists years to figure out the clinical pharmacology and neurological impact of ecstasy and other designer drugs, methamphetamines are blunt pharmaceutical instruments. The drug encourages the brain to flood the synapses with the neurotransmitter dopamine — the substance your body uses to reward itself when you, say, complete a difficult assignment at the office or finish a vigorous workout. And when the brain is awash in dopamine, the whole cardiovascular system goes into sympathetic overdrive, increasing your heart rate, your pulse, and even your respiration. You become, after that first hit of speed, gloriously, brilliantly, vigorously awake. Your horizon of aspiration expands outward, just as in your mind's eye your capacity for taking effective action to achieve your new, optimistic goals has also grown exponentially. Then, eventually, maybe in an hour, maybe in a day, maybe in a year, you run out of speed. And you crash.

In country after country throughout Asia, meth use skyrocketed during the '90s. And with the crash of the region's high-flying economies, the drug's use has surged again. The base of the drug — ephedrine — was actually first synthesized in Asia: a team of Japanese scientists derived it from the Chinese *mao* herb in 1892. Unlike ecstasy, which requires sophisticated chemical and pharmaceutical knowledge to manufacture, or heroin, whose base product, the poppy plant, is a vulnerable crop, ephedrine can be refined fairly easily into meth. This makes meth labs an attractive family business for industrious Asians, who set them up in converted bathrooms, farmhouses, or even on the family hearth.

There is something familiar to me about Jacky and her little hut and her desperate yearning for more speed and even for the exhilaration and intoxication she feels when she's on the pipe. Because I've been there. Not in this exact room or with these people. But I've been on speed.

During the early '90s, I went through a period when I was smoking *shabu* with a group of friends in Tokyo. I inhaled the smoke from smoothed-out tinfoil sheets folded in two, holding a lighter beneath the foil so that the shards of *shabu* liquefied, turning to a thick, pungent, milky vapor. The smoke tasted like a mixture of turpentine and model glue; to this day I can't smell paint thinner without thinking of smoking speed.

The drug was euphorically powerful, convincing us that we were capable of anything. And in many ways we were. We were all young, promising, on the verge of exciting careers in glamorous fields. There was Trey, an American magazine writer, like me, in his twenties; Hiroko, a Japanese woman in her thirties who worked for a Tokyo women's magazine; Delphine, an aspiring French model; and Miki, an A-and-R man for a Japanese record label. When we sat down together in my Nishi Azabu apartment to smoke the drug, our talk turned to grandiose plans and surefire schemes. I spoke of articles I would write. Delphine talked about landing a job doing a Dior lingerie catalog. Miki raved about a promising noise band he had just signed. Sometimes the dealer, a lanky fellow named Haru, would hang around and smoke with us, and we would be convinced that his future was surely just as bright as all of ours. There was no limit to what we could do, especially if we put our speed-driven minds to work.

It's always that way in the beginning: all promise and potential fun. The drug is like a companion telling you that you're good enough, handsome enough, and smart enough, banishing all the little insecurities to your subconscious, liberating you from self-doubts yet making you feel totally and completely alive.

I don't know that it helped me write better; I don't believe meth really helps you in any way at all. But in those months, it became arguably the most important activity in my life. Certainly it was the most fun. And I looked forward to Haru's coming over with another $150 baggie of *shabu,* the drug resembling a little oily lump of glass. Then we would smoke, at first only on weekends. But soon we began to do it on weekdays whenever I had a free evening. At first only with my friends. Then sometimes I smoked alone. Then mostly alone.

The teens and twenty-somethings in Ban Chua Gan also like to smoke *yubu,* but they look down on Jacky and Bing and their flagrant, raging addictions. Sure, the cool guys in the neighborhood, guys like Big, with a shaved head, gaunt face, and sneering upper lip, drop into Jacky's once in a while to score some drugs. Or they'll buy a couple of tablets from Bing's mother, who deals. But they tell you they're different from Bing and the hard-core users. "For one thing," Big alibis, "Bing hasn't left the slum neighborhood in a year. He doesn't work. He doesn't do anything but smoke." (Bing just shrugs when I ask if it's true that he hasn't left in a year. "I'm too skinny to leave," he explains. "Everyone will know I'm doing *yaba*.") Big has a job as a pump jockey at a Star gas station. And he has a girlfriend, and he has his motorcycle, a Honda GSR 125. This weekend, like most weekends, he'll be racing his bike with the other guys from the neighborhood, down at Bangkok's superslum, Klong Toey. That's why tonight, a few days before the race, he is working on his bike, removing a few links of the engine chain to lower the gear ratio and give the bike a little more pop off the line. He kneels down with a lighted candle next to him, his hands greasy and black as he works to reattach the chain to the gear sprockets. Around him a few teenage boys and girls are gathered, smoking cigarettes, some squatting on the balls of their feet, their intent faces peering down at scattered engine parts. The sound is the clatter of adolescent boys. Whether the vehicle in question is a '65 Mustang or a '99 Honda GSR motorcycle, the posturing of the too-cool motorhead trying to goose a few more horsepower out of his engine while at the same time look bitchin' in front of a crowd of slightly younger female spectators is identical whether in Bakersfield or Bangkok.

The slang for smoking speed in Thai is *keng rot*, literally "racing," the same words used to describe the weekend motorcycle rallying. The bikers' lives revolve around these two forms of *keng rot*. They look forward all week to racing their bikes against other gangs from other neighborhoods. And while they profess to have nothing but disgust for the slum's hard-core addicts, by 4 A.M. that night on a mattress laid on the floor next to his beloved Honda, Big and his friends are smoking *yaba*, and there suddenly seems very little difference between his crowd and Jacky's. "Smoking once in a while, on weekends, that really won't do any harm," Big explains, exhaling a plume of white smoke. "It's just like having a drink." But it's Thursday, I point out. Big shrugs, waving away the illogic of his statement, the drug's powerful reach pulling him away from the need to make sense. He says whatever he wants now, and he resents being questioned. "What do you want from me? I'm just trying to have fun."

In Jacky's hut, Bing and a few bar girls are seated with their legs folded under, taking hits from the sheets of tinfoil. As Jacky applies a thick layer of foundation makeup to her face and dabs on retouching cream and then a coating of powder, she talks about how tonight she has to find a foreign customer so she can get the money to visit her children out in Nakon Nayok. Her two daughters and son live with her uncle. Jacky sees them once a month, and she talks about how she likes to take them new clothes and cook for them. When she talks about her kids, her almond-shaped eyes widen. "I used to dream of opening a small shop, like a gift shop or a 7-Eleven. Then I could take care of my children and make money. I used to dream about it all the time, and I even believed it was possible, that it was just barely out of reach."

Jacky was a motorbike messenger, shuttling packages back and forth throughout Bangkok's busy Chitlom district, until she was laid off after the 1997 devaluation of the baht. "Now I don't think about the gift shop anymore. Smoking *yaba* pushes thoughts about my children to the back of my mind. It's good for that. Smoking means you don't have to think about the hard times." Bing nods his head, agreeing: "When I smoke, it makes everything seem a little better. I mean, look at this place — how can I stop?"

Bing's mother, Yee, slips off her sandals as she steps into the hut, clutching her fourteen-month-old baby. She sits down next to her son, and while the baby scrambles to crawl from her lap, she begins pulling the paper backing from a piece of tinfoil, readying the foil for a smoke. Her hands are a whir of finger-flashing activity — assembling and disassembling a lighter, unclogging the pipe, unwrapping the tablets, straightening the foil, lighting the speed, and then taking the hit. She exhales finally, blowing smoke just above her baby's face. Bing asks his mother for a hit. She shakes her head. She doesn't give discounts or freebies, not even to her own son.

I ask Yee if she ever tells Bing that he should stop smoking *yaba*. "I tell him he shouldn't do so much, that it's bad for him. But he doesn't listen."

Perhaps she lacks credibility, since she smokes herself?

"I don't smoke that much," she insists.

"She's right," Bing agrees. "Since she doesn't smoke that much, I should listen to her."

"And he's only fifteen years old," Yee adds.

Bing reminds her he's seventeen.

"I don't know where the years go," Yee says, taking another hit.

For the countries on the front lines of the meth war, trying to address the crisis with tougher enforcement has had virtually no effect on curtailing the number of users or addicts. Asia has some of the toughest drug laws in the world. In Thailand, China, Taiwan, and Indonesia, even a low-level drug trafficking or dealing conviction can mean a death sentence. Yet *yaba* is openly sold in Thailand's slums and proffered in Jakarta's nightclubs, and China's meth production continues to boom. Even Japan, renowned for its strict antidrug policies, has had little success in stemming speed abuse. Most likely these countries and societies will have to write off vast swaths of their populations as drug casualties, like the American victims of the '80s crack epidemic.

Asia's medical and psychiatric infrastructure is already being overwhelmed by the number of meth abusers crashing and seeking help. But in most of the region, counseling facilities are scarce, and recovery is viewed as a matter of willpower and discipline rather than a tenuous and slow spiritual and psychological rebuilding process. Drug treatment centers are usually run like a cross between boot camp and prison. Beds are scarce as addicts seek the meager resources available. In China, for example, the nearly 750 state-run rehab centers are filled to capacity; in Thailand the few recovery centers suffer from a chronic shortage of staff and beds. While the most powerful tools for fighting addiction in the West — twelve-step programs derived from Alcoholics Anonymous — are available in Asia, they are not widely disseminated and used.

What started out as a diversion for me and my Tokyo crowd degenerated in a few months into the chronic drug use of Jacky and her crowd. I began to smoke alone to begin my days. In the evening I'd take Valium or halcyon or cercine or any of a number of sedatives to help me calm down. When I stopped smoking for a few days just to see if I could, a profound depression would overcome me. Nothing seemed worthwhile. Nothing seemed fun. Every book was torturously slow. Every song was criminally banal. The sparkle and shine had been sucked out of life so completely that my world became a fluorescent-lighted, decolorized, salt-petered version of the planet I had known before. And my own prospects? Absolutely dismal. I would sit in that one-bedroom Nishi Azabu apartment and consider the sorry career I had embarked upon, these losers I associated with compounding the very long odds that I would ever amount to anything.

These feelings, about the world and my life, seemed absolutely real. I could not tell for a moment that this was a neurological reaction brought on by the withdrawal of the methamphetamine. My brain had stopped producing dopamine in normal amounts because it had come to rely upon the speed kicking in and running the show. Researchers now report that as much as 50 percent of the dopamine-producing cells in the brain can be damaged after prolonged exposure to relatively low levels of methamphetamine. In other words, the depression is a purely chemical state. Yet it feels for all the world like the result of empirical, clinical observation. And then, very logically, you realize there is one surefire solution, the only way to feel better: more speed.

I kept at that cycle for a few years and started taking drugs other than methamphetamine until I hit my own personal bottom. I spent six weeks in a drug treatment center working out a plan for living that didn't require copious amounts of methamphetamines or tranquilizers. I left rehab five years ago. I haven't had another hit of *shabu* — or taken any drugs — since then. But I am lucky. Of that crowd who used to gather in my Tokyo apartment, I am the only one who has emerged clean and sober. Trey, my fellow magazine writer, never really tried to quit and now lives back at home with his aging parents. He is nearly forty, still takes speed — or Ritalin or cocaine or whichever uppers he can get his hands on — and hasn't had a job in years. Delphine gave up modeling after a few years and soon was accepting money to escort wealthy businessmen around Tokyo. She finally ended up working as a prostitute. Hiroko did stop taking drugs. But she has been in and out of psychiatric hospitals and currently believes drastic plastic surgery is the solution to her problems. Miki has been arrested in Japan and the United States on drug charges and is now out on parole and living in Tokyo. And Haru, the dealer, I hear he's dead.

Despite all I know about the drug, despite what I have seen, I am still tempted. The pull of the drug is tangible and real, almost like a gravitational force compelling me to want to use it again — to feel just once more the rush and excitement and the sense, even if it's illusory, that life does add up, that there is meaning and form to the passing of my days. Part of me still wants it.

At 2 A.M. on a Saturday, Big and his fellow bikers from Do It Yourself Happy Homes are preparing for a night of bike racing by smoking more *yaba* and, as if to get their 125cc bikes in a parallel state of high-octane agitation, squirting STP performance goo from little plastic packets into their gas tanks. The bikes are tuned up, and the mufflers are loosened so that the engines revving at full throttle sound like a chain saw cutting bone: splintering, ear-shattering screeches that reverberate up and down the Sukhumvit streets. The bikers ride in a pack, cutting through alleys, running lights, skirting lines of stalled traffic, slipping past one another as they cut through the city smog. This is their night, the night they look forward to all week during mornings at school or dull afternoons pumping gas. And as they ride massed together, you can almost feel the surge of pride oozing out of them, intimidating other drivers to veer out of their way.

On Na Ranong Avenue, next to the Klong Toey slum, they meet up with bikers from other slums. They have been holding these rallies for a decade, some of the kids first coming on the backs of their older brothers' bikes. *Ken rot* is a ritual by now, as ingrained in Thai culture as the speed they smoke to get up for the night of racing. The street is effectively closed off to non-motorcyclists and pedestrians. The bikers idle along the side of the road and then take off in twos and threes, popping wheelies, the usual motorcycle stunts. But souped up and fitted with performance struts and tires, these bikes accelerate at a terrifying rate, and that blast off the line makes for an unstable and dangerous ride if you're on the back of one of them. It is the internal-combustion equivalent of *yaba:* fast, fun, treacherous. And likely to result, eventually, in a fatal spill. But if you're young and Thai and loaded on mad medicine, you feel immortal, and it doesn't occur to you that this night of racing will ever, really, have to end.

There are still moments when even hard-core addicts like Jacky can recapture the shiny, bright exuberance of the first few times they tried speed. Tonight, as Jacky dances at Angel's bar with a Belgian who might take her back to his hotel room, she's thinking that she'll soon have enough money to visit her children, and it doesn't seem so bad. Life seems almost manageable. A few more customers, and maybe one will really fall for her and pay to move her to a better neighborhood, to rent a place where even her children could live. Maybe she could open that convenience store after all.

By the next afternoon, however, all the promise of the previous evening has escaped from the neighborhood like so much exhaled smoke. Jacky's customer lost interest and found another girl. Even the bike racing fell apart after the cops broke up the first few rallying points. And now, on a hazy, rainy Sunday, Jacky and a few of the girls are back in her hut. They're smoking, almost desperately uploading as much speed as possible to ward off this drab day and this squalid place.

Jacky pauses as she adjusts the flame on a lighter. "Why don't you smoke?" she asks me.

She tells me it would make her more comfortable if I would join her. I'm standing in the doorway to Jacky's hut. About me are flea-infested dogs and puddles of stagnant water several inches deep with garbage, and all around is the stench of smoldering trash. The horror of this daily existence is tangible. I don't like being in this place, and I find depressing the idea of living in a world that has places like this in it. And I know a hit of the mad medicine is the easiest way to make this all seem bearable. Taking a hit, I know, is a surefire way of feeling good. Right now. And I want it.

But I walk away. And while I hope Jacky and Bing and Big can one day do the same, I doubt they ever can. They have so little to walk toward.

CAMDEN JOY

■

Hubcap Diamondstar Halo

FROM *Little Engines*

OUR STORY does not begin until the driver loses control, and for now, he has no idea that this is to happen. He's heading west from Massachusetts. He's driving this vehicle for the first time. He is alone.

The driver is G. Behind his square plastic glasses, such as one sees on CEOs above a certain age, G. possesses thick eyebrows, sadly raised, and large solemn eyes. This, with his undersized mouth, gives him the appearance of a guy too sincere for his own good. G.'s dress is unremarkable; a T-shirt, untucked over fraying blue jeans; a jacket, pale and lightweight, with a thin cotton lining; stiff, inexpensive shoes. His hair, once red, has turned bristly, has faded, and now resembles a mussed-up wad of Brillo. G. is not especially tall — he is, in the words of a former band member who telephoned to harass him before a gig, "a little shit of a guy" — and so is sitting propped up on a booster seat of Braintree-area yellow pages.

G. has traveled for eight hours or so without incident. Now it's past midnight. Ahead waits a grounded cloud, some heavy chill gray shroud drawn across the landscape. He clicks on his brights and reluctantly penetrates the milky haze, managing an expression both groggy and greatly pissed. He's driving out of focus into a half-developed Polaroid, like cobwebs on his glasses. The first thing he observes is a blur of ghostly red maple and ash foliage close on both sides of the interstate. This bleary tunnel of color continues. He travels the width of the Catskills to the plateaus of the Poconos with the damp, red-splotched forest pulled snug about him, glowing scarlet in his headlights.

Hours go by with G. ascending several inclines into still deeper fog. The vehicle's speed plummets. Roadside shacks offer gourds and squash. Work clothes are stuffed with brooms and straw to resemble figures in recline. Blown-out jack-o'-lanterns rest on bales of hay. Buckeyes, beech, and birch show leaves lit every shade from hemorrhage to bruise. G. yawns helplessly, limbs heavy. The dim haunt of the situation seeps into his lungs and blood, his brain. Going up it seems his initiative always goes out, plus his eyes tend to sting when he gets weary, which starts him blinking. He studies the people in automobiles across the highway, looking for clues as to what's ahead, but here the lanes are widely separated and he can see little past the windshield. To stay alert, he flips on the radio. He seeks ironic commentary like "I Can See Clearly Now" or "I Can See for Miles," things recorded mostly live with blended mike placement, swell warmth.

Instead, the radio presents him with voluptuous rhythms that make him feel insignificant. For a year, he feels, radio's been undergoing an ominous playlist standardization; in three years he'll find it worse — telecommunications laws will change, large broadcasters will be allowed an unlimited number of national stations. By decade's end, the frequencies belong to a tidy few. Positive role models dominate . . .

He wishes Thérèse could've been here. This fog: she was at her best in fog. She gauged the flight of birds, the direction of the winds; she lit a match to observe the shape of flames and timed the appearance of reptiles. It'll go soon, she said. Or: It'll be a while. She had not been mystical in most things, but in predicting the lifting of a mist she'd been divine.

Now the road narrows and the look of folks in cars driving back the other way strikes G. bleakly, their faces wan and dull as if they've witnessed a dismal horror and been drained of vigor. They return with broken spirits, it appears, the drivers remorseful and the passengers stunned.

Further down the road G. gets to the animals. The trees are not alone in their vivid deaths; there are beavers, opossums, even porcupines that have not survived their attempts to cross the asphalt. Their remains splatter the shoulder, unpleasantly disfiguring the highway lines. Captured in a glimpse while speeding past, it appears there has been, on the side of the road, a series of botched surgeries or a great many rhubarb pies kicked about. Juicy intestines; this paw, now useless; this startled frozen stare. *Embrace the lower animals,* G. recalls one Catholic saying. *Treasure even the vermin.* Francis of Paula spared the wasps in his garden as Anchieta the Hunchback spared the vipers. Hugh of Lincoln made friends with a wild swan that guarded his sleep and nuzzled his wide sleeves. Petroc, the sixth-century abbot, removed a splinter from the eye of a dragon that came to him for help. Columna had his white horse that wept.

G. senses movement. A shape materializes from a blood tree, a sudden flutter across the windshield. He swerves.

The van is boxy and slow to respond. It was manufactured in the early seventies. It belongs to the record label with which G.'s band has just signed. Its tires are bald, its body rattles. It stinks of stamped-out cigarette butts, crusted blood from picked scabs. This is its second engine. The odometer is on its third go-round.

Yet the van is infinitely better than G. ever expected it to be. He considers himself blessed. It was no secret how the president of the record company kept G.'s sister as his mistress. Maybe next he'd want G. taken out. Paranoid yes, but plausible. The marketing gets so easy with the musician out of the way (plus embarrassing comments about how G. really wants his sister back stop appearing in neighborhood gossip rags). When G. contemplated the deathtrap of a vehicle he'd likely receive, he first imagined it on the shoulder of a Las Vegas highway, in the heart of a heat wave, falling off the jack while Greg Dulli (who played one half of John Lennon's singing voice in the movie *Backbeat*) tried to fix its flat and, standing to one side, the rest of the Afghan Whigs watched the rear brake drum slam to the ground.

Christ, G. anticipated this van thing entirely wrong.

He had even, pathetically enough, experienced nightmares of

Chris Cornell loading in a Mesa Boogie amp for months while standing on the van's exhaust pipe, which eventually broke; the dream continued, with somebody else in Soundgarden driving it to the MTV awards show and leaving the overhead light on such that the battery never fully recovered; and finally, one rest-area evening, taunted all the while by resident taggers and huffers, you-know-who achieved impact while backing up the van (very badly) and collided with the too-narrow alley, and the drummer, making out with the tattoo artist from Toledo, knocked teeth and half an incisor chipped off and both side mirrors got cracked.

All worry proves ridiculous. For though this van, in the service of further popularizing rock-and-roll music around the continental U.S., has undertaken perhaps a hundred tours, ringing the bell of countless service stations, driving several bands to unforeseen breakthroughs (*pray it can handle one more*), the only documented trauma it'd endured was when the Fastbacks overheated the radiator while giving a lift to some radio pirates, and thinking quickly, not sharply, Lulu the guitarist had extended the Prestone coolant with ice-cold gin and Mountain Dew.

G. is trying to remember to stop next chance to check the level in the radiator —

It's a bird and he hits it. It hangs in the air behind him, heroic in the brake lights, maimed but still working to fly. How like an augury of ill it moves — a crumpled sheet of black construction paper, with no more command of flight. It descends in a twirl. Only one wing stays on its body. The other, freshly shorn, is folded around the van's windshield wiper.

Mortified, G. looks over his shoulder. He has no words for this sensation. He feels, if anything, short of belief. An abrupt defect in the road surface wrenches the wheel from his grasp with an ease that appears supernatural. The radio coughs up a T. Rex song. His vehicle spins ninety degrees. He brakes, unrighting the angle only slightly before the van leaves the asphalt. The hair stands up on the back of his neck. The instant is choked with consequence. The front left wheel meets a boulder. The nose, heavy with engine, plunges into a ravine. The vehicle's undercarriage launches high.

Wheels spin madly. Over it goes, a movement repeated a great number of times.

G. is unloosed about the van, for he has earlier unbuckled his seat belt (so as better to retrieve his cigarettes, which keep sliding down the dashboard into a shoved-aside pile of houseflies). He is a musician with interesting ideas — his sampled percussion tracks, for example, get compared to a shoe bouncing in a dryer — but side to side G. goes now, back and forth, vaulted into pressed steel. For a time he is the shoe in the dryer; the bean in the maraca; the rock in the cement mixer. Wingnuts fall from the wind wings and the vehicle violently falls apart — as if to say, what is any van, seeing that it is made by men? With progressively less jarring thumps, weight overcomes momentum, and what is left of the van comes to a rest on its back end.

At which point, our story begins.

G.'ll be working on a song when acutely he recalls a detail of the accident. The windshield buckling, for example, disassembling as it gushes back to shower him in a great many pebbles and splinters of glass. How to make that into music? He crosses his arms atop his head, closes his eyes, and feels again the impact of the wheelwell against his pinwheeling torso, thinking wet sandy thoughts, bouncing awkwardly around on an elbow, his chest, a foot, his knees, his chest (again), then his head. He gets so used to feeling these blows that when the van stops rolling, he doubts it. He does not question his inability to survive such a wreck and so, very naturally, accepts death. He is neither warm nor cold but persistently, frighteningly okay. He has lived twenty-six years, which apparently is enough. He can no longer feel his limbs but can hear, still, the radio going, as apparently it does in the afterlife.

To capture this in the studio will demand a very analog approach to recording — real drums, tape delay instead of digital delay. He'll reduce song tempos by half, introduce interfering notes, suspend chords every fourth beat, covet the racket of the console. He'll EQ the acoustic guitars to sound like cackling chickens, then saturate the tape, push it into the red, and forward the bass. He's been grunting along to the chord progressions. Now, needing lyrics, he'll find that images have arisen and somehow attached themselves. *The mayflies all explode,* he'll sing. *When they come to the coil at the driving range.*

The song possesses a healthy grime but remains much too ominous, and during the accident nothing feels ominous the way one expects. It's all very interesting and peaceful. To have the van take itself down an embankment, going not side over side but toppling in this unusual, drawn-out manner, like a sail ripping free from the topmost mast. Indeed, it's surprising how perfectly fine it feels to crash — years of driver's education and safety tips proved wrong! G. is unclear on why it took him so long to find this out. They taught him to drive safely. (They were wrong, per usual.)

Still seeking percussion beds that convey the color and character of that moment, G. will sample sounds (dropping a stapler on a pile of cymbals, ripping masking tape, holding a pick up to a ringing nylon string to make a buzz), and use those (edited a bit, pitched differently) in place of drums in a sequenced drum program.

Too much clang, rather like the tongues of angels who know not love.

Then a bandmate'll locate a Kotatone record player with a built-in speaker and a quarter-inch input. G. will run the tracks out of the computer into the beat-up Kotatone. Almost everything sounds right coming out of it. Cranked to ten with the turntable running, the Kotatone gives a swell rumble. It's soothing. It seems to shift and change. Eventually, G.'ll put about fifteen minutes of the rumble on the end of a CD called, naturally, *Kotatone.*

Satisfying.

A field recording.

The machine leaves the road and enters nature. All but the radio; the radio remains on. Mumbles, mutters, and priestly concerns as G. considers his situation. He sounds boxed in by the remnants of the machine, with nature abundant outside, and the radio going.

You lie as you have lain for ages, as a hermit in a house of clay and wattles made, in a slender patch of wilderness, heart open to the power of grace. The sourwoods and serviceberries glow crimson, and burning bushes abound. You sleep badly with the sense of missing someone. Distant thunder rumbles. The constellations dim and go out. The sun comes up two and one half hours late, and now scavengers form a circle in the sky. A certain serenity (until now scantly appreciated) is disturbed, nature's piety violated. Dragonflies exhibit unusual behaviors, as do grasshoppers. Songbirds are muted by field animals that claw the earth anxiously. The crab apples, having ripened to delectable scarlet at long last, attract no robins. Your prayers in the open thicket near the creek this morning go unanswered — but for an icy breeze coming off the shadows in the hollow, rising from a ravine where the night chill is camped, sick with the odor of gaseous vapors.

It is not long before you track down the source. There has been a traffic mishap last night and a vehicle, a sort of metal coach, rests within the steep valley of one of the tributary creeks just beyond the thicket. You follow a foot trail, sloping from your bluff down along the backbone of a ridge. Where the ravine suddenly steepens and narrows, where the shadows are long-lived and the dampness stays, the trees are different. Here are hemlock and poplar, straight and tall, reaching way up into the light. And here, below a stony notch, is the vehicle. As you approach the vehicle, it emits a soft hiss, a sound quite threatening until you recognize it as the dying signal of some broadcast.

You reach through what appears to've been a door and turn knobs until the sound of static has ceased. You glance down into the coach. That is when you come across a man, for the first time in quite a while. He rests on his back, with his legs uncomfortably bent up around his head. His left arm is black and blue, twisted up and wrung out. He's covered in glass. His mouth is bloody. His eyes eventually open. He extends a greeting, but mistakes you for a person named Thérèse. *Oh, it makes me catch my breath: small pretty nose and ardent gaze and molasses head of brunette hair.* He says he remembers how you looked at the end: *worn out, done in by a contaminant, hair like dead dune grass. But now* — he pronounces — *you appear as you did at the start. Face lit like a cola machine in the night. Command-eyed. Taken with the world.*

The wrecked man is dizzy and his chest aches. You inform him his system is undergoing a condition of supreme shock. He nods as if sympathizing with the complaints of a stranger, then gives a shudder and goes limp. For some reason this does not stir your concern. You find yourself without the urge to go for help. The man will be your companion, such as you have not had in a long time. The others are dead and buried. What joy it will be to reveal the wild glory of these environs to another! You can certainly fix what ails the wrecked man. You will find a certain place for him on your shelf alongside the bees who make a hive of your cupboard and the swallows who nest in your rafters. You admit this accident into what has become, since the closing of the nail factory, your one and only life. He was not brought to your attention by accident. For it is written, *None shall the Lord deliver through chance.*

Sometime later the wrecked man awakes. On this occasion he notices that his eyeglasses are fractured, with only one lens intact. He pokes his fingers straight through the frame's eye socket. He frets and mutters, then looks ruefully at a pocket watch. *I'm very late,* he explains. *I remember that much.*

You inquire if he'd like to eat something and what hurts. But he has no hunger and, for now, feels no pain. He is neither cold nor thirsty, and he longs for nothing. Again you assure him he is within a state of shock.

You experience a pang of regret over your egocentrism, and, surprising yourself, you declare, *I'll go for help.* But you won't, will you? Turmoil ensues. A great deal of you still wishes to maintain him as an accomplice of sorts, an experiment. A pet. You cannot decide what honor requires. *First,* you ultimately backpedal, *I'll remain until I'm certain you're stable.*

A deep autumn quiet descends. Down here along the creek, not so long ago, the narrow bottoms and ridge were cleared and cropped so cattle and hogs could pasture in the woods. Now the bottoms are thickety and weedy. Rhododendron hangs low. Mosses and ferns thrive.

In this moment you can almost imagine you are six again and

on vacation, watching a cast of thunderheads stage dramatic works over the Adirondacks, evening hearth flickering from fire while your parents squall through their stormy years and your sisters earn ribbons in appalling competitions, screen-door enthusiasms and easy pleasure. It calls up the space of time before you drop the spelling contest, in the fifth year of school, to the word *perspicacious,* when you still possess a naive sense of wisdom; again you taste the anticipation of crackle and ash from a finely fed furnace and the exultant shiver beneath a February blanket of snow; before everything got so wrong, a pileup of consternations, nights heavy with hate, before . . . — ah! The countenance trembles recalling hapless vixens such as were victims of your gingerbread, biscuits, and tasteless poisons, those wretched courtesans of few virtues and fewer morals, teeth like pearls, riding habits of pelisse cloth, lovely dolls of artifice who, once disposed of, were rarely missed; before you entered this life of sorrow and great compassion as if attending a funeral, before forsaking the world for vines and soil; then the conversion, the hesitations and timidities to be overcome, the penances to be paid, the austerities and agonies. The rash soul endures its dark night. The lion licks at its paw. The woods crawl with cops.

A wren sings in the underbrush.

That's the thing about consciousness, the wrecked man sighs. *It can never be trusted.*

Sunlight strikes the glass in the wrecked man's hair. It shimmers, as if he wears a halo. He is now sure you are the River Phoenix.

You must have been pissed not to get that Academy Award. What the hell, you were eighteen, and Kevin Kline deserved it too. The man snorts. *You must think I didn't recognize you, but you know, there's this thing that gives you away — this greasy blond American heart-throb attitude . . .*

Beneath the wrecked man's words runs the steady trilling of insects, and now and again the cry of a scavenger bird.

. . . Okay, personally, I liked you in Dogfight *more than in* Running on Empty, *or maybe even more than in* Mosquito Coast. *Boy, you and*

Martha Plimpton —! The man motions lewdly and laughs. *I'll never get that.*

A light wind picks up. It invites the tulip trees to dance. A small cloud drifts overhead and billows.

. . . So you were good as Chris Chambers in Stand by Me *— hell, my friend, you were good as Robert Kennedy, Jr. — but your best role just might've been Eddie Birdlace . . .*

You are exhausted by hearing so many words at once and by attempting to follow them all; but he will not be quieted.

The wrecked man next embarks upon a recollection inspired by the coach's pervasive odor of gasoline fuel, for gas fumes jar loose his early remembrances of church: *Infallible pontiffs named Innocent X and Urban I; guttering candles, ash and stone. Father Mac, a musty moth-eaten soul, he wants to teach me respect. I have dared to ask, 'Why is it that every time somebody dies they bury such perfectly nice wood with them?' I am eight. So now he says to me: 'Respect.' He suggests that I pray to Don John Bosco, eccentric defender of delinquent boys. Flustered, my mind goes blank — what (after all) is a mind? The brain makes the mind, and the brain is but a foundry of guiltbugs.*

The wrecked man pats the bumps that have blossomed on the crown of his head. With the nonchalance of a little boy, he pokes at the darkening black-and-blue marks on his ankles and calves. His manner suggests he remains unable to feel much.

So: Father Mac places his hands on my wrists. 'Humanity,' he grimaces, as if he'd intended to say, 'This hive of hand-buzzers.' I cough from the incense. Father Mac's grip is firm. 'A furnace of perfidy.' I cough again and start to speak. I see him clearly then as a bully with a weakness for boys. (That's the thing about consciousness, though, did I mention?) Father Mac bears down on the bones at the base of the hand, squeezing here, between the radial and ulnar arteries. 'This is where they crucified him.' His voice fairly hisses. No simple boy can denounce a man of the cloth (no one believes you, River Phoenix, not even your own mom) . . .

Presently, the wrecked man passes out.

After serving the wrecked man creek water which you bring to him cupped in your hands (hands you recognize now as horribly

filthy), you happily depart to pick him fruit, strolling to the or-
chard up the ridge, where the trees bear nectarines, little and pink-
fleshed. Fingers of autumn dusk creep dimly down the steep narrow hollows. The air smells of farmers burning corn stalks. You locate a Red Delicious tree and pick the man an apple.

Upon your return you appear to him, with violet cirrus framing
you, of course, and your sudden apple of deliciousness placed
squarely before him, as if you are the jealous schemer in a children's fable —! complete with warty nose and evil, satisfied
cackle. Or you're a tongue-darting serpent of temptation —! here
to revisit original sin, to invite the delight of renewing the great
mistake. Or an Eve — but one whose nudity is not yet shamed,
whose worldview has been tenderly arrested, who isn't afraid of leg
fasteners, who allows man to give her things, who long since
stopped growing and still wears outfits from grade school.

He fails to notice that you also bear nectarines. He hears you say
only, *I've got this apple I would like you to try,* before he blanches and
turns away. He traces the letters of words penned upon the vehicle. Where his finger now points it reads: I DON'T FEEL YOUR
LOUSY LOVE. You ask him why, for no love is lousy.

I didn't write that, the man says. *Mark Arm did.*

Oh?

He's another musician. Another guy. He sings too.

You sing?

The man holds a thoughtful pose, nods. *I . . . yes. I make songs.
And films. I make films.*

He studies you. *Have we met?* he asks, at long last. *I'm G.*

Hearing his name spurs you into action. It forces a troubling acknowledgment: the man does not belong solely to you; his arrival
is not meant to serve companionship; he is getting worse; you
must seek help.

You explain that he should wait here and you leave.

Your mission is a grave one, yet you feel anything but solemn.
Instead you experience a wondrous feeling of exhilaration. Moonlight drenches the land. The autumn maples stand etched in radi-
ance and shadows. Throughout these nearly inaccessible valleys

there is a low murmur of insects and the prevailing fragrance of nocturnal blossoms. Everything in the world tonight suggests that you can fly.

. . . And indeed, as you move across the countryside, you notice your toes now scarcely touch the ground. Over ash and oak you drift, above cliff faces and forested ridges, over Slocum Hollow, where the gristmill stood, and the charcoal furnace, and the long-ago homes of the immigrant miners and their silk-weaving wives. The full moon comes visible through the vague bones of your body as your essence recedes.

You have gone for help!

There was once a monk in Köln who could fly. It was said he possessed no control over it and ended up in the most embarrassing predicaments, with his garments snagged atop domes or his foot flailing through a pane of stained glass. He flew, quite apparently, at the Lord's sole discretion.

One doubts the monk enjoyed his gift very much . . .

MICHAEL KAMBER

■

Toil and Temptation

FROM *The Village Voice*

FOR SEVEN DAYS after his arrival from Mexico in mid-January, Antonio Gonzalez spent his time alone in the apartment, watching
Spanish-language soaps and game shows, occasionally looking
out the window at the snowy Bronx streets or gazing at the 6 train
as it clattered by on the el. Two years earlier, his older brother, Juan
Carlos, had learned the neighborhood by each day venturing a
block farther from the apartment, then returning home. When he
had mastered the surrounding streets, he traveled a stop on the
subway — then two, then three. But Antonio saw the police cars
passing by on the streets and, fearing deportation, he stayed inside. On the eighth day the skies cleared, and he went to work at
the car wash with his brother.

   Antonio and Juan Carlos left before dawn, walking north along
Westchester Avenue, past the candy store, restaurant, pizza parlor,
real estate office, and bodega, each business owned by immigrants: Indians, Dominicans, Italians, Guyanese, and Puerto Ricans, respectively. Antonio smiled as he passed the pizza parlor. A
fifteen-year-old acquaintance from Zapotitlán, Antonio's village of
4500 in southern Mexico, had vanished a year earlier, and a few
nights ago Antonio had gone to buy a slice and found the young
man there, sweeping bits of crusts and garlic salt from the floor.

   At Westchester Square, the two brothers caught the X31 bus
along Tremont and Williamsbridge Avenues to Eastchester, a

north Bronx neighborhood remarkable for its dreary nondescript-
ness: block upon block of squat one-story brick buildings, stores
selling auto parts and laminated furniture, a KFC, a Dunkin' Do-
nuts, some gas stations.

At the car wash, no one tells Antonio how much he is being
paid, and he does not ask. In lieu of training, he is handed a towel
and told to join a dozen others — all compact, brown-skinned
men like himself — who stand in the mist at the foot of the wash
tunnel, eyes sandy from sleep, waiting for the cars to roll out. The
men regard him coolly, saying nothing, but shout to one another
in Spanish over the roar of the machinery — the blowers, spray
jets, and huge flopping strands of soapy cloth that make sucking
noises as they slap against the cars.

At 7 A.M., a sedan rolls out of the tunnel, and six men swarm the
vehicle, quickly burnishing the exterior and wiping clean the windows from the inside. Thirty seconds later another vehicle is spit
out, and Antonio joins the second group, trying to walk alongside
the still-rolling car as the others do, wiping as they move.

The former slaughterhouse worker left school at thirteen. He
has been a laborer for five years, frequently averaging seventy or
more hours a week at jobs in Mexico. He has assumed that rubbing a car dry will be easy work, easy money. He is wrong. The
teenager stoops, bends, and reaches for the elusive water droplets;
an hour later his legs and back ache, and pain rockets through
his arm as he drags the waterlogged towel over the cars for the
thousandth time. The areas that he wipes are still damp, and the
others take up his slack and grumble about the poor job he's doing. He is nervous and afraid to disappoint his brother, who has
paid $1600 for Antonio's illegal passage to New York. He sees the
boss watching him from inside the glass booth, motionless and
grim-faced.

Another worker shows Antonio how to fold his towel to get
better coverage, but Antonio repeatedly drops the towel as he tries
to double it. Behind him, the cars are piling up in the tunnel, and
he works quickly, just short of frantic. He has eleven hours and
five hundred cars to go. Before the day is over, he is thinking that

his journey to New York is a mistake. He is thinking that he will return home soon, to Zapotitlán, his village in the state of Puebla, where the majority of New York's Mexicans come from.

If Antonio does return, he will be a man very nearly alone, in the company of young children and the elderly. Fully one third of Antonio's village — including nearly all of the working-age males and 20 percent of the women — is in New York City. Firm figures are hard to come by for a community that is largely illegal, but in the last decade, New York City's Mexican population has grown between 300 and 600 percent — depending on which experts are consulted — to a total of at least 300,000. Dr. Robert Smith, a Barnard College expert on Mexican immigration, calls the growth "astounding — the fastest of any group in the city." (So many Mexicans have left Puebla that they are called the Puebla York, in much the same way that New York City's Puerto Ricans are referred to as Nuyoricans, and Manhattan-based channel 47 hosts *Hechos Puebla,* a weekly show on Puebla current events.)

Like Antonio, nearly all the newly arrived Mexicans have traded one life of labor and poverty for another. They are young men and women who in their homeland have run up against the walls created by class, lack of education, and the detritus of seventy-plus years of one-party rule. In Mexico, there is no future; in New York, there might be.

The residents of Zapotitlán began arriving in New York eighteen years ago. A two-month investigation into the community reveals a clear majority who have fallen into a semi-permanent underclass: men and women here illegally, who trade seventy-hour workweeks for a handful of cash. A small but growing number of young men have drifted into drugs and gangs. But many others — maybe one in five — have found some degree of prosperity in New York, settling into comfortable middle-class lives and easing ties to their homeland. Still others have created a dual existence, maintaining families and even businesses in Zapotitlán. They fly home a few times a year, then travel back like thieves in the night, slipping past the Border Patrol into the Arizona desert. Of New York City's Mexican population as a whole, 75 percent are not upwardly mobile, as many as nine in ten are "illegal," and fully half the teens are not in school.

April 15 is opening day for the Liga Mexicana de Beisból, made up of sixteen teams, each representing a town in Puebla. (The baseball-crazy city of Tulcingo is fielding four separate teams.) Zapotitlán's team is making its league debut; they have new white uniforms, ordered from Mexico, bearing a cactus logo and the words *Club Zapotitlán.* On Sunday morning the players gather early at City Island and win an error-filled first game, 8–4, using a pitcher who was chased through the Arizona desert by the Border Patrol scant weeks ago. His nineteen-year-old son, also here illegally, works in a Dominican bodega on Tremont Avenue; the pitcher has come to help make money to pay for the son's house, under construction in Zapotitlán. He has come, he says, because he wants his son home soon, "before he becomes Americanized."

In years past, Zapotitlán's players were dispersed throughout other clubs in the league, yet a hundred or more Zapotecos would show up for a game if they heard a few of their *paisanos* were playing. "We love baseball," explains Angel Flores, one of Club Zapotitlán's founders. "But really we put the team together because the people from Zapotitlán need a place to gather." Hundreds of people from the village are expected to show up for games this year, which will be followed by barbecues and socializing.

Angel has spent twelve and a half of the past thirteen years in New York working as a laborer. For several years he has worked as a painter for an Irish contractor in Yonkers. He has watched as the man has gone from a rented house and car to an ornate home, three rental properties, and three new cars. "There is a network," Angel explains. "My boss gets all his contracts from other Irishmen."

Yet Angel is not envious of the Irishman's success; Angel makes $130 a day, tax free, a princely sum by the standards of illegal Mexicans in New York. And he has his own network; he has managed to stack the work crew with five others from Zapotitlán — including the pitcher, who is his cousin. Angel's father was a miner in Mexico, and he brags softly about his siblings there: a nurse, a lawyer, an engineer. He is not envious of them either; he put each through college with money he earned in New York. He is an un-educated laborer, they are professionals, yet he has enabled their social mobility. His one complaint about New York? "The people from Zapotitlán, I don't see some of them for years," he says. From the Bronx, they are slowly dispersing into Queens and Brooklyn, like water seeping into the earth after the rains.

Luis Garcia, the first resident of Zapotitlán to arrive in New York, in 1983, settled near Willis Avenue, in the Bronx, down the block from where the 6 train stops under the 40th Precinct. Within a few years, dozens of friends and relatives were arriving with little more than his phone number, and they slept on his couch or on mattresses lined up on the floor. Gradually the com-munity grew and relocated; some went out to Queens, and a few moved south to the burgeoning Mexican community in Sunset Park, Brooklyn. Most, however, stayed near the 6 train, following the el north along Westchester Avenue to Soundview and Castle Hill in the Bronx. They are there today, perhaps a thousand strong; at just one building, 690 Allerton Avenue, at the corner of White Plains Road, there are an estimated fifty families from Zapotitlán. (One of the few remaining Puerto Ricans in the building says, "You're looking for Mexicans? You came to the right place, and it's getting worse!") They find each other work, baby-sit one another's children. In a strange land, they take comfort in neighbors they have known since childhood.

And sometimes, in their insular community, they find love. In 1996, Alma Rosa, a tall, graceful teenager, placed second in the lo-cal beauty pageant in San Antonio, Mexico, a nearby village that makes Zapotitlán seem like a metropolis. Alfonso, the second oldest son of a middle-class family in Zapotitlán, found her there at the pageant, and the two began to date. Yet the young girl's family strongly disapproved of Alfonso, and they sent their nine-teen-year-old daughter away, to San Bernardino, California, where there is a small colony of townspeople. Alfonso followed and searched northern California in vain for several weeks, eventually losing hope, assuming she would be married if he ever found her.

He left for New York to seek work. The following spring, at a gathering of people from Zapotitlán, he heard two men speak of her. She too had come to New York, and he called her that evening. The couple live today in a building full of Mexicans on Dean Street, in downtown Brooklyn, with their two small children and three of Alfonso's brothers.

About one fifth of the immigrants from Zapotitlán are women, and the percentage is growing steadily. In the Mexican community as a whole, the number of women arriving in New York is higher, probably approaching 40 percent. They are working in factories, cleaning houses, and having children. The birthrate among Mexican women rose 232 percent between 1989 and 1996; they now rank third among immigrant groups in New York City — higher than Chinese, South Asians, or Haitians. "Most of these [Mexican] women are very young, and they have a high fertility rate; it's a double whammy," says Peter Lobo of the New York City Department of Planning. "This is going to have a huge impact on New York City."

At the car wash, a week has passed. The pain in Antonio's body has lessened; he has learned how to handle the towel, how to flip the car doors open, wipe the seals with one quick motion, then snap the towel over his shoulder and quickly wipe the windows with a softer blue rag. His coworkers are not so intimidating now; the other Mexicans see that he will work and begin to talk and joke with him — the Salvadorans also, though they speak differently and seem harder men, having been through a war that Antonio knows nothing about. And then there are the tall, dark-skinned men, men unlike any he has seen in Mexico, whom he has assumed are *morenos*, African Americans, but who turn out to be Africans, and at first he is confused by the distinction ("In the dark of the tunnel, you can see just their eyes," he says with some wonderment). Because they are African, they are very proud, he is told, and dislike taking orders. With the exception of a garrulous Nigerian who has learned to speak Spanish, the Africans are given jobs where they work alone.

Spend seventy-two hours a week wiping other people's cars, and resentment is a constant companion. Until recently, Antonio has known only Mexicans. Lunch and downtime at the car wash are filled with talk of money and race. Eastchester is a working- to middle-class neighborhood of West Indian and African American civil servants, secretaries, teachers, construction workers. Most work hard, many favor nice cars, and the line at the car wash is a parade of conspicuous consumption — Cadillacs, Lexuses, late-model SUVs. People come here because it is nearby, and because the "Super," which includes hot wax, polish, and wheels Armor-alled, costs $9, a savings of $3 over the other car wash, a half-mile down Baychester Avenue, where the white people go.

But the black people — especially the young black men — don't appreciate paying hard-earned money to have a bunch of illegals leave drops of water on their cars. If they feel they are not getting their money's worth, they wave their hands in the air and shout at the workers and then mock them: "No speek eengleesh." Antonio quickly learns the phrase "Yo, yo, yo" and an utterance that sounds to him like "fock" or "focking," which he believes to be a mean word. And noise is of particular concern. Antonio and Juan Carlos are soft-spoken and courteous. They would never raise their voices unless they were ready to fight. These black men raise their voices all the time.

The tips left by the black clientele run to silver and copper, with some dollar bills thrown in. At the end of a twelve-hour shift, Antonio takes home maybe $5 in tips. Down the hill, *los blancos* leave $5 bills, and rumor has it the workers average $30 a day in tips. Times six days, that's good money. But here Antonio is stuck with the cheap *morenos* who shout at him, wear their clothes baggy, and lounge against the wall. "Where do they get their money?" he wants to know. To him, and to the other Mexicans, the young black men seem lazy and dangerous.

The first week there are days when it rains and there is no work, but soon Antonio is averaging seventy-two hours a week. His hourly rate remains a mystery to him. He is simply handed an envelope with $270 in cash at week's end, which he accepts without complaint. Juan Carlos is the senior laborer at the car wash. With a year and a half of experience, he makes $4 an hour. The others, he believes, make $3.75 an hour. It is straight time — nothing extra after forty hours. A laborer working at the legal minimum wage, plus overtime, would be paid $497. The car wash has approximately twenty employees. By using workers without green cards, the owner, a Portuguese immigrant, is saving nearly a quarter of a million dollars a year.

Twenty years ago, Mexican workers had the second highest per capita income among Hispanics. Today they have the lowest. Their average earning power has dropped 50 percent, a result of the flood of illegal laborers like Antonio, who are readily exploited by tens of thousands of small businesses throughout the city — restaurants, delis, small factories, and building contractors who rely on their sub-minimum-wage labor to turn a profit.

But to Antonio, $300 a week is about $270 more than most men make in Mexico, where the minimum wage is $4 a day. After work one evening in mid-February, the two brothers walk down to the Western Union near Castle Hill Avenue. There, they send a money order for $300 to their mother in Mexico. It is their combined savings from three weeks of work. Theirs is a drop in the bucket: in 1996, the last year for which figures are available, $5.6 billion was sent home by Mexicans in the United States, making *remesas* the third largest factor in the Mexican economy.

Of Antonio's townspeople here in New York, there is a shoe-store owner in Queens who is building a gas station in the village; a busboy at a restaurant on Madison who is part owner of construction vehicles that are rented out in Zapotitlán for $2000 a month; a seventeen-year-old bodega worker on Tremont who makes $1200 a month and sends $1000 home to his mother — eating free food at his job and staying inside on his day off, lest he be tempted to spend money. They say that those who suffer the most in New York live the best when they return to Mexico.

When he left Zapotitlán for New York, Antonio stated that his dream was to build a kitchen for his mother. Upon receiving her son's money, she hires a local contractor to begin work on the addition, then abandons the project, to be completed another time. A few weeks later Antonio sends more money, and the mother of nine — who cannot read or write, but adds complex sums with lightning speed — buys several hundred dollars' worth of food and soda and opens a small store in the front room of her house.

By late February, Antonio has begun to feel secure in the Bronx. There is solace in the daily routine; he is no longer afraid of the police that pass by, and the dollar bills and coins are less confusing. Yet the frustration starts early each morning. At work, vacuum cleaner in hand, Antonio has learned to say, "Open the trunk." But the patrons frequently respond with a torrent of words, and he stands and listens helplessly. Buying coffee at the bodega is an ordeal; he gets nervous, procrastinates. What if the Puerto Rican woman is not working today? The other counter workers ask him questions that he does not understand. The customers stare as he grows flustered.

And Antonio begins to see the long-term limitations as well. The two brothers are living doubled up and being gouged on the rent, but cannot move; landlords won't rent to "illegals" with no credit history. Juan Carlos has a friend working at a midtown parking lot — a union job, $20 an hour, and they're hiring. But between Antonio and Juan Carlos, they have only one fake green card from Texas, with someone else's name on it. It will never do. So they stay at the car wash, surrounded by opulence and possibilities, caged by their illegal status and lack of English. A friend suggests English classes and Antonio laughs. "We leave the house before six in the morning and get home after eight at night — some nights we work until ten. When do we take the classes?" A week later he says, "We could just stay right here, buy from the Puerto Ricans, work with the Mexicans, stay right here." He means literally and figuratively, and he shakes his head. Right here is not going to be good enough.

For the first generation who arrived from Zapotitlán, in the 1980s, right here wasn't good enough either. Lupe Gonzalez came across in 1987, in the trunk of a car with holes cut in the floor. The coyotes gave him a straw through which he sucked fresh air as he bounced over the roads near San Diego. The eighteen-year-old entered the workforce as a messenger in midtown Manhattan — $100 a week plus tips. Yet the job suited him no more than the conservative lifestyle of his hometown. "I used to dress up in my sister's clothes and play with dolls when I was a child," explains Lupe. In 1991 he found a job as a hairdresser at a shop on a Bronx side street, near the Morrison Avenue stop on the 6 train. He slowly built up his clientele in the Hispanic neighborhood, and became best friends with two Puerto Rican stylists, who were also gay. "They taught me how to do my makeup, how to wear fake *tetas* and high heels. They took me to the gay clubs and balls," he says, explaining his entry into New York's gay community.

Eight years ago, he put down $5000, bought the shop he worked in, and renamed it Versace; in February of 2001, he opened a second, larger location, Style 2000. He now has five employees. On a recent April evening, the tall hairdresser with the lipstick and long hair formed elaborate curls with a hot comb in the crowded salon, the air filled with hairspray and merengue blasting from overhead speakers. The four chairs were full, and a crowd of people — Dominicans, Puerto Ricans, Mexicans, one Chinese woman — waited near the door for their hair to be cut.

As an openly gay man, a successful businessperson, a legal resident of the United States, and a fluent English speaker, Lupe is clearly an anomaly in the Mexican community, whose biggest holiday is December 12, the birthday of the Virgin of Guadalupe. One expects to hear painful stories of his exclusion among his fellow immigrants from Zapotitlán; there are none. "They wave at me on the street," he says. "They know that I'm one of the twelve sons and daughters of Delfino Gonzalez, from Zapotitlán. That's all that matters."

One Saturday night in late March, Los Tigres del Norte, a hugely popular Mexican *norteño* band, comes to New York. Antonio and Juan Carlos are there, and as the band takes the stage, the audience erupts, waves of adulation washing over the musicians.

They launch into a set of ballads about being from Mexico, having nothing there — no profession or future — and risking your life to cross the border illegally; about grueling workweeks and a life that is nothing more than "from home to work, from work to home." In the crowd there is a wave of emotion that Antonio has never felt before, a current very nearly electric. He is surrounded by thousands of cheering, nearly hysterical countrymen who share his life, his pain, his frustration. Grown men — macho Mexican men — are weeping all around him.

The following Saturday night, the eighteen-year-old's destination is the notorious Chicano Club. Three thousand miles away, in small Mexican villages, women speak of this Bronx nightspot in hushed tones. Men speak of it with smiles on their faces. They speak of the Dominican and Puerto Rican women in high heels, skin-tight pants, and halter tops. You can hold them as close as you want — at least as long as the song is playing. You're paying for it: $2 a dance. Antonio, Juan Carlos, and two friends sit at a table, drinking rounds of Corona and watching the women in the smoke-filled room. A live band is pounding out *bachatas, cumbias,* and covers of hits by Los Tigres. The music and bodies and laughter begin to run together. Money that could have been saved and sent to Mexico is spent on women and beer. It is the cost of feeling alive for a night. Antonio gets home about 4 A.M., sleeps for an hour, and leaves for work, exhausted, hung over, smelling of perfume, and feeling good.

Mexicans say that teenagers like Antonio lose their money and their innocence at the Chicano, but it is New York that takes these things. In Sunset Park, Brooklyn, Ignacio, a twenty-two-year-old man from Zapotitlán, knows the Chicano well — but he cannot go there, because it is in the Bronx, and people will kill him if they find him. A strikingly handsome, muscular man, he sits in a dreary apartment, roaches blazing trails over pinups of naked women on the walls. He sends $500 a month to his wife and three children in Zapotitlán. They live in a house overlooking the desert and the forests of giant saguaro cactus, in a place where, in the middle of the day, one hears total silence. His family is waiting pa-

tiently for his return. He is never going back. He cannot. He is addicted to New York.

Ignacio made his first trip to New York when he was seventeen. He worked delivering pizzas for an Italian place on the Grand Concourse, in the Bronx. One day the teenager made the mistake of looking inside the pizza box. "When you come from Mexico, your eyes are closed," he says of his early days in the city. "Now my eyes are open." His is a complex story involving drug deliveries, vendettas, betrayals, attempted murders. The details do not matter. What matters is that he stands at night on Brooklyn street corners in a tight T-shirt and baggy pants. He has a gold chain, a .25 automatic, and some bags of coke. Much of the profit goes up his nose, and he works a day job washing dishes to support his habit and his children. His life in New York is a secret he keeps from his family. "They have this dream of who I am — why ruin that?" he asks. He's made a couple of trips back, gotten his wife pregnant twice more. But he could not stay around the friendly, trusting people of his hometown. "Their eyes are closed," he repeats dismissively.

Living in New York is costing more than Antonio expected, much more. Rent, food, and transit take up over half of the $1200 a month that he earns. Then there are clothes to be bought, weekly phone calls to Mexico, haircuts, nights out, Laundromats, a large fake gold watch from Canal Street: it has been more than a month since he sent money home. Juan Carlos commiserates: "I've been here two and a half years," he says. "All I have to show for it is a pizza oven in Mexico." Though he doesn't say so, he has also purchased the building materials for his family's new concrete house, and now Antonio has helped pay for the kitchen and for his mother's new store, modest though it may be. But it is true; for themselves, they have nothing. Juan Carlos's dream of the two brothers opening a *taqueria* in Mexico seems to be years away. It is mid-April, however. Spring has come to the Bronx, and Antonio does not seem as fixated on his brother's dream as he once was. A Puerto Rican girl smiles at Antonio on a subway platform, he boldly asks for her number, and they talk on the phone. And there are more nights ahead at the Chicano Club, and at the nightspots that he has discovered along Roosevelt Avenue in Queens, where he danced for several hours one night with a pretty Peruvian woman.

At the car wash, his boss has seen that Antonio is good with his hands and is training him to compound paint, which entails running a large buffing wheel gently over the car's surface. Antonio has heard there is good money in this, that paint shops pay $500 or more a week for a good compound man. And he has heard that the boss may open another car wash, and that Juan Carlos will be manager if he can learn English. "Really, life in New York is pretty good," Antonio says one night, sitting on a park bench, Juan Carlos at his side. "All you need is a little money." Then he and his brother begin to discuss their latest plan, which is to save enough to bring their sixteen-year-old brother, Fernando, to the Bronx. He has already told them he wants to come.

■

Snacks

FROM *Jane*

EVERYBODY KEPT WAITING for me to get skinny. My dad said it could be any day. My mom said if I got skinny, it might help me with my moods. She promised me a new wardrobe, one more congruent with my era, my region. My sister said if I got skinny there would be the possibility of handjobs from her friends in the Jazz Dancing Club. Blowjobs, even. All the jobs. It was only fair, she said. They had older brothers, she'd done her part.

No one ever told me to stop eating, or even to curb it.

There was the occasional mealtime glance. Someone might say, "Stop playing with your food," which I could only reckon as code. Never in my life did I play with it.

Dinner was the least of it. Lunch was nothing. Breakfast was how I got to lunch.

Home from school, I'd stand at the refrigerator. Everything I needed in this life was there, cold, in plastic pouches, cylindrical tubs. I hated the word *snack*. It demeaned.

My mom liked to watch while I dipped the nachos into the jelly jar.

"Are you losing weight?" she'd say.

Somebody on TV said sex could make you skinny. I knew I'd have to go it alone.

Unfortunately, a certain technique of mine had consequences.

The hair on the parts of my arms that rubbed against the mattress rubbed off. It grew back as stubble. Someone started a rumor at school that I was shaving my arms.

All the time I spent denying it, tracing the source of the lie, I could have read some famous novel, had the world opened up to me. The world never opened up to me. It really just sat there. It needed a little salt.

Cigarettes, a girl I was eavesdropping on told her friend, cut down on your appetite. I thought I'd give them a whirl. I bought the brand I'd once spotted going through my babysitter's purse. Later someone told me they were "women's cigarettes."

This affected me.

Eventually, I moved into the basement. It was meant to be a sign of independence, I think, being nearer to the boiler. I could conceivably control the temperature of rooms. Here, walled in by the disingenuous mahogany, far from the sidelong sadness of my progenitors, I learned to ungirl my manner with a cigarette, to teach myself a disrespect for fire.

"Are you smoking?"

Dad was at the door. A shift in aromatics had brought him bounding down. He was always sniffing at things — his breakfast, his wife. He liked to pinkie out his ear wax, whiff it. He said he could tell from it if he was sick. Most of his knowledge was of this order. He was from strivers, Ivy League, but this is what he'd whittled it down to. I was a major admirer.

"I'm giving you a chance to answer me," he said now. "Are you smoking cigarettes down here?"

He'd been pre-law in college and I remember thinking about how since he was not a lawyer he would die pre-law, too. I crushed out the lit Capri in my pocket.

"I'll ask you one more time," he said. "Are you smoking down here?"

We squinted at each other through the smoke.

"No," I said.

I felt a part of his world then. Men lied to his face every day.

*   *   *

It was hard to believe how big I was. I wasn't quite obese. Those types were to be pitied, the ones we saw at the mall when my mom drove me over for new fat-boy pants. We'd circle for parking for a while, the seams of my corduroys planed down or outright split, my hands cupped over pressured bars of crotch flesh.

"It's glandular, poor things," she'd say, point them out for me, the obese kids, hobbling past our windshield with their moms. "It's not their fault."

Me, on the other hand, there was no question about me. I was definitely my fault.

I spent long minutes on the bench outside the ladies' room, listening to my mom's voice above the flushes, faucets. She'd strike up talk with all the other moms. Maybe some of them had come for fat-boy pants, but most of the fat-boy moms came alone. There weren't that many decisions to make at the fat-boy store. It was just a matter of getting really big pants. Maybe a sweater.

I knew some Catholic kids from the Catholic school down the block. They called me names, but not fat names. They called me kike, Christ-killer. Finally, real friends. I sat with them on the bike rack behind their school and smoked.

One of them was big, too. He said we were both going to hell for gluttony. The idea seemed to make him giddy. I told him my parents had parented me to understand you pay for everything here, in your own time, in your own home, even. They were humanists. They got special magazines in the mail.

My ass, my thighs, my belly, my breasts, it was all becoming an ethical question, a great humanist dilemma. Also, there were these huge, moist boils on my chest. My dad said not to worry. The same thing had happened to him. Then one magical summer, he told me, the fat just melted away. He'd even written a prizewinning book for children about it.

We had to read this book in school.

The boy chosen to give the report on it stood in front of the class and pointed me out for the others.

"The author hopes to show how fat his son is."

* * *

"Are you shaving your arms?" said my dad. He was staring at me while I spooned out the Thanksgiving yams.

"No," I said.

"Why in the hell would you shave your arms?" he said.

I looked to the women of our family. They seemed to prefer to wait this one out.

Now I saw my dad notice a discoloration in his serving, a burnt knot in his yams. He put his nose down to it.

"Just tell me why you would shave your arms," he said.

"There's no one answer," I said.

My dad pushed the bad yams away with his butter knife.

"I'll eat them," I said.

The new boy, he was Brody. He was mall obese. He was beyond mall obese. He had a new kind of body, something never before seen. When he walked through the hallway everyone whispered "glandular," as though they were saying "holocaust" or "slavery," all hushed and sorry about the way of things.

Brody was some kind of holy being, made by God, hands-on. They figured him for fattest boy in the world. Me, I was fat for the town, the county. I was Fat Shit, Lard Ass, Tits, Tub. But Brody was the wonder of glands. Brody could do no wrong. He'd been put on earth to teach us to be better people. Even the real torture freaks wouldn't touch him. They'd compliment his sneakers. If Brody dropped a ball in gym, some jock would jog over, hand it back to him. There was no way Brody could pick up the ball himself, but he had more important work to do. He was Gandhi in a fat suit. Me, when I dropped a ball, I tended to get it right back in the nuts.

Sometimes I wondered what Brody's mother told Brody at the mall.

Did she point me out, say, "You, my darling Brody, are glandular, but that boy there, he's weak"?

Is that what she said?

Whore.

They put us back to back, yards apart, each yoked to the looped end of a tug-of-war rope. This was physical education in our school.

The coaches least known for copping feels, the cruel, unperverted ones, had thought it up. Students cut lunch, free periods, to attend. They came in sick to see.

We stood there on the hardwood floor. Light poured down from the high gym windows. I couldn't see Brody, but I could feel him test the rope. It tightened at my hips, burned up my belly, went slack again. I heard his sneakers squeak.

We waited for the whistle.

They were chanting for him, for Brody, his glands.

They were sorry about Nagasaki, I guess, Babylon, Union City. They were sorry for everything.

I was sorry my father ever found my mother, smelled her, found her.

I heard that little ball stirring in the lip piece of the coach's whistle and I knew the next thing I heard would be Brody falling.

I could always hear things. Smell, I couldn't smell much since the cigarettes, but I could hear the quietest of things, things coming out of the quiet, sounds before they were sounds, names before they were even shouted after me.

It took all the coaches to carry Brody to the nurse's station. He'd hit his head.

One of the Jazz Club girls, a friend of my sister's, she called me Hebe. Hell, it was a start.

Brody was out for a week and then it was Christmas break. I'd waited days to be treated like a hero, but no dice. I was a dick. I'd hurt the huge Christ. I'd maybe damaged his glands.

I saw him at the mall a few days after Christmas. He had a neck brace, a plastic halo on his head. He waddled up in a version of my pants. A more benevolent color.

"Hey, Brody," I said.

He shot me this look of brotherhood, as though together we could shoulder the great weight of fat-boy sorrow. We could forget everything that had happened between us, enter the kingdom of kindness hand in hand.

I punched him in the gut. He leaned up on the wall, held his belly, kneaded it, as though to push the sting out. Blood was going out of his face. Glandular, I thought. Murdered. I pictured him home that night in bed, everything collapsing from a dead point in the center of him, dying like a star dies. Or maybe he could die right here, slide down dead against the wall.

I took up the rolls of his throat.

"Brody," I said.

I saw my arms out, the hair grown back. A revolution in technique, its dividends. Things change. A person can change.

"Brody," I said, squeezing, squeezing.

"Brody," I said, "you fat fucking fuck."

"Brody," I said, "you're killing me."

I was squeezing and squeezing.

Our mothers came out, ladies from the ladies' room, chatting.

ELIZABETH MCKENZIE

■

Stop That Girl

FROM ZYZZYVA

MY MOTHER AND I lived alone then, in a pink bungalow in Long Beach, with a small yard full of gopher holes and the smell of the refinery settling over everything we had. Couldn't leave a glass on the shelf a week without it gathering a fine mist of oil. I thought we had a real life anyway, before my mother started over.

I had a stocky Yorkshire nanny, who walked me home from school past the barbershop with the unhappy mynah bird. "Kill me!" it suggested as we passed by.

I never knew my father. He was some frat boy who danced well. Mom believed I'd have a leveler head.

My mother worked in petroleum research. She was a geology major in college and went to field camps in Wyoming and was renowned for shooting a bobcat at a hundred yards while it was cuffing around her professor's beagle. For the company, she looked through telescopes at the moon, as if there might be something useful up there. Mom felt her job was a joke. When she came home at night, she locked herself in the bathroom for an hour, taking a hot bath filled with salts.

She was said to look like Lauren Bacall in those days and dated a number of different engineers from the refinery. While Mom went searching for her purse and coat, they would bribe me with something, like it was up to me to release her — Silly Putty, a magnet, a comic book, a stuffed pig with a music box in it.

There we are in Long Beach the fall I start fifth grade, when the nights have grown cooler and our gas wall unit bangs out its stale-smelling heat and we're on the brink of changes so vast it's hard to believe we don't see them coming. One Saturday evening, we receive a new visitor in the form of Roy Ransom, a real estate broker, a handsome talker with dimples, cowboy boots, and a rounded ruby ring that looks like a bloody eyeball. He brings a bouquet as big as a baby, and my mother holds it that way. He slips me a piece of Double Bubble. By the following week it's a Slip 'N Slide. I suspect he appeals to that secret Wild West part of my mother, but it's more. A few months later my mother tells me, "Roy's taking us both out for a drive today, Ann. We're going to see a house."

I sit in the back seat of Roy's Caddy as we leave Long Beach behind. We aim for the San Fernando Valley. "You mean we're going to buy a house out here?" I ask Mom. We're in the Encino Hills; compared with Long Beach it looks like paradise: huge ranch houses and big yards; rose bushes, hibiscus, banana trees, palms.

"Well, maybe," my mother says, turning around in her seat like she has something to tell me. "We might buy a house — with Roy."

"With Roy?"

"Yes. We might all live out here together."

"Annie-girl, sound like a plan?" Roy says, eyeing me in his mirror.

I realize what they're trying to tell me.

We pull up in front of a huge, shingled yellow house, as long as the entire row of bungalows in Long Beach. My mother looks stunned as we wander into the place. It has beamed ceilings, parquet floors, a kitchen with an island and a double range, a breakfast nook and bar, a family room, three bedrooms, three baths, two fireplaces, and a den. They show me the room that would be mine — it has sheer pink curtains and wallpaper with ballerinas on it, something for a well-defined girl. When we finish inspecting the place, Roy Ransom says, "Hey, Annie, hit me right here! As hard as you can!" He is pointing at his stomach.

I don't ask why. I just do it.

"I'm waiting." He winks at my mother.

My hand hurts. I kick him in the shin.

A year later Mrs. Ransom has retired from petroleum work, pregnant. In the afternoons, she sews clothes and toys and bedding for the baby, placing them in the nursery-to-be, while I'm thinking of names. Percy is the one I'm rooting for.

Quiet collects in the rooms of that big house more than anywhere I've ever lived. I often tell my mother it's a suburban tomb, and she says, "Ann, I love this man. But you are still the most important person in the world to me." The words I live for, and I skate around the parquet floor in my socks, still feeling like it's all just temporary. I still can't believe that an extended family of Kuwaitis has moved into the pink bungalow, and that Nana has gone back to Leeds, and that a few friends from my school in Long Beach write me real letters with stamps on them like I've moved across the world.

"How about a swim?" Mom asks me after school nowadays.

"Maybe."

I come out into the back yard after a while and see my mother, in her white, flowered bathing cap, doing graceful laps up and down the pool. This is no kidney-shaped job, as Roy would point out. It's a classic rectangle of crystal blue, and I'm impressed by my mother's sidestroke.

"Come on in," Mom calls to me.

To surprise my mother, I say, "Okay" and walk straight into the pool with all my clothes on. She laughs and doesn't get mad at me for possibly ruining my leather shoes.

It's in the afternoons after school when I know I still have an impact on her. Once Roy's home, she'll even offer to help him clean up Open Houses or gather garbage from yards. She acts like he's our savior. One evening he insists we accompany him to pound in some fresh For Sale signs, and I climb onto the roof of the Cadillac and won't get off.

"Get down, Ann," my pregnant mother says, waiting sway-backed by the car. Like a prehistoric lobster, Roy snaps at my ankles.

"From up here I can see the reservoir," I say. "I think boys are peeing into it."

"That's nice, but let's go."

"Is that, like, what we drink?"

Roy stalks around the car and I hop to the other side. He charges back and this time I slip off. I fall onto the concrete, and no matter how much it hurts I decide I won't cry. Instead, I pretend I'm in a coma. "Ann?" my mother says. "Ann, are you all right? Look what you did!" she yells at Roy Ransom. "Faker," he replies. He tickles me. I sink my teeth into his arm. He slaps me across the top of the head, and my mother tells Roy never to lay a hand on me again. Roy tells my mother I'm a spoiled brat, and then I sit up and hear myself saying, "And you're a home-wrecker."

And thus, the following weekend, it's decided I'm spending some time with The Frosts. They are my grandparents, but when we talk about them we always call them The Frosts. Until then, I'd only seen them once or twice a year, because my mother hates them. They don't seem to miss us. They are too young and too busy for grandparents — Otto's a patent lawyer, Liz a pediatrician. Mom grew up a lonely daydreamer with no brothers or sisters. That's her rationale for the new baby — so things will be different for me.

Friday afternoon Dr. Frost shows up to collect me. She looks like my mother, but is smaller and more efficient, never a moment to kill. I don't know her very well. "Put on a dress with a nice collar, Ann. And comb your hair. I want you to look pretty for your passport."

"Why do I need a passport?"

"Hasn't your mother told you about our trip?"

"Trip?"

"You're coming to Europe with me. I'm attending a medical conference. You're going to straighten out and learn your place in the world. Good deal?"

"Europe?" I say, looking at my mother. "When?"

"Next month," Dr. Frost says.

Next month is May. May is a big month. May is when my mother is having the baby.

"I can't go," I say. "I need to be here for the baby."

"You've been a big help already," my mother says.

"I need to help more!"

Dr. Frost says, "After we have your picture taken, let's go buy some new clothes, shall we? I'm going to need some new things myself."

"I don't need any new clothes."

"All right, then we'll just get your picture taken."

I'm speechless, but finally I say, "This is definitely bizarre and grotesque," my favorite expression in many situations. Then I add my other: "It's also grossly mutilated and hugely deformed."

"Ann, your grandmother has offered to take you to Europe. You're a very lucky girl."

Lucky? Who needs parquet floors and a pool. Who needs Europe with the very person who makes my mother scream or cry whenever they talk on the phone. I try to catch my mother's eye, the special eye that knows me better than anyone, and I say, "I don't want to go." But the eye doesn't blink. There's no hope. Though they disagree on everything else, they're together on this one. My mother tells me, "The baby might not even come while you're gone, who knows."

Roy can't make it to the airport. Neither can Otto. I hug my mother and pat her stomach, which looks square now, like a little house. "Tell Percy to wait," I croak out.

"I'll try," my mother says.

Our travels take us first to Copenhagen, city of copper domes turned green and raw beef. I'm in Europe. I'm excited. I tell myself I'll see yodelers and eat lots of chocolate and buy souvenirs for my mother and the people I'm meeting at my new school. Even Dr. Frost seems to have loosened up a little. She's humming and smiling without explaining why.

Our second night there, in a quaint hotel with floors tilted like a fun house, we receive a telegram from Roy Ransom. "Wonderful news STOP We have a daughter STOP Catherine Louise STOP Mother and baby fine."

"Who's we?" I say, grabbing the telegram. It hits me for the first time that my sister's father is Roy Ransom. "Can I call my mother at the hospital?"

This is 1964. It isn't so easy. Dr. Frost says we'll send a telegram instead.

"Can we go home now?"

"Ann, you don't want to see a newborn baby. They're ugly little things with red faces. They don't even open their eyes."

"Really?"

I slide on the bare floors in my socks all the way to the lower wall. Tivoli Gardens flashes brightly across the street. From her bag my grandmother hauls out a textbook she has brought on this trip to instruct me with. It contains pictures of every bone, every muscle, every ligament, the cardiovascular, the respiratory, the digestive system, the works. "Tell me about dissecting cadavers," I ask her.

"Nothing to it," Dr. Frost says.

"But you were cutting open dead bodies. Wasn't it bizarre and grotesque?"

"Ann, the body is an amazing machine. It's not bizarre and grotesque at all," she says, pointing at a skeleton.

I want to hear interesting stories about guts, not her version of them. "Dead bodies are wonderful, newborn babies are really gross?"

"Goodnight, Ann," she says.

"Maybe we should go home," I murmur, but she ignores me in a different way, pretending not to hear. I pull the covers up around my neck and fall asleep hearing my grandmother listing bones.

The International College of Surgeons is meeting in Vienna, and we take three days driving there through Germany. I like stopping in towns and villages, jumping around cobblestone squares, dipping my hands in fountains, and eating pastries. I decide to stop thinking about home. The afternoon we arrive in Vienna, we check in at the Intercontinental across from the park, in plenty of time for the first night's event, and I'm fitting right in. Dr. Frost takes a long bath and changes into a blue chiffon dress, and I wear a green velvet frock with white gloves. We set out for our evening together in a taxi. She smells like hairspray and Windsong and talcum all mixed together. Her rings glint in the evening light. She taps her little heels.

We pull up at a real palace and proceed up a wide bank of marble steps. The roar of the doctors from around the world deepens as we get closer. Dr. Frost grabs the list of those in attendance and scans it. When we cross into the ballroom, I look up at my grand- mother and she has her nose at full tilt, her forehead high like a half-moon. A small orchestra is tuning up at the end of the room. Dr. Frost taps me on the shoulder and points to a tall, silvery- haired man standing alone in the crowd. "Go introduce yourself to that man," she urges me.

"Why?"

"Just do it," she whispers.

Luckily, I don't have to, because he turns and his face is radiant at the sight of Dr. Frost. "Liz," he says. He gives her a kiss and looks at her and laughs. "And this is your daughter?"

"My granddaughter."

"Impossible," he says, taking her hand. "You look wonderful."

"Ann, this is Dr. Von Allsberg."

I'm more interested in what we're having for dinner, and I lo- cate our table next to the dance floor. Eventually, a doctor takes the seat next to me. While Dr. Frost talks to the man with the silver hair, my doctor has a waxed mustache and smells like varnish. His name is Dr. Witkovitch and he's an internist from a small village in the Julian Mountains. He tells me he breeds roller-pigeons, which come in all colors and are iridescent. They rocket high into the sky, then come rolling down to earth in a free fall. It's a stunt and they enjoy it. I realize that Dr. Witkovitch is actually a very young man; it's the stiff mustache, oiled hair, and musty jacket that make him seem outdated and old. I'm thinking Dr. Frost will be impressed to see that I've befriended someone so quickly, but she's not watching. We slice up thin wafers of veal.

Later, the orchestra plays Strauss and I watch while Dr. Von Allsberg waltzes with Dr. Frost. She moves like a swan, her head back and eyes fastened on him.

"How do you know Dr. Von Allsberg?" I ask her that night.

"I know many people here."

"Can we go to Dr. Witkovitch's roller-pigeon farm?"

"Hardly," she says, examining her eyes in the mirror. "We have plenty to do as it is."

"Not even for a day?"

"Where is it?"

"Yugoslavia."

"Ha!"

The next day Dr. Frost leaves me with a baby-sitting service at the hotel. Over the phone, arranging it, someone calls her Mrs. Frost. "No! It's Dr. Frost." She never lets that mistake slip by. "Whenever your grandfather makes reservations, and he says it's for a Dr. and Mr. Frost, they behave very strangely, because they assume your grandfather must be the doctor and therefore is married to a man. People would rather believe your grandfather is married to a man than think a woman is a doctor!"

I am shocked.

"Say, after the conference, we'll take a boat trip on the Danube, how would that be?" she asks me.

"Good."

"Better than a bunch of roller-chickens?"

"Pigeons!"

"Same difference."

The babysitter is a glum old Austrian woman who likes to say "It is not allowed!" as often as she can clear her throat, and I read all day, looking out a window at the park. She feeds me some hard salty meat in a broth with little dumplings swimming around in it. By pointing at the park and annoying her with long sentences she doesn't understand, I get her to take me out, but I'm in such a bad mood I end up throwing rocks at a swan. And I'm disappointed Dr. Witkovitch hasn't hunted me down to find out if I can go to his

farm in Yugoslavia. The last night in Vienna, the night we are supposed to go to a special Hungarian restaurant and sample goulash,
my grandmother breaks the news to me she's going to an opera
with Dr. Von Allsberg instead.

"You can come too, of course, but I promise you, it will be very
long and boring."

"In that case, I'd love to."

"Seriously, Ann, I don't think you'd enjoy it. I'm all for exposing
you to cultural events, but you'll have a lot more fun running
around here."

"Running around?" This makes me grind my teeth, and I close
my eyes and imagine my grandmother being speared by head-
hunters. "What's the opera, anyway?"

"*Der Rosenkavalier,*" she tells me. Then she proceeds to offer up
the whole story, which is about mistaken identities. If she already
knows, why does she need to go? And I'm skeptical about the plot.
People can't be tricked that easily. If I came home in a costume, my
mother would still recognize me. It's changes on the inside she
won't be able to see.

There's a different babysitter at night. An old bald man with
only a pinkie and a thumb on his right hand. For some reason,
whiling away the evening with him in the smoky TV room, I feel
like crying for the first time in a long time. I'm not even sure why.
The seven-fingered man bites the nail on his lonely thumb. I keep
running to the window and looking out at the lamps in the park
and at every cab that pulls up to see if my grandmother is returning. At last, very late, I see Dr. Frost and Dr. Von Allsberg strolling
together out of the park, their heads close and crowned by lamp-
light. And it's bizarre and grotesque, because I can see that they're
holding hands.

When the conference ends, I'm glad to see the last of Dr. Von
Allsberg. My grandmother and I drive to a small village on the
Danube, where we board the boat. It is a hot May day. We spend
hours drifting past castles and abbeys and orchards, sitting on the
deck in the sun eating little napoleons and drinking tea. This is
what I've been waiting for.

"I wish there had been more women there for you to meet," my grandmother remarks. "You're to do great things. No man should stand in your way. And don't let Roy Ransom tell you otherwise! Think you'd like to be a doctor?"

"Maybe. What about industrial baking?"

"I want you to set your sights as high as you can. Your mother was sent to fine schools. I don't want you to think . . ." She pauses. "I happen to know that the man who was your father came from a very fine family."

I squint into the sun. "So what's a fine family like?"

"A fine family, Ann, is one with noble values and good ancestry. Like mine. Congressmen, attorneys and judges, officers in the Civil and Revolutionary Wars. Well educated and able to contribute to society."

"And did they get along with their kids?"

"I would think so."

I say, "That's good."

"Yes, it is good. I'm glad you and I are getting to know each other. Your mother was what they call a daddy's girl. Never liked me, truth be told. Even when she was a baby."

I look to see if Dr. Frost is kidding. "Babies always like their mothers."

"Not in this case. I'm afraid you've no idea what I'm talking about, coming from the spot she put you in."

And I say, "Well, I'm afraid you have no idea what I'm talking about, because all you ever cared about was your job."

"I see," Dr. Frost snorts.

For the rest of the boat ride, when I'm not snapping pictures in every direction, I'm trying to make my grandmother forget what I've said. My new sister might entice her. "She's much nicer than I am," I say. "She has red hair and speaks many languages. She can do magic tricks and dance."

"There'll be no stopping you two," my grandmother replies.

And finally, the day reaches its inevitable conclusion when we get off the boat and Dr. Von Allsberg stands waiting on the dock with flowers. "Why didn't you tell me he was going to be here?"

"Seriously, Ann. Are you my keeper?"

I march behind them, filtering everything I see through a blaze of fury. Spears are flying, and Dr. Frost is being lowered into a boiling cauldron. Tears are filling my eyes, and I don't want anyone to see them. And suddenly I get a strange urge to run up behind her and jump on her back and scream, "Piggyback ride!" Wham. Her small efficient body tumbles and cracks down on the cobblestones.

"Ouch," she groans.

"Sorry," I say, standing up.

"What were you thinking?" Von Allsberg says.

"My arm is broken," Dr. Frost announces.

"You're faking," I say.

"Afraid not," she says.

We spend hours in a local clinic while they set her arm. It's a clean break. The ulna. Ulna, ulna, I hear Dr. Frost say again and again. A neurologist, Von Allsberg supervises the exam, pricking her fingertips and banging a tuning fork on his shoe and then pressing the cool metal to her elbow and palms. How could a bone break so easily? Lying on the table, in the yellow light of the clinic, she looks old, finally — the way a grandmother should.

Now everything is different. My grandmother can't drive the car — not with a gearshift and a broken right arm. So Dr. Von Allsberg offers to get us back to Copenhagen. We'll spend just a few more days in Germany and Holland. We'll get home early. I'm now stuck in the back seat, where I have to stare at their necks. They talk and laugh and occasionally toss comments back to me like tidbits for a lost dog. Dr. Frost has bumps and creases on her neck — does Dr. Von Allsberg realize? Somewhere along the way, Von Allsberg buys me a doll: an Alpine girl in a dirndl, clutching a little straw basket. I immediately detest her like I detest the ballerinas in my room at home. But I have to admit, she's in a beautiful box. The box is green and has a delicate pattern on it, and is lined with velvet.

Twelve hours ahead of us on the polar route, and we want to make sure Dr. Frost will be as comfortable as possible. There's no doubt her arm is hurting. She takes the window seat so she won't be jostled, and the cast rolls between us with no one's signature on it except mine. I can't wait to get home.

At last we land in Los Angeles. I'm so excited I forget my carry-on bag and have to run back into the plane. Finally, walking out of customs, beaming with my experiences, returning to my homeland, I spot my mother and Roy in the crowd. They are waving, watching our glorious arrival. They are standing with a buggy.

"Mom!" I yell, running to her.

"Hey Annie-girl!" Roy Ransom says, hugging me first.

I get to my mother. I had imagined her grabbing me and squeezing me like there was no tomorrow, but instead she looks strange, an imposter in my mother's clothes. "Mom?"

"Did you change your hair?" she asks me.

"No."

"Mother, your arm!"

"Hello, Helen," Dr. Frost says. "Is this my new granddaughter?"

"Mom, I have a present for you!" I say, digging into my bag.

Everyone's peering into the buggy. I decide to wait on the souvenirs and wiggle in for a look. I see my sister for the first time. She's very small, surrounded by the blankets my mother made. She's wearing the yellow cap I sewed the piping on. I reach in to pick her up.

"No, dear," my mother says. "Not now. She's sleepy. Just leave her there."

I want to hold her.

"Ann, pay attention to your mother," Roy says. "You don't know how to hold her yet."

By then I am holding her just fine. "Percy," I say.

"Let me have her," my mother says.

"Just a second."

"Ann, now."

That's it. I start to run. After carrying my suitcase all over Europe, she's only a tiny bundle.

My mother says, "Wait! Stop!"

It was the beginning of my future, and I had the thought at that moment that there was no one around who would ever understand my version of things. So I darted in and out of the crowd, holding my sister close to me. I heard my mother calling out, and Roy Ransom shouting, "Stop that girl!" But the people I ran by were hurrying off to their own destinations, and no one stood in my way.

After scurrying down a flight of stairs and rounding a few corners, I found a vacant phone booth and closed the two of us in. My sister wasn't frightened. Why should she be? I held her out carefully and looked at her puffy blue eyes. She was staring right at me. Like she really wanted to know who I was. Though she had almost no hair or eyebrows, she looked exactly the way I'd imagined her. She lifted a small fist to her mouth and started sucking on it. "It's me," I taught her. "It's Ann. Ann. Ann."

It was a good thing I was home. My sister was growing up.

SETH MNOOKIN

■

The Nice New Radicals

FROM *Spin*

Less Rage, More Sage

WE LIKE our activists dangerous. We like our revolutionaries to
come armed. We like the radical elements of society to believe in
extremism. Well, most of us, anyway. It's why watching the news
and reading the papers during the weekend of April 21 was so satisfying. For two days, dangerous thugs wreaked havoc in Quebec
City, just as they had recently in Prague, Washington, D.C., and
Seattle. The *Boston Globe* wrote of "hundreds of self-described anarchists and revolutionaries" who unleashed "a hail of rocks, sand-
filled soda bottles, and flaming debris." The *Washington Post* described Quebec's Old City as "a war zone smothered in tear gas
and littered in defiance as thousands of protesters again tore down
the gates that separated them from prime ministers and presi-
dents meeting on the other side."

The occasion hardly seems to matter anymore: the script has
already been written. World leaders gather en masse — to discuss trade barriers, or debt relief, or nation-building — and thousands of young punks greet them with Molotov cocktails and
smashed plate-glass windows. This last time around, the protests
were against something called "the Summit of the Americas," a
meeting of heads of state from everywhere from Canada to Argentina who gathered to discuss the creation of one enormous free

trade zone in the Western Hemisphere. Not the sexiest meeting in the world, granted, but true to form, there were tens of thousands of protesters in Quebec City, from older tree-hugging hippies to a younger assortment of human rights activists. And together they unloosed those rocks and sand-filled bottles, tearing down those gates that separated the leaders from the masses. Right?

Not even close. Most of the thousands of protesters — about 99 percent — marched peacefully, demanding that this or that pet cause get more attention. The violence came courtesy of about two hundred fervent young men (mainly comprising a seemingly ubiquitous group of militant anarchists that calls itself the Black Bloc) who were trying valiantly to rip through barricades, throwing rocks at Royal Canadian Mounties, and reveling in each new tear-gas attack. Since Seattle's World Trade Organization riots in 1999 — the one time when vandals actually did do serious damage, to the tune of $3 million — scenes like this have become almost commonplace, and the articles that follow tend to be either mocking ("These kids are just along for the ride") or starry-eyed ("What passion! What conviction!").

But to get to the real heart of today's activists, you'd do better to put down the papers and stop by a sidewalk table at Manhattan's Caffe Pertutti, where twenty-one-year-old Barnard College student Jessica Coven likes to have lunch. She's wearing a spaghetti-string halter top and faded jeans, talking about what went down up north. "The mainstream media, they only want to cover the violence," she says. "They want the pictures of rocks and broken glass. But that's not what this movement is about."

Coven, the sector contact for the New York/New Jersey chapter of Students for a Free Tibet (SFT), seems very sure about everything, but her verbal mannerisms betray a hint of insecurity. "It's so unfortunate?" she says as she picks through her rotini with olive oil (no cheese, thanks; Coven's been a vegan since she was fourteen years old, when she was inspired by listening to radical hardcore bands such as Earth Crisis and Converge). "People who advocate the use of violence, they're really dangerous to the movement. But you can't dwell on it too much? In solidarity, we have all agreed to use nonviolence."

The Black Bloc anarchists may grab all the headlines, but it's people like Coven who are actually much more representative of today's activists. Noam Chomsky, the MIT linguistics professor and political dissident who has written extensively on "corporate media's" misrepresentation of American society, says, "The standard portrayal [of violent protesters] is so absurd as not to merit comment." Talking about recent protesters' goals, he says, "I could find virtually nothing about their actual concerns [in American media]." Ralph Nader, the longtime consumer advocate and recent Green Party candidate for president, agrees. "The media haven't done these people justice," Nader says, referring to the majority of those who showed up in Quebec City, Washington, D.C., and Seattle before that. "These activists have done their homework, but it's the smashing of windows that gets covered. And then, way down, the press finally gets around to talking about the overwhelming number of demonstrators who were peaceful."

Coven has chosen Tibet as her focal point, but she's conversant and at least nominally active in any number of causes, and she can spit out rote aphorisms with the slightly weary ease of an old pro. Indeed, today's activists are so interconnected that Paul Krassner — longtime editor of the political humor journal the *Realist* and a man who has done everything from editing Lenny Bruce's autobiography to protesting the Vietnam War with Abbie Hoffman and Jerry Rubin — refers to them as the "We Shall Overlap" generation. Krassner also sees the emergence of a much more practical, media-savvy activist culture. "Take the Ruckus Society," he says, referring to the group that runs training camps for people active in all sorts of left-leaning causes. "The stunts they pull are all media-oriented. And at the same time, they're contacting legislators. They know how to get things done."

The Art of "Pragmactivism"
(or: How to Otherwise Bring the Ruckus)

"Welcome to the Ruckus-SFT action camp! Give your name and let us know if you need a sleeping bag, and then go and set up on the hill." Lhadon Tethong, a twenty-five-year-old who is one of five full-time employees of SFT, is greeting the hundred or so college kids (along with a handful of high schoolers) who have committed to spending a week of their winter break in Malibu learning how to be better activists.

Based in Berkeley, California, the Ruckus Society was founded in 1995 by Mike Roselle, a legend in the environmental direct-action movement (in 1987, Roselle hung a banner off the face of Mount Rushmore to protest the government's lax approach to acid rain). While Ruckus does teach left-leaning activists how to stage "direct-action campaigns," the group stresses nonviolence and peaceful civil disobedience. As John Sellars, Ruckus's thirty-four-year-old director, says, "We talk about the fact that we want to build a nonviolent revolution that our parents will want to be a part of. I know that sounds kind of corny, but it's true."

Despite the do-right mission adhered to by the group's founders and followers, Ruckus is often portrayed as a breeding ground for anarchic thugs; indeed, after every Seattle or Quebec City, a new crop of breathless articles appears, each positioning Ruckus as a violent school for the radical fringe. This year's post-demonstration coverage was no different — the *New York Post* ran a headline days after Quebec that read RIOTERS ATTENDED ANARCHY CAMP. A journalist for London's *Daily Mail* wrote a blowsy first-person account that began "How I infiltrated the extremists who have been training London's May Day 'riot commandos.'" But the writer didn't infiltrate anything — he'd been invited to Malibu by Ruckus to learn more about the group.

The carpools continue to arrive throughout the afternoon on this chilly Friday in January, vans making the one-hour trek from the Los Angeles airport to a slightly rundown ranch several miles up in the hills of Malibu; the ranch's owner is donating use of the land for the week. Pulling into a dirt parking lot, the van's doors swing open, and two or three or six teens and twenty-somethings tumble out, bleary-eyed and shy, toting duffel bags stuffed with two-person tents, sleeping bags, and a week's worth of clothes. It feels like freshman orientation, except here, everyone is in the same clique.

Jessica Coven, fresh from a cross-country flight, arrives full of energy, ready to develop new strategies and form new bonds. Some of the hundred-plus campers — about seventy of whom are female — look stereotypically alternative, with tattoos down their forearms and tongue piercings; most, however, look like they could be extras in a Gap commercial. As they straggle toward a check-in table, most of their attention is focused on an ominous-looking scaffolding set up in the back of the parking lot. One of the few boys in attendance, a twenty-year-old from New Jersey, strains to appear nonchalant. "That's tall," he says, struggling not to swallow his Adam's apple.

This particular camp (Ruckus holds about six per year around the country) is cosponsored by SFT, a group whose supporters share sympathies with Tibet-supporting stars like Adam Yauch of the Beastie Boys and Uma Thurman. Other camps have less cachet. In March, Ruckus hosted an "Alternative Spring Break" action camp in Florida, centered on protests against the World Bank; in May, the group met in San Diego for a biotechnology action camp. People who come to Ruckus camps are asked to pay from about $75 to $500 for the week's training, but no one is turned away for lack of funds. (The group survives on a combination of these fees and grants from left-leaning foundations such as the Agape Foundation and the Foundation for Deep Ecology; Ruckus has also received donations from the Turner Foundation.)

Later that night, the volunteer kitchen crew begins what will soon become a ritual: blasting the opening strains of AC/DC's "You Shook Me All Night Long" to announce meals (mostly vegetarian). The following morning, groups of ten and twenty will climb the scaffolding, training for the occasion when they might be called upon to rappel down the Sears Tower or the World Trade Center to unfurl a banner. Other activities include dozens of workshops and seminars and training exercises in such topics as "Urban Climbing Techniques," "Arrest & Court," and "Political Theater." Many of this week's lessons will focus on specific campaigns — against Beijing's bid to host the Olympics, say, or against British Petroleum's investment in a Chinese pipeline into Tibet —

and Ruckus trainers talk about strategies as basic as "public humiliation" and e-mail bombing, which can potentially shut down companies' entire Web sites. Indeed, for the next week, we were going to learn how to be effective instead of merely enraged. Strong opinions, if unaccompanied by focused action, count for nothing in the Ruckus ethos. "I'm not here to just make a lot of noise and go home feeling good about what a great person I am," says Shayna Warshawsky, a sophomore at Boston University. "That's bullshit."

Unlike the activists of the '60s, who championed dropping out and not trusting anyone over thirty, the folks who go through Ruckus's crash courses are taught to work *with* the establishment. The *New York Times* recently wondered if activism has become so mainstream that on college campuses, "rallies and demonstrations are like so many other extracurricular activities." Coven's parents, if not gung-ho for her cause, are fully supportive. She flew to Malibu on their frequent-flier miles, and her dad sports a FREE TIBET bumper sticker on his Mazda Protegé.

This kid-tested, parent-approved support is exactly what Ruckus wants — and Sellars often talks about how ironic it is that the organization gets painted as an extremist group. Take his views on the Earth Liberation Front (ELF), the marauding band of arsonists that gained notoriety by torching a planned development site in Long Island, New York, earlier this year and a ski resort in Vail, Colorado, in 1998. The Vail fire, which caused $12 million in damage, was set to protest a planned development that would infringe on a lynx habitat. Its effect, however, was to solidify community sentiment on the side of the developers, and a restaurant that was destroyed in the blaze was rebuilt — four thousand square feet larger. "At the end of the day, did they save any lynx?" Sellars asks. "Did they get more political support? No, they didn't. They did the opposite."

Craig Rosebraugh, spokesman for the North American Earth Liberation Front, disagrees. He points out that ELF's use of "illegal direct action" in the form of "economic sabotage" has caused more than $40 million in damage to entities that are profiting off the natural environment. And by doing so, he says, the ELF has not only crippled the enemy, it's also raised awareness of the problem. "Ruckus definitely has a nonviolence philosophy that is different from the ELF's," Rosebraugh says. "They use civil disobedience and different sorts of tactics to achieve media attention and public education. But I think on their own, those tactics are not going to progress any social movement at this point in time in our society."

It's true, of course, that breaking stuff leads to breaking news, but Ruckus tries hard to stay on the positive side of the op-eds. It's not for nothing that each camp includes a four-hour session on "Media Training" that teaches, among other things, the best time to schedule a protest for maximum TV coverage (around noon) and provides a crash course in writing sound-bite-ready press releases. In Malibu, about seventy students gather under a gazebo for a lesson in political PR from Ruckus trainer Celia Alario, a friendly, thirty-something woman with thick curls of brown hair. "Whenever I'm planning an action," Alario says, "I call up my dad and read him my talking points. I want to make sure he can relate to them, that he gets what I'm trying to say."

As Alario talks, a group of girls huddle around a newly acquired heat lamp for warmth; the temperature has dropped below freezing, and it's raining outside. The Ruckus staff, to keep morale up, has begun staging skits about the importance of washing hands and keeping warm. For the first few days there are no showers available, and the students are left scrubbing themselves in the sinks and lathering on the deodorant. At night campers pull on multiple wool caps to fend off the cold, and every morning at seven, Annapurna Astley unsheathes her shrill bagpipes as a primal alarm clock. Astley, a recent Harvard grad, teaches at the Kashi Ashram at Florida's River School; she first hooked up with Ruckus when they held a camp on the ashram's site last year.

Following the bagpipes and a mushy breakfast, Coven and I join about forty other students at a "nonviolence training session." The seminar is led by two twenty-something women, both of whom are sporting overalls: Sprout, who has purple hair, and Moj. Heads nod as Sprout talks about "repressive, nonconsensual" power relationships, "like those between bosses and workers." Someone suggests adding "parents and children" to the list.

"Good thinking, good example," Sprout says.

"Right on," agrees Moj.

After the session, as she scans the group of students lining up for lunch, Coven tries to explain why such an "ordinary" — her word — group of people is so involved in issues that don't directly affect their lives. At the same time, and without realizing it, she's explaining the ideology that separates Ruckus devotees from the more widely photographed angry young men.

"People nowadays are up on what's happening in the world," she says. "Politicians just aren't doing anything. So all these groups — these groups that basically want global justice, that want powerful institutions to stop harming people that don't have as much power — are getting together and learning how to work together and force change."

Like in June 1999: John Hocevar, the head of SFT, and Han Shan, the Ruckus program director, hung a banner on the World Bank protesting the bank's possible funding of a Chinese project that would relocate thousands of Chinese into Tibet. A shot of the banner made it onto the front pages of several papers, including the *Washington Post,* but the action didn't stop at flashy signs. While hanging from the building, SFT leaders were negotiating for a sit-down with World Bank executives, and they got exactly that, as soon as Hocevar and Shan came down. World Bank president James Wolfensohn showed up; a year later, in July 2000, when the project came up for review, the bank voted it down.

"That's what we're doing," Coven says. "That's what we're *learning* how to do: force change."

All You Need Is Love (and Maybe a Bunny)

"Bobby, do you want to have sex?" Back in New York, Coven is kneeling in the corner of her dorm room. Bobby is Coven's pet rabbit, and he has a habit of humping an eighteen-inch-high rubber ball that Coven keeps in her room. She tries not to touch the ball if she doesn't need to.

Julia Butterfly Hill, whose two years spent living atop a Northern California redwood to protest destructive logging practices was chronicled in the movie *Butterfly*, says people like Coven are becoming more prevalent, and that they're the ones poised to make changes in the world. "It's easy to be angry, it's easy to just strike out," she says. "But it's a whole other thing to find the courage to be respectful, to be realistic, and to have these components in your activism."

Coven and her SFT comrades are currently looking to put pressure on corporations that do business with China, and they're busy planning ways to highlight China's human rights abuses to thwart the country's attempt to land the 2008 Summer Olympics. But right now, she has to finish up a paper — on Chinese history, natch — and then make the hour-long trek to her Tibetan boyfriend Tinley's apartment in the Bronx.

"You know, I feel like I couldn't be with someone who wasn't socially conscious," she says, although she admits that she and Tinley don't always agree on the best course of action in Tibet. Coven is an absolutist: she believes that Tibet must be wholly independent from China. Tinley, whose family lives in exile in India, supports a more moderate position in favor of autonomy for the Tibetan people. But they don't let it affect the relationship.

"It's okay," Coven says. "It's not something we're gonna *fight* over. We need to be realistic about it."

■

Local Hipster Overexplaining
Why He Was at the Mall

FROM *The Onion*

LOUISVILLE, KY. — Anders Larsen, known within Louisville hip-
ster circles as the bassist for Superfly Snuka and a contributing
music reviewer for the underground 'zine *Gun Shy,* spent several
hours Monday overexplaining why he was at Jefferson Mall over
the weekend.

"You know I normally wouldn't be caught dead in some corporate suburban hellhole like that," the twenty-four-year-old Larsen
told friends at Jack's Wax, an independent record store he fre-
quents. "But I was out near Jefferson Mall because I had to get a
new air filter for my car, and they're about five bucks cheaper at
that Crown Auto over there. Then, I got to thinking how my dad's
birthday's coming up, and I should probably get him something. I
figured I'd try the mall, since it's got tons of the kind of stupid crap
he likes.

"I can't believe I actually set foot in that place," added Larsen,
posting a flier for his band's upcoming gig in the Jack's Wax window. "If not for my dad and his dorko taste, I wouldn't have gone
within fifty miles of that den of lameness."

After briefly browsing B. Dalton, the Sunglass Hut, and Came-
lot Music for something for his father, Larsen said he became so
disgusted with "the unbelievable mainstreamness of it all" that he

couldn't bring himself to spend money at any of the stores. Giving up on finding a gift, Larsen decided to explore some of the mall's other outlets, "just as a joke."

He eventually wound up buying himself a silver-chain pocket watch, a purchase he spent nearly twenty minutes justifying to his fellow scenesters.

"I was walking around, just laughing my ass off at all the stores, when I decided to go into this place called the Wild Side, which is pretty much the lamest of them all," Larsen said. "It had all these 'leather' biker jackets that were made out of plastic, not to mention all this other cheesy, wanna-be-punk stuff. You know, poseur shit for the suburban rebel.

"But then, just as I was about to end my 'walk on the Wild Side,' I saw in a display case this German silver pocket watch, which, by some miracle, was actually kind of cool," Larsen continued. "Plus, it was on clearance for really cheap. Honestly, though, I only got it because I needed a new watch. I think my other one's about to break. It's been running really slow. Otherwise, I never would have given a penny to those losers."

While at the mall, Larsen also purchased a stainless steel coffee thermos from Williams-Sonoma, a copy of *Star Wars: Episode One* "because the movie was so bad, it's hilarious," and the Playstation game *Ape Escape*, which Larsen says is impossible to find used.

According to Rick Caras, Larsen's roommate and bandmate, this is not the first time he has overexplained a brush with mainstream culture.

"Last week, I noticed a Kid Rock CD on Anders's shelf, and I was like, 'Anders, you own a fuckin' Kid Rock CD?'" Caras said. "Well, I got this twenty-minute saga about how he bought it for his little brother, who's into that kind of rap-metal junk, but his brother already had it, so he was going to return it. But then he ended up opening it, just to hear that one stupid 'Bawitdaba' song that he heard on WTFX once — not that he ever listens to that 'shitty-ass corporate-rock station,' but he happened to be in a gas station when it came on and became 'entranced by its profound patheticness.'"

Among the other items Larsen has overexplained recently: how he knows who Keri Russell is, why he ate at Bennigan's, what he is doing with an *Entertainment Weekly* subscription, and why he saw the movie *Keeping the Faith.*

■

Marilyn Manson Now Going Door-to-Door Trying to Shock People

FROM *The Onion*

OVERLAND PARK, KAN. — Stung by flagging album sales and Eminem's supplanting him as Middle America's worst nightmare, shock rocker Marilyn Manson has embarked on a door-to-door tour of suburbia in a desperate, last-ditch effort to shock and offend average Americans.

Accompanied by bandmates Twiggy Ramirez, Madonna Wayne Gacy, and Zim Zum, Manson kicked off his fifty-city "Boo" tour January 26 in Overland Park, a conservative, middle-class suburb of Kansas City.

"When we first laid eyes on Overland Park, with its neat little frame houses, immaculately landscaped lawns, and SUVs in the driveways, we couldn't wait to swoop down on it like the Black Death," said Manson, born Brian Warner in Canton, Ohio. "We were like, 'Welcome to our nightmare, you bloated, pustulent pigs.'"

Last Friday at 4 P.M., Mark Wesley, forty-six, a resident of Overland Park's exclusive Maple Bluff subdivision, heard the sound of "animal-like shrieking" coming from the vicinity of his front lawn. Upon opening his front door, he was greeted by the sight of a pale and shirtless Manson carving a pentagram into his chest with a razor blade.

"Look at me, suburban dung," Manson told Wesley. "Does this shock you?"

When Wesley replied no, he said Manson became "petulant." Recalled Wesley: "He started stamping his feet and shaking his fists, saying, 'What do you mean, no? Aren't your uptight, puritanical sensibilities offended? Don't you want to censor me so you don't have to confront the ugly truth I represent?' So I say, 'Well, not particularly.' Then, after a long pause, he says, 'Well, screw you, jerk!' and walks off sulking."

That evening, Linda Schmidt was preparing to drive her daughter Alyssa to a Girl Scouts meeting when she found Manson standing on her porch draped in sheep entrails.

"I knew who he was, but I was kind of busy and didn't really have time to chat," Schmidt said. "He just kept standing there staring at me, expecting me to react in some way."

Added Schmidt: "I tried to be nice and humor him a little. I said, 'Yessiree, that sure is some shocking satanic imagery, no doubt about it. And that one eye with no color in the pupil, very disturbing. I'd sure like to suppress that.' I mean, what do you say to Marilyn Manson?"

A deflated Manson remained on Schmidt's porch as she and Alyssa drove off.

Subsequent attempts to provoke outrage were met with equal indifference.

"[Manson] was standing at my front door wearing those fake breasts he wore on the cover of *Mechanical Animals*," retiree Judith Hahn said. "He said, 'My name is Marilyn Manson, and I'm here to tear your little world apart.' I thought he was collecting for the Kiwanis food drive, so I gave him some cans of pumpkin pie filling."

Undaunted, Manson and his entourage stepped up their assault on mainstream American sensibilities. On Tuesday they arrived in the tiny Detroit suburb of Grosse Pointe Farms, where stockbroker Glenn Binford answered his doorbell to find Manson hanging upside-down on a wooden cross as Ramirez performed fellatio on him.

"I just stood there thinking, now there's a boy who tries way too hard," Binford said. "I mean, come on: homoerotic sacrilege went out in the late '90s."

Other provocative acts by Manson — including dismembering a chicken, bathing in pig's blood, and wearing a three-piece suit of human noses — failed to arouse anyone's ire, instead prompting comments such as "sophomoric," "trite," and "so Alice Cooper."

Manson's lone brush with controversy occurred in Edina, Minnesota, a suburb of Minneapolis. An unidentified Neighborhood Watch volunteer phoned police after seeing a nude, feces-smeared Manson being led around on a leash by a dwarf dominatrix. Officers arrived on the scene, but let Manson go with a warning for parading without a city permit.

"I could have given him a citation, but I figured, how much harm is he really causing?" Edina police officer Dan Herberger said. "I mean, he's just Marilyn Manson, for the love of Mike."

The "Boo" tour was dealt a further blow when Manson learned that Eminem's *The Marshall Mathers LP* had been banned from all K-mart stores. Manson's current album, *Holy Wood (In the Shadow of the Valley of Death),* is still available.

"Why are all you people outraged by Eminem? He's not scary!" Manson said. "He doesn't sport ghoulishly pale skin or wear gender-bending makeup. He's just some regular guy. I'm the one who people should be terrified by, not him! Me!

"If you ban me," Manson continued, "I promise to rail against censorship and hypocrisy. Please? Pretty, pretty please?"

By Monday the tour appeared to have lost all momentum. Sources close to Manson described him as "exhausted and discouraged," despite not having even completed the first leg of the three-month tour. By the time he arrived in Hoffman Estates, Illinois, Manson had resorted to leaving flaming bags of dog feces on doorsteps and shining a flashlight under his chin to make himself look "spooky." He was ultimately chased from a Hoffman Estates subdivision by a group of bicycle-riding teenagers who

advised him to "get [his] chalk-white goblin ass" out of their neighborhood.

On Friday, Manson is slated to appear in Bethesda, Maryland,
where many believe he will bring his tour to a premature end.

"Have you people forgotten already?" Manson told the *Washington Post*. "You all thought I was responsible for Columbine two
years ago. Well, I was! I was! I know I vehemently denied it at the
time, but really, I personally told those two kids to shoot up the
school. I'm serious. I sent them an e-mail. And I told them to wor-
ship Satan, too. You hear that, kids? Marilyn Manson says you
should shoot your friends in the head with a gun! And everyone
should eat babies! And rape their dead grandparents! And poop on
a church! There, now will someone please be offended?"

■

Journal of a New COBRA Recruit

FROM McSweeneys.net

May 1, 1986
Man. I'm so excited to graduate this month. It's been a fun few weeks, signing yearbooks and going to beer parties and such, but at the same time I keep feeling worried about what I'm going to do afterwards. I don't have the grades for college. Heck, when I talked to the army recruiter about becoming a GI, he said I don't even have the grades to serve my country. I sure don't want to work at the gas station like my brother.

May 2, 1986
Today this guy in a blue uniform came up and gave me a pamphlet. Said he was a recruiter for COBRA, an outfit a lot like the army but without all those government regulations to slow down the fun. We talked a little and he said he liked the cut of my jib, thought I'd be great COBRA material.

May 15, 1986
Signed up with COBRA today. I got real excited when they said I earned a signing bonus . . . figured it would be a couple hundred bucks that I could put toward a new bumper for my truck. Nope. Just a T-shirt with a funny-looking snake on the front. And I'm not supposed to wear it in public. Pretty weird stuff, but they seem like nice guys.

I report to COBRA boot camp out in Utah in the middle of June. The recruiter guy said that everyone around there thinks it's where some crazy old Mormon lives with all his wives. I'm not supposed to say anything about it to anyone. I'm supposed to tell Mom and Dad that I'm going off to work for the phone company.

June 16, 1986
First day of boot camp was a bear. All of the other boots seem like nice guys. Don't know what any of them look like because the first thing they did when we got here was give us blue helmets with black hankies to cover up our faces. I'm getting pretty good at recognizing people's eyebrows though.

Figured we'd do a lot of exercise today, but we didn't do as much as I thought. Mostly just running out of a door and yelling "CO-BRA!" at the top of our lungs. I got pretty good at it. Now I can sound awful scary when I yell "COBRA!" You wouldn't think it would wear you down, but boy, am I pooped.

June 18, 1986
Boot camp's still a lot of fun. And I'm learning a lot. Today we did more mental learning stuff than exercise. We received a lecture about our main enemy, the GI Joe team. Seems that Uncle Sam is so nervous about COBRA that he set up an elite team of soldiers just to try to fight us. I couldn't be more proud. I had no idea I was signing on with a bunch that was this important. I guess the Joes have stopped us at pretty much everything we've ever tried to do. But believe me, is that going to change now that Steve Loring is a member of COBRA!

Sarge said all kinds of funny things about how dumb the GI Joe team is. Like, they just have one person who's good at each thing they do. So they just have one guy who can fly a plane, and one guy who knows how to drive a tank, one guy who can fly a helicopter, one guy who can fight in the desert, and so on. They even have a whole aircraft carrier (for their one plane and one helicopter) with just a captain and one sailor to run it! Sarge was like, "What the heck kind of outfit is that?" and we were all just in stitches. Then this one recruit (I think it was Renfro, but I didn't get a good look at his eyebrows) says, "But if they're so dumb, how come they always beat us?"

Sarge made Renfro go out and run around the track and yell "COBRA!" for an hour.

June 20, 1986
Real boring day. I was all ready for some more physical training, but instead Sarge led us into a room full of phones and made us cold-call people and ask them if they wanted to switch their long distance to COBRA. During the break, Renfro asked Sarge when we became a long-distance provider. Sarge explained that we had to do something to make money if we were going to afford a private army with hundreds of tanks and planes and a Terrordome, not to mention all the expenses from the Serpentor genetic engineering project. Working the phones was demoralizing, and people were usually pretty mad when we called them, but it felt good to be doing my duty for COBRA. In between calls, I amused myself by thinking of cool one-liners I could say if I ever got the drop on one of those GI Joe bums.

June 21, 1986
Awful exciting day today. First we got to do our airborne training. They loaded us up into a plane, and we flew up and then jumped out. Our chutes had the big, scary COBRA symbol on them. It was awesome. But it was hard, because we were supposed to keep yelling "COBRA!" all the way down. It was tough to get enough breath to yell right at first. Sarge says it just takes practice.

After that we finally got to do weapons training. About time! They gave me a rifle and pointed at the target. I held the rifle up to my cheek and sighted down the barrel, just like I did when I went deer hunting with Grampa. Boy, did Sarge go apeshit over that! Got in my face and started yelling at me, asking how I expected to scare someone if I just stood there all quiet-like and shot so carefully. Sarge is a great teacher because he doesn't just criticize. He showed the right way to shoot. What you do is you start shooting your gun wildly and run towards the target as fast as you can, and in your scariest voice you yell "COBRA!" We worked on that all afternoon, and just before we broke for dinner, I actually hit the target! Sarge and everyone else were so happy for me that they were about to cry. Told me I'd just set the record for marksmanship in COBRA boot camp. I wanted to call Mom and tell her the good news, but she thinks I work for the phone company.

June 22, 1986
First payday. No check, just a couple more of those T-shirts. Doughty and me planned to drive into town and sell the shirts for spending money, but Sarge caught wind of our plan, reminding us that we weren't supposed to let anyone see the T-shirts because then they'd know we were in COBRA.

June 25, 1986
Tank training today! Wow, it was great! They didn't let us drive the HISS tanks ourselves, but we got to practice riding in the back turret and working the guns. By now we all knew what we were supposed to do without being told, and Sarge said he was so proud at the way we all just yelled "COBRA!" and shot wildly before he even showed us how.

Renfro tried to ruin the day with a whole bunch of his questions. First he asked Sarge why our combat fatigues were sky blue, saying we're visible from a mile away at least. Then, when we were practicing with the HISS tanks, Renfro started in on why the HISS driver wasn't protected by anything more than a piece of glass. And for that matter, he continued, why do we run the guns from an open turret with no protection at all? Sarge just about blew up.

I think Renfro's going to be running around the track and yelling "COBRA!" for a long, long time tonight.

RODNEY ROTHMAN

■

My Fake Job

FROM *The New Yorker*

I DON'T SMOKE, but I still take a cigarette break every day at four o'clock. I stand there and let the cigarette burn down. I pretend to inhale, lightly, so I don't trigger a coughing fit. The office smokers never notice; they're too busy complaining about their newly worthless stock options, or how the latest reorg left them with a job title they don't even understand, like "resource manager." I never speak up, because there is a crucial difference between my colleagues and me: I was never hired to work at this company.

I don't have stock options here. I don't have a job title here. *I don't have a job here.* A few weeks ago, I just walked into the office.

It was the first Internet office I'd ever seen. It takes up five floors of an old warehouse in downtown Manhattan's Silicon Alley. No one stopped me when I came in. The sense of transience was overpowering. Hundreds of employees worked at identical workstations. They sat in thousand-dollar ergonomic office chairs, but their nameplates were made with paper and Magic Marker. The message was clear: the chairs could be resold; the employees were expendable.

Twenty-five-year-olds in T-shirts and cutoff fatigues pinballed from computer monitor to coffee machine, staring at their feet. Scattered desks were unoccupied because of April's NASDAQ implosion. It struck me that somebody could easily just start showing up for work at this office. Sitting at an empty desk, minding his own business, he would never be noticed.

DAY 1, 10:30 A.M.: I recently left a sixty-hour-a-week job so I could have more free time and do freelance writing. It hasn't been going well. I have no free time, because I'm always trying to write. I get no writing done, because I'm always wasting time. What counts as wasting time? How about dozing off midday while reading *InStyle*? How about spending six hours deciding how best to spend six hours?

The building's lobby is a gray expanse of faux marble, sucking up daylight. There's no security guard. A small group of people wait for the elevator and sip iced coffee. Standing among them, I feel like a CIA operative, albeit one who scares easily and is wearing Teva sandals.

I spent the early part of the morning concocting a false identity. I decided that I had just been transferred from the company's satellite office in Chicago (I'd read about it on the Web site). Then I selected a fake job title. The more I thought about it, the more I liked the sound of "junior project manager." It seemed vague, perfect for flying under the radar.

The elevator empties into an airy loft, filled with desks. In front of me, a young receptionist is talking on the telephone. I try to look distracted, as if I were junior-managing a project deep inside my mind. I see her staring at me, but her face registers no concern. She turns back to her phone conversation, and I walk in undisturbed.

I have no idea where to go. I follow everyone down a hallway and into a bustling kitchenette. The kitchenette is spacious and revolves around a large common table that nobody sits at. There is a communal refrigerator stocked with a dozen brands of soft drink, but I take a sodium-free seltzer. I have never, ever liked seltzer. Everyone loads up on caffeine and moves on. People clutch mugs that say "Omnitech" or "Digitalgroup.com" instead of those "You Want It When?" Dogbert ones.

I drift freely around the office. It's like a campaign headquarters without buttons. The workstations are low to the ground and clustered in fours. Everyone is on the phone. I see a man in his forties with bare feet up on his desk. I see nose studs. Nobody looks at me twice. After a few laps around the office, I decide I've worked hard enough for today. As I walk out, I turn to the receptionist and say, "See you tomorrow."

DAY 2, 10:50 A.M.: There is a different receptionist today, and I walk by her too quickly to notice anything interesting. Everything feels different today, in a bad way. Back in the kitchenette, I take another repulsive sodium-free seltzer. It's now part of my office routine. Then I see a sign-up sheet posted on a bulletin board: FEELING STRESSED? JOIN US FOR LUNCHTIME YOGA!

It's too much to resist. I sign "Mike Kramer." As I finish, I realize someone is behind me, looking over my shoulder. "You don't have to sign up, you know," she says. "Only, like, four of us go."

I turn around. She's pretty, of course, even in harsh fluorescent lighting. The collar of her blouse is charmingly askew. I briefly imagine us doing downward dog pose on adjacent mats. Her name is Katie. (Actual names have been changed.) "Are you new here?" she asks.

"I've been here a week," I say. "I transferred from the Chicago satellite office."

I realize that employees my age probably don't use bland corporate-speak like "satellite office." "I'm a junior project manager," I add.

"Really?" she says. "I'm a project manager. What projects do you work on?"

It occurs to me now that I could have been more prepared. Perhaps I could have *learned what this company does.*

"I'm still finishing up Chicago projects." I begin shifting from foot to foot. Katie asks me where I live, and I tell her, "Downtown, with friends."

"No," she laughs, "where do you live *here*?"

"I, uh, don't have a desk yet," says the brilliant junior project manager, having worked for a week in an office with fifty empty desks.

* * *

DAY 2, 10:53 A.M.: I introduce myself to the receptionist. My thinking is that if I get her on my side, I'll be able to come and go as I please. Her name is Donna. "Nice to meet you, Donna," I say. "I'm Rodney Rothman." I immediately realize my mistake and panic. I've been here for three minutes and I've managed to establish two separate false identities, one of which is technically my real identity.

"Rodney, have you met Lisa yet?" she asks, motioning to a sturdy woman in a cardigan chatting ten feet away from us.

"Yes," I lie.

"Good. So you got an ID card?"

"Yes," I lie.

"Good. You'll need that after six." Donna's phone is ringing, and she's not picking it up.

"Do you have an extension yet?"

"They haven't given me one."

"And that's R-o-d-n-e-y?"

"Actually . . . it's Randy."

"Randy Rothman?"

"Ronfman. R-o-n-f."

Donna writes my name down on a pad of paper. Donna's phone is ringing. She's not picking it up. *Pick it up. Pick it up.* Donna extends her hand toward my sweaty palm. "Welcome to the office, Randy."

DAY 3: "Randy" is taking a much-needed personal day from fake work. I'm at an afternoon Yankee game with my friend Jay. Like many of my friends, Jay can't believe I'm really doing this; he regards me with a mixture of awe and concern. Jay was recently let go by an Internet startup. In between pitches and beers, he explains things like production tools and C++. Jay tells me that some of his former colleagues are continuing to go to work, even though they're not getting paid anymore.

Last night I checked out Web sites for some of the hundreds of Web consulting companies like mine. I learned about maximizing my knowledge system. I boned up on branding, decision support, and integrated E-solution deployment. Now, as I watch Tino Martinez take batting practice, I relate to his work ethic. We are strivers. We are brothers. We are improving our skill sets.

DAY 4, 7 P.M.: I ride up in the elevator with a tiny West Indian security guard in a heavy wool uniform. I'd like to see him try to wrestle me to the ground. I remember too late that the office is locked after six, but it doesn't matter. The guard swipes his own card and *holds the door open for me.*

I've always liked offices during the fringe hours, early morning and in the evening. It's liberating to spend peaceful time in a place that's normally frantic. To me, the sound of a night cleaning crew is like a rolling country stream.

The office is quiet and freshly mopped. I walk around and shop for my desk. It's hard to tell which desks are unoccupied. Some people refrain entirely from decorating their workspace. That way, they can pack up and leave quickly when the axe comes down. Other desks are decorated lavishly, although I can think of harsher words to describe a green plastic M&M playing a trumpet.

I hop from desk to desk. I sit in each chair, maximizing, deploying, wanting it to feel right. I finally select a desk at the end of a large room with thirty workstations. It's well situated, facing the entire room, with nobody in back of me. It has an operational computer, perfect for taking notes. I put my feet up and close my eyes, thinking of rolling country streams.

DAY 5, 10 A.M.: There's no seltzer in the kitchenette this morning. I have to take a Fresca, a beverage I loathe. It's a bad omen, considering what I have to do: sit down at my new workstation in front of an office full of employees.

I'm purposeful as I steam through the place, steering around bodies and desks. Nobody looks up. I reach my chair and sit down. I wait. I let out a loud sigh. I scan the room. Everyone is typing or on the phone. Two women in their early twenties huddle at a desk, eating breakfast and talking: "But what if I worked six hours on one, three on the other . . . I don't know, that's just what *they* told me to do."

Whoever *they* are, I don't see them. Nobody acknowledges me. The office has swallowed me up without a burp.

DAY 5, NOON: The phone rings. My imagination gets the better of me. I picture a squadron of security guards mobilizing upstairs. ATF agents clamber through air ducts, closing off my available exits. I wonder whether Teva sandals would cushion a twelve-story fall. I answer the phone. "This is Randy?"

"Randy. It's Donna."

I consider grabbing a spare rubber band for self-defense.

"Just confirming your extension."

"This is it."

"Great. Let me know if you need anything."

"Okay."

I know what I need. I need to take a break. I need to go outside and pretend to smoke a cigarette.

DAY 5, 6 P.M.: Today I followed a strict schedule of affectation. Every three minutes: stare dreamily into the distance. Every five minutes: flamboyantly rub eyes or chin, or tap finger thoughtfully on upper lip. Every ten minutes: make eye contact with someone across the room and nod in empathy. Every fifteen minutes: fill cheeks with air, then exhale while making a quiet *puh-puh-puh-puh* noise.

I take a beverage break every half-hour. Consequently, a bathroom break every hour. Establishing my own hourly bathroom routine within the pre-established routines of my coworkers is crucial to assimilation.

My small-talk break in the kitchenette was supposed to be every two hours, but sometimes I skipped it because of nerves. A small-talk break is a massive endeavor of strategizing. Every word is premeditated. A perfectly executed small-talk break goes like this:

> ME: How crazy is this coffee machine?
> WOMAN IN KITCHENETTE: Ha-ha, I know.

ME: It tastes like General Foods International Coffees.
WOMAN: Does it? Ha-ha.
ME: Ha-ha.

I've been at my desk for eight hours, and it already feels like home.

DAY 6, 8:45 A.M.: I came in early to beat the rush. The only other person here is a guy my age in a Mr. Bubble T-shirt. He sits under a large dry-erase board with an acronym-laden flowchart labeled "The Closed Loop Process." I'm noticing things I didn't yesterday, like the abandoned fire extinguisher on the floor next to my desk, and the office in the converted warehouse across the street, which looks nearly identical to this one. I find myself faintly bored, waiting for all the people to come in so I can act like I'm ignoring them.

DAY 6, 2 P.M.: When you work in a room with twenty other people, talking on the phone can be tricky. Every word you say can be heard and digested. It doesn't take much mental calculus for your neighbor to decipher the other end of the conversation. You learn to maximize your deployment of pronouns: "I got it . . . She said that? . . . Send me it before you do that with them there." Or you can be like the Mr. Bubble T-shirt guy and try to whisper inaudibly. His whisper was pretty audible this morning: "It's like, 'We're a news aggregator! We're a portal! We're a B2B thingy! Let's buy UPI!' *Total lack of focus!*"

My phone calls fall into three categories. Most of them are straight-up personal. I don't feel bad about this, because I believe that my colleagues would be more suspicious of me if I didn't spend half the day calling friends and family. Other phone calls relate to my real professional life: agents, other writers, etc. Because I work mostly in television, it's easy to make these calls sound Internet-related. I just use the word *network* as much as possible. My favorite phone calls are the ones that relate to my fake job. I set these up in advance by asking a few friends to call me. These calls make no sense at all, on either end, but they make me look busy.

"This is Randy."

"Randy, it's, uh, Kurt, at LogiDigiTekResources dot com, dot, uh, org."

"Hey, Kurt. The links are all crapped out. I think we need to check the URL again."

"Rodney, do I talk technical on this end, too?"

"Ha-ha-ha, Kurt. Good idea. I'll check that through with client services."

"Does it even matter what I say? Blah blah blah, la la la."

"Perfect. Cc. that to me. G'bye."

It all adds to the noise: the voices, the ringing, the hum of the air-conditioning, the clicking of heels on wood.

DAY 7, 7 P.M.: The Girl with Long Brown Hair has bar graphs on her computer. Bar graphs! I can see her through the glass partition next to my workstation. When I go to the bathroom, she looks up and says "Hi." Dear *Penthouse:* Every so often, she leans back in frustration, and her tailored white dress shirt tightens against her chest.

I generally avoid interoffice romances, but it's different when you're a guy working at an office without an actual job. As I think about the Girl with Long Brown Hair, though, a discomfort settles in. I increasingly feel that I've taken refuge in a self-constructed crappy high-concept movie. I picture us having a secret tryst. Then my conscience gets the better of me, and I tell her about my scam. She storms out, of course. I follow her down to Tampa, to the regional meeting. I stand on the conference room table with flowers and tap shoes, singing "My Cherie Amour." Then she forgives me, we embrace, an updated version of "My Cherie Amour" by the Goo Goo Dolls kicks in, the credits roll, and we thank the Toronto Chamber of Commerce.

Enough. I pack up my laptop and go home.

DAY 8, 10 A.M.: I ride up on the elevator with a fortyish-looking guy. He goes to five, I go to twelve.

"Morning," he says.

"Morning," I say.

Getting into the spirit of it, I add, "Hot one out there."
This is going great. He responds, "You work on twelve?"
"Yeah."
"What are you guys doing up there?"
"Uh . . . I have no idea."
He nods in understanding. He's been there. We hit floor five, and he steps off.
"Have a good one," he shouts over his shoulder.

DAY 8, 11:30 A.M.: The Man in the Blue Oxford Shirt is glaring. Every time he walks across the office, he fires a double-take at me. I have a premonition that he will be the dark agent of my downfall here. The Man in the Blue Oxford Shirt is doughy, with thinning, shiny hair. You get the feeling that his body type went from baby fat to middle-aged paunch all at once. He looks so ill at ease, I wonder whether he's a fake employee, too.

The Red-Haired Lady worries me even more. She's one of the older staff members. The more silent and inoffensive I am, the more I seem to threaten her. She probably thinks I'm an Ivy League consultant, here to observe her and weed her out. I see her reflection in the window whenever she creeps behind me. We've developed a little tango, she and I. She cranes her neck to look at my computer screen, and I lower my shoulder to block her view of my notes. Her oversized eyeglasses make me feel like I'm being cased by Sally Jessy Raphael.

DAY 8, 4 P.M.: While taking a cigarette break today, I meet a colleague named Lawrence, one of what seems like five hundred guys in my office who wear black nerd-chic eyeglasses. Lawrence says that his office responsibilities have recently been expanded beyond what he was hired for.
"What were you hired for?" I ask.
"Overseeing office support programs."
"What kind of programs?"
Lawrence takes a big drag off his cigarette. "Mostly Wellness."

* * *

DAY 9, 11:30 A.M.: Today I'm decorating my desk with whimsical junk I bought in a Sixth Avenue Chinese variety store. I arrange it precisely on the desk surface. On the right are two filthy pieces of rubber fruit: a smiling orange and a frowning pineapple. On the left is a pirated Winnie-the-Pooh figurine, for a touch of approach-ability. Last, I add a plastic Virgin Mary clock, to make sure I'm not too approachable. Nothing puts people off like the promise of spontaneous sermonizing. I figure the clock alone has added three days to my stay here. At the end of the day, I put a labeled personal item in the communal fridge. Hint: it was brewed in Latrobe, PA.

DAY 10, 7 P.M.: The Girl with Long Brown Hair is working late, so I am, too. A few minutes ago her boss was down here, standing over her, pacing. I struggled to hear what he was saying, but could make out only a few phrases and an undertone of irritation:

"Are you doing all this in Photoshop? I want to do it in Quark . . . There's no dialogue happening . . . Someone should go down to Staples and get this really sticky double-sided tape . . . We have to put this out."

Before he exited, he must have sensed that he was acting like an Old Economy jerk boss, because he turned and said, "You know, you don't have to do this tonight."

"Good." She laughed. "I have dinner plans."

"Groovy. Bye, sweetie!"

She packs up her handbag and walks up the steps. I watch her go, and stay another hour, glad I'm not a guy who says "groovy" or "bye, sweetie."

DAY 11, NOON: When I get back from lunch, there is a meeting of at least thirty staff members in the big conference room. Why am I not part of the company's knowledge-management system?

I work the resentment out through my work: an afternoon spent devising ways to deceive the increasingly menacing Red-Haired Lady. First I open up a Microsoft Excel spreadsheet docu-ment on my computer. I've never used a spreadsheet before, but I have no problem filling it in with random numbers. Whenever I see the Red-Haired Lady's reflection in the window, I click from my word-processor file to the spreadsheet file, drumming my fingers distractedly on the mouse. My only concern is that she'll think I'm auditing her expense reports and go on the warpath.

I also draw a meaningless flowchart, labeled "Starwood Project," on a legal pad, and leave it out on my desk to give me management credibility. I invent some acronyms, box them, and connect them with arrows. Then I write "August 2001" in big letters underneath, and underline it three times. This lets her know that I am very much on schedule, whatever it is that I am doing.

DAY 11, 5:30 P.M.: This afternoon, a group of middle-aged men show up in our work area and go from desk to desk talking to employees. Everyone looks terrified. I don't notice that they're approaching my desk until it's too late. "How are ya?" says one with swept-back hair. "Don't mind us, we're just taking a tour." I focus as hard as possible on my spreadsheet. My fingers dance a John Bonham solo on the mouse.

A member of the tour group speaks up: "Can I ask you a question?"

"Go right ahead."

"Is it true that there's massages on this floor?"

"That is true." And it is. Scattered throughout the office are fliers advertising "Back Massage by Melissa!" It's all part of chain-smoking Lawrence's Wellness empire. I've been building up the nerve to get one for days.

"Oh," the man says, already snickering. "Which floor has body piercing?"

The whole tour group explodes with laughter. I join in cautiously, then enthusiastically when I see that the tour group has begun riding the wave of hilarity to the next room.

"Take care, now," the man with the swept-back hair says, still laughing.

DAY 12, 10 A.M.: It's my twelfth day here, and the anonymity, once a pleasure, has become maddening. I feel a bubbling, reckless desire to make my existence known. Maybe that's why I've started signing my name to every sign-up sheet I see. Today I signed up for a charity walk. Yesterday I signed one labeled "May the E-Force Be with You."

Day 12, 2 p.m.: This week, Lawrence and Team Wellness posted the first two pages of *Moby-Dick* by the elevator, under the heading "Elevate Your Life with Literature!" I'm not sure if they have a nine-year plan for posting the rest. I am troubled by the implication that our elevator waiting time needed to be more useful. God forbid employees stop maximizing for a few seconds.

Did anyone bother to read the first two pages of *Moby-Dick* before posting it? Ishmael takes to the open sea on a whale-hunting expedition because he is fed up with the drudgery of office life, "of week days pent up in lath and plaster — tied to counters, nailed to benches, clinched to desks." Try thinking about that on the subway home from work.

What was Ishmael so afraid of, anyway? Are scurvy, whale attack, and pirate rape so much better than working in an office? At least our office is air-conditioned. At least our complimentary Thursday morning doughnuts haven't been befouled by bilge rats. Ishmael, poor sucker, was born a hundred years too early. He could have opened "the great flood gates of the wonderworld" right here in this wonderful wave tank of an Internet office.

Day 12, 3:30 p.m.: ". . . and so the universal thump is passed round, and all hands should rub each other's shoulder-blades, and be content." — Herman Melville, Chapter 1, *Moby-Dick*.

Melissa's hands are rubbing my shoulder blades. "You have a lot of tension in your neck and shoulders," she says. "You should get more massages." I couldn't agree with her more. I've been avoiding the massage room, perhaps because of a fear that Melissa would somehow sense my ruse through the deceitful flow of my lymphatic fluid. As she navigates her knuckles around my back, I meditate blissfully. Free massages. Free beverages. Companionship, flirtation, E-mail access. No disruptive phone calls, no meetings, no boss, no questions, no decisions to make. A perfect job, perfectly undisturbed by having a job.

"Sorry, Randy, back to work," Melissa says, finishing up with that weird karate-chop thing. "Lots of tired backs out there. Drink water."

DAY 12, 4:45 P.M.: I started the conversation, so I have only myself to blame. Laura, a friendly woman in her thirties with a broken wrist, has been working next to me all week long, and I haven't said a word to her.

"What happened to your arm?" I ask.

Laura skips the part where she got injured and just tells me her medical horror story. Andy, her "arm guy," wants to take bone from another part of her body, and she's mistrustful and scared.

"And who are you?" she adds.

"I'm Randy Ronfman."

"What do you do here?"

Lately, when I get this question, I lean heavily on the word *stuff*. I find it has a narcotizing effect.

"I'm here from the Chicago satellite office. I'm doing a bunch of stuff. Project managing stuff. Branding stuff."

"Branding stuff. *Really.*" Laura leans her good arm on the desk eagerly. "I'm in marketing and recruiting here. Do you mind if I pick your brain?"

A week ago this question might have terrified me, but now it excites me. I'm starting to believe that I actually do this for a living, that I am capable of having my brain picked about branding. Laura's question is a cataract of jargon: "Launching a B2B . . . E-commerce . . . inventive user experiences . . . success factors . . . so if you know any branding people in Chicago that could help us out with that, I'd really appreciate it."

"You don't want to work with the people there," I tell her conspiratorially. "They're not so great."

Laura's brow furrows in genuine disappointment. "Well . . . maybe you could come up with some people? Do you have a few minutes?"

"Not right now," I answer. "I have a meeting at five."

This is not a lie. I do have a meeting, for a real job. Typically, I've nearly missed it. "I should be back later. When do you leave?"

"Six."

I make a mental note to come back at six-thirty. "Think about people you know who are very well connected," Laura calls after me as I run out. "Who could send me off into *their* network of people."

Day 13, 5 p.m.: It's been twenty-four hours since my conversation with Laura, and I haven't seen her since. This doesn't surprise me. The office has a seizure-inducing strobe effect. People appear and disappear, switch desks, switch jobs. Today Rick, the head of the office, is walking around, asking where Lawrence is. He is informed that Lawrence has recently been "reshuffled" into a new department. Lawrence is now sitting fifteen feet from Rick's office, on the floor below us, a floor that has fewer than twenty people. *The head of the office.* And you wonder how I've been able to stay here for two weeks?

Day 13, 8 p.m.: If it's possible to be a workaholic at a job you don't actually have, that's what I've become. The thought of going back to my apartment is loathsome, and I don't even have a family I'm trying to avoid. In this office I feel productive, even when I'm doing nothing. In my apartment, even when I'm working, I'm idle, lazy, and always a hairsbreadth away from masturbation. In her book *The Overworked American,* Juliet Schor writes about workers at an Akron tire plant who won a six-hour day. Many of them used their increased leisure time to take on second jobs. I'm beginning to think that a second, or even a third, fake job sounds like a fine idea. How tremendous it would be, traveling from fake job to fake job, taking only Fresca, leaving only flowcharts.

Day 14, 2 p.m.: To make myself feel better, I've started holding my own meetings. All day long today, friends come in, in groups of varying sizes. Sometimes I hold the meeting at my desk, in full view of the office. I like this because it gives the impression that I'm bringing in my own department. It's usually small talk and the occasional "Well, it's great to finally meet you!"

Mostly, though, we meet in the barren, glassed-in conference rooms. We close the door and gossip. For authenticity, I pace around the room and gesticulate madly. It's a Kabuki theater rendition of how I think meetings should look. At one point a woman interrupts our meeting. It turns out that we weren't in an empty conference room. We were in her office. I swear you can't tell the difference.

DAY 15, 10 A.M.: Today I walk in and there's a staff-wide meeting in the conference room. Everyone is in there. My immediate concern is that they are meeting about me, preparing some form of ghastly homicidal vengeance, like locking me in the Xerox machine until I asphyxiate on toner powder.

There will always be drywall between me and them. That's the limitation of my perfect job. I can never join the inner circle. I can never become indispensable, because, no matter how hard I try, I don't really exist here.

DAY 15, 4 P.M.: There's no such thing as Casual Friday in a company that's casual all week long, but don't tell that to the Man in the Blue Oxford Shirt. He's wearing a short-sleeved blue polo shirt today. Recently I found out that he's a junior project manager, like me. His name is Dennis. It's hard to maintain an adversarial relationship with a guy named Dennis, particularly one who stopped caring about me a week ago. At this point, I'm rental furniture. I haven't seen the Red-Haired Lady for days. Maybe some Ivy League consultant sent her home to New Rochelle with the rest of the forty-year-olds.

DAY 16, 2:30 P.M.: The office smokers are abuzz today. Word is spreading that the rest of the fifth floor is going to be let go. Apparently the New York office is now officially the worst in the company. We're even lagging behind Denver, because "they're small market, but at least they control it." Each person present seems to have a compelling reason that they're the next in line for dismissal. Everyone is ticked off that most of the senior staff is conveniently on vacation and the mass firings are being handled by middle managers. Some new young guy with a patchy beard looks at me accusingly and says, "They're going after the high-salaried ones first." I don't get that. So I'm "high salaried"? Just because I happen to be the only smoker here who bothers to wear a belt?

DAY 17, 7:45 P.M.: When I arrive this morning, I sense that this will be my last day at fake work. What clinches it is the new phone list. Many names are no longer on it. My name is: Randy Ronfman, with my phone extension directly beside it. I feel an intense wave of emotion, guiltless and giddy. But before too long I start thinking about the Peter Principle and decide I have been promoted past my point of competency. I know how to be a fake employee, but this is too legitimate. The only thing left for me to do is actual work, with actual coworkers who will rely on me. I've done that before. It's not as much fun.

Someday, if I'm ever a death row inmate, or a guy who sneaks into prison and pretends to be a death row inmate, I know what my last meal will be. It will be sodium-free seltzer. I like how it cleans you out. I sip one as I go from desk to desk, telling my coworkers that I'm "going back to the satellite office." Many of them have never met me before, or seen me, for that matter, but they react cordially. They assume it's their mistake, not mine.

"Lucky bastard!" one guy says.

"Your own choice, or are you 'resigning'?" another says, making quotation marks with his fingers.

"Nice working with you," the Girl with Long Brown Hair says.

I pack up my things long after everyone else is gone, savoring the last of the quiet. As I leave, I stop at the dry-erase board with the "Closed Loop Process" flowchart. I add my initials, RMR, box them, and draw an arrow to the box. I will live on in the office as an acronym, forever. Well, for two weeks, at least, until someone takes down the board. That's as close as you get to forever in this office.

■

Fourth Angry Mouse

FROM *Zoetrope*

JEREMY JAX wanted to be funny, like his grandfather.

Jeremy's grandfather was Robby Jax, the famous comedian. In his seventies — which also happened to be the 1970s — Robby Jax was still performing at Cherrywood's Lounge, on 42nd Street, and Jeremy attended the shows with his parents.

Jeremy was ten, and when he sat on the couches in Cherrywood's, he expected that someone might read aloud to him from *The Chronicles of Narnia*. Bookcases lined the room. There were studs on the walls on which men hung their hats. The smoke in the air had a blue glow, and the smoke seemed to remain in the room day or night, even when no pipes were lighted. At Cherrywood's, women drank coffee with amaretto, and men drank ale. When someone sank a shot at the pool table, the ball fell snugly into one of six leather pouches.

In one corner, between two bookcases, was a small, hardwood stage bearing an upholstered chair. In this chair, drinking century-old Scotch, was Robby Jax. He sat down around eight on a Saturday night, drank silently until nine, then began to speak. If you were new to Cherrywood's, you wouldn't even know at first that a performance was under way. It would dawn on you gradually that the woman whose eyes you meant to seduce was having none of you. She was staring at the old gentleman in the corner, the one with the furry eyebrows. Everyone was staring at the old gentleman and beginning to smile, and the lights in the lounge had dimmed.

"And so," sighed Robby Jax, "I told Emma Jean Bryce of Vassar College that she reminded me of a stalk of celery. And Emma Jean Bryce of Vassar College looked at me quite seriously and said, 'Robert, I don't know what that means. I honestly don't.'" Robby Jax sipped his Scotch. He glanced slowly around at his audience. He adjusted his vest over his thick middle. "And I said to her . . . I said . . . 'Emma Jean. A man can do many things to a stalk of celery. But one thing a man cannot do to a stalk of celery is make love to it, Emma Jean.'"

The audience laughed.

Robby Jax shook his head. "The women at Vassar College," he said sadly, "are virginal stalks of celery."

The audience kept laughing.

"I'm in my first year at Vassar," a girl called out, "and I'm not a virgin."

"Not yet you aren't," said Robby Jax.

The audience roared.

Jeremy didn't understand how it happened. None of the things his grandfather said were actual jokes. They were just stories, little pieces of life that sounded true. For all Jeremy knew, his grandfather made them up as he talked. But somehow the Scotch and the smoke and his grandfather's tweeds warmed people up, got them laughing.

"What's the secret?" Jeremy demanded one night when he was twelve. His grandfather had just finished a set at Cherrywood's. He was drinking Scotch at the bar and whispering to a young woman in black velvet. The woman had a southern accent.

"Well?" said Jeremy.

"The secret to what?" said Robby Jax.

"How do you make people laugh?" Jeremy had his arms folded.

Robby Jax scowled. He loved Jeremy, but he was a widower and young women in velvet were rare occasions.

"What's the secret?" persisted Jeremy.

Robby Jax bent to his grandson. "Relax, kid," he whispered.

"What's the secret?" Jeremy whispered back.

Robby winked. "I just told you. Relax." Robby stood back up, held his palm open toward the woman. "And now, Jeremy, I'd like to introduce you to one of the finest creations our Lord ever set down on earth. She is called a brunette."

The young woman giggled. "Hush, Robby."

Relax, thought Jeremy. Relax, relax.

He thought this all through high school. He thought it when he worked stage crew for the productions of Smile and Frown, his high school's drama club. Jeremy would've auditioned himself, but his voice cracked into falsetto when he got nervous. Jeremy figured that once he was eighteen, officially a man, his voice would be strong. Plus he'd be at college, away from Manhattan. He could relax and become a brilliant comic actor.

Jeremy's chance came in October of his freshman year at Hobart College. He saw signs around campus advertising an annual student talent show called *The Follies,* and he decided to audition. There were slots for student singers, musicians, and performance artists, but the most coveted position in *The Follies* was master of ceremonies. It was in this role that Jeremy planned to make his comic debut.

The auditions were held in the Hovel, the on-campus student pub, on a Thursday night. The Hovel was dark and crowded. On most nights, it was a pit where students sought drinks and laughs. Tonight, though, it was meant to be a charmed, bewitching cave, full of human art.

"Don't suck," said Patrick Rigg. Patrick was Jeremy's roommate, along for moral support.

"I won't," said Jeremy.

Patrick and Jeremy sat in the corner. Jeremy wore his black suit, the one that matched the color of his hair. This suit, Jeremy believed, made his green eyes look jovial and menacing, as if he were a funny but dangerous man, like Lenny Bruce. It was this sinister edge, this tiny malevolence within himself, that Jeremy planned to exploit as a trademark of his performing style. Still, as a nod to his grandfather, the more traditional storyteller, Jeremy ordered Scotch at the bar.

"No Scotch," said the bartender.

"Perhaps Crown Royal?" said Jeremy.

The bartender snorted. "Perhaps beer," he said. "Perhaps Jäger-meister."

Jeremy ordered the Jägermeister, which was served in a plastic cup. He returned to his corner to watch the competition.

A quick-eyed juggler performed onstage. A dancer danced. Three frat boys in Marx Brothers garb jabbered and received applause. An awful singer named Freida forgot her lyrics and wept and ran away.

"Jeremy Jax," said the judges. "Auditioning for MC."

Jeremy took the stage. He set himself down in a chair amid the footlights. He smiled wearily at the audience, the way his grandfather always did. He drank his Jägermeister. Directly before him was a table where three judges sat.

"Say something," suggested a judge.

Jeremy nodded. He understood what was required of him. However, he hadn't planned any material. He'd expected a perfect, spontaneous anecdote to rise within him, but it wasn't happening. A minute passed. Jeremy gulped at his Jägermeister.

Relax, Jeremy told himself.

A judge wrote something down.

"Um," said Jeremy.

His heart lurched. He saw Patrick frowning. People stirred in their seats, whispering. Jeremy stared at the drink in his hand.

"What's the deal with malt liquor?" he stammered.

One of the kinder judges smiled. "We don't know," she called out. "What is the deal with malt liquor?"

Jeremy didn't answer. He sat motionless in his chair. There was a riot in his stomach, in his mind. He tried to think of a story, any story.

"Jägermeister," he said, "is German for 'master hunter.'"

Someone in the audience sighed. Seconds passed.

"Women are celery," blurted Jeremy.

The Hovel fell silent. Patrick Rigg left. People looked at the floor.

"Thank you," said the judges.

Outside the Hovel, in the darkness, in a clearing of trees,

Jeremy came to himself. His first instinct had been to run from the pub, to get out into the October air. He'd expected himself to throw up or cry or gnash his teeth. He was perhaps on the verge of doing these things when he made out another figure in the dark beside him. It was a girl kneeling on the ground, her face in her hands. It was Freida, the awful singer.

"Hey," whispered Jeremy. "Hey there."

Freida looked up. Her face was miserable, splotchy with eye shadow.

"Are you great?" she sniffled.

"What?"

Freida pointed at the Hovel. "I — I meant, were you great. In there. Onstage. Were you great?"

"No," said Jeremy. His voice was hard. "I sucked."

As he said this, Jeremy felt a chill inside himself. It was a cold, new rage of some sort. It was painful, but somehow good. It made him feel capable of startling feats, like bludgeoning his grandfather.

"I'm Jeremy Jax," said Jeremy. He was practically shaking. "I'm terrible."

Freida shivered. She wiped her face, took the hand of the furious young man.

"I'm Freida," she said. "Come on."

They went to Freida's dorm room. In what seemed an implicit, mutually understood gesture, Jeremy removed Freida's clothes. He did so violently, as Freida expected. Then they lay down.

Jeremy stared deep into Freida's eyes as they screwed. He wielded his body into hers, taking a certain vengeance on the night. Freida made awful noises that weren't so different from the awful noises she'd made at the Hovel. When it was over, they lay there. Jeremy's hands shook at his sides.

Freida's eyes were closed. Jeremy tried to think of something to say, but couldn't. So he got up, dressed, and left.

When he was twenty-three, Jeremy Jax returned to Manhattan. He had, by that time, a degree in Russian literature, a head of graying hair, and an Upper West Side apartment. He also had a job as assistant to the director of the Lucas, a theater on 51st Street that he admired for its history.

The Lucas was a dying theater. It had ruled Broadway in the 1930s, staging the world premieres of several famous productions, including Hunter Frank's *Killing Me Lately* and Dazzle MacIntyre's *Eight Boxes*. These plays and the Lucas itself had been renowned for their raw, aggressive candor. *Killing Me Lately,* in fact, had been investigated by the New York City Police Department in 1938 because the character of the murder victim was played by a different actor every night, after which that actor vanished from the cast. The owner of the Lucas at the time, Sebastian Hye, claimed it was merely a gimmick to fascinate the bloodthirsty. New Yorkers, of course, took the bait and bought tickets in droves.

By the early 1990s, when Jeremy Jax started work there, the Lucas had fallen from the grace of its early decades. The physical plant was in disrepair. The black plush seats needed reupholstering and the ceiling was full of echoes. Also, Michael Hye, the current owner and director of the Lucas, no longer wanted to produce sensationalist, frightening plays.

"Satire, fine," said Michael. "Irony, great. But no existentialism. No amorality. No ennui."

Michael was in his office, speaking on the phone to the playwright of the Lucas's latest show. Jeremy Jax sat in his cubicle outside Michael's office, eavesdropping.

"Now then," said Michael, "there are flaws in *Of Mice and Mice.*"

Jeremy sighed. *Of Mice and Mice,* the Lucas's new show, was scheduled to open in one month. It was a departure from traditional Lucas fare. It was a play in which all of the actors were dressed as giant mice.

"Act one is fine," said Michael. "It's act two. What's driving the mice in act two?"

Jeremy sighed again. Since its birth, the Lucas had been owned by the Hyes, a famous Manhattan theater family. The Hyes had always served as the producers and directors of the shows, and sometimes even as the editors of the playwrights. It was an unusual relationship, but Lucas Hye, who founded the theater in 1890, had been unusually wealthy and could afford to be overbearing. The contemporary Hyes could afford it, too.

"Fine," said Michael Hye into the phone. "I want the revised script by tomorrow." The phone clicked.

Jeremy sighed one final time.

"I heard that," called Michael. "What's your problem?"

"Nothing," muttered Jeremy.

Michael appeared in the doorway. He was six feet tall, like Jeremy, but pudgier and fifty years old. He had muttonchops and halitosis.

"Let's hear it, Jax," said Michael.

Jeremy had no love for Michael. However, Michael gave Jeremy good money and decent hours, and when Jeremy sat in on rehearsals, Michael often asked him what he thought.

"It just sounds," said Jeremy, "like you're trying to make *Of Mice and Mice* funny, and it's not supposed to be funny."

"Question," said Michael. "Is Jeremy Jax the expert on funny?"

"No," said Jeremy.

"Question," said Michael. "Was Ionesco's *Rhinoceros* funny?"

"Well . . ." began Jeremy.

"No," insisted Michael. "I saw it in London in seventy-nine. There were twenty people on that stage dressed as rhinoceroses and there wasn't a chuckle in the house." Michael put his hands to his hips. "The mice aren't funny. The mice are dire."

"Whatever," said Jeremy. "Forget I mentioned it."

In college, after his disastrous audition, Jeremy had turned his back on comedy. He found a home in Dostoyevsky and Chekhov. Russian writers, Jeremy felt, understood melancholy. They could be wry, but they believed in the Devil, and you didn't have to like black clothes or coffee to get their darkness. In what he considered a kindred Russian spirit, Jeremy had embraced the darkness he'd discovered in himself during that night years ago, his one night with Freida.

They'd never had a relationship, Jeremy and Freida. They'd come together once, as failures, and fucked each other as failures, and avoided each other thereafter. Jeremy remembered Freida as a ragged, tragic figure, like a doomed Karamazov or a Faust. He thought of her sometimes after work when he walked down Broadway to Cherrywood's Lounge, his late grandfather's haunt.

Jeremy drank Cutty Sark at Cherrywood's, sitting at the bar, glaring at the stand-up comedians who tried to take Robby Jax's place on the stage. The comedians were male, in their mid-thirties, with thinning hair and decent suits. They rolled their eyes and quibbled about women.

"Comedians aren't men," said Jeremy Jax. He was speaking to his old Hobart roommate, Patrick Rigg. Patrick was on Wall Street now. He was famous for his handsome bones, and he carried a gun.

"Russians are men," said Jeremy.

Patrick shrugged.

"Look at this guy." Jeremy nodded toward the stage, where the comedian was making baby sounds in the microphone.

"He's doing a bit about dating," explained Patrick.

Jeremy sucked ice and Scotch. He sucked till the cold hurt his teeth.

"He's mocking idyllic romance," said Patrick.

Russians, thought Jeremy, do not do bits.

It was on an ordinary Wednesday that Jeremy Jax became Fourth Angry Mouse. It happened quickly, and if Jeremy had had time to consult the darkness within him, he probably would have refused the role. But he was groggy from lunch when Michael Hye ran into the office.

"Call an ambulance," panted Michael. "Fourth Angry Mouse is down. Unconscious."

"What happened?" said Jeremy.

Michael shook his head. "He was berating First Kindly Mouse, and he collapsed. Hyperventilated or something."

Of Mice and Mice had eight characters, four Kindly Mice and four Angry Mice. All eight actors wore almost identical mouse outfits, but the mice were distinguishable by the colors of their trousers and their habits of movement. Second Kindly Mouse, for instance, was partial to softshoe. Third Angry Mouse rode other mice piggyback.

It turned out that things were serious. Fourth Angry Mouse, a habitual smoker, had suffered a collapsed lung.

"Jeremy." Michael pulled Jeremy into the office. It was four o'clock, still Wednesday. The ambulance had come and gone.

"Jeremy," said Michael. He spoke quietly, reverently. "The Lucas needs you."

"How's that?" said Jeremy.

Michael gripped Jeremy's arm. "You've got to be Fourth Angry Mouse."

"Like hell I do."

Michael's face was grave. "We have no understudy. The show opens Friday."

"Call Equity," said Jeremy.

Michael frowned. "Whenever it's possible, the Lucas does things in-house."

"Whenever it's possible," said Jeremy, "I don't play rodents."

"Don't be flip, Jeremy." Michael punched a calculator. "I'll give you one hundred and fifty dollars a night till we can train a professional in the role, if that's necessary. It's virtually a nonspeaking part, it's only a two-month run, and you know the show cold. Plus . . ."

"Plus what?"

"Plus I suspect you understand Fourth Angry's sensibility."

"He doesn't have a sensibility, Michael. He's a fucking mouse."

Michael snapped his fingers. "That. Right there. The way you just spoke to me. That's Fourth Angry's tone. His Weltanschauung."

"Forget it," said Jeremy.

"Three hundred a night," said Michael.

"Done," said Jeremy.

Rehearsals began twenty minutes later. Jeremy suited up in a giant mouse outfit and took the stage. The other mice gathered around.

"Who's this guy?" they asked.

"It's me," said Jeremy. His breath felt warm and close inside the mouse head, which was held to the costume's body by hinges. Jeremy's eyes peeked out through a grille in the costume's mouth.

"I'm Jeremy Jax," said Jeremy.

Third Kindly Mouse put his paws on his hips. "Michael. This is absurd."

"Yeah," said First Angry Mouse. "We're professionals. You can't just stick some random employee into —"

"The kid knows the part," said Michael Hye. "Besides, Fourth Angry only has one line."

Fourth Kindly Mouse patted Jeremy's back. "Let's give him a chance."

"What's his background?" said Third Angry Mouse.

"He's Robby Jax's grandson," said Michael.

The mice all nodded, impressed.

"Let's hear him," said First Angry. "Let's hear him try his one line."

Michael urged Jeremy onto the roof, which was a giant promontory piece of the set. It was from this roof that Fourth Angry Mouse proclaimed his line.

"Go on, Jax," said Michael.

Jeremy climbed the roof, looked out at the empty seats of the Lucas. A spotlight came on in the ceiling, singled him out.

Three hundred a night, Jeremy told himself.

"Do it up, kid," yelled Fourth Kindly Mouse.

Jeremy took a breath.

"'I have arrived!'" he shouted.

Within two weeks, an extraordinary thing happened. New York City fell in love with *Of Mice and Mice*.

There was no rational accounting for it. Manhattan's theater tastes had ranged over the preceding decade from men drenched in blue paint to maniacs thumping garbage cans, so the popularity of eight giant mice was perhaps only a matter of savvy timing. On the other hand, *Of Mice and Mice*'s playwright was furious. He'd intended *Of Mice and Mice* as a somber allegory about the divisiveness of the human heart, and audiences were finding the play outrageously funny. Children and adults loved the show with equal ardor, the way they might a classic Looney Tunes. Susan March, who wrote the editorial column "March Madness" for the *New York Times,* claimed that "these eight mice show us, with their tongues in their divine little cheeks, how laughable are all our attempts at serious human contention. Who would've expected such charm from the Lucas?"

Receiving particular laud was the character of Fourth Angry Mouse. He wore unassuming blue trousers and had only one line, but there was something about his befuddled manner, his confused scampering to and fro among his fellow mice that endeared him to audiences and won him standing ovations.

"Fourth Angry Mouse," wrote Susan March, "is petulant, skittish, bent on private designs. But he is so convincingly lost in his own antics that we can't help but laugh at the little guy. He could be any one of us, plucked off the street, tossed into public scrutiny. Would any of us seem less goofy, less hysterically at sea?"

Compounding the intrigue around Fourth Angry Mouse was the fact that the program listed the actor's name as Anonymous. This was unheard-of. Benny Demarco, the character actor of film and stage fame, was carrying the role of First Kindly Mouse and garnering good reviews. Trisha Vera, as First Angry Mouse, had some brilliant moments, including a Velcro routine on the walls. But it was the unknown man behind Fourth Angry Mouse that Manhattan wanted to meet most. Some critics speculated that it was Christian Frick, reprising his Tony Award–winning role as the Familiar in *Coven.* Most reviewers, though, suspected that a newcomer lurked behind Fourth Angry Mouse, a dark-horse tyro with few credentials beyond instinct.

As for Jeremy Jax, he was flabbergasted. He tried in each performance to implement the critical notes he'd been given by Michael Hye and *Of Mice and Mice*'s livid playwright. However, Jeremy was no actor. He had no knack for detail, no timing, no sense of his body as perceived by others, and so no clear motives for how to move when dressed as a seven-foot mouse. He got upset at the laughter he aroused — he didn't want his fellow mice to think him a showboat — but the more upset he got, the harder people laughed and the more money the Lucas made.

Relax, Jeremy told himself. Relax.

But Jeremy couldn't relax. His fame was a farce to him. He wanted no one to acknowledge it until he decided if it was shameful. If he'd been a praying man, Jeremy might've consulted the spirit of his dead grandfather directly for some assurance that he was authentically comic. Instead, he got drunk at Cherrywood's with Patrick Rigg.

"You no longer suck," said Patrick. "Why not spill your name?"

"Because," hissed Jeremy. "Because I'm a fucking mouse, that's why."

Patrick shrugged. Outside of Michael Hye and the other cast members — whom Michael had contracted into secrecy — only Patrick knew Jeremy's alter ego.

"You might be a mouse," said Patrick, "but you're definitely the man. Everybody loves you."

Jeremy scowled. If I were a man, he thought, I'd be drinking vodka in Siberia. I'd be living on tundra, with a beefy wife.

To cheer his buddy up, Patrick dragged Jeremy to Minotaur's, a basement nightclub in the meatpacking district. Minotaur's was a labyrinth of halls and dark corners. There were doors off the halls, some of which led to rooms of bliss. Other doors led nowhere. If you got separated from someone at Minotaur's, you might not see him or her till morning or ever again. The idea, though, was to dabble in as many corners as you could, then follow the maze to its center, a wide clearing called the Forum. In this room were several bars, a high ceiling, a dance floor, and a stage that had revolving entertainment: house on Mondays, blues on Tuesdays, swing on Thursdays, ska on Fridays. Patrick took Jeremy to the Forum on a Wednesday. Wednesday was Anything-Can-Happen Night.

Jeremy groaned again. "Why am I here?"

Patrick whinnied a high, eerie laugh. He pointed at the stage.

"Watch," he said.

Jeremy watched. A person named Harold read erotica. A girl named Tsunami danced.

"They suck," said Jeremy.

"Watch," insisted Patrick.

"Ladies and gentlemen," said the MC, "please welcome back to Minotaur's The Great Unwashed."

A whoop went up. The lights dimmed. Three young women took the stage, one at the drums, two on guitar. The girl on lead guitar had long black hair combed over one eye in a sickle that hid most of her face. Seconds later, she and her band were at it. They played simple, throbbing music, but what got Jeremy's ear was the singer, the lead guitarist. Her face was hidden by her sickle, and her voice was awful but arresting, like Lou Reed's. She told lyrics in a simple monotone, then her words rose and cracked and broke your heart. Jeremy felt the hairs on his neck ripple. He turned to Patrick.

"She's . . . she's . . ." Jeremy wanted to say she was terrible. He wanted it to be a compliment.

"She's Freida," said Patrick. "Freida from Hobart."

Jeremy's mouth opened. Patrick was right. It was Freida.

"She's great," whispered Jeremy.

"I know," said Patrick. "I saw her here last month."

"Why didn't you tell me?"

Patrick grinned, sly and easy. He knew things about Manhattan that only dead people should know.

Jeremy found Freida after the show. She remembered him, and shook his hand. They went through a door, bought some drinks, went through another door, sat on a couch.

"I can't believe it's you," said Jeremy. "You were great out there."

Freida brushed back her sickle. "Your hair got gray," she said.

"So what do you do with yourself now?" asked Jeremy.

Freida tapped her guitar. "I do this, stupid. I sing."

"Full-time?"

"Well, I'm a saleswoman at Saks. But who cares about that?"

Jeremy stared at her. He wanted to tell her how supple her thighs looked under her miniskirt, how terrific it was that she was profiting from her awful voice.

"What are you doing?" asked Freida.

Jeremy downed some Ballantine. "I'm assistant to the director at — well, I work at the Lucas theater."

Freida nodded. "The Mouseketeer Club."

"Ha," said Jeremy. He took another look at Freida's thighs, which, if he remembered right, had a tiny spray of freckles on them up around the hips. He remembered his grandfather, who'd loved whispering to pretty girls. Jeremy glanced around. The room they were in was dark and empty.

"Freida," he whispered. He placed his hand on her thigh.

Freida immediately removed it. "Nope," she said. She smoothed her skirt and looked at Jeremy, her eyes all business.

Jeremy was surprised. He'd heard anything went in the back rooms at Minotaur's, and he'd once taken this girl quite aggressively. He reached toward Freida's lap again. Freida slapped his hand easily away. She made a little sound that could have been a laugh, then stood up.

"What's wrong?" demanded Jeremy.

Freida shook her head. "Nothing's wrong, stupid." She picked up her guitar and walked away.

The more Jeremy thought about Freida, the madder he got.

"She called me stupid," Jeremy muttered. "Twice."

"What are you mumbling about?" asked First Angry Mouse.

The mice were backstage, in the greenroom, stretching, getting their heads on straight. The Saturday evening curtain was rising in five minutes, and rumor had it that Mayor Fillipone was in the audience.

"Nothing," snapped Jeremy.

"Hey, Jax," said Benny Demarco, "don't step on my tail during the butter dance."

"I won't."

"Well, you did this afternoon."

"Bullshit," snapped Jeremy.

Michael Hye popped his head in the door. "Places," he said.

Jeremy sighed heavily.

"What's your problem?" said Michael.

"Fourth Angry's pissed off," said Benny.

Jeremy gave Benny the finger.

"All right, all right," said Michael. "Everyone, relax. We've got the mayor out there. Places."

The mice scurried out.

Jeremy moved upstage to the giant cheese grate, took his position behind it.

The curtain rose. The audience applauded. The mice began their story, strutting and fretting upon the stage. Jeremy remained cloaked in darkness. He didn't appear until twenty minutes into act one. Most nights, while he stood waiting, he peeked through the cheese grate and scanned the audience for famous people. Tonight he looked for the mayor. What he discovered instead was a young woman in the tenth row with a sickle of hair across her face.

"Freida," whispered Jeremy.

She wore a crimson gown and gloves that came up her forearms. Beside her was a handsome man in a tuxedo who had one hand locked around Freida's wrist. With his free hand, using his fingertips, he stroked her bicep casually, possessively.

Jeremy scowled. Relax, he told himself. Relax, relax.

But he couldn't relax. Not only had Freida called him stupid, she'd laughed at him, laughed at the immense, sexual, Russian darkness inside him. And now here she was, the lead singer of The Great Unwashed, hiding her awful voice behind her crimson dress and her sickle of hair. Freida was a celebrity, apparently, a healthy Manhattan aesthete out on the town with her lover. It made Jeremy furious.

He rushed into view, two full minutes ahead of cue. The audience exploded with applause. The other seven mice stared at Jeremy.

Michael Hye stood at the back of the Lucas.

"Oh, no," he whispered.

Jeremy panicked. He squeaked loudly, twice, which was the signal for the butter dance, which wasn't even part of act one. Chaos ensued. Half of the mice followed Jeremy's lead and improvised a makeshift butter dance, while the other mice threw up their paws in protest. The audience laughed.

Benny Demarco, as First Kindly Mouse, leaned close to Jeremy.

"You're ruining it," he hissed.

Out of frustration, Benny gave Jeremy a kick in the ass. Fourth Angry Mouse responded by shoving Benny into the butter churn.

The audience roared. The playwright, standing beside Michael Hye, seethed and cursed.

First Kindly Mouse began chasing Fourth Angry Mouse. The chase rambled through the butter dancers, over the cheese grate, onto the lower portion of the roof, off of which Jeremy flipped Benny. Benny landed on top of two other mice, collapsing them to the floor.

The crowd was in stitches, even those who'd seen the show before and knew a bungle was under way.

Jeremy stood panting in his mouse outfit, his face — his human face — gone beet red.

Relax, he ordered himself. Relax.

But even as he thought this, Jeremy caught Freida's face in the crowd. Her mouth was thrown open, bucking with laughter. Her teeth seemed to eat the air ravenously as she howled. The mouth of her lover was howling, too.

Jeremy closed his eyes, hard, hating what he was: a funny man. He was funny in a tense, awful way, a way that infuriated him and delighted others. These others, the audience, were delighted even now. They laughed, pointing at him. He couldn't bear it. He ran to the top of the roof.

"I have arrived," hissed Jeremy.

He put his hands to his mousy head, tried to unscrew it. He cuffed at his face, boxed his ears, yanked at his headpiece.

"What's he doing?" squeaked the mice below.

Michael Hye and the playwright caught their breath.

"Oh God," whispered Michael.

The audience hushed. Fourth Angry Mouse was clawing at his cheeks, apparently trying to tear his own skull off.

The other mice dashed for the roof.

"Don't do it," squealed Third Kindly.

"Wait," barked Third Angry.

"I have arrived," warned Jeremy. He swatted stubbornly at his neck, loosening the hinges there.

First Kindly Mouse was only feet away.

"Character," hissed Benny. "Stay in character."

"I have arrived," shouted Fourth Angry Mouse. He popped the final hinge in his neck.

No, prayed Michael Hye, but it was too late. In a beheading that shocked the masses, Jeremy Jax revealed his feeble self.

ERIC SCHLOSSER

■

Why McDonald's Fries
Taste So Good

FROM *The Atlantic Monthly*

THE FRENCH FRY was "almost sacrosanct for me," Ray Kroc, one
of the founders of McDonald's, wrote in his autobiography, "its
preparation a ritual to be followed religiously." During the chain's
early years french fries were made from scratch every day. Russet Burbank potatoes were peeled, cut into shoestrings, and fried
in McDonald's kitchens. As the chain expanded nationwide, in
the mid-1960s, it sought to cut labor costs, reduce the number of
suppliers, and ensure that its fries tasted the same at every restaurant. McDonald's began switching to frozen french fries in 1966
— and few customers noticed the difference. Nevertheless, the
change had a profound effect on the nation's agriculture and diet.
A familiar food had been transformed into a highly processed industrial commodity. McDonald's fries now come from huge manufacturing plants that can peel, slice, cook, and freeze 2 million
pounds of potatoes a day. The rapid expansion of McDonald's and
the popularity of its low-cost, mass-produced fries changed the
way Americans eat. In 1960 Americans consumed an average of
about eighty-one pounds of fresh potatoes and four pounds of
frozen french fries. In 2000 they consumed an average of about
fifty pounds of fresh potatoes and thirty pounds of frozen fries. Today McDonald's is the largest buyer of potatoes in the United
States.

The taste of McDonald's french fries played a crucial role in the chain's success — fries are much more profitable than hamburgers — and was long praised by customers, competitors, and even food critics. James Beard loved McDonald's fries. Their distinctive taste does not stem from the kind of potatoes that McDonald's buys, the technology that processes them, or the restaurant equipment that fries them: other chains use Russet Burbanks, buy their french fries from the same large processing companies, and have similar fryers in their restaurant kitchens. The taste of a french fry is largely determined by the cooking oil. For decades McDonald's cooked its french fries in a mixture of about 7 percent cottonseed oil and 93 percent beef tallow. The mixture gave the fries their unique flavor — and more saturated beef fat per ounce than a McDonald's hamburger.

In 1990, amid a barrage of criticism over the amount of cholesterol in its fries, McDonald's switched to pure vegetable oil. This presented the company with a challenge: how to make fries that subtly taste like beef without cooking them in beef tallow. A look at the ingredients in McDonald's french fries suggests how the problem was solved. Toward the end of the list is a seemingly innocuous yet oddly mysterious phrase: "natural flavor." That ingredient helps to explain not only why the fries taste so good but also why most fast food — indeed, most of the food Americans eat today — tastes the way it does.

Open your refrigerator, your freezer, your kitchen cupboards, and look at the labels on your food. You'll find "natural flavor" or "artificial flavor" in just about every list of ingredients. The similarities between these two broad categories are far more significant than the differences. Both are manmade additives that give most processed food most of its taste. People usually buy a food item the first time because of its packaging or appearance. Taste usually determines whether they buy it again. About 90 percent of the money that Americans now spend on food goes to buy processed food. The canning, freezing, and dehydrating techniques used in processing destroy most of food's flavor — and so a vast industry has arisen in the United States to make processed food palatable. Without this flavor industry today's fast food would not exist. The names of the leading American fast-food chains and their best-selling menu items have become embedded in our popular culture and famous worldwide. But few people can name the companies that manufacture fast food's taste.

The flavor industry is highly secretive. Its leading companies will not divulge the precise formulas of flavor compounds or the identities of clients. The secrecy is deemed essential for protecting the reputations of beloved brands. The fast-food chains, understandably, would like the public to believe that the flavors of the food they sell somehow originate in their restaurant kitchens, not in distant factories run by other firms. A McDonald's french fry is one of countless foods whose flavor is just a component in a complex manufacturing process. The look and the taste of what we eat now are frequently deceiving — by design.

The New Jersey Turnpike runs through the heart of the flavor industry, an industrial corridor dotted with refineries and chemical plants. International Flavors & Fragrances (IFF), the world's largest flavor company, has a manufacturing facility off Exit 8A in Dayton, New Jersey; Givaudan, the world's second largest flavor company, has a plant in East Hanover. Haarmann & Reimer, the largest German flavor company, has a plant in Teterboro, as does Takasago, the largest Japanese flavor company. Flavor Dynamics has a plant in South Plainfield; Frutarom is in North Bergen; Elan Chemical is in Newark. Dozens of companies manufacture flavors in the corridor between Teaneck and South Brunswick. Altogether the area produces about two thirds of the flavor additives sold in the United States.

The IFF plant in Dayton is a huge pale-blue building with a modern office complex attached to the front. It sits in an industrial park, not far from a BASF plastics factory, a Jolly French Toast factory, and a plant that manufactures Liz Claiborne cosmetics. Dozens of tractor-trailers were parked at the IFF loading dock the afternoon I visited, and a thin cloud of steam floated from a roof vent. Before entering the plant, I signed a nondisclosure form, promising not to reveal the brand names of foods that contain IFF flavors. The place reminded me of Willy Wonka's chocolate factory. Wonderful smells drifted through the hallways, men and women in neat white lab coats cheerfully went about their work, and hundreds of little glass bottles sat on laboratory tables and shelves. The bottles contained powerful but fragile flavor chemicals, shielded from light by brown glass and round white caps shut tight. The long chemical names on the little white labels were as mystifying to me as medieval Latin. These odd-sounding things would be mixed and poured and turned into new substances, like magic potions.

I was not invited into the manufacturing areas of the IFF plant, where, it was thought, I might discover trade secrets. Instead I toured various laboratories and pilot kitchens, where the flavors of well-established brands are tested or adjusted, and where whole new flavors are created. IFF's snack-and-savory lab is responsible for the flavors of potato chips, corn chips, breads, crackers, breakfast cereals, and pet food. The confectionery lab devises flavors for ice cream, cookies, candies, toothpastes, mouthwashes, and antacids. Everywhere I looked, I saw famous, widely advertised products sitting on laboratory desks and tables. The beverage lab was full of brightly colored liquids in clear bottles. It comes up with flavors for popular soft drinks, sports drinks, bottled teas, and wine coolers, for all-natural juice drinks, organic soy drinks, beers, and malt liquors. In one pilot kitchen I saw a dapper food technologist, a middle-aged man with an elegant tie beneath his crisp lab coat, carefully preparing a batch of cookies with white frosting and pink-and-white sprinkles. In another pilot kitchen I saw a pizza oven, a grill, a milkshake machine, and a french fryer identical to those I'd seen at innumerable fast-food restaurants.

In addition to being the world's largest flavor company, IFF manufactures the smells of six of the ten best-selling fine perfumes in the United States, including Estée Lauder's Beautiful, Clinique's Happy, Lancôme's Trésor, and Calvin Klein's Eternity. It also makes the smells of household products such as deodorant, dishwashing detergent, bath soap, shampoo, furniture polish, and floor wax. All these aromas are made through essentially the same process: the manipulation of volatile chemicals. The basic science behind the scent of your shaving cream is the same as that governing the flavor of your TV dinner.

Scientists now believe that human beings acquired the sense of taste as a way to avoid being poisoned. Edible plants generally taste sweet, harmful ones bitter. The taste buds on our tongues can detect the presence of half a dozen or so basic tastes, including sweet, sour, bitter, salty, astringent, and umami, a taste discovered by Japanese researchers — a rich and full sense of deliciousness triggered by amino acids in foods such as meat, shellfish, mushrooms, potatoes, and seaweed. Taste buds offer a limited means of detection, however, compared with the human olfactory system, which can perceive thousands of different chemical aromas. Indeed, "flavor" is primarily the smell of gases being released by the chemicals you've just put in your mouth. The aroma of a food can be responsible for as much as 90 percent of its taste.

The act of drinking, sucking, or chewing a substance releases its volatile gases. They flow out of your mouth and up your nostrils, or up the passageway in the back of your mouth, to a thin layer of nerve cells called the olfactory epithelium, located at the base of your nose, right between your eyes. Your brain combines the complex smell signals from your olfactory epithelium with the simple taste signals from your tongue, assigns a flavor to what's in your mouth, and decides if it's something you want to eat.

A person's food preferences, like his or her personality, are formed during the first few years of life, through a process of socialization. Babies innately prefer sweet tastes and reject bitter ones; toddlers can learn to enjoy hot and spicy food, bland health food, or fast food, depending on what the people around them eat. The human sense of smell is still not fully understood. It is greatly affected by psychological factors and expectations. The mind focuses intently on some of the aromas that surround us and filters out the overwhelming majority. People can grow accustomed to bad smells or good smells; they stop noticing what once seemed overpowering. Aroma and memory are somehow inextricably linked. A smell can suddenly evoke a long-forgotten moment. The flavors of childhood foods seem to leave an indelible mark, and adults often return to them, without always knowing why. These "comfort foods" become a source of pleasure and reassurance — a fact that fast-food chains use to their advantage. Childhood memories of Happy Meals, which come with french fries, can translate into frequent adult visits to McDonald's. On average, Americans now eat about four servings of french fries every week.

The human craving for flavor has been a largely unacknowledged and unexamined force in history. For millennia royal empires have been built, unexplored lands traversed, and great religions and philosophies forever changed by the spice trade. In 1492 Christopher Columbus set sail to find seasoning. Today the influence of flavor in the world marketplace is no less decisive. The rise and fall of corporate empires — of soft-drink companies, snack-food companies, and fast-food chains — is often determined by how their products taste.

The flavor industry emerged in the mid-nineteenth century, as processed foods began to be manufactured on a large scale. Recognizing the need for flavor additives, early food processors turned to perfume companies that had long experience working with essential oils and volatile aromas. The great perfume houses of England, France, and the Netherlands produced many of the first flavor compounds. In the early part of the twentieth century Germany took the technological lead in flavor production, owing to its powerful chemical industry. Legend has it that a German scientist discovered methyl anthranilate, one of the first artificial flavors, by accident while mixing chemicals in his laboratory. Suddenly the lab was filled with the sweet smell of grapes. Methyl anthranilate later became the chief flavor compound in grape Kool-Aid. After World War II much of the perfume industry shifted from Europe to the United States, settling in New York City near the garment district and the fashion houses. The flavor industry came with it, later moving to New Jersey for greater plant capacity. Manmade flavor additives were used mostly in baked goods, candies, and so-das until the 1950s, when sales of processed food began to soar. The invention of gas chromatographs and mass spectrometers — machines capable of detecting volatile gases at low levels — vastly increased the number of flavors that could be synthesized. By the mid-1960s flavor companies were churning out compounds to supply the taste of Pop Tarts, Bac-Os, Tab, Tang, Filet-O-Fish sand-wiches, and literally thousands of other new foods.

The American flavor industry now has annual revenues of about $1.4 billion. Approximately ten thousand new processed-food products are introduced every year in the United States. Al-most all of them require flavor additives. And about nine out of ten of these products fail. The latest flavor innovations and corpo-rate realignments are heralded in publications such as *Chemical Market Reporter, Food Chemical News, Food Engineering,* and *Food Product Design.* The progress of IFF has mirrored that of the flavor industry as a whole. IFF was formed in 1958, through the merger of two small companies. Its annual revenues have grown almost fifteenfold since the early 1970s, and it currently has manufactur-ing facilities in twenty countries.

Today's sophisticated spectrometers, gas chromatographs, and headspace-vapor analyzers provide a detailed map of a food's flavor components, detecting chemical aromas present in amounts as low as one part per billion. The human nose, how-ever, is even more sensitive. A nose can detect aromas present in quantities of a few parts per trillion — an amount equivalent to about 0.000000000003 percent. Complex aromas, such as those of coffee and roasted meat, are composed of volatile gases from nearly a thousand different chemicals. The smell of a strawberry arises from the interaction of about 350 chemicals that are present in minute amounts. The quality that people seek most of all in a food — flavor — is usually present in a quantity too infinitesimal to be measured in traditional culinary terms such as ounces or tea-spoons. The chemical that provides the dominant flavor of bell pepper can be tasted in amounts as low as 0.02 parts per billion; one drop is sufficient to add flavor to five average-size swimming pools. The flavor additive usually comes next to last in a processed food's list of ingredients and often costs less than its packaging. Soft drinks contain a larger proportion of flavor additives than most products. The flavor in a twelve-ounce can of Coke costs about half a cent.

The color additives in processed foods are usually present in even smaller amounts than the flavor compounds. Many of New Jersey's flavor companies also manufacture these color additives, which are used to make processed foods look fresh and appealing. Food coloring serves many of the same decorative purposes as lipstick, eye shadow, mascara — and is often made from the same pigments. Titanium dioxide, for example, has proved to be an especially versatile mineral. It gives many processed candies, frostings, and icings their bright white color; it is a common ingredient in women's cosmetics; and it is the pigment used in many white oil paints and house paints. At Burger King, Wendy's, and McDonald's coloring agents have been added to many of the soft drinks, salad dressings, cookies, condiments, chicken dishes, and sandwich buns.

Studies have found that the color of a food can greatly affect how its taste is perceived. Brightly colored foods frequently seem to taste better than bland-looking foods, even when the flavor compounds are identical. Foods that somehow look off color often seem to have off tastes. For thousands of years human beings have relied on visual cues to help determine what is edible. The color of fruit suggests whether it is ripe, the color of meat whether it is rancid. Flavor researchers sometimes use colored lights to modify the influence of visual cues during taste tests. During one experiment in the early 1970s people were served an oddly tinted meal of steak and french fries that appeared normal beneath colored lights. Everyone thought the meal tasted fine until the lighting was changed. Once it became apparent that the steak was actually blue and the fries were green, some people became ill.

The federal Food and Drug Administration does not require companies to disclose the ingredients of their color or flavor additives so long as all the chemicals in them are considered by the agency to be GRAS ("generally recognized as safe"). This enables companies to maintain the secrecy of their formulas. It also hides the fact that flavor compounds often contain more ingredients than the foods to which they give taste. The phrase "artificial strawberry flavor" gives little hint of the chemical wizardry and manufacturing skill that can make a highly processed food taste like strawberries.

A typical artificial strawberry flavor, like the kind found in a Burger King strawberry milkshake, contains the following ingredients: amyl acetate, amyl butyrate, amyl valerate, anethol, anisyl formate, benzyl acetate, benzyl isobutyrate, butyric acid, cinnamyl isobutyrate, cinnamyl valerate, cognac essential oil, diacetyl, dipropyl ketone, ethyl acetate, ethyl amyl ketone, ethyl butyrate, ethyl cinnamate, ethyl heptanoate, ethyl heptylate, ethyl lactate, ethyl methylphenylglycidate, ethyl nitrate, ethyl propionate, ethyl valerate, heliotropin, hydroxyphenyl-2-butanone (10 percent solution in alcohol), α-ionone, isobutyl anthranilate, isobutyl butyrate, lemon essential oil, maltol, 4-methylacetophenone, methyl anthranilate, methyl benzoate, methyl cinnamate, methyl heptine carbonate, methyl naphthyl ketone, methyl salicylate, mint essential oil, neroli essential oil, nerolin, neryl isobutyrate, orris butter, phenethyl alcohol, rose, rum ether, γ-undecalactone, vanillin, and solvent.

Although flavors usually arise from a mixture of many different volatile chemicals, often a single compound supplies the dominant aroma. Smelled alone, that chemical provides an unmistakable sense of the food. Ethyl-2-methyl butyrate, for example, smells just like an apple. Many of today's highly processed foods offer a blank palette: whatever chemicals are added to them will give them specific tastes. Adding methyl-2-pyridyl ketone makes something taste like popcorn. Adding ethyl-3-hydroxy butanoate makes it taste like marshmallow. The possibilities are now almost limitless. Without affecting appearance or nutritional value, processed foods could be made with aroma chemicals such as hexanal (the smell of freshly cut grass) or 3-methyl butanoic acid (the smell of body odor).

The 1960s were the heyday of artificial flavors in the United States. The synthetic versions of flavor compounds were not subtle, but they did not have to be, given the nature of most processed food. For the past twenty years food processors have tried hard to use only "natural flavors" in their products. According to the FDA, these must be derived entirely from natural sources — from herbs, spices, fruits, vegetables, beef, chicken, yeast, bark, roots, and so forth. Consumers prefer to see natural flavors on a label, out of a belief that they are more healthful. Distinctions between artificial and natural flavors can be arbitrary and somewhat absurd, based more on how the flavor has been made than on what it actually contains.

"A natural flavor," says Terry Acree, a professor of food science at Cornell University, "is a flavor that's been derived with an out-of-date technology." Natural flavors and artificial flavors sometimes contain exactly the same chemicals, produced through different methods. Amyl acetate, for example, provides the dominant note of banana flavor. When it is distilled from bananas with a solvent, amyl acetate is a natural flavor. When it is produced by mixing vinegar with amyl alcohol and adding sulfuric acid as a catalyst, amyl acetate is an artificial flavor. Either way it smells and tastes the same. "Natural flavor" is now listed among the ingredients of everything from Health Valley Blueberry Granola Bars to Taco Bell Hot Taco Sauce.

A natural flavor is not necessarily more healthful or purer than an artificial one. When almond flavor — benzaldehyde — is derived from natural sources, such as peach and apricot pits, it contains traces of hydrogen cyanide, a deadly poison. Benzaldehyde derived by mixing oil of clove and amyl acetate does not contain any cyanide. Nevertheless, it is legally considered an artificial flavor and sells at a much lower price. Natural and artificial flavors are now manufactured at the same chemical plants, places that few people would associate with Mother Nature.

The small and elite group of scientists who create most of the flavor in most of the food now consumed in the United States are called "flavorists." They draw on a number of disciplines in their work: biology, psychology, physiology, and organic chemistry. A flavorist is a chemist with a trained nose and a poetic sensibility. Flavors are created by blending scores of different chemicals in tiny amounts — a process governed by scientific principles but demanding a fair amount of art. In an age when delicate aromas and microwave ovens do not easily coexist, the job of the flavorist is to conjure illusions about processed food and, in the words of one flavor company's literature, to ensure "consumer likeability." The flavorists with whom I spoke were discreet, in keeping with the dictates of their trade. They were also charming, cosmopolitan, and ironic. They not only enjoyed fine wine but could identify the chemicals that give each grape its unique aroma. One flavorist compared his work to composing music. A well-made flavor compound will have a "top note" that is often followed by a "drydown" and a "leveling-off," with different chemicals responsible for each stage. The taste of a food can be radically altered by minute changes in the flavoring combination. "A little odor goes a long way," one flavorist told me.

In order to give a processed food a taste that consumers will find appealing, a flavorist must always consider the food's "mouthfeel" — the unique combination of textures and chemical interactions that affect how the flavor is perceived. Mouthfeel can be adjusted through the use of various fats, gums, starches, emulsifiers, and stabilizers. The aroma chemicals in a food can be precisely analyzed, but the elements that make up mouthfeel are much harder to measure. How does one quantify a pretzel's hardness, a french fry's crispness? Food technologists are now conducting basic research in rheology, the branch of physics that examines the flow and deformation of materials. A number of companies sell sophisticated devices that attempt to measure mouthfeel. The TA.XT2i Texture Analyzer, produced by the Texture Technologies Corporation, of Scarsdale, New York, performs calculations based on data derived from as many as 250 separate probes. It is essentially a mechanical mouth. It gauges the most important rheological properties of a food — bounce, creep, breaking point, density, crunchiness, chewiness, gumminess, lumpiness, rubberiness, springiness, slipperiness, smoothness, softness, wetness, juiciness, spreadability, springback, and tackiness.

Some of the most important advances in flavor manufacturing are now occurring in the field of biotechnology. Complex flavors are being made using enzyme reactions, fermentation, and fungal and tissue cultures. All the flavors created by these methods — including the ones being synthesized by fungi — are considered natural flavors by the FDA. The new enzyme-based processes are responsible for extremely true-to-life dairy flavors. One company now offers not just butter flavor but also fresh creamy butter, cheesy butter, milky butter, savory melted butter, and super-concentrated butter flavor, in liquid or powder form. The development of new fermentation techniques, along with new techniques for heating mixtures of sugar and amino acids, have led to the creation of much more realistic meat flavors.

The McDonald's Corporation most likely drew on these advances when it eliminated beef tallow from its french fries. The company will not reveal the exact origin of the natural flavor added to its fries. In response to inquiries from *Vegetarian Journal*, however, McDonald's did acknowledge that its fries derive some of their characteristic flavor from "an animal source." Beef is the probable source, although other meats cannot be ruled out. In France, for example, fries are sometimes cooked in duck fat or horse tallow.

Other popular fast foods derive their flavor from unexpected ingredients. McDonald's Chicken McNuggets contain beef extracts, as does Wendy's Grilled Chicken Sandwich. Burger King's BK Broiler Chicken Breast Patty contains "natural smoke flavor." A firm called Red Arrow Products specializes in smoke flavor, which is added to barbecue sauces, snack foods, and processed meats. Red Arrow manufactures natural smoke flavor by charring sawdust and capturing the aroma chemicals released into the air. The smoke is captured in water and then bottled, so that other companies can sell food that seems to have been cooked over a fire.

The Vegetarian Legal Action Network recently petitioned the

FDA to issue new labeling requirements for foods that contain natural flavors. The group wants food processors to list the basic origins of their flavors on their labels. At the moment vegetarians often have no way of knowing whether a flavor additive contains beef, pork, poultry, or shellfish. One of the most widely used color additives — whose presence is often hidden by the phrase "color added" — violates a number of religious dietary restrictions, may cause allergic reactions in susceptible people, and comes from an unusual source. Cochineal extract (also known as carmine or carminic acid) is made from the desiccated bodies of female *Dactylopius coccus Costa,* a small insect harvested mainly in Peru and the Canary Islands. The bug feeds on red cactus berries, and color from the berries accumulates in the females and their un-hatched larvae. The insects are collected, dried, and ground into a pigment. It takes about seventy thousand of them to produce a pound of carmine, which is used to make processed foods look pink, red, or purple. Dannon strawberry yogurt gets its color from carmine, and so do many frozen fruit bars, candies, and fruit fillings, and Ocean Spray pink-grapefruit juice drink.

In a meeting room at IFF, Brian Grainger let me sample some of the company's flavors. It was an unusual taste test — there was no food to taste. Grainger is a senior flavorist at IFF, a soft-spoken chemist with graying hair, an English accent, and a fondness for understatement. He could easily be mistaken for a British diplo-mat or the owner of a West End brasserie with two Michelin stars. Like many in the flavor industry, he has an Old World, old-fash-ioned sensibility. When I suggested that IFF's policy of secrecy and discretion was out of step with our mass-marketing, brand-conscious, self-promoting age and that the company should put its own logo on the countless products that bear its flavors, instead of allowing other companies to enjoy the consumer loyalty and affec-tion inspired by those flavors, Grainger politely disagreed, assur-ing me that such a thing would never be done. In the absence of public credit or acclaim, the small and secretive fraternity of flavor chemists praise one another's work. By analyzing the flavor formula of a product, Grainger can often tell which of his counter-parts at a rival firm devised it. Whenever he walks down a super-market aisle, he takes a quiet pleasure in seeing the well-known foods that contain his flavors.

Grainger had brought a dozen small glass bottles from the lab. After he opened each bottle, I dipped a fragrance-testing filter into it — a long white strip of paper designed to absorb aroma chemi-cals without producing off notes. Before placing each strip of pa-per in front of my nose, I closed my eyes. Then I inhaled deeply, and one food after another was conjured from the glass bottles. I smelled fresh cherries, black olives, sautéed onions, and shrimp. Grainger's most remarkable creation took me by surprise. After closing my eyes, I suddenly smelled a grilled hamburger. The aroma was uncanny, almost miraculous — as if someone in the room were flipping burgers on a hot grill. But when I opened my eyes, I saw just a narrow strip of white paper and a flavorist with a grin.

HEIDI JON SCHMIDT

■

Blood Poison

FROM *Epoch*

"YOU PROBABLY DON'T BELIEVE this is my daughter," my father
said to the cabdriver. "You're wondering, where did a broken-down
old guy like him come up with a gal like that?"

It was only an hour since I'd gotten off the train and already my
father had explained to two strangers that we weren't having an affair. The first was the bartender at the Oyster Bar, where Pop had
pulled out my stool as if New York was his overcoat and he was
spreading it over a puddle for me. The bartender looked as if he
had long since stopped seeing individual faces or thinking of anything except whatever he himself was obsessed with — money or
football or his prostate or maybe some kind of love or ideal. He
nodded without listening, dealing out some packets of crackers
like cards. The place was full — of men and women who looked
busier and more purposeful than I'd ever been — and the chalk-
board listed oysters named for all the places I'd have felt more at
home: Cotuit, Wellfleet, Chincoteague — low-tide towns where
the few people left behind through the winter huddled in the souvenir shop doorways, stamping their feet and swearing under the
clouds of their breath.

To the bartender I'd given an apologetic smile, which went,
of course, unnoticed. Ahmed Sineduy, license number 0017533,
cried "Yes!" with wonderful enthusiasm, as if he had indeed been
trying to imagine what would attract me to my father.

"In fact," Pop crowed, "I *created* her!"

I'd convinced him to have a drink at lunch — a mistake, but I wanted one myself. He makes me nervous — I don't know him very well. He and my mother married young, and after I was born he drifted away, taking long and longer visits to his mother in the city until finally we noticed that he was living with her and visiting us. I'd study the New York news every night, first thinking I might see him, later that if I came to understand the city, I'd get a sense of my father, too. Phrases like "truck rollover in the Midtown Tunnel" were invested with incalculable glamour for me, and when people spoke of the Queensboro Bridge or the East River they might as well have been talking about the Great Obelisk of Shalmanezar and the Red Sea.

Twice a year my mother put me on the train to the city so I could spend the weekend with him. In my grandmother's apartment it was still 1945, and I pushed the mother-of-pearl buttons on the radio set, expecting to hear FDR, while Pop made supper and Grammy offered me hoarded bits of chocolate and cake. We tried to act familiar, which meant we couldn't ask the kind of questions that might have helped us figure each other out, and year after year the distance grew. If Pop was doing well in the market he talked a mile a minute, spreading out maps and showing me pictures of the houses — sometimes whole islands — he meant to buy. When he was losing he was silent, and would start out of his trance every few minutes to ask how I was doing in school. As soon as I could I'd escape to the guest room, pull the velvet drapes, and fold myself into the heavy bed linens, where in my fantasies some man as commanding and enveloping as Zeus the swan held me in the tightest grip you can imagine, while all the lights of the city whirled over our heads.

So, yes, I was an overheated child, and so fervid an adolescent I became accustomed to seeing my teachers squirm and look away from me, praying I'd go elsewhere for the extra help next time. By college the pedagogical discomfort was happily transformed, and there was no end to the office hours available for a girl whose palpitating heart was quite nearly visible through her blouse. How I loved school!

With my father I keep my hair shaken down over my eyes like a dog, though I still come twice a year to visit. It pleases him to think of himself as a father, and God has damned me to try and please him. When my mother gave up her quest to draw him back to us and started the divorce, he sobbed like a lost little boy. And now that my grandmother's dead, I'm the only family he has.

This time I was even "on business" — I was flying to Cincinnati in the morning for a job interview — a visiting assistant professor job of the sort that a person like me would be very lucky to have; a job I needed to escape a debilitating love: a professor, of course, my Louis — an authority on Balzac, about whom no one else gives a damn. When I first met him he was railing at some translator's disrespect for an original text, and I remember thinking that he was *really angry,* that a crime against meaning was no less brutal to him than a physical assault. Needless to say I threw myself at him, and at Balzac. I swam through *The Human Comedy* as if it were a river I had to cross to reach him, but when I reached the other shore he was gone. By then I'd studied long enough to see Louis had such feeling for literature because ordinary life seemed so empty to him. And I was the very emissary of the ordinary — eating, bleeding, laughing, et cetera — a constant reminder of how much better Balzac had done than God. Louis began to inflict little cruelties, insults and condescensions, like cigarette burns, wherever he knew I was tender, and I slowly found myself entirely absorbed in these wounds — with each I became sicker, but it seemed an ailment only Louis's gentle care could cure. In a minute of clarity I realized I'd have to tear myself out of his life by the roots, and taking a job in a distant city looked like the surest way.

The cab zipped uptown, switching lanes and skirting bike messengers and double-parked delivery trucks with an ease I should have found alarming, but I leaned back. I had faith in Ahmed. As long as he was talking to my father I was safe.

"Seventy-nine?" Ahmed asked.

"Fifty-six and a half!" my father replied. His age.

"Fifty-six?" Ahmed hit the brake. We were already somewhere in the sixties.

"Seventy-ninth Street," I said. "Museum of Natural History."

Natural History in springtime; in September, the Met. Once, when I was maybe ten, we tried something different, a piano concert at Lincoln Center. I had a velvet dress, and Pop kept whispering things about the music to me, pointing out the movements in a concerto, praising the pianist's fine technique. He had never said a word about music before, and certainly I'd never heard him speak with rapture — he was trying to impress me, I realized; he wanted my esteem. And I tried — I worked at admiring him the way a doubting priest works at faith.

"But you must see plenty of men out with girls who aren't their daughters," he was saying to Ahmed, thinking perhaps of Louis, who's fifty-three. "It happens all the time."

He made it sound like a horror: something too awful to think about, like a child crushed under a bus or chained in a basement, one of the travesties he absorbs out of the paper, and can't stop talking about, almost as if he'd suffered them himself. He keeps his eye trained on the pain in the newspaper; he can't bear to look at real life.

He quit his job during the divorce; he couldn't stand to give money to people who rejected him. After that he went into business for himself, borrowing office space from acquaintances, empty desks he could use for a few months or a year, in a cubicle on the eighteenth or twenty-fifth or forty-seventh floor where a couple of sour men smoked cigars and followed the ticker tape all day. Visiting, I'd stand at the window, watching the secretaries gather like pigeons on the pavement below, thinking that someday I'd become one of them and work silently all day among people who took no notice of me. Then we'd go home to Grammy, who still called him Skipper, his childhood name. They fought over trifles as if they were married, but she had no notion of money and was happy as long as he didn't waste food or throw away any reusable string. When she died she left him a pantry full of egg crates and plastic containers, but he had already spent her fortune.

In his new flat on Staten Island, he was perfectly content, he told me again and again. Yes, it faced north, but he wasn't one of these people who had to have sunlight, and what a relief just to cook for himself. It wasn't as if he were isolated — he had the *Times* and fifty-two channels. He would have been amazed to realize that the pretty morning news anchor he admired was younger than I was, that if he were to meet her by one of the fabulous accidents he imagined, he, too, would be "out with a girl" right now.

"Have any children yourself?" he asked Ahmed, with his salesman's hearty voice.

"Seventy-nine!" Ahmed declared.

"No English," I mouthed to Pop, twice before he understood.

"Aha!" he said. He cleared his throat. He had that tutelary gleam in his eye — he was going to show me how little distance there is between cultures, how much can be accomplished with a smile, a concerned tone. He thought, quite rightly, that I was an awkward, inward girl, in need of social training. Where did Ahmed come from, he asked — Syria? Lebanon? India, perhaps?

When Ahmed said Karachi, my father turned out to have a few words of Punjabi, and an enthusiastic accent, too. Ahmed burst into speech.

"Whoa, whoa, you're way beyond me!" Pop said. "Slow down, wa-a-a-y down."

By Seventy-ninth Street Ahmed had taught him some basic insults, and the words for *father* and *daughter.*

"Nice guy," Pop said as the cab fishtailed away from us. "Wish I could have tipped him."

"What did you say to him?" I asked.

"'Isn't it a beautiful evening,'" he told me. "The janitor at the office taught me. He has a wife and three kids back there . . . He doesn't have much hope of getting them over, but he sends money . . ."

He sighed so heavily, thinking of this family torn apart, that I was afraid he was going to cry. He's so tall, has such broad shoulders, that when he gets weepy it's like seeing a statue melt. Even now I'll be doing the dishes or walking the dog and I suddenly feel his sadness go through me. I think of him as a little boy, his own father dying — he'll say "when I died," by accident, when he speaks of it — I never know what to do to assuage it, any more than I did when I was ten. One morning back then he told me that my mother didn't want to make love to him anymore. I had only the vaguest idea of what he meant, and I sat stupidly over my cinnamon toast searching for something helpful while his lip began to tremble, as if I was his last hope and had failed him.

By now he's so solitary he expects no consolation, and he walked along tightly for a minute, entirely constricted by sadness, and then threw it off with a quick little gesture, like breaking a chain.

"He taught me to say 'Wow, get the legs on that babe,' too." He laughed, holding the door to the automatic teller open for me. There was hardly room for two people in the booth. I edged into the corner while he fed his card to the machine.

"We'll have to see," he said. "Last week they credited me with fifty dollars by mistake. In fact, I'm overdrawn." He punched in his number: 1014, the date of his marriage to my mother.

"I've got money," I said. I was embarrassed how much — Louis never let me help with the rent, so my salary went straight into the bank.

"No, no, honey," he told me. "I think we'll be fine here. I've *been* making money. I started with five thousand and I was doing great all through March — I was up to twenty-five. Then I lost a few thousand last week, a few more Monday, and Friday another seventeen . . ."

By my math this meant he was broke. I'd guessed it, seeing his posture from the train window as he waited on the platform, and when, over the whole course of lunch, he never spoke of buying any islands at all.

"As long as they didn't catch the error," he said, "we ought to be all right." We heard the rollers inside the machine as they shuffled the bills; then it spat three starched twenties at us through pursed rubber lips.

"The town's ours," said Pop, as if we'd drawn three cherries on a slot machine. His luck was turning, he could feel it. I could hardly keep up with him as he strode back toward the museum.

"Two adults," he said to the cashier, and "Can it really be, you're an adult?" to me, and then, to the cashier again, "She's my daughter. What do you think?"

Her badge read CYNTHIA POST, DOCENT. She had a kind of brisk official grace, and she glanced at me and gave him a perfunctory smile. As I accepted my museum pin from her, I thought that although she might have been unhappy in her life, she did not look as if she'd often been confused. She would have spent her whole life here, walking to the museum past her grocery, her florist, her dry cleaner, the school she and her children had attended, the church she had been married in. I regarded her with both condescension and jealousy — I would never belong so squarely to anything. I'd put on a hat that morning because it seems to me that only very confident people wear hats — so that I'd appear to be self-assured — but I felt only foolish and ostentatious, like a child dressed up in her mother's clothes.

My father, of course, looked great. Age has given him the look of dignity, and he takes a professional pleasure in conversation. No one has ever sounded more reasonable, more calm and knowing. If he told you to buy something, you'd buy, or he'd explain it slower, with more stubborn patience, until you did. He solicited Cynthia Post's suggestion of the best exhibit, and as we took the direction she suggested (something interactive in the Rocks and Minerals), her smile was newly warm. Following him down the corridor, one hand on my hat as I tried to keep pace with his stride, I felt for a minute as I used to when I visited: happy and excited just to be in his company, sure that if I could only manage to keep my hand in his he'd pull me around the corner into a new world.

"Did she say the second right, or the third?" he asked me. The hallway ended in three closed doors. Two were locked, so we went through the third and down another long passage toward a sign that read ENTRANCE, which turned out to be one of a pile of ENTRANCE signs stored against another locked door. There was hardly any light and I felt terribly claustrophobic suddenly, as if we were locked here forever. After all the years of visiting museums I'm still never comfortable in one — even in a roomful of Renoirs I long for a window, and the Museum of Natural History, the final repository of moon rocks and extinct sparrows and other small, dun-colored things whose significance one would never believe if it weren't written out for you, always seemed to me the loneliest place in the world. To stand here now with my father was to guess what it might feel like in my grave.

Pop took a credit card out of his wallet and slid it down the doorjamb.

"Voilà!" he said, pushing the door open and ushering me through. "I'm way over the limit on that card anyway," he said.

We were in my favorite room — the dioramas of aboriginal life. It was empty except for us and a troop of black Girl Scouts whose noses were pressed to the glass to see Cro-Magnon man forage and the Vikings set to sea. I peered in over their heads; I love ant colonies, too, and model trains, quattrocento crucifixions — those representations of life where everyone takes part, whether sowing or winnowing, rowing or raising the sail. You never see anyone like me, loitering at the edge of the scene, too fearful to make an effort, wishing only to escape his little glassed-in world.

My father checked his watch. He had done the fatherly thing by bringing me: now what? He turned his attention to the scouts. He's friend to all little girls now, watching them on the street, in the library or the supermarket, befriending them in elevators, smiling down over them with an unbearable nostalgia. Nostalgia for me, I suppose, though like most nostalgia this was not yearning for something lost but for something that had never been, an old wish so deeply etched into memory that finally it was clear as if real. Every one of these children was the child I might have been — a child who flew off the school bus into her father's arms and who was gentle and delicate, shy and kind. I had been most disappointing, talking too much, laughing too loudly, though "unnaturally" silent with him. He was still saving elephant jokes for me while I was soldiering my pompous twelve-year-old way through *The Feminine Mystique,* and I could tell from his face, when he walked in to find me reading it in the bathtub, that he was certain it must be filth. He stood there looking down at me with his characteristic puzzled, hurt expression, wondering what could be wrong, how I could have become the way I was. "Does your mother know you're reading that?" he asked finally, but he left before I could answer, as if he had to get away from me. Even my body was becoming obscene.

Now he looked down over these little girls in their uniforms and berets as if he might find a new daughter among them. Two of them, whispering together, became gradually aware of him and grew silent.

"Why you staring?" one of them asked, sharp as her own mother, I supposed. The mother who had woven those hundred braids and fastened them with red and yellow beads.

"I was wondering which badges you have there," he told her.

She was maybe seven; pride quickly overwhelmed her suspicion. She lifted her sash and began, in a careful, earnest voice, to describe them, pressing a finger to each embroidered circle: there was one for reading, one for learning to swim, one for refusing drugs. He bent to look more closely, asking how she had earned them, expressing amazement that such a small girl could have accomplished such difficult tasks. The whole troop, wary at first, then eager, reconstellated around him.

"Girls?" Their leader fixed a level gaze on them — they had been taught not to take up with strangers; in fact there was a badge for that, too. They turned unwillingly from my father's attention and reformed their line of pairs, holding hands as they went on toward the Bird Room. The one with the red and yellow beads took a last quick glance over her shoulder at us as she left the room.

"It's terrific," he said, watching them. "They're from Paterson. You know what a sewer Paterson is? But that little girl, she looked me right in the eye when I spoke to her, she —"

He broke off. His eyes were brimming.

"If I could find the right woman," he said, "I'd start all over again, and this time it wouldn't be one child, I'd like to have four or five — or six! or seven! I suppose that surprises you . . ." he said with some kind of belligerence.

"Not at all," I said. I'd have been surprised if he didn't dream of such things, but it seems his penance for never having completely entered into marriage is that he can't get completely divorced. He never dated anyone after my mother. He told me once that as a young man he had assumed that husband and wife became, sexually, one being, so that if split, both halves must die. Adultery must then be physically appalling: when a colleague of his had casually mentioned a mistress, my father had begun to retch as if he'd heard of a bestial crime.

"I'm so glad we can *talk* to each other!" he said now. We had come to the Hall of Dinosaurs, and I made a show of studying a stegosaurus spine.

"People have such awful relations with their children these days," he went on. "But I feel there's nothing I wouldn't be comfortable telling you."

I was afraid this might he true, and indeed, a minute later he was feeling comfortable enough to tell me about a sore he had on his back, somewhere near the seventh vertebra — no, he hadn't been to the doctor — and here, with his arm twisted and groping in the back of his shirt, he stopped to ponder medical costs and the arrogance of the educated, and to remind me that he had treated his own athlete's foot for years with a simple formula of diluted sulfuric acid. But this thing was painful, and he couldn't see it, that was the real problem.

"It's there, there, a little up," he said, turning his back to me and trying to reach it with his thumb.

"A little *up*," he said again, with irritation, because I was supposed, apparently, to examine it. I looked around in the vain hope that someone might come through, some white rabbit of a scientist carrying a large bone, the kind of man I always dream will save me.

"Up, up, *there*," Pop said, giving a little moan as I touched the sore. "It hurts," he said, in the voice of a child.

"I'll look at it when we get back to the island," I promised, thinking he'd forget it by then.

The Hall of African Mammals opened before us, long, cool, and dark like the nave of a cathedral, its polished marble walls glistening, its chapels dedicated not to saints but to species endangered or extinct. In the center was a stuffed woolly mammoth lifting its trumpeting head. A young waiter in a tuxedo shirt was arranging café tables around it.

"Hello!" my father called to him, across the room. "Is this a private party?"

No, it was a regular thing on Fridays, came the answer, though not until five.

It was a quarter past four. Could my father prevail upon him —? He'd been bringing me here since I was six —

The waiter interrupted him — sit anywhere, he said. It was easier to pour a couple of early drinks than listen to the story. He brought us two gin-and-tonics and a cup of Goldfish crackers and left us alone.

As I lifted my drink my father looked me up and down quickly, startled, as if he had just realized again that he was out with a woman. I was glad the waiter had gone — I didn't think I could bear to have myself explained again.

"So, what's this job in Columbus?" Pop asked, the way he used to ask me about school.

"Cincinnati," I said, but though he had asked the same question, with the same error, at lunch, I was relieved to hear it. It's the sort of thing fathers and daughters talk about, and I had, for once, a good answer.

"Assistant professor," I told him. "I mean, it's mainly teaching composition, but —"

"But it's a job," he said. "You won't be on the dole anymore."

"A teaching fellowship isn't quite the dole."

"It's all Greek to me, sweetie," he said with a laugh. "I'm sure it's very important. Nothing wrong with a little work, though."

If he saw the irony in this, it didn't show in his face. These were phrases he'd heard, "Greek to me" and "Nothing wrong with a little work." He repeated them just to have something to say. He hadn't gone to college — his mother thought it extravagant, so he'd never quite understood what I'd been doing studying all the time. To deal him a sharp reply would have been like striking a child.

"It'll be a lot of work," I said, careful to keep the eager, Horatio Alger note in my voice. "But it's great just to get an interview. You wouldn't believe it, but they said almost two hundred people applied. And now it's just between me and two others. And they've been so nice, you should have heard what they said about my articles ... Considering the market," I said, thinking now that in fact I hadn't done so terribly badly, had accomplished a little and had time to accomplish more, that I could really give him something to be proud of, that he might even see that if there was promise in my life, his, too, could be redeemed, "I'm doing pretty well."

"You can go pretty far with a nice set of tits these days," he said.

He was smiling as if he had just gotten off a wonderful *mot,* and I wanted to smile, too, because if I smiled we could go on as if he hadn't said this, and soon it would really seem he had not. I couldn't manage it, but I carefully avoided looking down to see if my sweater was too tight, or crossing my arms over my chest, or cringing or shrinking in any way. I looked past him for a minute, at a kudu, lithe and proud in its glass enclosure, looking out over a glittering lake.

You're all he's got, I said to myself. *Be kind.*

"Do you suppose that's real water?" I asked, hoping to lead him back to safety. He likes a mechanical question, and can spend hours explaining about pistons and spark plugs, how the keystone holds the arch and the moon pulls the tide. Now he began on the properties of chlorine, but a morose fog settled into his voice and he stared a long time into the scene.

"No," he said suddenly, rousing himself. "By God, I *wouldn't* mind marrying again, not one little bit." His voice rang against the marble walls. "I'd like to find a woman who loves to cook, and loves to talk, and loves to hike, and loves to fuck —"

He paused, darting a glance toward me, worrying I might be offended? Hoping so? Testing, to see if I might be the woman described?

"And then I'd like to buy a piece of property on the sunny side of a good, serious hill, and we'd start building a house there."

He drained his drink and looked around for the waiter.

"I was right," he told me. "I *knew* T-bills were going to turn around this week. If only I'd been able to get a solid position, we could be having this drink . . . on Antigua! Or, how would you like Positano? Looking out over the Bay of Naples? Bougainvillea cascading down the hillsides? What would you think about that?

"I've *been* making money," he said again. "This time next year, who knows?" He lifted the empty glass to his lips again.

"Where *is* he?" I asked, but the waiter was gone.

Then came the Girl Scouts, two by two, swinging their clasped hands, unable to quite keep themselves from skipping until they stood before the woolly mammoth, whereupon a hush seized them as if they were in the presence of a god or a living dream. Daneesha, the one with the red and yellow beads, greeted my father now as an old friend, shaking off her partner and running to him to show off a new gyroscope from the souvenir shop.

He woke up. For a minute he was in the thrall not of the past or the future but of Daneesha and her gyroscope, which he spun for her on his fingertip, then along its string. Soon he was writing out his phone number, inviting her to dinner the next time she came into town.

"Your whole family," he told her. "Do you like spaghetti?"

It was just her mother and herself, she said, and they loved spaghetti. She was hungry, as I'd been: she wanted to draw her hand along a man's scratchy cheek, to be lifted in a pair of arms that could carry her anywhere. As she took the business card with his number, her clear smile faded into an expression of secret greed. She pocketed it quickly, and, as if afraid he would snatch it back from her, ran back to the troop, whose leader turned a hard warning glance at him. I remembered that the mother of a little girl in his building had told him if she found her daughter at his place one more time she'd call the police. Nobody gets it, I thought — it's not that he wants sex with little girls, it's that he wants to live like they do, in a world before all that.

"It's hard to believe that you used to be that age," he said, as the scouts went off toward the planetarium. He checked his watch.

"If we leave now," he began, "we can change at the World Trade

Center before the crush . . ." Call Hunan Kitchen from the ferry terminal, catch the 5:40 boat, be on the island by 6:15, and pick up dinner on the way home. And he was off into the city with me only one step behind. The subway station felt just like always, comforting in its clangor, the crowd of preoccupied faces pressing onto the escalator, the couple of latecomers running edgewise down the stairs. The doors of one train closed with hydraulic authority and it slid smoothly off as another slammed in around the bend. Pop put one token in the stile for me, waved me through, and strode ahead of me again toward the first car. From here we could easily cross to the express at Grand Central. And it was waiting, already packed. I folded myself between two men in suits and swayed with them all the way downtown. I *do*, I thought, *I love it here*. At South Ferry we ran up the ramp, and though the boat was boarding Pop dialed Hunan Kitchen: he could see by the size of the crowd that there was plenty of time.

We were the last up the gangplank, and the first to disembark, running down the iron stairway to the street, crossing with the light, turning up the street past the Hadassah Thrift Shop and Winnie's Bridal and Formal, and Island Cleaners, where suits and dresses moved in stately procession on their conveyor, and as we opened the door at Hunan Kitchen they were calling our number.

"Steaming!" Pop said, opening the little cartons and setting them in the center of the table, as proud as if we had ridden unscathed through the gears of a great machine.

"It's all in the timing," he told me, feeling paternal now, ready to share the wisdom of his lifetime with me. "It's an instinct — you have to have a sense for it. The crowd is going one direction, everyone's jumping on the bandwagon, and you have to be willing to stop and think, 'Maybe there's another way.' I'm always ready to take the risk, move against the prevailing winds, and it's paid off for me."

He gestured in the direction of the newspaper, still folded to the market tables. "What I would have done this week, if I'd had the money," he said, "nobody else even considered, but it would have been *very* profitable."

He shook his head. "But for a lack of cash, really, I'd be on top of the world today. I've just gotta get back in there, sweetie, and with this kind of opportunity, you know, by November, the clouds are closing in here, and I can be thinking where I'd like to retire to."

He popped the beer top as if it were champagne, but in another minute he was lost to his thoughts again. The lamp over the table, all four hundred watts of it (he had hated my mother's dinners by candle), shone pitilessly down on his face. Everything in his apartment — the bare bulbs, the month's worth of newspapers piled by the couch, the box of sugar he plunked down defiantly before me as if to say, "I suppose you expected a bowl" — still set itself against my mother. But on the wall facing his chair hung her engagement photograph, taken when she was twenty and secure in a luxuriant beauty. I had nothing of her in me, I thought — I was his daughter exactly, and it made me want to rip at my skin.

"Curaçao is nice," Pop said suddenly. "Coves, inlets, nice private spots. I don't need a glittering nightlife, wide beaches, high-rise hotels . . ." His voice swelled. "Some people have to have that, the glamour — it makes them feel like they are somebody, I guess . . . I never felt that way. That's one thing I like about Beverly Dill" — this was the news anchor he admired — "she's down-to-earth. She's smart, but not so smart you wouldn't trust her. She's not looking for fame or money, not the kind of gal who would turn up her nose at —"

"I have found you ridiculous since the time I was old enough to laugh." I could taste these words on my tongue, and they were delicious. To have nothing to be proud of but the fact that you didn't like high-rise hotels! To be cooped in your deathly apartment beneath a photograph of your former wife, sketching, sketching on the blueprints for the next one as if anyone at all could bear to love you!

But it was valor, almost, his relentless optimism, the way, though his life had eroded beneath him, he refused to feel the loss, counting his blessings, keeping his eye on the future even if by now he could see no more in the future than these worn old fantasies, the escape to the island, the beautiful woman's love. To despise him was to remember, suddenly, a time when I was twelve and he had driven me to the dentist for an extraction that went awry. An hour of bloody probing and wrenching ended in an operation with scant anesthesia, but the worst part was seeing Pop stand by helpless, one minute trying to make light of it, the next turning away, aghast. If I'd ever dreamed he could take care of me, I had to admit myself wrong that day. On the way home we passed a K-mart and suddenly he was doubling back, determined to buy me a gift. Dazed and aching, I waded in behind him among racks of too-blue jeans and stacks of lawn furniture poised to fall. In the music department I grabbed the first thing on the rack, just to get it over with. It was *Yellow Submarine,* and I still can't hear it without thinking of everything I wanted that purchase to assuage: he was failing, at marriage, at work, at fatherhood, and he had one hope left, the hope that I was too young to see.

Now I continued to pretend. "— at the simpler things in life," I said. This was a phrase of his, and to speak it was a way to say, covertly, "It's okay, it's only money you've lost, nothing important."

"The *simpler things in life.* Exactly," he said. "*Exactly.* There are so few people, sweetie, who really understand . . ." He turned to me with a true smile, even a loving smile, and I felt, and despised myself for feeling, overjoyed. His discourse on simplicity carried us to bedtime, when he cleared the newspapers off the sofa, pulled it out for me, and gave me sheets, the same ones Grammy had ripped up their worn middles and restitched for him before she died. As I made up the bed, I heard him brush his teeth while the bathroom radio gave the financial news. A cold rain pricked at the window, and under the marquee of the defunct moviehouse across the street a tired prostitute looked up and down the empty street. I went to pull the curtain, but of course there wasn't any.

"You know, the way you're standing, you could almost have been your mother for a minute there."

I jumped. I hadn't heard him come out of the bathroom.

"Sweetie," he said, coming toward me, "it's only me." I was afraid for a minute he was going to put his arms around me, but instead he took off his shirt.

"Would you mind just looking at my back for me? This — boil, or whatever it is — I . . ." He trailed off — I could see he didn't like to ask.

"Oh, Pop, I don't know anything about boils," I said, but after all he was alone, while I had Louis to look at any boils of mine, so I sat him down to examine him. His skin was coarse and oily — I remembered all I knew about skin, how it's the body's largest organ and full of various glands. How heavy a skin is, like a wet suit: I pictured his folded over the back of a chair. The sore was a round raw center in a nimbus of pus, and I saw he'd been picking at it, like a child who can't leave a scab alone.

"Press it and see what's in it, sweetie," he said. "I thought something crawled out of it yesterday."

He looked up at me and some ancient, familiar shadow crossed his face. Was he cut so absolutely free of his moorings, so adrift in fantasy, that his night terrors were as alive to him as his island dreams? I felt frightened myself, suddenly — he seemed a mire that might any minute pull me in, and I tried to remind myself that he was only a man, a lost, confused man who had no one to care for him but me.

I set my finger to the edge of the inflammation, and the pain pleased him. "It doesn't sting," he said. "More like a burn . . ."

"It just needs to be disinfected," I said. "There's only a little swelling here, nothing to worry about." Truly, I thought it might want lancing, but I knew if I suggested that he'd ask me to do it, and dabbing it with a bit of cotton soaked in witch hazel was almost more than I could bear.

"That's good," he said with a little shudder. "That's so good."

"There," I said. Blood poison was unlikely, and no one would count me responsible if his blood was poisoned, or neglectful if he died. I probably wouldn't feel more than the occasional prick of guilt myself — nothing compared to the way I felt for hating him so. "I think it's going to heal up fine."

"It's wonderful to have family, isn't it, sweetie?" he said, standing up, relieved, it seemed, of every fear and sorrow by my little ministration. "So few people understand that, that it's family, not glamour, or money, or fame, that's the important thing."

He turned, glowing with good feeling, to hug me.

I knew it would be insane to scream. I leaned stiffly toward him, patting his back above the sore, concentrating on my breath so as not to panic, doubly gentle because I felt as if my fingers might sprout claws.

"Is there a sheet or something I could tack up over the window?" I asked when he released me.

He looked puzzled. "Nobody can see in here, sweetie," he said. "We're on the sixth floor."

He was right, of course. Still I felt exposed.

"If you're nervous," he said, "you can come in and sleep with me."

His voice was studiedly casual, but his eyes had the angry gleam of a man who has bet everything on a single number and is watching the wheel spin. It was a proposition, and I felt the room swinging around me like a nauseating carnival ride, in the center of which I — my heart, breath, mind, and most of all my eyes — must keep fixed absolutely still.

"I'm okay," I said. Very lightly, hoping I could somehow back away from him without moving. It was the first such suggestion I had ever declined. Professors were so magnificently arrogant, they'd leave the marks of their grip on my arm, asking me to bed as if they were challenging me to a duel — it would have been cowardice to refuse. And the others, the timid boys who tried a little ruse, like my father — I could never bear to turn them down. Men — you can feel their sadness, but how to assuage it? You have to do it through sex, they can't take nourishment any other way. And I was always so grateful to be wanted, to feel them drinking their strength from my beauty, drinking and drinking until they seemed powerful as gods.

Pop shrugged. "We used to do it, when you were two years old," he said.

"So, Columbus tomorrow!" he said when I didn't answer. "Teaching, you say?"

I nodded.

"What would you teach?" he asked, sounding baffled.

"Comparative literature."

"You don't need some kind of certificate for that?"

"No," I said, knowing he didn't count the Ph.D.

"Amazing. Hey, you don't think there might be a something out there for me, do you? I've got a real soft spot for the Midwest. Good people, salt of the earth. Nothing keeping me here — you might say I'm footloose and fancy free. We could get a nicer place if there were two of us. I've *been* making money . . ."

To invite him would be suicide. To say no was more of a homicide. I settled for silence; cowardice seemed a bloodless crime.

"Well, just something to think about . . ." he said. "It's just great to have you here, sweetie."

He spoke so sincerely that I was afraid he was going to hug me again, but no, he went into his bedroom and closed the door, and a few minutes later I saw the light blink out beneath.

I curled against the far arm of the couch, pulling my knees to my chest, keeping the blanket tight around me, the way I used to sleep as a child. I had a recurring dream then that some awful force had come to suck me out the window, and I'd hold my breath, playing dead until it went away. I was always looking for a charm, something to wrap myself in for safety, the image of Zeus or Louis or whoever — everyone needs something like that, something to grab hold of in the dark. Now I tried to think of Cincinnati — a sleepy river town, sun on the factories, the pleasure of getting to know a new city — but all I could feel was that I didn't dare leave Louis, I needed him to keep my father at bay. After a long time I fell not asleep but into a kind of purgatorial consciousness, full of specters but still at one remove from that room.

"There's no one else," a voice said, so clear it seemed to rouse me. "*You'll* have to marry him."

Then I heard my father's bedsprings and his feet as they touched the floor. Soon he would pad past me on his way to the bathroom. I held myself tighter, trying to take the deep, slow breaths of a sleeper. He might be only inches away from me, but he wouldn't guess I'd awakened, and I'd never let him know.

DAVID SEDARIS

■

To Make a Friend, Be a Friend

FROM *Esquire*

EVERY NIGHT before going to bed, my boyfriend, Hugh, steps outside to consider the stars. His interest is not scientific — he doesn't pinpoint the constellations or make casual references to Canopus. Rather, he just regards the mass of them, occasionally pausing to sigh. When asked if there's life on other planets, he says, "Yes, of course. Consider the odds."

It hardly seems fair we'd get the universe all to ourselves, but on a personal level I'm highly disturbed by the thought of extraterrestrial life. If there are, in fact, billions of other civilizations, where does that leave our celebrities? If worth is measured on a sliding scale of notoriety, what would it mean if we were all suddenly obscure? How would we know our place?

In trying to make sense of this, I think back to a 1968 Labor Day celebration at the Raleigh Country Club. I was at the snack bar, listening to a group of sixth graders who lived in another part of town and sat discussing significant changes in their upcoming school year. According to the girl named Janet, neither Pam Dobbins nor J. J. Jackson had been invited to the Fourth of July party hosted by the Pyle twins, who later told Kath Matthews that both Pam and J. J. were out of the picture as far as the seventh grade was concerned. "Totally, completely out," Janet said. "Poof."

I didn't know any Pam Dobbins or J. J. Jackson, but the reverential tone of Janet's voice sent me into a state of mild shock. Call me naive, but it had simply never occurred to me that other schools might have their own celebrity circles. At the age of twelve I thought the group at E. C. Brooks was, if not nationally known, then at least its own private phenomenon. Why else would our lives revolve around it so completely? I myself was not a member of my school's popular crowd, but I recall thinking that, whoever they were, Janet's popular crowd couldn't begin to compete with ours. But what if I was wrong? What if I'd wasted my entire life comparing myself with people who didn't really matter? Try as I might, I still can't wrap my mind around it.

They banded together in the third grade. Ann Carlsworth, Christie Kaymore, Deb Bevins, Mike Holliwell, Doug Middleton, Thad Pope: this was the core of the popular crowd, and for the next six years my classmates and I studied their lives the way we were supposed to study math and English. What confused us most was the absence of any specific formula. Were they funny? No. Interesting? Yawn. None owned pools or horses. They had no special talents, and their grades were unremarkable. It was their dearth of excellence that gave the rest of us hope and kept us on our toes. Every now and then they'd select a new member, and the general attitude among the student body was *Oh, pick me!* It didn't matter what you were like on your own. The group would make you special. That was its magic.

So complete was their power that I actually felt honored when one of them hit me in the mouth with a rock. He'd gotten me after school, and upon returning home I ran into my sister's bedroom, hugging my bloody Kleenex and crying, "It was Thad!!!"

Lisa was a year older, but still she understood the significance. "Did he *say* anything?" she asked. "Did you save the rock?"

My father demanded I retaliate, saying I ought to knock the guy on his ass.

"Oh, Dad."

"Aww, baloney. Clock him on the snot locker and he'll go down like a ton of bricks."

"Are you talking to *me*?" I asked. The archaic slang aside, who did my father think I was? Boys who spent their weekends making banana-nut muffins did not, as a rule, excel in the art of hand-to-hand combat.

"I mean, come on, Dad," Lisa said. "Wake *up*."

The following afternoon I was taken to Dr. Povlitch for x-rays. The rock had damaged a tooth, and there was some question over who would pay for the subsequent root canal. I figured that since my parents had conceived me, given birth to me, and raised me as a permanent guest in their home, they should foot the bill, but my father thought differently. He decided the Popes should pay, and I screamed as he picked up the phone book.

"But you can't just . . . call Thad's house."

"Oh, yeah?" he said. "Just watch me."

There were two Thad Popes in the Raleigh phone book, a Junior and a Senior. The one in my class was what came after a Junior. He was a Third. My father called both the Junior and the Senior, beginning each conversation with the line, "Lou Sedaris here. Listen, pal, we've got a problem with your son."

He always said the name as if it meant something, as if we were known and respected. This made it all the more painful when he was asked to repeat it. Then to spell it.

A meeting was arranged for the following evening, and before leaving the house, I begged my father to change his clothes. He'd been building an addition to the carport and was wearing a pair of khaki shorts smeared with paint and spotted here and there with bits of dried concrete. Through a hole in his tattered T-shirt, it was possible to see his nipple.

"What the hell is wrong with this?" he asked. "We're not staying for dinner, so what does it matter?"

I yelled for my mother, and in the end he compromised by changing his shirt.

From the outside, Thad's house didn't look much different from anyone else's — just a standard split-level with what my father described as a totally inadequate carport. Mr. Pope answered the door in a pair of sherbet-colored golf pants and led us downstairs to what he called the "rumpus room."

"Oh," I said. "This is nice!"

The room was damp and windowless and lit with hanging Tiffany lampshades, the shards of colorful glass arranged to spell the words *Busch* and *Budweiser*. Walls were paneled in imitation walnut, and the furniture looked as though it had been hand-hewn by settlers who'd reconfigured parts of their beloved Conestoga wagon to fashion such things as easy chairs and coffee tables. Noticing the fraternity paddle hanging on the wall above the television, my father launched into his broken Greek, saying, *"Kalispera sas adelphos!"*

When Mr. Pope looked at him blankly, my father laughed and offered a translation. "I said, 'Good evening, brother.'"

"Oh . . . right," Mr. Pope said. "Fraternities are Greek."

He directed us toward a sofa and asked if we wanted something to drink. Coke? A beer? I didn't want to deplete Thad's precious cola supply, but before I could refuse, my father said sure, we'd have one of each. The orders were called up the stairs, and a few minutes later Mrs. Pope came down carrying cans and plastic tumblers.

"Well, *hello* there," my father said. This was his standard greeting to a beautiful woman, but I could tell he was just saying it as a joke. Mrs. Pope wasn't *un*attractive, just ordinary, and as she set the drinks before us I noticed that her son had inherited her blunt, slightly upturned nose, which looked good on him but caused her to appear overly suspicious and judgmental.

"So," she said. "I hear you've been to the dentist." She was trying to make small talk, but due to her nose, it came off sounding like an insult, as if I'd just had a tooth filled and was now looking for someone to pay the bill.

"*I'll* say he's been to the dentist," my father said. "Someone hits you in the mouth with a rock, and I'd say the dentist's office is pretty much the first place a reasonable person would go."

Mr. Pope held up his hands. "Whoa, now," he said. "Let's just calm things down a little." He yelled upstairs for his son, and when there was no answer he picked up the phone, telling Thad to stop running his mouth and get his butt down to the rumpus room ASAP.

A rush of footsteps on the carpeted staircase, and then Thad sprinted in, all smiles and apologies. The minister had called. The game had been rescheduled. "Hello, sir, and you are . . . ?"

He looked my father in the eye and firmly shook his hand, holding it in his own for just the right amount of time. While most handshakes mumbled, his clearly spoke, saying both *We'll get through this* and *I'm looking forward to your vote this coming November.*

I'd thought that seeing him without his group might be unsettling, like finding a single arm on the sidewalk, but Thad was fully capable of operating independently. Watching him in action, I understood that his popularity was not an accident. Unlike a normal human, he possessed an uncanny ability to please people. There was no sucking up or awkward maneuvering to fit the will of others. Rather, much like a Whitman's Sampler, he seemed to offer a little bit of everything. Pass on his athletic ability and you might partake of his excellent manners, his confidence, his coltish enthusiasm. Even his parents seemed invigorated by his presence, uncrossing their legs and sitting up just a little bit straighter as he took a seat beside them. Had the circumstances been different, my father would have been all over him, probably going so far as to call him son — but money was involved, so he steeled himself.

"All right, then," Mr. Pope said. "Now that everyone's accounted for, I'm hoping we can clear this up. Sticks and stones aside, I suspect this all comes down to a little misunderstanding between friends."

I lowered my eyes, waiting for Thad to set his father straight. "*Friends?* With *him?*" I expected laughter or the famous Thad snort, but instead he said nothing. And with his silence, he won me completely. A little misunderstanding — that's *exactly* what it was. How had I not seen it earlier?

The immediate goal was to save my friend, so I claimed to have essentially thrown myself in the path of Thad's rock.

"What the hell was he throwing rocks for?" my father asked. "What the hell was he throwing them at?"

Mrs. Pope frowned, implying that such language was not welcome in the rumpus room.

"I mean, Jesus Christ, the guy's got to be a complete idiot."

Thad swore he hadn't been aiming at anything, and I backed him up, saying it was just one of those things we all did. "Like in Vietnam or whatever. It was just friendly fire."

My father asked what the hell I knew about Vietnam, and again Thad's mother winced, saying that boys picked up a lot of this talk by watching the news.

"Aww, you don't know what you're talking about," my father said.

"What my wife meant —"

"Aww, baloney."

The trio of Popes exchanged meaningful glances, holding what amounted to a brief, telepathic powwow. "This man crazy," the smoke signals read. "Make heap big trouble for others."

I looked at my father, a man in dirty shorts who drank his beer from the can rather than pouring it into his tumbler, and I thought, You don't belong here. More precisely, I decided that he was the reason *I* didn't belong. The hokey Greek phrases, the how-to lectures on mixing your own concrete, the squabble over who would pay the stupid dentist bill — little by little, it had all seeped into my bloodstream, robbing me of my natural ability to please others. For as long as I could remember, he'd been telling us that it didn't matter what other people thought: their judgment was crap, a waste of time, baloney. But it did matter, especially when those people were *these* people.

"Well," Mr. Pope said, "I can see that this is going nowhere."

My father laughed, saying, "Yeah, you got that right." It sounded like a parting sentence, but rather than standing to leave, he leaned back in the sofa and rested his beer can upon his stomach. "We're all going nowhere."

At this point, I'm fairly sure that Thad and I were envisioning the same grim scenario. While the rest of the world moved on, in a year's time my filthy, bearded father would still be occupying the rumpus room sofa. Christmas would come, friends would visit, and the Popes would bitterly direct them toward the easy chairs. "Just ignore him," they'd say. "He'll go home sooner or later."

In the end, they agreed to pay for half the root canal, not because they thought it was fair, but because they wanted us out of their house.

Some friendships are formed by a commonality of interests and ideas: you both love judo or camping or making your own sausage. Other friendships are forged by mutual hatred of a common enemy. On leaving Thad's house, I decided that ours would probably be the latter. We'd start off grousing about my father, and then, little by little, we'd move on to the hundreds of other things and people that got on our nerves. "You hate olives?" I imagined him saying. "I hate them, *too!*"

As it turned out, the one thing we both hated was me. Rather, I hated me. Thad couldn't even work up the enthusiasm. The day after the meeting, I approached him in the lunchroom, where he sat at his regular table, surrounded by his regular friends. "Listen," I said. "I'm really sorry about that stuff with my dad." I'd worked up a whole long speech, complete with imitations, but by the time I finished my mission statement, he'd turned to resume his conversation with Doug Middleton. Our perjured testimony, my father's behavior, even the rock throwing: I was so far beneath him that it hadn't even registered.

Poof.

The socialites of E. C. Brooks shone even brighter in junior high, but come tenth grade, things began to change. Desegregation drove a lot of the popular people into private schools, and those who remained seemed silly and archaic, deposed royalty from a country the average citizen had ceased to care about.

Early in our junior year, Thad was jumped by a group of the new black kids, who yanked off his shoes and threw them in the toilet. I knew I was supposed to be happy, but part of me felt personally assaulted. True, he'd been a negligent prince, yet still I believed in the monarchy. When his name was called at graduation, it was I who clapped the longest, outlasting even his parents, who politely stopped once he'd left the stage.

I thought about Thad a lot over the years, wondering where he went to college and if he joined a fraternity. The era of the Big Man on Campus had ended, but the rowdy houses with their pool tables and fake moms continued to serve as reunion points for the once popular, who were now viewed as date rapists and budding alcoholics. While his brothers drifted toward a confused and bitter adulthood, I tell myself he stumbled into the class that changed his life. He's the poet laureate of Liechtenstein, the surgeon who cures cancer with love, the ninth-grade teacher who insists that the world is big enough for everyone. When moving to another city, I'm always hoping to find him living in the apartment next door. We'll meet in the hallway and he'll stick out his hand, saying, "Excuse me, but don't I — *shouldn't I* — know you?" It doesn't have to happen today, but it does have to happen. I've kept a space waiting for him, and if he doesn't show up, I'm going to have to forgive my father.

The root canal that was supposed to last ten years has now lasted more than thirty, though it's nothing to be proud of. Having progressively dulled and weakened, the tooth is now the brownish gray color the Conran's catalog refers to as "kabuki." While Dr. Povlitch worked out of a converted brick house beside the Colony Shopping Center, my current dentist, Docteur Guige, has an office near the Madeleine, in Paris. The receptionist calls my name and it often takes a while to realize she's referring to me.

On a recent visit, Dr. Guige gripped my dead tooth between his fingertips and gently jiggled it back and forth. I hate to exhaust his patience unnecessarily, so when he asked me what had happened, it took me a moment to think of the clearest possible answer. The past was far too complicated to put into French, so instead I envisioned a perfect future, and attributed the root canal to a misunderstanding between friends.

GARY SMITH

■

Higher Education

FROM *Sports Illustrated*

THIS IS A STORY about a man, and a place where magic happened. It was magic so powerful that the people there can't stop going back over it, trying to figure out who the man was and what happened right in front of their eyes, and how it'll change the time left to them on earth.

See them coming into town to work, or for their cup of coffee at Boyd & Wurthmann, or to make a deposit at Killbuck Savings? One mention of his name is all it takes for everything else to stop, for it all to begin tumbling out . . .

"I'm afraid we can't explain what he meant to us. I'm afraid it's so deep we can't bring it into words."

"It was almost like he was an angel."

"He was looked on as God."

There's Willie Mast. He's the one to start with. It's funny, he'll tell you, his eyes misting, he was so sure they'd all been hoodwinked that he almost did what's unthinkable now — run that man out of town before the magic had a chance.

All Willie had meant to do was bring some buzz to Berlin, Ohio, something to look forward to on a Friday night, for goodness' sake, in a town without high school football or a fast-food restaurant, without a traffic light or even a place to drink a beer, a town dozing in the heart of the largest Amish settlement in the world. Willie had been raised Amish, but he'd walked out on the religion at twenty-four — no, he'd peeled out, in an eight-cylinder roar, when he just couldn't bear it anymore, trying to get somewhere in life without a set of wheels or even a telephone to call for a ride.

He'd jumped the fence, as folks here called it, become a Mennonite and started a trucking company, of all things, his tractor-trailers roaring past all those horses and buggies, moving cattle and cold meat over half the country. But his greatest glory was that day back in 1982 when he hopped into one of his semis and moved a legend, Charlie Huggins, into town. Charlie, the coach who'd won two Ohio state basketball championships with Indian Valley South and one with Strasburg-Franklin, was coming to tiny Hiland High. Willie, one of the school's biggest hoops boosters, had banged the drum for Charlie for months.

And yes, Charlie turned everything around in those winters of '82 and '83, exactly as Willie had promised, and yes, the hoops talk was warmer and stronger than the coffee for the first time in twenty years at Willie's table of regulars in the Berlin House restaurant. They didn't much like it that second year when Charlie brought in an assistant — a man who'd helped him in his summer camps and lost his job when the Catholic school where he coached went belly-up — who was black. But Charlie was the best dang high school coach in three states; he must've known something that they didn't. Nor were they thrilled by the fact that the black man was a Catholic, in a community whose children grew up reading tales of how their ancestors were burned at the stake by Catholics during the Reformation in Europe more than four hundred years ago. But Charlie was a genius. Nor did they cherish the fact that the Catholic black was a loser, sixty-six times in eighty-three games with those hapless kids at Guernsey Catholic High near Cambridge. But Charlie . . .

Charlie quit. Quit in disgust at an administration that wouldn't let players out of their last class ten minutes early to dress for practice. But he kept the news to himself until right before the '84 school year began, too late to conduct a proper search for a proper coach. Willie Mast swallowed hard. It was almost as if his man, Charlie, had pulled a fast one. Berlin's new basketball coach, the man with the most important position in a community that had dug in its heels against change, was an unmarried black Catholic loser. The only black man in eastern Holmes County.

It wasn't that Willie hated black people. He'd hardly known any. "All I'd heard about them," he'll tell you, "was riots and lazy." Few had ever strayed into these parts, and fewer still after that black stuffed dummy got strung up on the town square in Millersburg, just up the road, after the Civil War. Maybe twice a year, back in the 1940s and '50s, a Jewish rag man had come rattling down Route 39 in a rickety truck, scavenging for scrap metal and rags to sell to filling stations thirty miles northeast in Canton or sixty miles north in Cleveland, and brought along a black man for the heavy lifting. People stared at him as if he were green. Kids played Catch the Nigger in their schoolyards without a pang, and when a handful of adults saw the color of a couple of Newcomerstown High's players a few years before, you know what word was ringing in those players' ears as they left the court.

Now, suddenly, this black man in his early thirties was standing in the middle of a gym jammed with a thousand whites, pulling their sons by the jerseys until their nostrils and his were an inch apart, screaming at them. Screaming, "Don't wanna hear your shoulda-coulda-wouldas! Get your head outta your butt!" How dare he?

Worse yet, the black man hadn't finished his college education, couldn't even teach at Hiland High. Why, he was working at Berlin Wood Products, the job Charlie had arranged for him, making little red wagons till 2 P.M. each day. "This nigger doesn't know how to coach," a regular at the Berlin House growled.

Willie agreed. "If he wins, it's because of what Charlie built here," he said. "What does he know about basketball?"

But what could be done? Plenty of folks in town seemed to treat the man with dignity. Sure, they were insular, but they were some of the most decent and generous people on earth. The man's Amish coworkers at the wood factory loved him, after they finally got done staring holes in the back of his head. They slammed Ping-Pong balls with him on lunch hour, volleyed theology during breaks, and dubbed him the Original Black Amishman. The Hiland High players seemed to feel the same way.

He was a strange cat, this black man. He had never said a word when his first apartment in Berlin fell through — the landlord who had agreed to a lease on the telephone saw the man's skin and suddenly remembered that he rented only to families. The man had kept silent about the cars that pulled up to the little white house on South Market Street that he moved into instead, about the screams in the darkness, the voices threatening him on his telephone, and the false rumors that he was dating their women. "They might not like us French Canadians here," was all he'd say, with a little smile, when he walked into a place and felt it turn to ice.

Finally the ice broke. Willie and a few pals invited the man to dinner at a fish joint up in Canton. They had some food and beers and laughs with him, sent him on his merry way, and then . . . what a coincidence: the blue lights flashed in the black man's rear-view mirror. DUI.

Willie's phone rang the next morning, but instead of its being a caller with news of the school board's action against the new coach, it was him. Perry Reese, Jr. Just letting Willie know that he knew exactly what had happened the night before. And that he wouldn't go away. The school board, which had caught wind of the plot, never made a peep. Who was this man?

Some people honestly believed that the coach was a spy — sent by the feds to keep an eye on the Amish — or the vanguard of a plot to bring blacks into Holmes County. Yet he walked around town looking people in the eyes, smiling and teasing with easy assurance. He never showed a trace of the loneliness he must have felt. When he had a problem with someone, he went straight to its source. Straight to Willie Mast in the school parking lot one night. "So you're not too sure about me because I'm black," he said, and he laid everything out in front of Willie, about racism and how the two of them needed to get things straight.

Willie blinked. He couldn't help but ask himself the question folks all over town would soon begin to ask: Could I do, or even dream of doing, what the coach is doing? Willie couldn't help but nod when the black man invited him along to scout an opponent and stop for a bite to eat, and couldn't help but feel good when the man said he appreciated Willie because he didn't double-talk when confronted — because Willie, he said, was real. Couldn't help but howl as the Hiland Hawks kept winning, forty-nine times in fifty-three games those first two years, storming to the 1986 Division IV state semifinal.

Winning, that's what bought the black man time, what gave the magic a chance to wisp and curl through town and the rolling fields around it. That's what gave him the lard to live through that frigid winter of '87. That was the school year when he finally had his degree and began teaching history and current events in a way they'd never been taught in eastern Holmes County, the year the Hawks went 3–18 and the vermin came crawling back out of the baseboards. Damn if Willie wasn't the first at the ramparts to defend him, and damn if that black Catholic loser didn't turn things right back around the next season and never knew a losing one again.

How? By pouring Charlie Huggins's molasses offense down the drain. By runnin' and gunnin', chucking up threes, full-court pressing from buzzer to buzzer — with an annual litter of runts, of spindly, short, close-cropped Mennonites! That's what most of his players were: the children, grandchildren, and great-grandchildren of Amish who, like Willie, had jumped the fence and endured the ostracism that went with it. Mennonites believed in many of the same shall-nots as the Amish: a man shall not be baptized until he's old enough to choose it, nor resort to violence even if his government demands it, nor turn his back on community, family, humility, discipline, and orderliness. But the Mennonites had decided that unlike the Amish, they could continue schooling past the eighth grade, turn on a light switch or a car ignition, pick up a phone, and even, except the most conservative of them, pull on a pair of shorts and beat the pants off an opponent on the hardwood court without drifting into the devil's embrace.

The Hawks' Nest, Hiland's tiny old gym, became what Willie

had always dreamed it would be: a loony bin, the one place a Mennonite could go to sweat and shriek and squeal; sold out year after
year, with fans jamming the hallway and snaking out the door as
they waited for the gym to open, then stampeding for the best
seats an hour before the six o'clock jayvee game; reporters and visiting coaches and scouts sardined above them in wooden lofts they
had to scale ladders to reach; spillover pouring into the audito-
rium beside the gym to watch on a video feed as noise thundered
through the wall. A few dozen teenage Amish boys, taking advantage of the one time in their lives when elders allowed them to behold the modern world, and sixteen-year-old cheerleaders' legs,
would be packed shoulder to shoulder in two corners of the gym at
the school they weren't permitted to attend. Even a few Amish
men, Lord save their souls, would tie up the horses and buggies
across the street at Yoder's Lumber and slink into the Nest. And
plenty more at home would tell the missus that they'd just remembered a task in the barn, then click on a radio stashed in the hay
and catch the game on WKLM.

Something had dawned on Willie, sitting in his front-row seat,
and on everyone else in town. The black man's values were virtually the same as theirs. Humility? No coach ever moved so fast to
duck praise or bolt outside the frame of a team picture. Unselfish-
ness? The principal might as well have taken the coach's salary
to pep rallies and flung it in the air — most of it ended up in the
kids' hands anyway. Reverence? No congregation ever huddled
and sang out the Lord's Prayer with the crispness and cadence that
the Hawks did before and after every game. Family? When Ches-
ter Mullet, Hiland's star guard in '96, only hugged his mom on
parents' night, Perry gave him a choice: kiss her or take a seat on
the bench. Work ethic? The day and season never seemed to end,
from 6 A.M. practices to 10 P.M. curfews, from puke buckets and
running drills in autumn to two-a-days in early winter to camps
and leagues and an open gym every summer day. He out-Amished
the Amish, out-Mennonited the Mennonites, and everyone, even
those who'd never sniffed a locker in their lives, took to calling the
black man Coach.

Ask Willie. "Most of the petty divisions around here disappeared because of Coach," he'll tell you. "He pulled us all together. Some folks didn't like me, but I was respected more because he respected me. When my dad died, Coach was right there, kneeling beside the coffin, crossing himself. He put his arm right around my mom — she's Amish — and she couldn't get over that. When she died, he was the first one there. He did that for all sorts of folks. I came to realize that color's not a big deal. I took him for my best friend."

And that man in Willie's coffee clan who'd held out longest, the one given to calling Coach a nigger? By Coach's fifth year, the man's son was a Hawk, the Hawks were on another roll, and the man had seen firsthand the effect Coach had on kids. He cleared his throat one morning at the Berlin House; he had something to say.

"He's not a nigger anymore."

The magic didn't stop with a nigger turning into a man and a man into a best friend. It kept widening and deepening. Kevin Troyer won't cry when he tells you about it, as the others do. They were brought up to hold that back, but maybe his training was better. He just lays out the story, beginning that autumn day ten years ago when he was sixteen, and Coach sat him in the front seat of his Jeep, looked in his eyes, and said, "Tell me the truth."

Someone had broken into Candles Hardware and R&R Sports and stolen merchandise. Whispers around town shocked even the whisperers: that the culprits were their heroes, kids who could walk into any restaurant in Berlin and never have to pay. They'd denied it over and over, and Coach had come to their defense . . . but now even he had begun to wonder.

A priest. That's what he'd told a few friends he would be if he weren't a coach. That's whose eyes Kevin felt boring into him. How could you keep lying to the man who stood in the lobby each morning, greeting the entire student body, searching everyone's eyes to see who needed a headlock, who needed lunch money, who needed love? "Don't know what you did today, princess," he'd sing out to a plump or unpopular girl, "but whatever it is, keep it up. You look great."

He'd show up wearing a cat's grin and the shirt you'd gotten for

Christmas — how'd he get into your bedroom closet? — or carrying the pillow he'd snagged right from under your head on one of his Saturday morning sorties, when he slipped like smoke into players' rooms, woke them with a pop on the chest, then ran, cackling, out the door. Sometimes those visits came on the heels of the I A.M. raids he called Ninja Runs, when he rang doorbells and cawed "Gotcha!," tumbling one family after another downstairs in pajamas and robes to laugh and talk and relish the privilege of being targeted by Coach. He annihilated what people here had been brought up to keep: the space between each other.

His door was never locked. Everyone, boy or girl, was welcome to wade through those half-dozen stray cats on the porch that Coach gruffly denied feeding till his stash of cat food was found, and open the fridge, grab a soda, have a seat, eat some pizza, watch a game, play cards or Ping-Pong or Nintendo . . . and talk. About race and religion and relationships and teenage trouble, about stuff that wouldn't surface at Kevin Troyer's dinner table in a million years. Coach listened the way other folks couldn't, listened clean without jumping ahead in his mind to what he'd say next, or to what the Bible said. When he finally spoke, he might play devil's advocate, or might offer a second or third alternative to a kid who'd seen only one, or might say the very thing Kevin didn't want to hear. But Kevin could bet his mother's savings that the conversations wouldn't leave that house.

Coach's home became the students' hangout, a place where they could sleep over without their parents' thinking twice . . . as long as they didn't mind bolting awake to a blast of AC/DC and a 9 A.M. noogie. There was no more guard to drop. Parents trusted Coach completely, relied on him to sow their values.

He sowed those, and a few more. He took Kevin and the other Hawks to two-room Amish schools to read and shoot hoops with wide-eyed children who might never get to see them play, took the players to one another's churches and then to his own, St. Peter, in Millersburg. He introduced them to Malcolm X, five-alarm chili, Martin Luther King, Jr., B. B. King, crawfish, Cajun wings, John Lee Hooker, Tabasco sauce, trash-talk fishing, Muhammad Ali.

And possibility. That's what Coach stood for, just by virtue of his presence in Berlin: possibility, no matter how high the odds were stacked against you, no matter how whittled your options seemed in a community whose beliefs had barely budged in two hundred years, whose mailboxes still carried the names of the same Amish families that had come in wagons out of Pennsylvania in the early 1800s — Yoders and Troyers and Stutzmans and Schlabachs and Hostetlers and Millers and Mullets and Masts. A place where kids, for decades, had graduated, married their prom dates, and stepped into their daddies' farming or carpentry or lumber businesses without regard for the fact that Hiland High's graduating classes of sixty ranked in the top ten in Ohio proficiency tests nearly every year. Kevin Troyer's parents didn't seem to care if he went to college. Coach's voice was the one that kept saying, "It's your life. There's so much more out there for you to see. Go places. Do things. Get a degree. Reach out. You have to take a chance."

The kids did, more and more, but not before Coach loaded them with laundry baskets full of items they'd need away from home, and they were never out of reach of those 6 A.M. phone calls. "I'm up," he'd say. "Now you are, too. Remember, I'm always here for you."

He managed all that without raising red flags. He smuggled it under the warm coat of all that winning, up the sleeve of all that humility and humor. Everyone was too busy bubbling over the eleven conference titles and five state semifinals. Having too much fun volunteering to be henchmen for his latest prank, shoving Mr. Pratt's desk to the middle of his English classroom, removing the ladder to maroon the radio play-by-play man up in the Hawks' Nest loft, toilet-papering the school superintendent's yard and then watching Coach, the most honest guy in town, lie right through all thirty-two teeth. He was a bootlegger, that's what he was. A bootlegger priest.

"Kevin . . . tell the truth."

Kevin's insides trembled. How could he cash in his five teammates, bring down the wrath of a community in which the Ten Commandments were still stone, own up to the man whose explosions made the Hawks' Nest shudder? How could he explain something that was full of feeling and empty of logic — that somehow, as decent as his parents were, as warm as it felt to grow up in a place where you could count on a neighbor at any hour, it all felt suffocating? All the restrictions of a Conservative Mennonite church that forbade members to watch TV, to go to movies, to dance. All the emotions he'd choked back in a home ruled by a father and mother who'd been raised to react to problems by saying, "What will people think?" All the expectations of playing for the same team that his All-State brother, Keith, had carried to its first state semi in twenty-four years, back in 1986. Somehow, busting into those stores in the summer of '91 felt like the fist Kevin could never quite ball up and smash into all that.

"I . . . I did it, Coach. We . . ."

The sweetest thing eastern Holmes County had ever known was ruined. Teammate Randy Troyer, no relation to Kevin, disappeared when word got out. The community gasped — those six boys could never wear a Hawks uniform again. Coach? He resigned. He'd betrayed the town's trust and failed his responsibility, he told his superiors. His "sons" had turned to crime.

The administration begged him to stay. Who else was respected enough by family court judges, storekeepers, ministers, and parents to find resolution and justice? Coach stared across the pond he fished behind his house. He came up with a solution both harder and softer than the town's. He would take Randy Troyer under his own roof, now that the boy had slunk back after two weeks of holing up in Florida motels. He'd be accountable for Randy's behavior. He'd have the six boys locked up in detention centers for two weeks, to know what jail tasted and smelled like. But he would let them back on the team. Let them feel lucky to be playing basketball when they'd really be taking a crash course in accountability.

Kevin found himself staring at the cinder-block wall of his cell, as lonely as a Mennonite boy could be. But there was Coach, making his rounds to all six lost souls. There was that lung-bursting bear hug, and another earful about not following others, about believing in yourself and being a man.

The Berlin Six returned. Randy Troyer lived in Coach's home for four months. Kevin walked to the microphone at the first pep rally, sick with nerves, and apologized to the school and the town.

Redemption isn't easy with a five-foot-eleven center, but how tight that 1991–92 team became, players piling into Coach's car every Thursday after practice, gathering around a long table at a sports bar a half-hour away in Dover, and setting upon giant cookie sheets heaped with five hundred hot wings. And how those boys could run and shoot. Every time a twenty-footer left the hands of Kevin Troyer or one of the Mishler twins, Nevin and Kevin, or the Hawks' star, Junior Raber, Hiland's students rose, twirling when the ball hit twine and flashing the big red 3s on their T-shirts' backs.

Someday, perhaps in a generation or two, some Berliner might not remember every detail of that postseason march. Against Lakeland in the district championship, the Hawks came out coma-tose and fell behind 20–5, Coach too stubborn to call a time out — the man could never bear to show a wisp of doubt. At halftime he slammed the locker-room door so hard that it came off its hinges, then he kicked a crater in a trash can, sent water bottles flying, grabbed jerseys, and screamed so loud that the echoes peeled paint. Kevin and his mates did what all Hawks did: gazed straight into Coach's eyes and nodded. They knew in their bones how small his wrath was, held up against his love. They burst from that locker room like jackals, tore Lakeland to bits, and handily won the next two games to reach the state semis. The world came to a halt in Berlin.

How far can a bellyful of hunger and a chestful of mission take a team before reality steps in and stops it? In the state semifinal in Columbus, against a Lima Central Catholic bunch loaded with kids quicker and thicker and taller and darker, led by the rattle-snake-sudden Hutchins brothers, Aaron and All-Stater Anthony, the Hawks were cooked. They trailed 62–55 with thirty-eight sec-onds left as Hiland fans trickled out in despair and Lima's surged to the box office windows to snatch up tickets for the final. Lima called time out to dot its *i*'s and cross its *t*'s, and there stood Coach in the Hiland huddle, gazing down at a dozen forlorn boys. He spoke more calmly than they'd ever heard him, and the fear and hopelessness leaked out of them as they stared into his eyes and drank in his plan. What happened next made you know that everything the bootlegger priest stood for — bucking the tide, believing in yourself and possibility — had worked its way from inside him to inside them.

Nevin Mishler, who would sit around the campfire in Coach's back yard talking about life till 2 A.M. on Friday nights, dropped in a rainbow three with twenty-seven seconds left to cut the deficit to four. Time out, calm words, quick foul. Lima's Anthony Hutchins blew the front end of a one-and-one.

Eleven seconds left. Junior Raber, whose wish as a boy was to be black, just like Coach, banked in a driving, leaning bucket and was fouled. He drained the free throw. Lima's lead was down to one. Time out, calm words, quick foul. Aaron Hutchins missed another one-and-one.

Nine ticks left. Kevin Troyer, who would end up going to college and becoming a teacher and coach because of Coach, tore down the rebound and threw the outlet to Nevin Mishler.

Seven seconds left. Nevin turned to dribble, only to be ambushed before half-court by Aaron Hutchins, the wounded rattler, who struck and smacked away the ball.

Five seconds left, the ball and the season and salvation skittering away as Nevin, who cared more about letting down Coach than letting down his parents, hurled his body across the wood and swatted the ball back toward Kevin Troyer. Kevin, who almost never hit the floor, who had been pushed by Coach for years to give more, lunged and collided with Anthony Hutchins, then spun and heaved the ball behind his back to Junior Raber as Kevin fell to the floor.

Three seconds left. Junior took three dribbles and heaved up the impossible, an off-balance thirty-five-footer with two defenders in his face, a shot that fell far short at the buzzer . . . but he was fouled. He swished all three free throws, and the Hawks won, they won — no matter how many times Lima fans waiting outside for tickets insisted to Hiland fans that it couldn't be true — and two days later won the only state title in school history, by three points over Gilmour Academy, on fumes, pure fumes.

In the aisles, people danced who were forbidden to dance. The plaque commemorating the crowning achievement of Coach's life went straight into the hands of Joe Workman, a water and towel boy. Kevin Troyer and his teammates jumped Coach before he could sneak off, hugging him and kissing him and rubbing his head, but he had the last laugh. The 9 A.M. noogies would hurt even more those next nine years, dang that championship ring.

Someone would come and steal the magic. Some big-cheese high school or college would take Coach away — they knew it, they just knew it. It all seems so silly now, Steve Mullet says. It might take Steve the last half of his life to finish that slow, dazed shake of his head.

Berlin, you see, was a secret no more by the mid-1990s. Too much winning by Coach, too many tourists pouring in to peer at the men in black hats and black buggies. Two traffic lights had gone up, along with a Burger King and a couple dozen gift shops and God knows how many restaurants and inns with the word *Dutch* on their shingles to reel in the rubberneckers. Even the Berlin House, where Willie Mast and the boys gathered, was now the Dutch Country Kitchen.

Here they came, the city slickers. Offering Coach big raises and the chance to hush that whisper in his head: why keep working with disciplined, two-parent white kids when children of his own race were being devoured by drugs and despair for want of someone like him? Akron Hoban wanted him. So did Canton McKinley, the biggest school in the city where Coach had grown up, and Canton Timken, the high school he attended. They wanted to take the man who'd transformed Steve Mullet's family, turned it into something a simple and sincere country fellow had never dreamed it might be. His first two sons were in college, thanks to Coach, and his third one, another guard at Hiland, would likely soon be, too. Didn't Steve owe it to that third boy, Carlos, to keep Coach here? Didn't he owe it to all the fathers of all the little boys around Berlin?

Coach had a way of stirring Steve's anxiety and the stew of rumors. He would walk slow and wounded through each April after he'd driven another team of runts to a conference crown, won two or three postseason games, and then yielded to the facts of the matter, to some school with nearly twice as many students and a couple of six-foot-five studs. "It's time for a change," he'd sigh. "You guys don't need me anymore."

Maybe all missionaries are restless souls, one eye on the horizon, looking for who needs them most. Perhaps Coach was trying to smoke out even the slightest trace of misgivings about him, so he could be sure to leave before he was ever asked to. But Steve Mullet and eastern Holmes County couldn't take that chance. They had to act. Steve, a dairy farmer most of his life, knew about fencing. But how do you fence in a man when no one really understands why he's there, or what he came from?

Who was Coach's family? What about his past? Why did praise and attention make him so uneasy? The whole community wondered, but in Berlin it was disrespectful to pry. Canton was only a forty-five-minute hop away, yet Steve had never seen a parent or a sibling of Coach's, a girlfriend or even a childhood pal. The bootlegger priest was a man of mystery and moods as well as a wide-open door. He'd ask you how your grandma, sister, and uncle were every time you met, but you weren't supposed to inquire about his — you just sensed it. His birthday? He wouldn't say. His age? Who knew? It changed every time he was asked. But his loneliness, that at last began to show.

There were whispers, of course. Some claimed he'd nearly married a flight attendant, then beat a cold-footed retreat. A black woman appeared in the stands once, set the grapevine sizzling, then was never glimpsed again. Steve and his pals loved to tease Coach whenever they all made the twenty-mile drive to Dinofo's, a pizza and pasta joint in Dover, and came face to face with that wild black waitress, Rosie. "When you gonna give it up?" she'd yelp at Coach. "When you gonna let me have it?"

He'd grin and shake his head, tell her it would be so good it would spoil her for life. Perhaps it was too scary, for a man who gave so much to so many, to carve it down to one. Maybe Jeff Pratt, the Hiland English teacher, had it right. Loving with detachment, he called it. So many people could be close to him, because no one was allowed too close.

A circle of women in Berlin looked on him almost as a brother — women such as Nancy Mishler, mother of the twins from the '92 title team, and Peg Brand, the school secretary, and Shelly Miller, wife of the booster club's president, Alan. They came to count on Coach's teasing and advice, on his cards and flowers and prayers when their loved ones were sick or their children had them at wit's end, and they did what they could to keep him in town. "I wish we could find a way to make you feel this is your family, that this is where you belong," Peg wrote him. "If you leave," she'd say, "who's going to make our kids think?" The women left groceries and gifts on his porch, homemade chocolate chip cookies on his kitchen table, invited him to their homes on Sundays and holidays no matter how often he begged off, never wanting to impose.

But they all had to do more, Steve decided, picking up his phone to mobilize the men. For God's sake, Coach made only $28,000 a year. In the grand tradition of Mennonites and Amish, they rushed to answer the community call. They paid his rent, one month per donor; it was so easy to find volunteers that they had a waiting list. They replaced his garage when a leaf fire sent it up in flames; it sent him up a wall when he couldn't learn the charity's source. They passed the hat for that sparkling new gym at Hiland, and they didn't stop till the hat was stuffed with 1.6 million bucks. Steve Mullet eventually had Coach move into a big old farmhouse he owned. But first Steve and Willie Mast had another brainstorm: road trip. Why not give Coach a couple of days' escape from their cornfields and his sainthood, and show him how much they cared?

That's how Steve, a Conservative Mennonite in his mid-forties, married to a woman who didn't stick her head out in public unless it was beneath a prayer veil, found himself on Bourbon Street in New Orleans. Standing beside Willie and behind Coach, his heartbeat rising and stomach fluttering as he watched Coach suck down a Hurricane and cock his head outside a string of bars, listening for the chord that would pull him inside.

Coach nodded. This was the one. This blues bar. He pushed open the door. Music and smoke and beer musk belched out. Steve looked at Willie. You could go to hell for this, from everything they'd both been taught. Willie just nodded.

They wedged into a whorl of colors and types of humanity. When Steve was a boy, he'd seen blacks only after his parents jumped the fence, became Mennonites, and took the family in their car each summer to a city zoo. Nothing cruel about blacks was ever said. Steve's parents simply pulled him closer when they were near, filled him with a feeling: our kind and theirs don't mix. Now there were blacks pressed against his shoulders, blacks on microphones screaming lust and heartache into Steve's ears, blacks pounding rhythm through the floorboards and up into his knees. People touching, people gyrating their hips. You could go to hell for this. Steve looked at Willie as Coach headed to the bathroom. "I can't take this," Steve said.

"It's Coach's time, bub," Willie said.

Coach came back, smelled Steve's uneasiness, and knew what to do. "Liven up," he barked, and grinned. They got some beers, and it was just like the Hawks' radio play-by-play man, Mark Lonsinger, always said: Coach stood out in a room the instant he walked in, even though he did everything to deflect it. Soon Coach had the folks nearby convinced that he was Black Amish, a highly obscure sect, and Steve, swallowing his laughter, sealing the deal with a few timely bursts of Pennsylvania Dutch, had them believing the three of them had made it to New Orleans from Ohio in a buggy. Before you knew it, it was nearly midnight, and Steve's head was bobbing, his feet tapping, his funk found deep beneath all those layers of mashed potatoes. You know what, he was telling Willie, this Bourbon Street and this blues music really aren't so bad, and isn't it nice, too, how those folks found out that Mennonites aren't Martians?

When they pulled back into Coach's driveway after days filled with laughter and camaraderie, Steve glanced at Willie and sighed, "Well, now we return to our wives."

"You're the lucky ones," said Coach. "Don't you ever forget that."

Steve realized something when they returned from the road: it wasn't the road to ruin. He felt more space inside himself, plenty enough room for the black friends his sons began bringing home from college for the weekend. He realized it again the next year, when they returned to Bourbon Street, and the next, when they went once more, and the one after that as well. "Some things that I was taught were strictly no-nos . . . they're not sins," Steve will tell you. "All I know is that it all seemed right to do with him."

Funny how far that feeling had fanned, how many old, deep lines had blurred in Berlin, and what occurred in a dry community when Coach overdid it one night four years ago and tried one last time to leave. "I screwed up," he told school superintendent Gary Sterrett after he got that second DUI, fourteen miles up the road in Sugar Creek. "You need to take my job."

What happened was sort of like what happened the time the ball rolled toward the Hawks' bench in a game they were fumbling away that year at Garaway High, and Coach pulled back his leg and kicked the ball so hard that it hissed past a referee's ear and slammed off the wall, the gym hushing in anticipation of the technical foul and the ejection. But nothing happened. The two refs had such enormous respect for Coach, they pretended it away.

He apologized to every player and to every player's parents for the DUI. Steve never mentioned it. The community never said a word. It was pretended away.

They've combed through the events a thousand times, lain in bed at night tearing themselves and God to shreds. There were clues, after all, and it was their job to notice things Coach was too stubborn to admit. They thought, when he holed up in his motel room for three days in Columbus last March, that it was merely one of his postseason moods, darker than ever after falling one game shy, for the third straight year, of playing for the state title. They thought he was still brooding two months later when, preoccupied and suffering from a cold he couldn't shake, he started scrambling names and dates and getting lost on country roads.

It all came to a head one Saturday last June, when he climbed into another rented tux because Phil Mishler, just like fifty or sixty kids before him, had to have Coach in his wedding party. At the reception, Coach offered his hand to Tom Mullet and said, "I'm Perry Reese, Jr., Hiland High basketball coach." Tom Mullet had been Hiland's assistant athletic director for ten years.

Phone lines buzzed that Sunday. People began comparing notes, discovering new oddities. On Monday night two of Coach's best friends, Dave Schlabach and Brian Hummel, headed to Mount Hope and the old farmhouse Coach had moved into just outside Berlin, the only house with lights in a community of Amish. They found him shivering in a blanket, glassy-eyed and mumbling nonsense.

Their worst possible fears . . . well, it went beyond all of them. Brain tumor. Malignant. Inoperable. Four to eight months to live, the doctors at Canton's Aultman Hospital said. You can't bring down a sledgehammer faster than that.

Jason Mishler, Coach's starting point guard the past two years, was the first kid to find out. He stationed himself in the chair beside Coach's bed, wouldn't budge all night and most of the next day. His cousin Kevin Mishler, from the state championship team, dropped his vacation on Hilton Head Island, South Carolina, and flew back. Dave Jaberg, who had played for Hiland a few years before that, dropped the bonds he was trading in Chicago and drove for six hours. Junior Raber was on the first plane from Atlanta. Think a moment. How many teachers or coaches would you do that for?

The nurses and doctors were stupefied — didn't folks know you couldn't fit a town inside a hospital room? Coach's friends filled the lobby, the elevator, the halls, and the waiting room. It was like a Hiland basketball game, only everyone was crying. Coach kept fading in and out, blinking up at another set of teary eyes and croaking, "What's new?"

What do people pray for when doctors don't give them a prayer?

They swung for the fences. The Big M, a miracle. Some begged for it. Some demanded it. A thousand people attended a prayer vigil in the gym and took turns on the microphone. Never had so much anger and anguish risen from Berlin and gone straight at God.

Steroids shrank the tumor enough for Coach to return home, where another throng of folks waited, each telling the other tales of what Coach had done to change his life, each shocked to find how many considered him their best friend. When he walked through his front door and saw the wheelchair, the portable commode, the hospital bed, and the chart Peg Brand had made, dividing the community's twenty-four-hour care for Coach into six-hour shifts, he sobbed. The giving was finished. Now all he could do was take.

Go home, he ordered them. Go back to your families and lives. He called them names. They knew him well enough to know how loathsome it was for him to be the center of attention, the needy one. But they also knew what he would do if one of them were dying. They decided to keep coming anyway. They were family. Even more in his dying than in his living, they were fused.

They cooked for him, planned a trip to New York City he'd always dreamed of making, prayed and cried themselves to sleep. They fired off e-mails to churches across the country, recruited entire congregations who'd never heard of Coach to pray for the Big M. Louise Conway, grandmother of a player named Jared Coblentz, woke up three or four times a night, her heart thumping so hard that she had to drop to her knees and chew God's ear about Coach before she could drop back to sleep. People combed the Internet for little-known treatments. They were going to hoist a three at the buzzer and get fouled.

Coach? He did the strangest thing. He took two radiation treatments and stopped. He refused the alternative treatments, no matter how much people cried and begged and flung his own lessons in his face. Two other doctors had confirmed his fate, and damned if he was going to be helpless for long if he could help it. "Don't you understand?" he told a buddy, Doug Klar. "It's okay. This is how it's supposed to be."

He finally had a plan, one that would make his death like his life, one that would mean the giving wasn't finished. He initiated a foundation, a college scholarship fund for those in need, started it rolling with his $30,000 life savings and, after swallowing hard, allowed it to be named after him on one condition: that it be kept secret until he was dead.

He had no way to keep all the puzzle pieces of his life in boxes now; dying shook them out. Folks found out, for instance, that he turned forty-eight last August. They were shocked to meet two half-sisters they'd never heard of. They were glad finally to see Coach's younger sister, Audrey Johnson, whose picture was on his refrigerator door and who was studying to be a social worker, and his younger brother, Chris, who helps run group homes for people who can't fend for themselves and who took a leave of absence to care for Coach.

It turned out that Audrey had made a couple of quiet visits a year to Coach and that the family had gathered for a few hours on holidays; there were no dark or splintering secrets. He came from two strict parents who'd died in the '80s — his dad had worked in a Canton steel mill — and had a mixed-race aunt on one side of the family and a white grandfather on the other. But there were never quite enough pieces of the puzzle for anyone to put them together on a table and get a clean picture.

Coach's family was shocked to learn a few things, too. Like how many conservative rural white folks had taken a black man into their hearts. "Amazing," said Jennifer Betha, his half-sister, a supervisor for Head Start. "And so many loving, respectful, well-mannered children around him. They were like miniature Perrys! Our family was the independent sort, all kind of went our own ways. I never realized how easy it is to get to Berlin from Canton, how close it is. What a waste. Why didn't we come before?"

Coach had two good months, thanks to the steroids. Berlin people spent them believing that God had heard them, and that the miracle had come. Coach spent the months telling hundreds of visitors how much he cared about them, making one last 1 A.M. Ninja Run, and packing his life into ten neat cardboard boxes.

The first week of August, he defied doctors' orders not to drive and slipped into the empty school. Gerald Miller, his buddy and old boss at the wagon factory, found him later that day at home, tears streaming down his cheeks. "Worst day of my life," Coach said. "Worse than finding out about this thing in my head. I cleaned out my desk. I can't believe it. I'm not gonna teach anymore. I'm done."

In early September the tumor finally had its way. He began slurring words, falling down, losing the use of his right hand and leg, then his eyesight. "How are you doing?" he kept asking his visitors, on blind instinct. "Is there anything I can do for you?" Till the end he heard the door open and close, open and close, and felt the hands, wrapped around his, doing that, too.

On the day he died, November 22, just over a week before the Hawks' first basketball game and seventeen years after he first walked through their doors, Hiland looked like one of those schools in the news in which a kid has walked through the halls with an automatic weapon. Six ministers and three counselors walked around hugging and whispering to children who were huddled in the hallway crying or staring into space, to teachers sobbing in the bathrooms, to secretaries who couldn't bear it and had to run out the door.

An old nettle digs at most every human heart: the urge to give oneself to the world rather than to only a few close people. In the end, unable to bear the personal cost, most of us find a way to ignore the prickle, comforting ourselves that so little can be changed by one woman or one man anyway.

How much, in the end, was changed by this one man? In Berlin, they're still tallying that one up. Jared Coblentz, who might have been the Hawks' sixth man this year, quit because he couldn't play for anyone other than Coach. Jason Mishler was so furious that he quit going to church for months, then figured out that it might be greedy to demand a miracle when you've been looking at one all your life. Tattoo parlors added Mennonites to their clientele. Junior Raber stares at the RIP with a P beneath it on his chest every morning when he looks into the mirror of his apartment in

AtlantaThe

ritual they had been led to believe it was, wasn't all that different from their own. Still, Steve hesitated. He glanced at Willie Mast. "Would Coach want us to?" Steve whispered.

"You got 'er, bub," said Willie.

So they rose and joined all the black Baptists and white Catholics pouring toward the altar, all the basketball players, all the Mennonites young and old. Busting laws left and right, busting straight into the kingdom of heaven.

■

"Jiving" with Your Teen

FROM *Modern Humorist*

Chapter 4: Vocabulary

ANYONE WHO has observed the youths of America knows they frequently take liberties with the English language in order to flaunt their illiteracy and impress the opposite sex. As a parent, it is vital that you understand their vocabulary — like a cheetah, your teen can sense your confusion and fear. When you master their vocabulary you can finally tell them, in their own language, that the police at the front door are for them.

Here are a few mandatory words and phrases to use when speaking to your teen:

Dope — A slang word that refers to every teenager's horrific need to associate what he or she considers "good" with deadly narcotics. When this phrase is uttered, do not panic. Simply reply with: "Yeah, dog, I got the stash up my cavity."

It's all good — A shortened term from its original version, "It's all good when you're employing illegal narcotics and engaging in immoral sexual activity." Your teen doesn't mean that everything in the world is "good." He or she means that everything in the poverty-stricken inner-city ghetto is "good."

Cool — One of the most enduring slang terms in American culture. The word "Cool" has seen many forms. As a youth, you probably used the term sensibly: "Hot dog! It's cool outside, Mabel." Your teenager uses it in a different context:

"That's Cool."
Translation: Marijuana is being smoked.

"That is so Cool."
Translation: A lot of marijuana is being smoked.

"Not Cool."
Translation: The dog is being smoked.

Use this vocabulary with caution, as we "old people" often misuse it. Here are a few frequently asked questions and answers to guide you:

Q: I thought I asked my teen to take out the garbage, but she ended up getting pregnant. What did I say wrong?
A: Effective communication can be difficult. It is best that you start out slowly. Clearly, you rushed this process, perhaps saying, "Come on, ride the train" when you meant, "Hit the skins, bitch." Remind your teen: Take out the trash, don't fornicate with the trash.
Q: I told my teen that I loved him, but he became a heroin addict. What did I say wrong this time?
A: Your teen's heroin addiction is probably your fault. The things you tell your teen are vital in making sure he or she takes a pass on that crack pipe when attending a friend's drug party. Here are a few phrases to say to your teens to keep them drug-free:

> "I love you like a play cousin."
> "You're my favorite trick."
> "The Pimp Daddy is in the hizz-ouse."
> "Yeah, dog, I got the stash up my cavity."

Q: I bought my son a pair of pants, but he keeps wearing them below his waist. How do I tell him to straighten up?
A: Simply ask your foolhardy son, "Where my dogs at?" He should comply immediately.

While learning how to talk to your teen, you must be able to "stay cool." Panic attacks do not help. Just because your teen speaks a different language than you doesn't mean that you are out of touch with your teen. It just simply means that you are too busy to care what is happening in your child's life.

Next: Chapter 5 — How to talk to your teen through the bulletproof window at the rehab clinic.

ADRIAN TOMINE

■

Bomb Scare

Optic Nerve #8

...AS THE U.N. DEADLINE FOR AN IRAQI WITHDRAWAL APPROACHES, PRESIDENT BUSH HAS NOW ORDERED OVER 400,000 U.S. TROOPS INTO THE PERSIAN GULF...

LOOK AT THIS... THEY COULD RE-INSTATE THE DRAFT ANY DAY NOW AND WE'D BE **FUCKED!**

AREN'T WE TOO YOUNG?

THERE WERE GUYS WHO WERE ONLY SEVENTEEN AT THE START OF VIETNAM...NEXT THING THEY KNOW, THEY'RE GETTING **EVISCERATED** IN SAIGON!

I'M *SIXTEEN.*

WELL, IF THIS GOES ON LONG ENOUGH...

JEEZ...I GUESS I'D HAVE TO HIDE OUT IN CANADA OR SOMETHING...

YEAH, AND WHEN YOU'RE INEVITABLY APPREHENDED, YOU SPEND THE REST OF YOUR LIFE IN SOME *DISEASE-RIDDLED* PRISON!

I'D BLOW MY OWN BRAINS OUT BEFORE I FOUGHT IN SOME WAR.

PSHHT

HERE... JUST TRY ONE SIP.

NO.

OKAY...THIS IS THE DRUM MACHINE. YOU JUST HIT THESE PADS...

AND YOU CAN LOOP IT.

BOOM
BOOM
TCH!
BA-BOOM TCH!
BA-BOOM BOOM
TCH

HERE'S THE SAMPLER. SAY SOMETHING INTO THE MIC.

LIKE WHAT?

HOW ABOUT YOU? WHAT DID YOU DO TONIGHT?

OH, I MET A FRIEND FROM WORK FOR COFFEE.

IT WAS NICE.

WELL, I'M GONNA PUT MY HEADPHONES ON AND GO TO BED...

SLEEP TIGHT.

BOYS' LOCKER ROOM

I FEEL LIKE I CAN LITERALLY **SMELL** THE BACTERIA WAFTING AROUND ME...

THANK **GOD** THIS IS THE LAST SEMESTER OF THIS TORTURE I'LL EVER HAVE TO ENDURE!

WHAT AM **I** GONNA DO NEXT YEAR? MAYBE I CAN GET SOME KIND OF DOCTOR'S EXCUSE...

"OH, ALEXTH...I'M GETTING **THO** HORNY!"

HA HA HA

"ME TOO, THCOTTY!"

"I'D TAKE A THOWER, BUT I'M AFRAID EVERYONE WILL THEE MY HARD-ON!"

HA HA HA HA

HEY GUYS... ENJOYING THE SHOW?

CAREFUL, BRYAN... THEY MIGHT DOUBLE-TEAM YOU!

I'M JUST **DYING** FOR ONE OF THESE STEROID-INJECTED **FUCKS** TO THREATEN ME PHYSICALLY...

WHAT ARE YOU TALKING ABOUT?

BECAUSE THEN I WOULD BE LEGALLY ENTITLED TO USE **THIS**...

YOU'RE CARRYING AROUND A *GUN*?

WOULD YOU SHUT UP?

IT'S A *TASER*. TEN SECONDS OF CONTACT AND YOUR ADVERSARY IS INCAPACITATED. TWENTY SECONDS AND THEY'RE UNCONSCIOUS.

KOFF
KOFF aggots

HA HA HA HA

HI CAMMIE!

OH...HEY, SCOTTY. GOD, HOW LATE AM I?

ONLY LIKE TWENTY MINUTES. IT'S BEEN PRETTY DEAD ANYWAY...

MY HEAD *KILLS*... I PARTIED WAY TOO MUCH LAST NIGHT.

YEAH...

SPECIALS

SOUP

CAN I ASK YOU SOMETHING? YOU'RE FRIENDS WITH BRYAN VANDERMEER, RIGHT?

WE HANG OUT.

HOW CAN YOU *STAND* THAT GUY? I MEAN...

BRYAN? HE'S OKAY.

WELL, THE NEXT TIME HE MAKES SOME FAG JOKE ABOUT ME, REMIND HIM THAT *HE'S* THE ONE ROLLING AROUND WITH GUYS ON THE WRESTLING TEAM.

YOU KNOW, IT'S NOT REALLY *YOU* HE'S MAKING FUN OF. IT'S MORE LIKE YOU AND THAT ALEX GUY...TOGETHER.

OH...WELL THAT CHANGES EVERYTHING!

PFF...

SO, THEN...YOU AND ALEX...

AREN'T...?

OH MY GOD!

DO PEOPLE SERIOUSLY THINK WE'RE *GAY*? WHAT... JUST BECAUSE WE'RE NOT OBNOXIOUS, ATHLETIC JERKS LIKE BRYAN?

IT'S JUST THAT YOU TWO ARE *ALWAYS* TOGETHER, AND YOU NEVER HANG AROUND WITH ANY GIRLS...YOU JUST SEEM LIKE A...COUPLE!

LOOK, JUST BECAUSE WE'RE EACH OTHER'S ONLY FRIEND, THAT *DOES NOT MAKE US*—

SHHH

IT DOES NOT MAKE US HOMOS.

OKAY, OKAY.

MOM?

ARE YOU GONNA EAT ANY OF THIS PASTA?

WHAT?

NO...YOU GO AHEAD.

IS THAT GUY PICKING YOU UP?

HIS NAME'S *PHIL*, AND NO...I'M MEETING HIM AT THE THEATER.

I THINK ALEX SAID SOMETHING ABOUT GOING TO SOME... PARTY.

SO IF IT ENDS UP GETTING LATE, I MIGHT JUST CRASH AT HIS PLACE.

THAT'S FINE.

MM... SMELLS GOOD.

I'M GLAD THAT YOU'RE GOING TO PARTIES AND HAVING FUN.

WELL... WE'LL SEE ABOUT THE "FUN" PART.

SO, ARE THERE GONNA BE PEOPLE FROM SCHOOL THERE?

YOU MUST BE JOKING.

SUTTER HIGH IS AN INFINITESIMAL PART OF MY WORLD.

BANG! BANG! K·CLANG CLANG BANG!

K·CLANG CLANG ANG!

DOES ANYBODY HAVE ANY... ANY BREAD? MY TOFU DOGS ARE GETTING ALL BURNT!

HOW ABOUT A... A PLATE OR SOMETHING?

I CAN'T BELIEVE YOU'VE NEVER HEARD THIS!

MOM?

OH MY GOD, CAMMIE... HOW *ARE* YOU?

I'M FINE. IT WAS NOTHING A LITTLE STOMACH-PUMPING COULDN'T FIX.

HA HA

HEY, BRYAN. I GUESS I'M THE TALK OF THE SCHOOL THANKS TO YOU.

UM... I THINK HE'S WAITING FOR AN APOLOGY.

HA HA

YOU EXPECT AN APOLOGY FROM *ME*?

I THINK THAT'S KINDA WHAT YOU DO WHEN YOU SMEAR DIARRHEA ON SOMEONE'S COUCH.

HA HA

:SNORT:

FUCK OFF, BRYAN. HOW ABOUT *YOU* APOLOGIZING FOR TAKING MY CLOTHES OFF AND INVITING EVERYONE IN FOR A LOOK?

YOU DON'T EVEN KNOW WHAT HAPPENED, BITCH. I PROBABLY SAVED YOUR FUCKING LIFE.

AND WHERE WERE *YOU* AT LUNCH TODAY?

I COULDN'T FIND YOU.

YEAH...I HAD TO FINISH THIS ASSIGNMENT FOR PHOTO. SO I WAS IN THE DARKROOM.

SOU

HI! HOW'S IT GOING? I—

I DON'T WANT TO TALK ABOUT IT.

OKAY.

Sorry, We're CLOSED

NO, NO... IT WOULDN'T BE LIKE HITTING "PAUSE" ON THE VCR. I MEAN, EVERYTHING WOULD STILL BE MOVING AROUND...

IT'S JUST LIKE... EVERYTHING STAYS BASICALLY THE SAME. NO AGING, NO DYING, NO BIG CHANGES...

GOD... THAT'S A PRETTY FUCKED-UP FANTASY.

WELL, I JUST THINK ABOUT IT SOMETIMES.

AND YOU'D WANT THIS TO HAPPEN, LIKE, NOW?

NO WAY!

MORE LIKE... FOUR OR FIVE YEARS AGO.

THAT SEEMS LIKE A GOOD TIME TO FREEZE.

WHAT ABOUT NEW EXPERIENCES?

YEAH...

I GUESS I'M JUST NOT INTO THAT.

WHAT?

I KNOW, I KNOW...

I'M PROBABLY THE ONLY 16-YEAR-OLD IN THE WORLD THAT DOESN'T WANT TO GET DRUNK AND DO DRUGS AND GET LAID.

WAIT...

YOU DON'T WANT TO GET LAID?

I MEAN, IN THEORY... MAYBE. IT JUST SEEMS TOO MONUMENTAL.

HA HA HA

GOD... I'M HORNY ALL THE TIME! DON'T YOU EVER AT LEAST, UH...

WHAT?

NOTHING.

JUST SORT OF A FALLING OUT, I GUESS.

WELL, IF BY SOME MIRACLE YOU FEEL LIKE TALKING ABOUT IT...

I KNOW. IT'S FINE.

I'VE GOT TO JUMP IN THE SHOWER, BUT IF PHIL SHOWS UP, LET HIM IN.

AND BE NICE!

UH, HI...

HI! YOU MUST BE SCOTTY, RIGHT? I'M PHIL.

YEAH... COME ON IN. MY MOM'S STILL GETTING READY.

GREAT.

YOUR MOM TOLD ME THAT YOU'RE REALLY INTO MUSIC.

YEAH.

WELL, HERE... THIS IS FOR YOU.

OH...

C+ C+ music factory

GONNA MAKE YOU SWEAT

THANKS, BUT... I'M NOT REALLY INTO THESE GUYS.

WELL, THEY TOLD ME IT'S NUMBER ONE RIGHT NOW.

I KNOW IT'S POPULAR, BUT...

LOOK... JUST TAKE THE GOD DAMN TAPE, OKAY?

Scotty—
It's a terrible feeling when you have to try to avoid someone constantly, so don't worry about it. I'll make it easy and avoid you. Who would've thought that you'd try to climb the social ladder? Well, good luck... I know how bothersome those "fag" jokes can be. By the way, I'm not exactly sure what you've been telling people, but we both know what happened that night. Eventually you'll look back on all this with embarrassment and guilt, but for now, enjoy yourself.

Alex

...WE HAVE REPORTS TONIGHT THAT SADDAM HUSSEIN HAS ORDERED A FULL WITHDRAWAL OF TROOPS FROM KUWAIT...

SCOTTY, I WANT TO TALK TO YOU ABOUT SOMETHING...

I JUST WANT YOU TO HEAR ME OUT AND TRY TO KEEP AN OPEN MIND, OKAY?

YOU KNOW THAT PHIL AND I HAVE BEEN SPENDING A LOT OF TIME TOGETHER LATELY...

AND I FEEL VERY LUCKY THAT I MET HIM. IT'S BEEN A BIG CHANGE FOR ME.

I JUST WANTED TO SEE HOW *YOU* FELT ABOUT HIM BECOMING MORE...A PART OF OUR LIVES.

NOW, I DON'T WANT YOU TO THINK I'M TRYING TO...*REPLACE* DAD IN ANY WAY...

WHAT DO YOU MEAN?

THAT'S *EXACTLY* WHAT YOU'RE TRYING TO DO.

≈SIGH≈

IS IT SO HARD FOR YOU TO BE JUST A LITTLE BIT SUPPORTIVE AND... OPTIMISTIC ABOUT ALL THIS?

SKKRK: PARDON THE INTERRUPTION, BUT THIS IS PRINCIPAL JARMAN SPEAKING. IF I COULD PLEASE HAVE EVERYONE'S ATTENTION...

WE HAVE A, UH, UNEXPECTED SITUATION ON OUR HANDS. FACULTY, COULD YOU PLEASE HAVE ALL YOUR STUDENTS FILE OUT TO THE SOCCER FIELD IMMEDIATELY?

I HEARD SOMEONE CALLED IN A BOMB THREAT!

DUDE! THEY ACTUALLY FOUND THE BOMB ON CAMPUS!

ALL THE WAY OUT TO THE SOCCER FIELD, GUYS! KEEP MOVING!

PRETTY WEIRD, HUH?

OH, HEY...

IF THERE REALLY IS A BOMB, DON'T YOU THINK THEY'RE KIND OF ENDANGER-ING OUR LIVES BY KEEPING US HERE?

YEAH...BUT THINK HOW AMAZING IT WOULD BE IF WE ACTUALLY GOT TO SEE THE SCHOOL BLOW UP!

YOU SURE YOU WANT TO BE SEEN SITTING WITH ME?

TCH... SHUT UP.

SO IT LOOKS LIKE I'M GONNA BE MOVING PRETTY SOON.

WHAT?

I'M MOVING WITH MY MOM AND BROTHER... TO L.A. PROBABLY.

ARE YOU SERIOUS? WHY?

≋SIGH≋ IT'S REALLY FUCKED-UP AND COMPLICATED, BUT BASICALLY... WE'RE, LIKE, LEAVING MY DAD.

HE DOESN'T EVEN KNOW YET.

BUT WHAT HAPPENED? I MEAN...

PFF...I DON'T REALLY WANT TO GET INTO IT, BUT...

I DON'T KNOW...I'M KIND OF HAPPY ABOUT IT. I'M SICK OF THIS SHIT-HOLE.

GREAT.

WELL, I GUESS IT'S BACK TO EATING LUNCH IN THE DARKROOM.

WHAT?

THAT'S WHAT I USED TO DO BEFORE I MET ALEX. I'D EAT MY LUNCH IN THE DARKROOM AND PRETEND TO PRINT PHOTOS.

YOU KNOW... THAT WAY I WOULDN'T HAVE TO SIT ON THE QUAD BY MYSELF.

OH MY GOD... THAT'S SO PATHETIC!

YEAH, WELL...

GOD, I CAN'T BELIEVE THIS!

OH, YOU'RE GOING TO BE FINE. YOU'LL MEET NEW PEOPLE...

CAMMIE... I DON'T **WANT** TO MEET NEW PEOPLE.

LISTEN UP! THE SHERIFF'S DEPARTMENT HAS ASSURED US THAT THE SITUATION IS UNDER CONTROL...BUT AS A PRECAUTION, WE ARE GOING TO DISMISS CLASS FOR THE REST OF THE DAY!

PLEASE LEAVE THE CAMPUS IN A QUICK AND ORDERLY MANNER, AND WE'LL SEE YOU BACK HERE TOMORROW!

ZOE TROPE

■

Selections from
Please Don't Kill the Freshman

FROM Future Tense Press

List of Characters

Linux Shoe — fourteen years old. freshman. best friend. homosex-
ual. beautiful. has made me cry many, many times. disgustingly
insightful. plays cello. reads philosophy. asked me why Tosca
had to die.

Plum Sweater — eighteen years old. senior. of the literary persua-
sion. very dry laugh. very soft (muddy brown) hair.

Wonka Boi — fifteen years old. freshman. very *fifteen*. listens to angry music. thinks his parents are out to make his life a living
hell. whines. needs someone. a teenager. has completely random moments of blue-eyed beauty.

Case Boy — fifteen years old. freshman. quiet in his own re-
pressed way. listens to angry music. speaks of random things.
we could kill each other with our words but we choose not to.
likes anime, guinea pigs, and the Metallica t-shirt I gave him for
his birthday. also prone to expressing his violence through video
games.

Techno Boy — seventeen years old. junior. has a red car. works at a
restaurant. it hurts when he smiles. very, very beautiful. dan-
druff. likes computers, electronic music. seeking a girl that
won't eat his heart with a steak knife.

Fishsticks — English teacher with pedophilic tendencies. also known as the blond Beck wannabe. listens to Radiohead. likes *The Odyssey* way too much.

Cherry Bitch — most beautiful girl ever. sixteen years old. sophomore. wears juicy red lipstick. smokes cigarettes like she wants to fuck them with her bright red mouth. makes art with her hands. makes sounds with her hands. makes beauty with her hands.

Jar Guard — English teacher who is far too nice. too young to be burnt out yet. listens to U2. enjoys the occasional back rub. has a wife. lets anyone write anything on the dry erase board in his classroom.

Curry — fifteen years old. freshman. mother is literally insane. very conservative family. he likes dressing up in women's clothing (watched *Rocky Horror* too many times). also enjoys listening to bad punk rock music.

trois.dix-huit

Mocking me for my strength. They have none, only a lack of dignity which allows them to make fools of themselves publicly. Too much to ask for them to play OUR music as they filed into the gym. Too much to ask that they stop talking for FIVE seconds while we try to. Microphones are useless. School assemblies, even when I'm a part of them, are nauseating. They are vegetables; they should throw themselves at us. We tried. It was a multimedia presentation of guilt tactics. "Recycle or die" would have been a better slogan. I am such a loser geek. I'd burn this earth club t-shirt but I'm too lazy. And the toxins from the smoke would pollute the air. I try to remember to breathe . . . Words are scarce, dreams are many. Blond curls in blue VW bug flipping over and over, unable to drive. Can't handle control. I pray not to die. This was only Saturday.

trois.vingt-quatre

My biology teacher is trying to give a review lecture for the test on Friday. I could get a zero on the test and still have an A in the class. It's kind of depressing. I think my time is spent much more productively by writing, glaring at her, sipping orange juice, and nibbling on cheerios. I am not an elitist. I am just a cheerio junkie. I wish I had my *Mother Jones*. It's easier to read and drown out her voice. Rejected by the Plum Sweater and muddy brown hair. Loved and then rejected. Chastised and then stroked. STOP ABUSING ME!!! Oh, but I want more. Please don't stop. Fishsticks (blond Beck wannabe) on videotape, Aerie Poetry Slam 2000. He reads his sexy poem in his sexy voice. "You know he's talking about his ten-year-old niece, don't you?" People laugh, then ashamed silence. Unable to laugh out loud at the truth. The man *is* a pedophile. No! No more di-hybrid crosses or punnet squares or sex-linked double allele chromatic heterozygous codominant genotypic ratios! I'm going to start drooling like the rest of my classmates. And then, after that, she'll break out the safety crayons and we can have art time. Orange juice and honey nut cheerios are a delicacy. I had to argue with my science teacher last year to get into this class and now I sit here with these morons who don't give a fuck. Argh. I will not be an angry twenty-something. I will not grow into an angry twenty-something. I will not . . . meet. my. fate.

trois.vingt-sept

Plum Sweater on my voice mail. Heart palpitations induced. What a punk rawk goddess. I'm going to faint. My fingers are shaking. I can't decide whether to squeal excitedly with a friend or call her back. I decide to call her. We laugh. Our voices are fake. She sounds so young. Painting pottery tomorrow? Great. Okay. I'll call you when I get home. I can't get over it. Is it a date? Is she interested in me? I'm so fucked up. I am SOOO . . . fourteen. I can't stop shaking. She said she finds me "interesting." My heart is pounding. I can't believe this. It's Plum Sweater.

trois.vingt-huit

Fucking Plum Sweater. What a bitch. She has company, church, cleaning, *The West Wing*. After more than twenty-four hours of a girl-scout-knotted stomach and shaking hands, I am told I have to wait until Saturday. I'm going to wring her neck after I hold her forever. My fingers click idly. I find this boy I know. I ask him to come over. I tell him I can't be alone. My shiny black Linux Shoe agrees and scurries. We eat toasted cheese sandwiches and I rub my nose into his 100% cotton trousers. Such a marvelous fag. He tells me about making love on fresh-cut grass. I want to cry. I'm supposed to be hugging a Plum Sweater. These gray trousers will have to do.

trois.trente-et-un

I take a shower and sigh. I am not looking forward to Plum Sweater, amazingly. We chase each other through the phone lines. Eventually, 2:45. I get as little work done on my eight-minute speech as possible. We lazily paint pottery. She tells me about choosing a school, her best friend's competitiveness, birth control, her mother walking in on her when she was having sex. I feel so small. I realize I have no chance. I return home to my friends and they console me. I attempt to write my eight-minute speech. I hate my biology teacher. My brother packs to go back to college. I flip through the pictures he brought home. I smile at the picture of his friend, Rob. I want to steal one but I am too nice. I shouldn't pine after college boys, anyway. I have no chance. After useless hours spent typing and clicking, I curl into my empty double bed and the TV comforts me. The noise becomes softer and I fade into the darkness.

quatre.quatre

I promise myself I'm going to laugh about this someday. My dreams are obscure and frightening but I refuse to leave them. Linux Shoe greets me in the hallway. We pace to the choir room and gnaw on our cuticles. I shuffle to the classroom of France and Midwestern Tackiness. I ask her if I can turn something in and she tells me not to be rude. I promise myself I'm going to laugh about this someday . . . Elijah Wood can't act. His portrayal of Huck Finn makes me want to vomit. My Linux Shoe sits by me at lunch in his classic black jacket. I squeeze his blue-jean-covered knee and hate the Case Boy for trying to tell me that Linux Shoe will not find anyone. To quote Wonka Boi: "LYING BITCH." He is right. So right. I can't wait to program a computer and get yelled at by a boring ex-hippie (a substitute, obviously) . . . Linux Shoe follows me home and into my bed. We waste time, drinking too much, holding each other. We finally give up and walk around the neighborhood, softly revealing secrets to each other in the clean quiet of the evening. Fresh-cut grass is everywhere. We laugh. We sip cold water and continue to giggle. I try, so hard, not to cry when he leaves.

quatre.onze

Linux Shoe whines loudly about his inability to write, lack of a boyfriend, overinterest in the straight boys. I sigh and hit his cheek with the back of my hand. He honestly believes that if he does not have a boyfriend before he turns fifteen, his entire life will be over. No reason to live. No will to go on. Because, so far, this is his entire life. And he's gone his entire life without a boyfriend. I laugh and shake my head. When he sits still, he wears a cloak of longing that presses down on his shoulders, pushing him into the ground, weighing down the corners of his mouth. I keep my mouth closed, because if I opened it, tears would come out. Some beautiful man is going to steal him away from me someday. Too soon. Far, far too soon.

quatre.dix-huit

Camped out in front of my locker like a homeless person. Waiting for a security guard to yell at me. They pass by numerous times and do not even look at me. I should be in class. Instead, I open Bukowski's *Tales of an Ordinary Madness* and read with a look of confusion on my face. I find this beautiful. No. one. notices . . .

Cherry Bitch lets me wear her cat-eyed glasses. I feel silly and vain and I like it. I walk home and eventually kiss the Wonka Boi (supposed to be gai). He shoves his tongue in my mouth anxiously, awkwardly. Too much like a child ripping open a shiny Christmas present only to be disappointed. I don't understand my need to mess with unattractive people. Curry wore a candy necklace today and I tried to bite off some candy and ended up making his neck bleed. What a tragedy. My hands are cold. My feet hurt. Career week only gets worse, I think. Tomorrow we have to write notes to the presenters we saw today (like the woman from State Farm who tried to convince us that selling insurance was a fun, interesting career field . . . LYING WHORE). That could take at least two hours . . . Vivarin. I believe this calls for Vivarin.

quatre.vingt-trois

The weekend finally ends. Before the memories melt together like globs of chicken fat, I would like to press my hands into the sticky wet cement for a few moments:

- Sleeping on the floor of Cherry Bitch's beach house right next to the giant window. Throwing my arm over her side and holding her against me. Her fingers hold my hand until they become limp one by one and I know she's fallen asleep.
- Wearing my brand-new Powell's sweatshirt for three days in a row. It had taffy, bodily fluids, food, sand, and dirt on it by Sunday evening.
- Eating ice cream cones and squeaky cheese at the Tillamook Factory.
- Plum Sweater being cold and then forgiving. I nearly died.
- Holding Linux Shoe as I fall asleep, saddened when he's forced to go back to the boys' side of the house.
- Eating. SO MUCH FOOD. Teenagers. are. cows.
- Laughing at Cherry Bitch: "Fuck tha po-lice."
- Wandering up and down the beach at night in the dark listening to the waves.

- Bumper cars and Anti-Crombie t-shirts bought on a rainy seaside boardwalk.
- Cherry Bitch lighting cigarettes. Breath smelling of charcoal and ashes . . . Smelling black.
- Riding in special ed buses.
- Linux Shoe. Linux Shoe. Linux Shoe.
- Reading tarot cards for Linux Shoe and a boy who cried on the beach while holding a knife.
- Sitting on a boy's lap and being groped randomly.
- Reading Cherry Bitch's volumes of art.
- Almost too much acceptance.

Monday feels like nothing in comparison. Linux Shoe dresses too nicely. I feel vague and ask for love. I am always hugging. Few arms find their way around my waist. The words become dry.

quatre.vingt-quatre

Seven weeks left of this building. I am frightened. Very frightened. Sometimes the entire world scares the crap out of me. I still feel vague and cryptic. Season finales for all my favorite TV shows. The never-ending purr of lawn mowers in my neighborhood. Sky continually a beautiful shade of light blue. More reasons for fear. Some of my friends are driving, smoking pot, piercing their lips. I vaguely remember finger-painting with tempera paints when I was seven years old. Sometimes the cycle of life makes my fingers twitch and wrists ache. A wad of dictionary pages grows larger in my stomach. I fear driving. I fear senior prom. I fear graduation. I fear college. I fear relationships. I fear life. I curl up in the fetal position on my bedroom floor, the one in the first house I lived in, the one with the elephant painted on the wall.

quatre.vingt-cinq

Enough of my philosophical rambling. Okay, that's a lie. Sometimes I'm sick of loving everyone. I'm sick of being the one people depend on. I'm sick of depending on people. I care so much the skin under my fingernails bleeds and turns black, but I am rarely held, recognized, encouraged. Sometimes loneliness makes me more vague and cryptic. Aerie people suggest I have my own book. I laugh and tell them yes. I narrow my submissions down to four. It is difficult, like losing children. I am aborting my words.

cinq.huit

My Linux Shoe is melancholy and I do not know how to help it. I get annoyed, push him away, give up. I tell him he is margarine, that he is my only joy and other contradictory things. Aerie's poetry slam in thirteen days, woo. Even though I'm sure it will mostly be trembling teenagers reciting poorly written love poems in crackly voices, I think it will be marvelous. I'm going to read one of Linux Shoe's poems and a few other writings . . . I have this feeling that I am running around and accomplishing nothing. This is springtime. I must resist the urge to place daisies in gun barrels. Last night my dad was driving me home from band practice and we passed by a fast food joint. EIGHT FUCKING COP CARS WERE THERE TO BUST TWO GUYS! TWO! I counted. Pigs. Goddam pigs. I felt like screaming but I couldn't. My dad is the only one who would say, "Hey, wanna go back and look at what happened?" My mother would never do such a thing. She usually comes home, lights a cigarette, drinks liquor diluted in cheap soda, and reads crime novels. She is not a bad person. I worry that she is too unhappy. Case Boy has decided to make a political statement by wearing the same outfit every day until school ends. I admire his philosophy, though fear it is misguided. A girl named Louisa wore the same green dress every day in the fall. These girls in my biology class were talking about her. "Isn't that strange? I want to ask her about it, blah blah blah." I calmly interrupted, "Why does it matter? Why do you care?" And the girl with flat brown hair and boring lips, "Oh, I don't care, I just want to know why she'd do that. It's weird." These people drive me crazy.

cinq.onze

I worry about very, very tedious things. My friends are very, very horny. And sometimes, if I listen closely enough, I can't hear anything at all. I can hear black. Linux Shoe nods and tells me I think too much and say too little. I never thought of myself as such a person but he is right. Sometimes I don't say what I think. That makes me human. He comes over and we sit in my nineteen-seventy-something Bug and listen to the radio. The seats aren't even cracked. We ride public transportation and eat Mexican food and look at books and boys. He is not perfect. But he's the closest thing I've found.

cinq.vingt-et-un

I do not spend time in class today . . . I spend time in the lecture room, arranging black lights, feathers hanging from the ceiling, scribbling art with chalk. The room is art nouveau. Wonderful, as Cherry Bitch would say. Later that evening, she adorns a pair of wings and white clothing which electrifies under the black light (scotch tape does too). It is a slam. A slamming sort of slam. I read first, pieces I pretend are my own. Lips I pretend are my own. A voice I pretend is my own. The band drifts between my words (the beat of a drum and the hum of a strum of a guitar , , ,) Absolutely fabulous, as Cherry Bitch would say. Later, I win a prize for best reading voice. Curry wins a prize for best overall piece. Flecks of spit hit the microphone as he recites his acceptance speech: "Holy crap." I laugh. Linux Shoe wears a wine-colored shirt (I swoon) and the evening is absolutely wonderful. The room is humid and quite moist, but the atmosphere is perfect . . . I'd die in that room, if I had a choice.

cinq.vingt-trois

There is an English teacher named Jar Guard. He doesn't teach my English class, but I certainly enjoy him more than Fishsticks. His wife has him on a diet. Every day at lunch, he eats two pieces of fruit, fat-free yogurt, or some other tasteless dish. He screws up his face in disgust. I tell him that I would never put him on a diet. I want to marry a man like him. Soft but not fat. Intelligent but not arrogant. Owns a sticker that says "Tough Guys Write Poetry." Black hair and funky glasses. Wears pin-stripe pants, shiny black shoes, and casual-dress shirts. He's only been teaching for three years, so he isn't burnt out yet. One of the few teachers who still seems alive. If I were a teacher, I would lose all hope very quickly. I lost all hope as a student quite a while ago. He continues to smile and walks with his shoulders back, hips moving. And maybe because he remembers those random things that mean everything, "You're a very beautiful woman," he tells me. I smile too, for the first time in months.

cinq.vingt-quatre

Techno Boy, the one who took me to McDonald's so long ago, gives me a ride home in his air-conditioned car. Reluctantly, I agree to go home with him. He does not want to be alone but he does not say so. His parents collect porcelain figures with rosy cheeks. Cats, women, bears, pigs. All made of pale ceramic. He claims they are worth upwards of three hundred dollars. I've never trusted people who so greatly value material possessions. Value them enough to choke their homes with them. He shows me the basement: twenty thousand heaving worn brown boxes filled to the brim with Christmas decorations, more porcelain figurines arranged on shelves, and two separate bullet-making contraptions. I feel overwhelmed. I think his house would make a wonderful bonfire. I simply nod. His hands shake very, very badly all the time. He tried to move out of his parents' house because they are verbally abusive. He tried to smile when he showed me his bedroom, Shari's menu lying on the floor. (I have to memorize it for work, he tells me. I open it up and ask, How much is a Denver omelette? He smiles painfully, 6.49? I tell him he is right, even though he is forty cents off.)

cinq.vingt-six

Curry wears his Old Navy and drinks his 24 oz. lattes from Starbucks while hatefully condemning all of society. Why? Because THEY are so trite and ignorant. Like listening to Bad Religion makes him some sort of pseudo anarchist god. Okay, so maybe I exaggerate a little. He isn't that bad. But some people are. A stoner girl in a few of my classes hates the popular people who wear Converse shoes. Like when you go to buy Converse shoes, she thinks you should have to show your anarchy-punk ID card. Another girl in our class wears Converse shoes and Gap jeans, an ultimate sin to the punk stoner girl. All I wanna know, all I really wanna know is: When the fuck is this shit going to matter? Jesus Christ, people, let it go. Let it be.

cinq.trente

I watch a movie called *Edge of Seventeen*. I feel like I'm going to be sick and that's okay. Instead of eating too much, I'm thinking too much and I need to throw up some of these thoughts before something vile happens. I am thinking that I don't need to prove myself to the people who don't matter. I am thinking that I love Linux Shoe and he could be taken away from me at any moment. I am thinking of longing. I am thinking that I would like to be six years old or nineteen years old. I am thinking I am indecisive. Mostly I am longing. I am convincing myself of many, many things, but my longing is a constant. My longing is riding my bike with pink streamers on the handles to 7-Eleven and buying a Slurpee. My longing is a soft boy to hold me. My longing is to be rid of my empathy. Out of all the things I am thinking and convincing myself of, the only thing I know for sure is that it's okay. It's okay to convince and to long and to think. And perhaps most importantly, I know what matters. Linux Shoe matters. My words matter. The people I love matter. Not that building, not those letters on that piece of paper, not the teachers who yell, not the teachers who tape pictures of pretty blond girls to their podiums, not the crackly voice on the PA, not the scores from the "state," not the stupid girls or the angry boys. As simple as this may be, I sit and cry because no one else will know this for a very, very long time . . . I know a billion other truths and philosophical ramblings. But what do I really know? Nothing. I'm fourteen. I am a girl in a pretty little public high school in a pretty little house in a pretty little neighborhood. What do I know?

six.neuf

Stepping in horseshit is never as glamorous as it seems. Stepping in horseshit when you're behind a float that leaks water is even less glamorous, if you can imagine. I have no appetite when it is over. I just want to go home and sit. I want to pretend that I am not such a band geek and that I do not spend my Saturdays wearing a shako and playing a brass instrument. But sometimes life is like that. I don't get much choice. I come home, try to clean myself of the stench (band geek or horseshit . . . Sometimes I can't tell which is worse, so I scrub extra hard). I have to leave soon, anyway, to go burn dead animal flesh with the literary department from school. We listen to Bob Dylan and talk about what is important and play basketball and I touch my Linux Shoe until my hands bleed rose petals. He is leaving for Singapore on Wednesday. He matters to me like my shoelaces. Always there, always wrapped between the holes. Everything falls apart when he's gone. I can't walk. I trip and fall and lick the ground. After the BBQ, I continue to be a teenager. We go to a double feature at a cheesy theater in the ghetto part of the suburbs. I remember being little and thinking that the teenagers who sat in the back row were obnoxious and stupid and I never wanted to be like them. I am, now. We laugh and rest our feet on the back of the seats. We throw candy and poke each other. I wonder how long I can do this before I am the adult sitting in front of myself, rolling my eyes and just wanting to watch the movie. The second movie is so bad we leave during the middle and wander around the empty streets. I'm not too scared because one boy has a knife. We act like teenagers. We do stupid things. One girl steals a letter off a sign and puts it in her purse. We go into a food mart at a gas station and laugh at the condoms for sale. We walk by a pizza joint and I wave like a freak at a friend inside. I run in and talk with her, thinking that I never would have done this a year ago when I hated these sorts of people. When I called them stupid and immature. When I hated them so much for having fun. I've only got three years, one month, and sixteen days left of this. I'm not going to waste it anymore.

CONTRIBUTORS' NOTES

Jenny Bitner is a San Francisco–based writer and visual artist. She received an MFA in creative writing from the University of Virginia, where she was a Hoyns Fellow. Her short stories and articles have appeared in *To-Do List*, *Comet*, and the *San Francisco Bay Guardian*. A chapbook of her poetry, *Mother*, was published by Pine Press. Currently she is working on an illustrated novel titled *Notes to a Potential Lover*.

Sara Corbett is a contributing writer at the *New York Times Magazine* as well as a contributing editor at *Sports Illustrated Women* and *Skiing*. Her nonfiction pieces have appeared in *Esquire*, *Elle*, *Men's Journal*, and *Outside*. Her short fiction has appeared in *Story*, the *New England Review*, the *Gettysburg Review*, and the *Indiana Review*. Corbett was a finalist for the Livingston Award for young journalists and was nominated for a Gay and Lesbian Alliance for Anti-Defamation prize for outstanding magazine work. Her book *Venus to the Hoop: A Gold-Medal Year in Women's Basketball* was published in 1997. The author of five children's books as well, Corbett lives in Maine with her husband and son and is currently at work on a novel.

Michael Finkel is a freelance writer and small-scale chicken farmer who lives in western Montana. He has been on assignment on six continents, and his articles have appeared in the *Atlantic Monthly, National Geographic Adventure, Rolling Stone,* and the *New York Times Magazine.* He is the author of *Alpine Circus,* a book of wintertime adventures, and has previously been anthologized in *The Best American Sports Writing* and *The Best American Travel Writing.*

Meenakshi Ganguly is the South Asia correspondent for *Time* and lives in New Delhi, India. She has many friends among the Tibetan refugee community and travels often to Dharamsala, where the Dalai Lama, the temporal and spiritual head of the Tibetans, lives and runs his government in exile. Ganguly began her career as a journalist in 1988 after earning a master's degree in sociology from the Delhi School of Economics. She is married to the cinematographer Sanjay Kapoor.

Karl Taro Greenfeld's *Standard Deviations: Growing Up and Coming Down in the New Asia* was published in July 2002. ("Speed Demons" was adapted from part of that book.) He is the editor of *Time Asia* and also wrote *Speed Tribes: Days and Nights with Japan's Next Generation.* A former correspondent for *The Nation* and staff writer at *Time,* he has also written for *GQ, Vogue, Men's Journal, Outside,* and the *New York Times Magazine,* among other publications. He often wonders why he is not more famous.

Camden Joy is a novelist, pamphleteer, and so-called guerrilla critic. Recognized for his rock-and-roll fictions, he has written numerous radio dramas, liner notes, record reviews, and short stories. His efforts to blend these media into what is termed "pop fabulism" or "lo-fi literature" have resulted in the composition of three critically acclaimed novellas and two novels. Joy initially came to prominence through a series of street-postering projects he undertook in New York City from 1995 to 1997. He currently lives on the outskirts of Boston.

Michael Kamber is a freelance writer and photographer based in New York City. He has documented the immigrant population in

New York and has made numerous trips to Mexico to research articles about the enormous migration of laborers to the United States and the effects of this exodus on Mexican society. A 2001–2002 Revson Fellow at Columbia University, he has published work in the *Village Voice,* Wired.com, *Brooklyn Bridge,* and Mother Jones.com. He is a recipient of the Columbia University School of Journalism's Mike Berger Award.

Sam Lipsyte was born in New York in 1968 and grew up in New Jersey. His first book, *Venus Drive,* a collection of short stories, was named one of the twenty-five best books of 2000 by the *Village Voice.* His second book, a novel titled *The Subject Steve,* was published in 2001. He lives in Queens, New York.

Elizabeth McKenzie was born in Los Angeles. She received her M.A. in creative writing from Stanford University and was a staff writer at the *Atlantic Monthly.* Her fiction has appeared in *The Pushcart Prize XXV, TriQuarterly,* the *Threepenny Review, ZYZZYVA, Shenandoah,* and *Witness.* She lives in Santa Cruz, California.

Seth Mnookin lives in New York City with his cat. He is a senior writer at *Newsweek* and writes frequently about national affairs, music, and popular culture.

The Onion is a satirical newspaper and Web site published in New York City, Chicago, Madison and Milwaukee, Wisconsin, and Denver, Colorado. It can be found on the Web at www.theonion.com.

Keith Pille grew up next to a nuclear power plant in eastern Nebraska. Since then he has been waiting for his radiation-spawned mutant powers to develop but to date has nothing but an uncanny ability to give driving directions. He currently lives in south Minneapolis with his lady and thirty pounds of cat.

Rodney Rothman was the head writer of *The Late Show with David Letterman* until 2000 and most recently wrote and produced the

TV show *Undeclared*. His writing has appeared in the *New York Times*, *McSweeney's*, *The New Yorker*, the *New York Times Magazine*, and *Men's Journal*. His first book, tentatively titled *Early Bird*, is forthcoming.

David Schickler writes fiction and screenplays. His short stories have appeared in *Zoetrope: All Story*, *Tin House*, and *The New Yorker*. He received an MFA in creative writing from Columbia University and in 2001 published his first book, *Kissing in Manhattan*, which contains the story "Fourth Angry Mouse." He lives in New York.

Eric Schlosser is a correspondent for the *Atlantic Monthly* and the author of the best-selling book *Fast Food Nation*. After the publication of "Why McDonald's Fries Taste So Good," McDonald's restaurants were destroyed by radical Hindus, class-action lawsuits were filed against the restaurant, and riots broke out in India. These actions forced apologies from McDonald's, as well as a corporate acknowledgment that there was beef in the fries and donations to vegetarian and Hindu causes. Schlosser lives in New York City.

Heidi Jon Schmidt is the author of *Darling?* and *The Rose Thieves*. Her stories have been widely published and anthologized, most recently in *Prize Stories 2002: The O. Henry Awards*. Her novel, *The Bride of Catastrophe*, is forthcoming in 2003. She lives in Provincetown, Massachusetts, with her husband and daughter and teaches in the MFA program at Queens College in Charlotte, North Carolina.

David Sedaris is a humorist and social critic whose commentaries are heard on National Public Radio. He is the author of the bestsellers *Barrel Fever*, *Naked*, and *Me Talk Pretty One Day*, and he contributes essays to such magazines as *Esquire*, *Allure*, *The New Yorker*, and *Travel and Leisure*. Under the name The Talent Family, he and his sister, Amy Sedaris, collaborate on plays, one of which

— "One Woman Shoe" — received an Obie Award. He lives in Paris.

Gary Smith is a senior writer for *Sports Illustrated* and a three-time winner of the National Magazine Award for feature writing. He has made seven appearances in *The Best American Sports Writing* — more than any other writer.

Seaton Smith was born on February 4, 1982, in San Diego, California, and raised in many parts of the country. (Okay, a couple). He attended high school in Montclair, New Jersey, and is currently in his third year at Howard University, pursuing a major in film. His interest in writing came from an on-campus magazine called *The Illtop*, which was founded and funded by the actor/comedian Chris Rock. Through the magazine he learned of *The Modern Humorist* and applied for an internship, which he received. Currently he is working on a play, more essays, and a career in stand-up comedy.

Adrian Tomine has been producing his *Optic Nerve* series for more than ten years. One of America's best-known comics artists, he also contributes illustrations to such publications as *The New Yorker, Details,* and *Rolling Stone.* His stories have been collected in three books. Born in Sacramento, California, in 1974, he now lives in Berkeley.

Zoe Trope is the pseudonym of a writer in the Portland area who is still in high school and protecting her privacy. Her account of her freshman year, *Please Don't Kill the Freshman,* will be published as a book in 2003. Her e-mail address is zoe_trope@hotmail.com.

THE B·E·S·T AMERICAN SERIES ™

THE BEST AMERICAN SHORT STORIES® 2002

Sue Miller, guest editor • Katrina Kenison, series editor

"Story for story, readers can't beat the *Best American Short Stories* series" (*Chicago Tribune*). This year's most beloved short fiction anthology is edited by the best-selling novelist Sue Miller and includes stories by Edwidge Danticat, Jill McCorkle, E. L. Doctorow, and Akhil Sharma, among others.

0-618-13173-6 PA $13.00 / 0-618-11749-0 CL $27.50
0-618-13172-8 CASS $26.00 / 0-618-25816-7 CD $35.00

THE BEST AMERICAN ESSAYS® 2002

Stephen Jay Gould, guest editor • Robert Atwan, series editor

Since 1986, the *Best American Essays* series has gathered the best nonfiction writing of the year. Edited by Stephen Jay Gould, the eminent scientist and distinguished writer, this year's volume features writing by Jonathan Franzen, Sebastian Junger, Gore Vidal, Mario Vargas Llosa, and others.

0-618-04932-0 PA $13.00 / 0-618-21388-0 CL $27.50

THE BEST AMERICAN MYSTERY STORIES™ 2002

James Ellroy, guest editor • Otto Penzler, series editor

Our perennially popular anthology is a favorite of mystery buffs and general readers alike. This year's volume is edited by the internationally acclaimed author James Ellroy and offers pieces by Robert D. Parker, Joyce Carol Oates, Michael Connelly, Stuart M. Kaminsky, and others.

0-618-12493-4 PA $13.00 / 0-618-12494-2 CL $27.50
0-618-25807-8 CASS $26.00 / 0-618-25806-X CD $35.00

THE BEST AMERICAN SPORTS WRITING™ 2002

Rick Reilly, guest editor • Glenn Stout, series editor

This series has garnered wide acclaim for its stellar sports writing and top-notch editors. Now Rick Reilly, the best-selling author and "Life of Reilly" columnist for *Sports Illustrated,* continues that tradition with pieces by Frank Deford, Steve Rushin, Jeanne Marie Laskas, Mark Kram, Jr., and others.

0-618-08628-5 PA $13.00 / 0-618-08627-7 CL $27.50

THE B·E·S·T AMERICAN SERIES ™

THE BEST AMERICAN TRAVEL WRITING 2002
Frances Mayes, guest editor • Jason Wilson, series editor

The Best American Travel Writing 2002 is edited by Frances Mayes, the author of the enormously popular *Under the Tuscan Sun* and *Bella Tuscany*. Giving new life to armchair travel for 2002 are David Sedaris, Kate Wheeler, André Aciman, and many others.

0-618-11880-2 PA $13.00 / 0-618-11879-9 CL $27.50
0-618-19719-2 CASS $26.00 / 0-618-19720-6 CD $35.00

THE BEST AMERICAN SCIENCE AND NATURE WRITING 2002
Natalie Angier, guest editor • Tim Folger, series editor

This year's edition promises to be another "eclectic, provocative collection" (*Entertainment Weekly*). Edited by Natalie Angier, the Pulitzer Prize–winning author of *Woman: An Intimate Geography*, it features work by Malcolm Gladwell, Joy Williams, Barbara Ehrenreich, Dennis Overbye, and others.

0-618-13478-6 PA $13.00 / 0-618-08297-2 CL $27.50

THE BEST AMERICAN RECIPES 2002–2003
Edited by Fran McCullough with Molly Stevens

"The cream of the crop . . . McCullough's selections form an eclectic, unfussy mix" (*People*). Offering the best of what America's cooking, as well as the latest trends, time-saving tips, and techniques, this year's edition includes a foreword by Anthony Bourdain, the best-selling author of *Kitchen Confidential* and *A Cook's Tour*.

0-618-19137-2 CL $26.00

THE BEST AMERICAN NONREQUIRED READING 2002
Dave Eggers, guest editor • Michael Cart, series editor

The Best American Nonrequired Reading is the newest addition to the series — and the first annual of its kind for readers fifteen and up. Edited by Dave Eggers, the author of the phenomenal bestseller *A Heartbreaking Work of Staggering Genius*, this genre-busting volume draws from mainstream and alternative American periodicals and features writing by Eric Schlosser, David Sedaris, Sam Lipsyte, Michael Finkel, and others.

0-618-24694-0 PA $13.00 / 0-618-24693-2 CL $27.50 / 0-618-25810-8 CD $35.00

HOUGHTON MIFFLIN COMPANY   www.houghtonmifflinbooks.com